Missing

Time

Terry Edwards

© Terry Edwards 2019

All rights reserved.
Subject to statutory exception and to provisions of relevant collective licensing agreements, no part of this publication may be reproduced without the prior written permission of the author.

The moral right of Terry Edwards
to be identified as the author of this book has been asserted in accordance with the Copyright, Designs and Patents Act 1988.

This is a work of fiction.
Names, characters, businesses, places, events and incidents are either the products of the author's imagination or used in a fictitious manner. Any resemblance to actual persons, living or dead, or actual events is purely coincidental.

ISBN 978-1-9162114-0-7

Also by this author:

Available on kindle

*Consciousness in a Virtual Reality
Holographic Universe*

Dedication

To my wife June with eternal love

Acknowledgements

Allan Smith, my stepson and friend, for believing in and encouraging my writing.

Magnús Þór Sigmundsson of Iceland, my friend and musical collaborator on *The Mandroid*. Thank you for your wonderful music. The song writing process concentrated the story down to its essential elements.

John Richardson and Alan Williams, my friends in the Rubettes who proposed and supported a musical version of *The Mandroid*.

Tim Woods for *The London Slang Dictionary* © (2008) and access to the language of London teenagers at that time.

Kim Kimber
(www.kimkimber.co.uk)
for copy-editing and technical support.

James Fanthorpe
(www.xlbookcoverdesign.co.uk)
for the cover design.

Claire Rushbrook
(reedsy.com/claire-rushbrook)
for proofreading.

Part 1
Missing Time

Prologue

2008, Somewhere In South London

Darkness surrounded him like midnight in a coalmine. The only sound was his breathing. All he could see was blackness, an empty void; sight without image, mind without thought. Was he *somewhere* or *nowhere*? This was no place on earth, for sure. This was far out in deep space beyond the confines of any star system. He was in a spacesuit, alone and drifting.

In the distance he saw a dot of deep blue light. The dot began to expand, slowly at first and then incredibly quickly. Almost instantaneously, it became a massive blue object hurtling towards him, expanding into unimaginable enormity. With no reference, no sound, just black emptiness, he could not judge its size – perhaps thousands of miles in diameter, perhaps billions. It came so close; he thought he could touch it, barely having time to feel the terrifying certainty of impending oblivion.

It seemed like a dark blue sun with speckles of intense white light. There was no heat, no gravity to crush him, just an overpowering feeling of love beyond endurance. The surface seethed and writhed. Then a hole appeared in front of him – a folded orifice disappearing into the distance – a tunnel leading into the object. An irresistible force latched on to him and drew him inside. Faster and faster he flew as it sucked him along. He travelled down a tunnel of white and blue light towards a centre that seemed far, far away.

A voice filled his consciousness. *Do not fear me. I am your friend.* He heard the words with his mind rather than his ears.

"Who are you?" he asked.

My name would mean nothing to you. You know me as the Old One.

"I know you? Are you inside this sphere of light? Will I meet you when I reach the centre?"

He heard pleasant, cheerful laughter in his mind. *I AM the sphere of light. When you reach the centre we will be one; but not yet, my friend. Not yet. There is much to do first.*

The discordant ringing of a cheap alarm clock shattered the lucid dream and dragged him back to reality. He felt jaded as if he had been awake all night. He looked at the time and remembered his appointment in the City of London. Groaning, he arose from his bed and headed for the shower.

Chapter One

"Do you have any questions for us, Mr Crandle?"

Roger regarded the man in the expensive suit and shook his head. "No, thank you."

Another black mark, he thought, but what did they expect? He knew the job; he knew the salary; he could do the work. He'd once had a colleague who abandoned his usual job to study interview techniques to pass promotion panels. To Roger's amazement the colleague had passed the next board and the one after that. By then he had reached his personal threshold of incompetence and settled for the higher salary and longer holidays.

Roger resigned eventually and went to America, the land of opportunity, for a better education. He had returned home five years later with a blank memory, no money, no friends and no qualifications. He boarded a plane in England; he alighted a plane in England. There was nothing in between but an empty void.

Something must have happened to him during this obscure period of his existence. Much about him had changed before and after. Sometimes knowledge came to him that he didn't know he knew. His memory concealed experiences he would not have believed; too outlandish to be true. It was as if a wake had reached the shore with no ship to account for it, a giant submarine passing through the darkness of his unconscious mind. It was like the 'dream' or inexplicable experience of the previous night, a cold blue star, a voice, a feeling of love and peace; home.

The chairman said, "Very well."

Roger sat for a while, unsure what to do. He waited patiently for a signal. Had they finished interviewing him? His principle interrogator whispered to the colleague on his left, a dark-haired sombre woman who seemed to have forgotten how to smile. Maybe she only smiled out of working hours or when the managing director made a joke.

Failure at interviews was almost inevitable. Try as he might, Roger could not play the employment game but he needed a job to escape the clutches of the benefit system. What did *these* people want to hear? "Where do you see yourself in five years' time?" meant nothing to him. If he got the job, he would be doing it. If he didn't get the job, he would be doing something else. He might be dead. Who knew?

In spite of the tension, Roger felt detached and calm inside. He knew they looked down on him. Yes, they were important people but only in their own heads; "I am an important person because I have a managerial job; you are nothing." They wanted somebody to maintain their database system; Roger had the necessary skills. What was the problem?

He understood their reluctance. There was a big question mark; a gap in his CV. Could he have been in prison? He said he had worked in America but gave no positive information about what he'd done there or who his employers had been. His knowledge of software and methodologies was out of date. Most damning of all, he had not worked for over a year since his return to England. Even if they gave him the job, would he turn up? Would he run out screaming after the first morning? For Roger, that was not an option. Nobody can live without some money. Deep down inside he despised 'the system'. Maybe they sensed it. He was aware that people gave off subtle messages that belied what they said. Perhaps...an insight penetrated Roger's mind; they feared him! Why was that? He was harmless. He was tall but he wasn't a heavyweight. Somebody once described him as an extremely large stick insect. He certainly didn't have a black belt in an arcane martial art. He was no hero!

After a long pause, Roger got up from the chair and headed for the exit. As he turned the door handle, he looked back, giving his interrogators one last chance to say something. Nothing doing! The chairman turned to the colleague on his right, a black man with silver hair who nodded in approval at something Roger could not hear. He walked out of the room.

So much for his first job interview in seven weeks. They were seven short weeks by his reckoning but counted as eternity to the Benefit Agency that paid him a pittance to survive. But he was grateful for anything. His skills and qualifications seemed to be more of a hindrance than a blessing. In Roger's view a specialist was somebody who knew more and more about less and less. Perhaps it was time to remove his qualifications and technical experience from his CV? It might increase his opportunity of finding less cerebral labour – he could load a dishwasher with the best of them.

Corporate slavery oppressed the human species. Somehow Roger knew this. He understood systems and how they work. He thought, *this is how life is, get on with it.* He smiled ruefully to himself as he emerged from the office block and headed homewards. *Does it have to be like this?*

The bus took him to the tube station. He went through the barriers and walked around a disparate gaggle of ticket inspectors, reincarnated in contemporary jargon as Revenue Protection Officers. The name had changed but not the role. They still found endless fascination in the humble train ticket; connoisseurs of the genre you might say. They subjected each one to minute scrutiny. Perhaps there was a mythical ticket to Cockfosters that held the meaning of life?

During the tube ride home, Roger found himself in the same carriage as his brother-in-law. Billy Morris was fast asleep at the far end of the carriage. Roger stood up, struggling with his own inertia as he progressed towards his sister's spouse. He gave Billy a light tap on the shoulder. The sleeping man snorted and raised his eyes blearily. His vacant gaze fell on Roger and his face cracked into a smile of recognition. Then, with surprise, he noted that the train was pulling into his station. "Oh, we're here. Better get up I suppose."

Roger nodded. "How true those words are, even today as we speak," he said, imitating a verbose speechmaker they both knew who liked the sound of his own voice.

Billy chuckled and dived for the opening. Roger, following close on his heels, only just cleared the exit as the doors closed.

"Hey, bruv! What's up?"

"Round here – mostly mobile phone masts and house prices," said Roger.

Billy stretched as he walked, straightening the kinks in his spine. "Been looking for you, I have," he declared to Roger.

"Why's that then?"

"Yeah, I been on the Internet."

"I'm very pleased for you. Does that mean you're coming home with me?"

Billy nodded.

Right now, Roger wanted to get to his flat and unwind. He really did not want to go to Billy's house. Billy's domestic felicity was rather too noisy for Roger's taste.

"Is something wrong?"

"Shh, can't talk here. Wait till we get inside your place."

Roger glanced at his brother-in-law curiously, noting his conspiratorial stance and the finger planted slyly by the side of the nose. Nobody watching could have mistaken his body language. Billy was an avid conspiracy theorist. Roger didn't believe more than ten per cent of Billy's ideas but he always enjoyed hearing them.

"Got any beer?" Billy asked hopefully.

This was not something a man on Benefit would admit to without hesitation.

"Might have."

"Good-oh. Your sis sends her best."

"Thanks."

They walked along the row of flats and terraced houses until they arrived at the entrance to Roger's block of flats. Most of the people they passed were of ethnic origin.

"You're a bit of a minority round here," Billy commented.

"Suits me," Roger replied.

"Doesn't it make you feel like an alien?"

Roger glanced at Billy; for some reason his remark stirred an odd feeling.

"No, mate. I really like it here – most of the time."

"Bet you're glad you moved south of the border." The border in this case was the River Thames.

"You make it sound like Texas."

Roger searched his pocket for the key to his flat. He did not need to punch the pin number in the outer door; nobody bothered to lock it. A squashed beer can wedged it open. The passageway contained the usual collection of bicycles, flung down indiscriminately by aggravating youngsters, the *ASBO* generation for whom anti-social behaviour appeared to be the norm. Roger knew it was futile to complain. They would only take it out on him later by vandalism or violence. Roger stepped over the bikes to climb the stairs. Billy simply stepped on them. Roger didn't much like using the lifts. They made him claustrophobic. These lifts were long and narrow, just adequate for a coffin. On the third floor, they encountered two local gang members, one black, one white, both wearing grey hoods.

"Mr Crandle," said the white man. "Always a pleasure to see you, sir."

"Hello, Barty," Roger said warily, hearing sarcasm in the politeness.

"I told you the other day that I might need to put some stuff in your lockup."

"I said it is not possible."

"Oh, it's possible. Wouldn't you agree, Cade?"

"Yeah, man. You'd better do as we ask. The alternative would be…"

"Unfortunate?" suggested Barty.

Cade laughed. "Yeah, unfortunate in the extreme." He pulled a knife out of his pocket and tossed it in the air. He caught it neatly by the hilt and quickly put it away again.

Roger said nothing and turned away. Barty murmured something to Cade and they both laughed and walked on. Roger unlocked the door to his apartment and led Billy inside. Billy wandered through to the living room and dropped on to the couch. The décor of the flat was basic and unexceptional; the contents tidy but not fastidiously so.

Billy brought out a wad of tobacco from an inner pocket and started to roll a cigarette.

"This is a no smoking establishment, if you don't mind," Roger reminded him from the doorway, holding his last bottle of beer in one hand and an opener in the other.

"I don't mind," said Billy, pulling away a small amount of tobacco and placing it in the paper. "You still like living here with those scumbags?"

"They're not all like that. Most of the people round here are decent and kind."

Billy looked sympathetic. "I was never good at fighting. Didn't you meet all this in America? If you believe the telly programmes, they all carry guns. I suppose it's one way of settling an argument."

Roger was about to say 'of course not' but stopped when he recalled that he couldn't remember. Much of what happened during his time in America was a complete blank, an enduring amnesia. "No... I don't know. I don't think so."

"Memory not come back yet?" Billy asked. "You been wiped by a man in black."

"What do you mean?"

"Missing time! You got missing time. Remember Tommy Lee Jones and Will Smith in the movies. They used those flashy-flashy things – remember?"

Roger laughed. "Yeah, I remember that. Have you been looking at websites about aliens again?"

"Don't mock. It's not a joke to all those Americans who've been abducted by aliens. They come back with missing time."

Roger smiled. "With 'missing time'? You can't possess a negative. Besides, I don't believe in aliens or flying saucers."

"When people see UFOs it's because they're there," Billy insisted. "I don't say it's always a spaceship. Sometimes the unidentified turns out to be something ordinary like a Chinese lantern. You can't imagine a radar trace from one of those. By the way, has anybody seen a UFO round here?"

"Of course not."

"Men in black?"

"No…"

Billy got up and peered out of the third-floor window at the street below.

"Then who's that down there?"

Roger walked to the window and looked down to where Billy was pointing. He saw a man in a black suit, white shirt and thin, dark tie sitting in some sort of black limo, unusual for this part of South London. The tinted side window was open so he could see the driver who was smoking a cigarette.

"No, it's a coincidence," he said.

"Maybe," Billy agreed. "But doesn't he look like the typical man in black you see on MUFON? He even looks ugly."

"What's MUFON?"

"The Mutual UFO Network."

The man in the car looked up, saw them and immediately turned his eyes downwards. As the car window began to rise, Roger saw him texting on his mobile phone.

Roger shook his head. "It's a coincidence," he repeated.

Billy lit his cigarette, took a drag and then gestured with it, like a man proved right. "Yeah. Whatever."

Shrugging indifferently, Roger moved away from the window and handed over his single remaining bottle of lager. Offering a glass would constitute an insult in Billy's circle of acquaintance.

"Glad you opened it," Billy remarked. "My teeth aren't what they used to be."

Roger laughed. "That's one thing you can't do with a mobile phone. A virtual bottle opener wouldn't get you far."

Roger sat down in the armchair, armed with a large mug of tea, his only compensation in times of penury. Billy sat opposite him in a halo of smoke and raised the bottle to his mouth. He looked pensively at his brother-in-law.

"Have you thought of hypnosis? I read a book by Dolores Cannon. She recovers missing time for people who've seen flying saucers and stuff like that. Someone like her could get back those years in America."

Roger shook his head. "I don't fancy it. I have experienced occasional flashes…strange things like a castle and knights in armour. I don't really believe them. They don't seem real – how could they be?"

"Perhaps they're not. If you have worked for the

American government in secret Black Projects they can implant fake memories. That way you can't believe anything you do recall and it reduces your credibility if you tell your story."

"We don't have that sort of technology," said Roger.

"Not that we *know of*. You should look at the Disclosure Project website. It's very convincing."

"Whatever you say, Bill. I'll do that when I get a computer."

"When will that happen? You're skint. Come and use mine."

There was a tap at the door. Instantly, Roger tensed up.

"Aren't you going to see who it is?" asked Billy.

Reluctantly, Roger got up and went out to the hallway. He peered through the spyhole and saw that it was only Mavis Pargiter from next door. At least it wasn't a hoodie but with Billy there it could turn out to be embarrassing. Roger opened the door and stepped outside, uncomfortable about blocking her from entering his flat.

"Hello, Mavis. My brother-in-law is visiting right now. I know you don't like smoking." More to the point, she didn't like Billy.

"No problem, Roger. I just wanted to talk to you. Can you drop by later?"

"Yes, of course."

Mavis gave Roger a long, serious look. "Please make sure you do," she said, before turning and going back inside her own flat.

Roger returned to Billy.

"Who was it?"

"Just a neighbour."

"Oh, it was that Mavis, was it? She fancies you."

Roger groaned.

"You know what they say about old fiddles and good tunes," Billy added with a wink.

"Yes – they get you six months."

"Why don't you get a girlfriend then? There are some good-looking girls hanging around downstairs."

"Great! They're not girls looking for romance, Bill. Most of them belong to street gangs. They'd be more likely to mug me. Anyway, what's the point? Being sociable costs and I'm out of work," Roger explained patiently. "Besides, I've got enough to worry about already."

Billy sighed in sympathy. "Yeah, what with men in black outside and hoodies inside, I agree."

Roger bit his tongue. He thought the idea of 'men in black' was nonsense.

"Did you come here to cheer me up or is that simply a bonus?"

"Consider it on the house," said Billy grandly. "I really came to tell you that Liz knows a girl whose friend told her about a relative who knows a woman who hypnotises people into finding lost memories and stuff. She wondered if she could help you get your marbles back."

"Sometimes I think the Greeks will get their Elgin Marbles back from the British Museum before that happens. Look, I'm perfectly sane! I don't need curing of anything."

"Well, let's face it. You haven't been cutting the mental mustard since you returned from the other side of the pond. You were so clever – too clever for your own good. You're a bit of a dead beat now. Just look at this drum; Del Boy Trotter would be at home here," said Billy who watched a lot of reruns on TV.

Roger was about to say that it was all nonsense but something in his mind said *do it*.

"I can't pay."

"We'll negotiate. She might fancy you! Stranger things have happened. That would make it a lot cheaper," he said, winking and leering in an irritating way. Billy drained the bottle and dropped the butt of his rollup in it.

"I'll take that," said Roger, who liked things to be tidy, especially cigarette ash and beer bottles.

"Okay, bruv. I gotta go now."

Billy strolled to the door with his hands in his pockets.

"Say hello to Liz for me," said Roger.

Billy nodded. "Yeah. See you around."

Roger closed the door behind his brother-in-law and bolted it firmly. He sat down in the armchair, breathing a sigh of relief, and relaxed. He pondered the significance of this new development. What had he to lose other than money he hadn't got?

"Oh, *bother*!" Roger said to himself suddenly, remembering his promise to visit Mavis when Billy had gone.

He got up, grabbed his keys, went to his neighbour's door and knocked.

Usually, Mavis Pargiter greeted him with a bright smile; this time she wore a frown. She let him in. Roger headed for a chair by the electric heater with the decorative fake coals. They glowed orange beneath the flying ducks on the wall. Mavis sat down opposite him and studied his face.

"You know I'm quite psychic."

Roger nodded.

"Some of the local lads have been pushing you around."

"Yes, I did mention it to you the other day. Is that what you wanted to tell me?"

"You must be careful. They have guns."

"I know; they want to stash them in my lockup along with drugs and other stuff. They've got a complete arsenal. One even has a knuckle duster from the fifties."

Mavis regarded him intently for a while before continuing. "I think you could hurt them. I don't know what it means but I get the feeling you could be extremely dangerous."

Roger was totally confused. "Dangerous? *Me*? What do you mean?"

"I don't know. Have you learned a martial art? Do you keep a gun? Anything...?"

"No. I could use protection, but I don't get into fights if I can help it. Guns get you ten years in this country. When I was in America they came with cornflakes." Roger paused for a second. "I think I almost remembered something then."

Mavis was insistent. "I just get this feeling that you could harm them. You might do something you would regret for the rest of your life."

"I think it's the other way around. They're more likely to harm me."

"I don't pretend to know what it means. Don't be tempted to do it. That's the message I get. But that's not all. There are others who are interested in you. You have many enemies and friends too."

"You must be mistaking me for somebody else. Who would know me?"

Mavis shook her head. "It was so clear, so strong. I

felt obliged to tell you but don't know why. If only you could remember your past – when you lived abroad."

"I don't know what to make of all this. Billy keeps on at me about missing time and aliens. He thinks I'm being followed. I didn't believe him but there was somebody outside looking up at the window. Was it a coincidence? What's it all about?"

Mavis looked as if she wanted to tell him something and then thought better of it. Roger saw a fleeting emotion cross her face before she almost pushed him out the door. "You'd better go home now. I've got things to do. Just remember, don't fight anybody. You might not lose."

Confused and weary, Roger returned to his flat. He decided it was time to shrug aside the cares of the world; enough is enough! He would forget the deluded ramblings of his well-meaning brother-in-law and the dubious advice from his so-called 'psychic' neighbour. It was all nonsense.

He made another mug of tea and sat down to enjoy it, sighing in relief. Before he could fall asleep, there was a light tap at the door.

Should he ignore it?

With a deep sigh, he went to the door, opened it and looked out. Standing before him was the largest, tallest, darkest hoodie imaginable. Even Roger had to tilt his head upwards to view his visitor. They looked at each other for a moment. Then Roger said, "Aren't you rather old for a hoodie?"

The visitor's face cracked in a smile. "A tad, perhaps. I thought I'd blend in with the natives, old boy."

They laughed and exchanged brief token hugs.

"Melvyn! Come in. It's always a pleasure to see you

even though you *are* a lawyer."

"One gets paid a frightful amount of money and gets called to the bar to spend it. What more could you ask for?"

"It's the bit in between that I wouldn't like. Want some tea?"

"That would be nice. I'm staying at my mum's place for a few days."

"Your mum's wonderful."

"Yeah, yeah, I know. It's funny being back though. The place is the same but there's something different here. All this violence – it never used to be so bad."

Roger smiled. "Your family doesn't change. They are the best people around here. Sugar?"

"Just milk thanks."

They sat down. Roger did not rush the conversation. Melvyn would come out with his reason for visiting when he felt ready.

"So you're a busy man?"

Melvyn nodded as he sipped. "I have more work than I can handle. Sorry about the sartorial disaster. I didn't want to stand out."

Roger gazed at him, sheathed in light grey, six foot seven and built like a heavyweight boxer. "You! Stand out? Heaven forfend."

Melvyn laughed. "The things you come out with. 'Heaven forfend'! Are you still reading old writers like Jane Austen?"

"That was Shakespeare. But, yes. I like old books. Authors really knew how to write back then – or some of them did."

"Aren't Jane Austen's books just romances?"

Roger bristled. "Of course not. Austen wrote about the limited world she knew. She wrote brilliant observations of the hypocrisy and humour of a society hidebound with rules and restrictions, especially for women. The only marriage proposals she bothered to narrate explicitly are the funny, unsuccessful ones. The romances in her books are about as significant to the plot as the horse in a Western."

There was a long pause and then Melvyn came out with it.

"Rog, talking of proposals, I'm getting married. I wanted to tell you myself."

"That's wonderful. I haven't seen Serena for years."

"Nor have I. I'm marrying Paula. You haven't met her yet. She's a colleague."

"Ah, I just assumed…"

"Yeah. I think everybody 'assumed' but people change. Besides, something happened that made me realise it wasn't going to work out with Serena." He sounded emotional and Roger felt quite sorry for him. He remembered how close they had been.

"Do you want to talk about it? What happened to make you think it wasn't going to work?"

There was a pause; then Melvyn smiled. "She got married."

Roger slapped him on the arm. "You could always take a hint, Melvyn. You seem happy about Paula. I am so pleased for you."

"Yeah, man. Life is great. Thanks." Melvyn took a sip of his tea. "Should I send you an invitation to the wedding once it's arranged? It'd mean a lot to me."

"I guess I can't refuse, as it's you. When is it?"

"Oh, not for some time. We've got to get a deposit together to buy a place. Even on my outrageously inflated salary that's going to take another year or two, or twenty. We're looking for a really nice detached house in Berkshire. When we've put down the deposit, I'll let you know the date of the wedding."

"Berkshire," Roger said, "*Royal* Berkshire. Your going up in the world,"

Melvyn grinned. "Yeah but I'm not looking where any film stars or royals live. I don't want to bring down the prices. Not everybody wants to live next door to a lawyer."

Roger laughed. "Okay, if I've got to go to a wedding, it might as well be yours."

"Right. And don't worry about a present. I know you haven't found a job yet. Your presence will be a gift for me. Besides, we've already got a toaster…and two children. We've got two girls Paula made earlier."

Melvyn smiled. "Now tell me what's happening with you. How did your course in America work out? Did you get the degree?"

Chapter Two

Roger walked to his sister's home through the gloom of a damp, cloudy morning in South London. He stopped outside the terraced house she shared with her husband and two children. Knowing the reason for going there, he felt more than a little uncomfortable. Resisting a strong impulse to turn back home, he pressed the button on the door and was rewarded by the sound of a Tardis landing. Billy was devoted to Dr Who. A ten-year-old boy opened the door, saw it was only Uncle Roger and ran back to his video game, leaving him on the doorstep.

"Who is it?" called Liz from the kitchen.

"Only me."

"Did Robin say hello?"

"Not in as many words."

"Billy, tell your son to say hello to his uncle," said Liz, shifting responsibility on to a husband who couldn't hear her.

Ungreeted, but not unwelcome, Roger headed to the kitchen.

"Don't worry about it, Liz," said Roger. "I'm sure Robin and I will have a conversation by the time he's thirty-five."

Liz gave him a quick hug and peck on the cheek and resumed tossing the salad. Billy, in the middle of buttering bread, rolled a cigarette and listened to his iPod, humming tunelessly to something that only he could hear, apart from an irritating buzz emitting from his headphones. He gave Roger a casual wave.

"I can see who Robin takes after," said Roger.

"Oh, Billy never hears a word I say. Access to his planet is by invitation only. Toss this salad for me, dear. There's more dressing in that bottle over there. Deborah hasn't arrived. I hope she does. I've made all this healthy food especially."

"I'm happy to eat a salad but I must say, I'm not convinced about this hypnotism thing."

"She hasn't agreed to do it yet. This is just to meet you. Anyway, it's called regression – not hypnotism."

"What's the difference?"

"About £50 an hour," said Billy loudly. He could hear them talking in the lull between tracks.

Liz gave her husband a sharp slap. "He only listens to heavy metal, somebody called Dead Leopard I think."

"I can hear the base line and something like a swarm of locusts," Roger said.

"Don't worry about money," Liz continued. "She said she'd waive the fee in this case."

"She did! Why?"

"I got her interest with missing time and aliens," shouted Billy, loud enough to hear himself above Def Leppard.

"You didn't! I'm getting this under false pretences," said Roger. "I feel a fraud."

"For once I must disagree with you," yelled Billy, who always disagreed with him as a matter of course. "I bet you were on a secret mission to Mars."

"We've never sent a spaceship to Mars."

"Oh yes we have. It's all on the Internet. They went in a reverse-engineered, antigravity machine in 1962 with the Soviets. There's a video on YouTube of them landing taken through the cabin window."

"That's rubbish, Billy. We had enough trouble getting to the moon in 1969."

The door opened and another child walked through the kitchen and grabbed a doughnut.

"Hello, Uncle Roger."

"Hi, Tracey."

"I'm going back upstairs, Mum."

"They've got everything they could ever need in their bedrooms," Billy explained. "Computers, TVs, DVD players, satellite, cable."

"Wasn't it rather expensive?"

"Yeah, not half, but they compare notes at school these days. If their phones are not worth stealing they're not considered to be cool."

"Consumerism is the new religion," muttered Roger.

"Of course," said Liz. "What else is there?"

The sound of a landing Tardis interrupted further discussion.

Liz raced Robin to open the door to avoid creating the wrong impression. Her son's lack of the social graces was okay for his uncle but wouldn't do for a stranger. Billy led Roger to the living room and dimmed the lighting. Roger sat down in an armchair and waited. The voices in the hallway moved towards them and the door opened. Roger stood up again – uncertain and embarrassed.

"This is Deborah," said Liz. "This is Billy – my husband, and this is–"

"Roger. Hi!" She spoke as if she knew him already. Then slightly apologetically she added, "At least, I presume this is Roger." Her voice was mildly accented. Her clothes were elegant and well cut without being flashy.

Roger stood up and shook hands. Billy waved affably.

"Please, sit down," said Liz in her best telephone voice.

"How did you hear about me?" Deborah asked.

"My mother's friend recommended you," Liz replied. "I don't know where she found out about you. Did you help somebody she knows?"

"Yes, something like that. The important question is whether I can help Roger." She turned towards him. "Do you want to be helped?"

"I guess so. I suppose it would be good to get my memories back."

Deborah smiled. "You don't sound sure about that. Maybe you had a good reason for forgetting them in the first place."

Roger shrugged. "Maybe."

Liz glanced at Roger and gave him a meaningful look. As far as she was concerned, he was not showing the right sort of enthusiasm. "Of course he does. He needs to know so that he can fill in his CV at the job centre."

Deborah smiled at that. "For his CV! Hmm, we'll see. It depends on how deeply his missing memories are buried – and what kind of blocks are in place."

"Blocks?" said Roger suspiciously.

"Oh, just technical jargon," Deborah said dismissively.

"Shall we eat now?" asked Liz brightly, changing the subject.

The children moaned about being forced to eat a meal without the television on. By the time they started the main course, Liz was growing tired of the grumbling, especially when it dwelt on the horrors of eating salad. Deborah looked politely away while Liz leaned close to Robin and severely reprimanded him about his behaviour. Then she repeated the exercise for Tracey. She gave her guest an embarrassed smile.

"You have very nice children," Deborah remarked tactfully. "I like your home. It has a good feeling about it."

"Oh, do you really think so?" asked Liz sounding surprised. "I thought you'd– Oh, never mind." She glanced at her husband and noticed that he was staring at Deborah. She poked him in the ribs with her elbow. "Billy, your mouth is hanging open. Please close it. We don't need to see what you're eating."

"Sorry…"

Deborah and Roger smiled at one another. The ice was breaking a little.

"Roger. What do you do?"

Inwardly he groaned. He realised Deborah was just making polite conversation but wondered why people categorise you by your employment. It was irksome to somebody in his situation.

"I am unemployed at the present time. It's not easy to find a job these days."

"That could be a result of your memory loss. You might have capabilities you have forgotten." She hesitated before adding meaningfully, "Sometimes even the greatest men or women can be reduced in circumstances by a traumatic experience."

"Great men!" said Billy. "This is Roger we're talking about!"

"Bill!" Liz gave him another dig in the ribs.

"I was generalising," said Deborah. "We do not

know what Roger might have achieved during his missing period, do we?"

"I suppose not," Billy acknowledged doubtfully.

"I don't think I've ever had greatness thrust upon me," Roger pondered. "My life is mundane and always has been, I think."

Deborah smiled. "I was simply using an example to describe the possible effects of malevolent intervention on the human psyche. I did not mean to suggest more."

Roger looked at his food with a puzzled expression. What did *malevolent intervention* mean?

The meal continued in a more innocuous vein as they chatted politely.

Liz brought in the coffee and a cup of boiled water for Deborah. No longer able to contain her curiosity, she asked, "Are you married, Deborah?" There was no ring but that was not conclusive evidence either way.

Deborah studied the cup before her before answering. "I *am* in a committed relationship, yes." She anticipated the follow-up and added, "And *no*, I do not have children."

Her tone discouraged further probing and Liz dropped the interrogation.

At the evening's end, Liz tactfully dragged Billy away to herd the children upstairs to their respective gadgets, while she cleared away the dinner plates and cutlery.

"So, Roger, would you like me to help you probe your missing memories?" Deborah asked. "I cannot guarantee success but I would be happy to try."

Roger hesitated. "I can't pay you much. You know my circumstances."

"I do. It is not a question of money. Now that I have met you, I have... formed a favourable opinion. But I need to assess the nature of the problem before making a firm commitment. It really depends on you."

"How much do you know about me? Who told you about my time in the States?"

"It is not important. I *know* – that is all. Do you want me to try?"

"I'm not sure…" Roger looked into her eyes and a rush of emotion washed over him, a pain of anguish deep inside. Tears filled his eyes. His breathing became laboured. Deborah saw it, stood up and approached where he sat. Leaning over, she placed both hands on the sides of his face. Gazing into his eyes, she said, "I think I've got my answer."

"I really don't understand any of this," he said, embarrassed by his own emotion.

"Don't think about it. Just do it." She stepped back, reached into her bag for a visiting card and held it out to Roger. "That's my cell phone number," she said. "If you need me, just ring."

Roger looked at the card. It read 'Deborah Farnham, Regression Therapist', followed by the mobile number. "Shall we make an appointment now?" he asked with some ambivalence.

Deborah took out a diary and gave him a date and time the following week. Roger made a note on a scrap of paper from his sister's sideboard and tucked it in his shirt pocket.

"You'll need my telephone number and address," Roger said.

"I already have it," she said softly.

Right on cue, Liz and Billy returned.

Deborah stood up. "I'd better be going. Thank you for dinner and for your hospitality," she said to Liz. She shook hands with Billy, who blushed and stuttered something vague, and hugged Liz briefly before turning to Roger. He put out his hand awkwardly just as Deborah reached forward for a hug. They managed an embarrassed compromise and she was gone.

Roger said, "I think I'll get back home now. Thanks for...for helping. I suppose anything is worth trying."

"I think she might be able to get your memory back," said Liz.

"Maybe. Bye, sis. See you around, Billy."

"Stay cool, mate."

Roger walked out of the house and headed towards the high street in the direction of home. He felt that his life was turning a corner. It was a positive feeling. The sky was more or less dark but there was a gentle glow from the lights of London. He looked up to see if he could see any stars. A bright light attracted his attention. He observed it closely, trying to decide if it was a star or an aircraft, as it moved closer towards him. As it drew near he could swear it was a silvery disc. It was unlike any aircraft he could identify. That made it a UFO. It appeared to be slowing down directly above him. He stopped walking and stared upwards. The object drew closer but judging distance was difficult with no scale of reference. Was it large and far off or near and quite small? The light from it seemed part reflection and part emission. Suddenly, Roger remembered his brother-in-law's obsession with the phenomenon. He ran back to his sister's house, pressed the button that activated the Tardis sound and knocked furiously in his impatience.

"Billy! Billy! Come here – quick!"

After an age, the door opened and Billy emerged, confused by the commotion.

"What's going on?"

"Look up there – what do you see?"

Roger turned back and the object vanished. From the corner of his vision he saw a row of dots of light shooting like intermittent punctuations into the sky, almost too fast for his sight to accommodate.

"I can't see anything." Billy sounded peeved.

"It's just gone," said Roger in frustration. "I think it was what you would describe as an unidentified flying object. At least, I couldn't identify it. It was not an aircraft that I recognised. I don't know what it was. That's why I called you out. I hoped you could assure me that I'm not going mad."

"What's to assure? You *are* going mad. That's why we've found you a therapist. If you did see a UFO, I am jealous because you don't believe they exist. I do and I have never seen one."

"I did call you."

"I know you did, Rog. Thanks for that. Cheers, mate. Maybe next time…"

"Yeah, see you later."

Roger resumed his walk home in a daze; overwhelmed by the events of the day and challenged emotionally. His entire view of the world felt brittle somehow. Eventually, he approached his apartment block with little thought of what might await him. He opened the outer street door and entered the vestibule, straight into the clutches of two hoodies. They pushed him around, flung him down on the cold, hard stairs and delivered a series of kicks. Roger grunted with pain and tried to cover his vital areas by rolling over and pulling his arms and legs into his body. The hard edges of the concrete steps were as unforgiving as his assailants.

"I asked you if we could use your lockup garage

and you said no. Remember? If you don't do what we ask you won't *need* a garage. Got it?"

"He *don't* need no garage. He's got no wheels."

"But he does have legs – for the time being. Know what I mean?"

Roger groaned with each kick. When the beating stopped, he looked up and saw Barty Loughlin and Cade Mitchell waiting, watching; determined to have their way. Cade had a knife in his hand and Barty was toying casually with an automatic pistol. There was no choice. Roger pulled himself painfully to his feet and reached into his pocket. He fumbled with the garage key but he was shaking too much to prise it off the ring. Cade grabbed the bunch of keys, took off the one he wanted and threw the remainder on the ground. They could have taken them all and left him stranded but they didn't want to draw too much attention to his circumstances. They just needed to use his garage. Having got what they wanted, they ran off.

"You have a nice day, my man," Cade called as he disappeared.

Roger struggled to stand, slowly and painfully, and climbed the stairs to his flat. He opened the door and walked in, ready to collapse on his bed to recover.

"Oh no, not more trouble."

Somebody had been inside the flat during his absence and turned the place over. It looked like vandalism but why did they lock the door behind them? Had anything been taken? How did they open the lock? Was it Barty and Cade again?

Roger groaned wearily, in total despair, and sank down on the nearest chair. He should phone the police but he didn't want to make the hoodie problem any worse. It was a dilemma. If he called in the law about his burglary, the hoodies might think he had grassed on them. He dismissed the idea that it was Barty and Cade. They wanted to use his garage, not rob him. What did he have to steal? The police would want to know what had been taken. Nothing? He'd get six months for wasting police time.

Roger sat there for a while, too hurt and too shocked to do anything. He considered going to his neighbour, Mavis.

On impulse he stood up and walked to the window. His ribs hurt where Barty and Cade had kicked him. He thought something might be broken. He could not face going to A&E but it might be necessary to seek medical attention. He looked down at the street and, sure enough, there was a car bearing the faint outline of two men in black suits and dark glasses. It was almost dark so why sunglasses? Were they his burglars or did they know the culprit?

At that moment there came a loud, harsh rapping on the door.

"This is the police. Open up in there. Keep your hands where we can see them."

Roger was amazed. Did they know he had been burgled? The banging and shouting continued. Roger unlatched the door and stood back. The police had arrived.

"How did you know…?"

Whatever Roger expected to happen, it was not this. Four policemen in body armour rushed into the room pointing handguns at him, demanding he lay flat on the floor. One twisted his arms up behind him and put on handcuffs, tightly and painfully, pinching his flesh. Then all of them grabbed him at once. They lifted him bodily with such violence that one of the policemen hurt his own wrist. Roger's feet hardly touched the ground as they rushed him down the stairs into a van with a grill across the back window.

The black car pulled away in one direction, the police van drove off in the other, with Roger in the back, battered and bruised. By now he was totally confused and in shock. The policeman that had grabbed him too vigorously had fractured a wrist bone. So, to the charges of possessing drugs and guns they added aggravated assault and resisting arrest. All he knew was that resistance had been futile under the circumstances.

Roger tried to explain, politely, that he was innocent but to no avail. They ignored everything he said and talked about him as if he wasn't there. He ended up in a cell at the police station. He complained about his injuries, some from the hoodies' attack, others from the arrest. They took no notice of him and left him in the cell overnight. The rough bed was uncomfortable. The dim light did nothing to relieve the gloom of the décor.

As he lay there, struggling to relax, Roger thought about the events of the day. The way the police had treated him came as no surprise. They were merely exercising the common practice of the system. There was no malice in their actions. Their attitudes were implicit in the culture. They did what their superiors expected, no more and no less. They did not know him as a person. The time-honoured phrase 'innocent until proved guilty' was hardly at the forefront of their minds when they set out to nick a villain. That is all Roger was from their point of view, even if he hadn't done anything wrong. He bore no grudge against them. Casting his mind back to the attacks of Barty and Cade he could not contemplate *them* without resentment. Try as he might, his instinct to disregard their attacks was unequal to the task. They were his *neighbours*. What greater reason should they require to be kind and helpful to one another? Why did he even think he *should* accommodate the transgressions of those who mistreated him? He was not religious. Perhaps it had something to do with the events of his missing time? No – that is how he had always been – tolerant and non-judgemental. He fell into a fitful sleep and dreamed about the horror of handcuffs.

The next morning they brought him a breakfast that, as a vegetarian, he couldn't eat because it was mostly bacon and sausage. He picked ruefully at some scrambled egg on the side of the plate and drank the cold tea. After a couple of hours, they took him to an interview room. A silent, uniformed constable stood and ignored him with determined intensity. Eventually a young detective came in with a file and sat down at the desk. There was a surveillance camera high on the wall.

Detective Constable Parsons opened the paperwork and put on a recording device to log the interrogation, stating his name and rank and the time. He said that the subject was Roger Crandle and gave his address. Then he turned his attention to Roger.

"You own a lockup garage behind the block of flats where you reside. Acting on information received we obtained a warrant and forced open the door. Inside we discovered proscribed substances with an estimated street value of twenty thousand pounds. We also found three firearms and two knives. Can you explain how these items came into your possession?"

"They were never in my possession. I have never

seen them." *That was quick!* he thought. *Was this whole thing a set up? Barty and Cade only took the key a few minutes before the police arrested me.*

"They were in your garage so technically they were in your possession. Do you deny putting them there?"

"Yes."

"Then how do you account for them?"

"I can't. They were not there on Tuesday when I last looked."

The interrogation went on for over an hour – the questions, the accusations. Reluctantly, in fear of reprisals, Roger explained that he was the victim of intimidation and violence. He told them of the break in by persons unknown but they ignored him on that subject. Apparently, burgling his flat was not significant to their enquiry. Eventually, the detective made his play.

"You know you are likely to get ten years for possessing guns and Class A drugs. We could, of course, make a deal and see that you only get eighteen months at the most."

"Detective Constable Parsons, what about my burglary? How long will the people who broke into my home get?"

"You can forget that. How do we know you were burgled? You might just be untidy."

"I'm not a criminal and you know it," said Roger with fragile dignity.

"Tell me who your accomplices are and we will put in a word for you."

"For a start, I had no accomplices because I didn't do anything. Secondly, if I tell you who I believe to be responsible they will probably kill me. Will you protect me? No, I think not."

The policeman did not look surprised. It was not an uncommon situation. It was not his fault, it was the system; it was the job. He looked at the young man and sighed. Roger bore the scars and wounds of a bad day, beaten up by hoodies and then rough-handled by the police.

Parsons paused for some time before asking a question that totally confused Roger.

"What did you do to the four police officers who arrested you yesterday?"

"Do? What do you mean, what did I do? Everything that was done was done *to* me, not *by* me."

Parsons looked serious as he said in a sombre voice: "Then why are all four of them in hospital in a coma?"

Roger was genuinely shocked.

"But I was locked up in here all night. How could I do that? And how would I go about it anyway? Are they ill?"

"Nobody really knows," said the detective. "One officer in a coma might be chance but all four is more than a coincidence. If you hadn't been locked up all night, we would be pinning it on you – if we knew *what* we were pinning."

"I'm terribly sorry," Roger said with feeling. "I have no idea what's going on."

The detective had another humdinger of a question to throw at him. "Who is Deborah Farnham?"

"Who?"

He threw a business card on the desk. "We found this."

"Oh, just somebody I met at my sister's house. I don't know anything about her. She certainly has nothing to do with this." Even as he said it, Roger wondered if that was true. With all the chaos Roger had completely forgotten about his new acquaintance.

"I can soon run some checks on her background. Is she a dealer?"

"Drugs! Of course she isn't. But you can check up on her if you want to waste more time and money. Sure – why not?"

The detective continued talking to him about irrelevant things, people and crimes he had never heard of, more repetition of threats. Roger detached himself from the scene. A strange calmness came over him and he heard the droning voice as if down a long tunnel. His brain took on a strange tingling as if a light had gone on inside his head. It was as if he was merging with the room, the policeman and everything in it. His own body was just an object in the space and 'he' was something much greater, almost nebulous, a field of awareness.

Detective Parsons began to sense his lack of attention. "Mr Crandle, what are you looking at?" he asked uneasily, turning in the direction of Roger's gaze.

"Sorry, nothing really. I suppose I'm in shock after all that has happened." Roger focussed on Parsons and the feeling faded. He had not the faintest idea what the policeman had been saying to him. It meant nothing at all. Now he was back to normal consciousness.

Parsons snorted and switched off the recorder. He picked up his file of papers and left Roger with his silent uniformed supervisor. Roger glanced at the policeman and was surprised to see him staring at him with something like fear on his face. What was happening? No doubt Parsons would be back with a bigger stick or a more compelling carrot. Roger was on the verge of despair. He could not think of any strategy that would improve his situation. There was no way he could phone anybody and no point anyway; whom could he call? He did not wish to alarm his sister. Their parents lived abroad. He had never felt his social isolation more keenly than at this moment.

Something strange had happened during the interrogation. He could not explain it. Was it a hallucination? What had driven the detective out of the room? Roger had perceived a sudden discomfort in the man, almost panic. It made no sense.

Then he thought of Deborah Farnham. Did this have something to do with her? He couldn't see how. Eventually, another officer arrived to take him back to his cell. It seemed that he was going to spend a second night in custody. Then events took an unexpected turn and a uniformed sergeant opened his door and told him he could go.

"You've been bailed."

"Bailed? By whom?"

The sergeant did not reply but led him to the front reception desk and gave him back his belongings, including Deborah's business card, and made him sign various papers.

"Have you got a solicitor?" the sergeant asked.

"No. They cost money and I don't have any. If I was really a drug dealer or a gun runner I suppose I would have a brief but I'm not."

"You will be hearing from the Crown Prosecution Service in due course. In the meantime, please try to stay out of trouble, Mr Crandle."

"Thank you, sir," Roger said politely. He gathered his possessions from a box and walked towards the door. Conveyance to the station had not been as problematic as getting home. Police transport was a one-way courtesy. Roger was trying to decide whether to walk or take a bus and generally feeling depressed about the events of the past two days. He descended the steps, deep in thought. He heard a cheery voice ring out.

"Hi, Roger!"

He looked up with a start.

"Deborah!"

"I thought you might need a ride home."

"But…"

"I've brought my car. It's just being fixed up. How are you doing, boys?"

Roger turned in the direction she was looking to see a pink Mercedes sports model with a policeman changing the wheel and a traffic warden fiddling under the bonnet. All this was happening in the police station car park.

Deborah looked stunning in a tailored business outfit with a short skirt and carefully arranged hair. Her style and demeanour were totally different from their previous encounter at his sister's. Roger wondered which version was real. It struck him then that sartorial appearance is illusion anyway. Her presence outside the police station brought light into his darkness.

"How did you know I was here?" he asked. "Did you stand bail for me?"

"Shh! Don't speak yet. I have been doing my helpless American woman abroad act. It's a hire car. I think I drove over a nail outside the station. I don't want to change a wheel in this rig. I bought these clothes to impress so they're not cheap."

Roger studied her closely. "They certainly impress me," he said.

She smiled faintly. Roger decided that this was the real Deborah, not the one who was manipulating the police force. But then…perhaps they were both real. *How confusing life is,* he thought.

"You're taller than I expected," Roger said and then paused. "Now, why did I say that? How could I possibly have expectations? We've never met before Liz introduced us yesterday."

She nodded. "Yes. Strange isn't it? You're taller than I expected too. It's a mystery, I guess. I think they've nearly finished changing my wheel."

Twenty minutes passed before she drove out of the station car park and headed towards his home. She seemed to be accustomed to London traffic but drove carefully. She said American roads were wide and straight, without bollards and other sundry obstacles at every corner and junction. Roger didn't like driving in the metropolis unless it was absolutely necessary. The question didn't arise at the moment; he couldn't afford a car. As he neared home, he scanned the street warily for signs of his hoodie 'friends'. He wished to avoid two hoodies in particular – not all young people who wore the uniform were paid-up members of a gang.

He ushered Deborah up the communal stairwell to his apartment as quickly as possible. He assumed it would contrast unfavourably with her accustomed style of décor. Yet he could remember enough from his earliest time in America to know that it wasn't the Promised Land. His student apartment in New York had been quite tacky.

He groaned when he saw the state of his flat. He'd almost forgotten the burglary.

Cheerfully, Deborah slapped him on the back. "Now, let's try to sort this mess. Then you can tell me what happened."

Deborah set about tidying the flat and cleaning up the damage. Roger joined in but inside he felt uneasy. This intrusion in his life and the desecration of his home by person or persons unknown unsettled him.

"Who told you I was at the police station? Does my sister know?"

Deborah shook her head. "I guess you haven't told her?"

"No. I didn't want to worry her. Liz might have paid a solicitor to rescue me and I don't have the means of paying her back."

"I heard about it from a friend of mine. Nobody you would know. He has – let's say – connections in the police. Well, he has connections everywhere. Funnily enough he looks a bit like you," she added, grinning.

Roger nodded absently but had no idea what she was talking about. He was too shocked by the day's events to think clearly. Why would she know somebody connected with a police station near his home in South London?

"So he bailed me out? Why would he do that?"

"Oh, you and he go back aways."

"He knew me in America?"

"Not exactly. He just said that he owes you. I can't say more. But he did say that you travelled quite a lot during your time out of the UK. That's what he told me anyway."

Roger pondered these things for a while. It was obvious that she knew more about him than she was prepared to divulge so he changed the subject. "What is the difference between regression therapy and hypnotism?" he asked.

"In hypnosis you suggest the subject goes to sleep.

You want to bypass the conscious mind and talk directly to the unconscious. In regression you simply relax them. You try to keep the conscious mind involved in the process. Deep hypnosis has its uses but I am not anxious to raise any demons from *your* subconscious. Are you sure this a good time to try? You look like you've been through hell."

"Yes. Let's do it."

"When we've straightened out your place," she said.

Roger's agreement had more to do with being sociable than any strong desire to undergo therapy. Deborah had gone to all this trouble to help him and he felt obliged to go along with it. For some reason, Roger felt that the burglar had broken in to find something specific. He owned nothing of significant monetary value and could not imagine why anyone would bother with his possessions. He shared these thoughts with Deborah as they cleared up.

"Maybe they are also interested in your memories – and want to find out if you've recovered anything."

"But how and why?"

She shrugged. "No idea. A diary perhaps? Do you write down your thoughts?"

"No, I don't, and I can't see why anybody would want to know about *my* memories."

"It doesn't seem likely on the face of it," she agreed, straightening a photograph on the bedroom wall. Roger's missing time began to take on a new and disturbing dimension. He felt a fresh curiosity about it – mingled with fear.

Roger was grateful for Deborah's help. He hadn't expected it. It made him realise that his first impression of her had been rather shallow. It took an hour to tidy and clean the flat and when it was restored to satisfactory order, Roger suggested having coffee. While he made it, they talked about his life in London and what little he could recall of America. He noticed that she avoided talking about herself. She seemed quite skilful at deflecting conversation away from anything personal.

"When I was walking home yesterday – after you left us – I saw a flying saucer."

"Really."

"You didn't laugh."

"No, Roger. I didn't laugh. It was a saucer and not a triangle?" she asked.

"Yes. What do you mean?"

"People sometimes see flying triangles as well as discs and orbs. I've read up on it. That's all."

"I would have scoffed if Billy had told me a story like that. I'd have said he saw it because he wanted to. I don't even believe there are such things. I suppose I'm a sceptic."

Deborah nodded. "There was a time when a sceptic was somebody with an open mind. Nowadays it means somebody who doesn't believe in anything that doesn't fit the current scientific paradigm. That is why science is trapped inside a prison of its own making. Occam's Razor cuts both ways."

"I wouldn't know about that," said Roger rather irritably.

Deborah shrugged. "You are defending your position, I suppose. So, what else happened?"

Roger described how his consciousness had altered in the interview room at the police station.

"Actually, it seemed to bring a chill to the room. The young detective noticed it and left as quickly as he could."

Deborah's composure slipped for a moment. She looked uneasy. "Did you feel anger towards *him*?"

"Not really. He was just doing his job. Do you think it had something to do with me?"

"Maybe," she said but she didn't sound thrilled by this thought. "It certainly suggests that deep hypnosis is out."

"He said something else that disturbed me," Roger said, shifting uncomfortably in his chair. "He told me that the four policemen who were first through the door when they arrested me are all comatose in hospital. Can you make any sense of that?"

Deborah looked up sharply. "Really! That's *very* interesting. Do they know why or how?"

Roger shook his head. "No. They said they would have arrested me if I hadn't been locked up at the time."

"Huh! What could they have proved against you?" she said sceptically. "How did you feel about those men?"

"Nothing really. I blame the system, the macho culture. I suppose some people resist arrest so they go in expecting the worst. But it angers me that they didn't give me a chance to go with them voluntarily."

Deborah looked pensive and said nothing for a minute or two. "I understand you were attacked recently. How did you feel about the young men responsible?"

Roger shrugged. "I felt resentful. These flats could be a good place to live if everybody pulled together. I think some people get a kick out of creating fear and hurting others. Nobody helps you if the gangs pick on you. Some of them call me 'posh' because I sound different to them."

Deborah summed up the situation. "So you took it personally when the hoodies hurt you and nothing happened to them. You did not take it personally that the policemen bullied you and they ended up in a coma?"

"Well, yes, but I don't see any direct connection there. I couldn't have been involved in what happened to the coppers."

She nodded slowly. "Perhaps not. I need to take advice on this. Can you give me a couple of minutes to phone somebody?"

"Of course."

Deborah took out a mobile phone and went outside the flat for a few minutes. On returning she said, "Let's start the regression. I want you to sit on a hard-backed chair. I want you to be relaxed but not comatose."

The session lasted about an hour. She talked him into a state of deep relaxation; mostly by saying, 'relax'.

She asked him to go back in time to the year he first decided to go to America to study for a PhD at New York University. It was not successful from Roger's point of view. He didn't remember much more in the regressed state than he could in his usual awareness. She asked him about people he met at the university. It was standard stuff. He spoke of his project supervisor and one or two other students. Deborah closed the session down when he came to the barrier he referred to as 'the wall', the point in time where his memory stopped dead. Before ending the session, she asked him to think about the policemen in a coma and make a positive decision to forgive them for what they did. It seemed an odd request but he did as she asked. Then she counted him out of relaxation into full wakefulness. At no time was he unconscious or unable to control his mind. It did enable him to recall events and people in greater clarity. It was not a magic doorway to the past.

Once the session was over, Deborah decided it was time to leave.

"Do you think it's worth continuing?" he asked.

"Oh yes. Don't you want to go on?"

"Of course. Do you think I will succeed?"

"It might take some time," she acknowledged. "Most people can access hidden memories under light hypnosis. Others need a deeper state. I can put you right to sleep to set aside your conscious mind but I am not ready to do that yet. Your case is a bit different. Besides, you don't mind my company, do you?"

He laughed. "Not at all."

"Well, that's all right then." She looked deep into his eyes as if reading something profound in the depths of his soul. Then she turned and left the flat.

Roger stared after her for a few moments, his toes curling from unfathomable emotions.

Chapter Three

Crowds of shoppers bustled around the high street where Roger searched for bargains and special offers to eke out his meagre income. 'Buy one, get one free' is all very well but why don't they just give you the free one? Why would he want two packs of avocados? He lived alone!

Roger had just emerged from the monthly ritual of humiliation at the job centre. The system was fine-tuned to embarrass and inflict the maximum stress on people in unfortunate circumstances. Roger wrote to companies that advertised for people with computer skills but seldom received a reply. When he did get an interview, he was severely disadvantaged by his inability to 'play the game'. Also there was the gap in his employment record. Saying that he had a memory loss went down even worse. That put him in the shadow of mental illness and the attitude of most employers towards that was generally prehistoric. Another classic line was 'you should consider retraining'. It had taken years to build up his skills and experience in cutting-edge systems. Now they expected him to take a two-day course in word processing and start a new career; 'unlimited opportunities for one-fingered typists'.

Now he was free for a whole month – apart from writing pointless letters of application to people who wouldn't reply. Roger made a last call to the chemist where the profit mark-ups were astronomical and then set off for home with a cluster of carrier bags. He dodged the traffic and skirted the crowds on the pavements.

"Roger!"

He looked around and saw his brother-in-law coming out of a pub.

"Hi, Billy."

"I spotted you through the window. Come and have a drink. You've got time. You've got nothing else to do."

"I can't, Bill. I haven't got any money."

"I can buy me wife's brother a drink without expecting one back. Besides, I've got something to talk to you about. It's important."

Roger smiled and relented. Billy did not have much in common with him but he was family. He was good company too, a nice thought on a dull day; not that he was averse to dull days after recent events. A drop of real ale would wash the taste of the job centre out of his mouth. They turned into Billy's local that Liz described as his natural home. She referred to their family house as his second home. The girl behind the bar didn't need to ask what Billy wanted but Roger was not a regular. "Yeah, another one of the same please, Patty."

Billy rolled a cigarette while he waited and stuck it behind his ear for later. Then he took the drinks to where Roger sat. Normally, Billy stood at the bar but this was not appropriate for this particular conversation.

"Cheers, Bill. You must miss being able to smoke in the pub," Roger remarked.

"Yeah! Tony Blair's greatest victory," muttered

Billy. "He found his weapons of mass destruction after all – cigarettes!"

Roger smiled. "What did you want to talk to me about?"

"I wanted to ask you why you behaved so strangely this morning. I see you went home to change afterwards. Was that sharp suit you had on to impress the job centre? I told you you'd never be employed wearing pullovers. And those cool dark glasses!"

"What do you mean? I put these on first thing this morning."

"No, mate. I saw you meself. You were in the high street near McDonald's. I spoke to you and you looked at me as if I was a total stranger and asked who I was. I said I'm your brother-in-law, you moron."

"You said that, did you? What did I say?"

Billy looked either side conspiratorially. He lowered his voice to a whisper. "You said something like, 'Moron? You think me of diminished intelligence? Do you know Roger Crandle?' So I said, 'Fuck off, it's me you berk.' Well, what could I say? I assumed you were out of your tree and went along with it. Then you said, 'I hear Roger still lives at his old address' – as if you were somebody else. Of course, by then I decided you were barking. Then it got really weird."

"*Then* it got weird!"

"Much weirder! I said, 'I like the whistle.' I meant the suit, of course."

"Whistle and flute. It looked good then?"

"Yeah! It was new – or looked it. Anyway, I've never seen you in it before. Actually, it was much too good for you."

"It can't have been me. I don't have a new suit.

What colour was it?"

"Black," said Billy. "You had cool dark glasses sticking out of your breast pocket. Hah! Come to mention it, you looked like one of them men in black. Think you could fool me like that? Pretending not to know me." He paused as a thought struck him. "Perhaps you've gone on from loss of memory to multiple personalities. Oh dear. Perhaps that American woman wasn't such a good idea. Poor old Rog, fancy going *doolally tap!* Lost your marbles now as well as your memory."

"So, your theory is that I went through a personality change and magically acquired a new suit to go with it? That's neat. What did I say to you after that?"

"You said, 'How did I know you could whistle?' Then you gave me a tune – a normal whistle at first; then it turned into a three-part harmony like you were accompanying yourself."

"I can't whistle in three parts. I can just about manage one."

"I said, 'That's amazing, Rog. What is it?' So, guess what happened then? While you were still whistling, you said it was the 'Hallelujah Chorus'. You know, that Handle Messy Thing. Suddenly, I heard the whole piece of music coming out of you in surround sound – orchestra and choir an' all. I flipped my lid then and scarpered. So, which one of us is mad?"

Roger looked at his brother-in-law and grinned. "Definitely you, mate. You're mad as a hatter. Is this a wind-up?"

"No – I swear on me mother's grave…"

"Bill. Your mother's still alive and she wants to be cremated."

"I know; I'm just careful about committing myself."

Nevertheless, it gave Roger disquiet. He didn't know what to believe. Nothing in his life made sense any more.

"I'm not making it up, honest," Billy insisted.

"I don't think anybody could," Roger said. "I don't believe in UFOs but I saw one. Something strange is going on. Do you think Deborah knows more than she is letting on?"

"I dunno but I'm going to buy you another drink because I need one," Billy said, sucking the dregs of his first pint. "Thank goodness for emergencies!" he uttered, raising the empty glass.

"Thanks, mate. Buying me two drinks! Most appreciated. Normally I'd say no but these are exceptional circumstances." Then he added softly, "My God, are they."

***

'CRANDAL IS DED'

It was daubed on the wall of his flat in red paint along with ugly squiggles and a swastika. The swastika he knew had been a symbol of auspicious fortune and positive goodness going back at least twelve thousand years until the Nazis hijacked it. They tainted its meaning forever through acts of appalling evil. It didn't take a genius to guess the authors of this crudely daubed version. It bore the hallmarks of Barty and Cade's style. They probably believed he had told the police about the stuff in his lockup. Either that or they had told them themselves. Great!

Mavis Pargiter emerged from her flat and shook her head sadly.

"Not very nice is it, Roger?"

"No. It might win a Turner Prize if we could transport it brick by brick. There should always be a benefit to misfortune."

Mavis smiled. "You're taking it extremely well but I don't think you feel as confident as you sound."

"No. I don't know what to do, Mavis. I'm no fighter."

"I wish I could help but I can't think of anything either. Come and have a cup of tea. I'll see if I can see anything in the tea leaves."

"Why not? It doesn't look like I'm going anywhere in a hurry."

Roger followed Mavis into her flat. He was quite pleased to collapse into her armchair and relax while she brewed tea. He preferred 'real' tea from a pot rather than a squeezed bag. Mavis didn't use a strainer when she was reading the leaves. As soon as they sat down, Mavis took the cover off the teapot and poured.

They drank from cups and saucers rather than mugs. Roger liked mugs but Mavis was even more of a traditionalist than he was. When they had finished their tea, Mavis told Roger to swill the dregs around and pour the liquid into a spare cup, leaving the leaves at the bottom. He handed it over for inspection.

"I don't think I have ever seen a reading like this. If I didn't know better I'd say that that outline is a spaceship but that *can't* be so, can it? And there's a troublemaker out there who's got it in for you. It could be more than one. There's a group of them. The black men?"

Roger remembered Billy's comments about the men in the limo. "Men in black, perhaps?"

Mavis shrugged. "Maybe, whatever that means. There's an 'H'? I think it's a name beginning with that letter. I'm sure he's a friend."

"Deborah said I have a friend out there. He bailed me out of police custody. I don't know his name. What does it all mean, Mavis?"

"This is beyond me. I'm out of my depth with you."

Roger's mobile phone rang.

"Hello. Oh hi, Deborah. What? Where? Okay, see you."

"Trouble?" asked Mavis.

"For once, no. My friend Deborah is nearby and wants to pop in. I'd better get back to my flat."

As he turned to leave, Mavis said, "I keep getting Gemini; the sign of twins. You don't have a twin brother, do you?"

"No, just a sister. We're not twins."

Mavis shook her head, frustrated. "I don't understand. You can't have a twin and not know about it. And something about a great big moon at Saturn. What's it called?"

"Do you mean titan?" Roger asked. "That's the biggest moon. Titan doesn't mean anything to me."

"Oh, well, either it will or it won't. See you later."

"Bye."

Deborah drew a few stares from the flat dwellers that loitered in the forecourt and the stairwell. It was the customary lot of strangers to be scrutinised. She showed no sign of nervousness and took it all in her stride. Roger let her in the front door of his flat and followed her into the lounge. She stood looking at him without taking off her lightweight coat. She held his gaze for a moment.

"What do you say to going out for a meal somewhere?"

"It sounds very nice but I can't."

"Why not?"

"I'm skint. Remember?"

"That is not a problem. I do not see you as a client. You are a research project. That means I can put it on my expense account."

"Okay. I accepted a couple of beers from Billy. I suppose I can let you buy me a meal. I just don't want–"

"What?"

"I don't want to get too used to enjoying the things in life I can't afford."

"That's fine. Look on the bright side, I might never do it again," she said with a smile.

Three blocks away, there was an Indian restaurant that Roger used to frequent in wealthier days. The décor was somewhat ancient and the food traditional. It was where many Indian families chose to eat, which was a recommendation in itself. He didn't like his curries over-cooked and over-spiced. Flavour was more important to him than having his taste buds incinerated, which was the norm in most restaurants serving spicy cuisine.

Roger opened the door for Deborah to enter. They waited to be seated. A waiter responded and led them towards a small table in the centre. Deborah called him back, asking to be seated by a wall. It was the optimum location for surveying the interior and the street outside. The waiter lit a candle and then tried to take her coat when she took it off.

"No thanks, I'll keep it," she said, placing it over the back of her chair. She put her handbag on the table, close to where she would eat. Roger noticed that she took in the entire room with a glance, apparently checking the exits. Her behaviour was not so obvious that anybody would notice unless they were in close proximity.

"You can help me order," she said casually. "I still haven't found my way around these menus. We don't have so many Indian restaurants in America as you do here."

"I bet you get more Indian restaurants than British. You'd starve to death *here* if you wanted an 'English Takeaway'. I remember hearing of some London lads who went to France for the first time. They said that the only English item on the menu was *gateau*."

Roger helped her to make a selection and place her order. At least he had a choice of vegetarian options. She ordered wine for herself and Roger had Indian beer.

"Any luck finding a job?" she asked while they sipped their drinks.

"No. I even called in a temping agency recently to see if I could get a low-grade office job. They put me through basic tests, spreadsheets and a simple database – stuff like that. It seemed to be going well until they gave me a page of text to type up on a word processor. This was to quantify my speed and accuracy. I'm a pretty fast typist because of my previous work on systems; writing specs and process outlines. I went back to the woman who gave me the tests. She looked at how much I'd typed and said that I must have cheated. 'Men can't type,' she said. 'How could I possibly do that,' I asked? There was no desktop scanner. I even offered to type something in front of her but she told me to get out like I was some sort of criminal. You can imagine how I felt. So I got up and left. I can't tell you how much that rankled. It's like being accused of theft or fraud."

"Would you be happy working as an office assistant, Roger?" Deborah asked. She could see how upset he was by the incident.

"I'd take a lower paid job but I can't even do that because I'm overqualified. I might take my qualifications off the CV even though you're not supposed to. At least I might get off the dole."

"You've become very cynical, Roger, but I understand why. You have a great void in your life."

The waiter came over with the first course. Roger looked down at his starter and pondered her words. "You do know me from somewhere, don't you? You knew me during my missing years, I think."

"We have never met before your sister introduced us. But we did...*know* about each other a long time ago."

"That makes no sense. How can you know somebody you haven't met?"

Deborah paused then smiled. "Let's say we corresponded on a regular basis."

"You mean we wrote letters to each other?"

"Something like that. I can't say any more. You've got to find your own answers."

"I heard a story once about a man who wrote hundreds of letters to a girl in another country. It didn't quite work out as he intended."

"What happened?"

"She married the postman. Such is life," he sighed philosophically. "This whole business is quite frustrating. I feel like a pawn in somebody else's game. Let's talk about something different."

"Sure, how about the British weather? How weird is that?"

They enjoyed the meal, declined the sweet menu

and ordered coffee. Roger poured milk in his and wished for cream. He looked out of the window. It was dusk bordering on night. Across the road the street lamps came on, dimly glowing red. In a few minutes they would change to bright yellow-orange. He caught a glimpse of a man who looked oddly familiar. He stood, silhouetted by a shop window. His head moved casually from side to side and then he walked away down the street and out of sight. Roger turned back to Deborah but she was lost in thought, occasionally looking around the room at other diners. Eventually, she turned to him and smiled self-consciously. "I guess I'm distracted. I haven't had a chance to relax lately. My life has been very intense for some time now."

Being out of work, Roger dreaded being asked, 'what do you do?' So he said, "How do you pass your time?"

Deborah laughed. "You've probably guessed that hypnotherapy is not my main occupation. I investigate temporal anomalies, ET abduction and alien interventions. I advise on interstellar treaty negotiations – the usual mundane women's work."

"Temporal anomalies?"

"Time travel often results in inconvenient divergences in the predominant timeline. Whenever we make a decision or intervene in an action, the universe explores all significant options by fragmenting into parallel versions. The field of consciousness craves understanding. It experiments with us, with events, with choices and puts us through experiences to find out what we are made of – our characters if you like. The timelines do not come back together until the conclusion of our lives here. Does that make sense to you?"

"I suppose so," he said doubtfully. In truth, he thought she was insane.

"It's not my idea. I had a good teacher."

"Oh, who was that?"

"*You!* I've still got the letters you wrote to me nearly thirty years ago."

"Me! I would have been three years old then."

"Yes – *here* but not in *that* timeline. You said there's probably a parallel universe where you were not raised vegetarian just to see what difference it makes. Once you've unravelled your memory gap, I might let you read those letters."

"So, did I send you a letter explaining the meaning of life?"

"No, but you did say that the meaning of life is what *we express* through ourselves in our lives. The question remains open for eternity as the answer manifests in infinite variety, complexity and originality."

"*I* said *that!*"

"Yes. You said that something greater than ourselves expresses us as physical, thinking beings."

"That being?"

"Everything that is *not* you in this present moment of time. That is the *real* you. Each one of us is a version of the entire pattern of space and time minus our physical form with its finite mind. *You* are a pattern of conscious existence in physical form expressing your desires, thoughts and feelings as your story unfolds in this wonderful holographic virtual reality. The whole expresses its parts and collectively the parts express the whole. When we are born here, we forget who and what we really are. Simple!"

"Scientists won't like that idea," Roger said.

"That goes without saying," Deborah agreed. "But

even if they do open their minds to the possibility that reality is virtual, they won't understand the consequences. They won't just bury their heads in the sand; they will set them in concrete before they accept the implications."

"Did I say anything about consciousness?"

"Quite a lot. For example, you said that *consciousness* is *not thought* although we do experience thoughts in consciousness. The distinction here is subtle and not easy to express in words. Consciousness rides on the back of thought in order to create experience for itself."

"You say I told you this?"

"In letters, yes." She could have said an early version of email but that defied simple explanation.

Roger didn't believe a word of it. He supposed she was making fun of him.

"And how did I know all this?" he asked.

Deborah detected the tone of disbelief in his voice. "You said it came from the Old One."

"The Old One?"

"You have remembered something?"

He shook his head. "No, but I did have a dream. At least, it seemed like a dream but it was very real."

"Lucid dreaming can be like that," she said. "Were you fully conscious during the experience?"

"Yes." Then he added softly, "Like a blue star."

Deborah decided to change the subject. "Do you recall telling me about those policemen who arrested you?"

"You mean the ones who fell into some sort of coma?" he asked.

"Yes. They're okay now. They all came out of it at the same time."

"I don't understand," said Roger. "Are you saying there is a connection with me?"

"I instructed you to forgive them while you were under regression therapy. That was the time it happened. All four of them awoke in their respective hospitals, none the worse for their experience."

"That is strange," Roger said.

"Yes, I suppose it would seem so to most people."

"How did you find out?" Roger asked.

"My friend monitors all official radio traffic, especially the police, and intercepts everything that passes across their data networks," she said.

"So what does it mean? Are you saying I did something to put them in an unconscious state? How can that be? What happens in my brain stays in my brain," Roger declared positively.

"My friend says all existence is based on a single idea, the number one, the unit of existence and consciousness. Everything is consciousness because it transcends time and space. The one unit has the infinite quality of oneness or love. So every action we make is either for oneness or for separation. Karma is the process by which the universe adjusts the consequence of a negative action to restore the balance. It also reinforces positive actions to the benefit of all. Do you know about karma?" she asked.

"I've heard of it. I can't say I believe in it. I think of it as primitive superstition. I don't subscribe to any religion."

"According to my friend, karma has nothing to do with religion; it means *action*. He says that we all exist in a virtual reality game structured from *mathematics*, which is really a universal *operating system* like Android or Windows. The game has rules and consequences. Karma is not usually instantaneous; it works over periods of time from a few days to a whole lifetime."

"Hmm, I'm not sure about this," Roger murmured. "How is that relevant here?"

"You accepted what those men did without resentment. Karma operates more quickly when we don't bear grudges or judge those that hurt us. You *did* feel anger towards the hoodies so nothing happened to them. You and they will need to resolve any residual consequences between you in the future, either in this life or another. Circumstance will bring you together to do this. It was different with the policemen. The policemen didn't hurt you as badly as Barty and Cade but karma did come into play. Under normal circumstances these things happen in a way that seems purely coincidental – no identifiable chain of cause and effect. However, *you* have certain abilities as a result of things that happened during your period of missing time. It was an unconscious reflex action. When you forgave the policemen, the debt dissolved. You set them free and, more importantly, you freed yourself."

"They were just doing their jobs," Roger said.

Deborah nodded. "I have done things in my career that I'm not proud of. Karma doesn't deal with reasons and motives. It simply looks at actions and their consequences. Life makes adjustments to educate and enlighten rather than punish. Sometimes enlightenment can be painful. It's much better to do good than harm if you wish to progress in the greater scheme of things."

Roger's mind was in turmoil by these revelations. None of it made sense in the light of his beliefs and previous experiences – at least not with the past he could remember. It made the period of his missing memory seem all the more mysterious.

Roger looked back to the window as twilight gave way to darkness. His reflection glowed in the candlelight. Suddenly, he froze for as he moved to pick up his coffee cup his reflection stayed where it was. It was as if his face had somehow divided into two versions. In the reflection, his hair was longer and parted down the middle. In the other, the hair was short without a parting.

"Bloody hell! Look! That's me! In a decent suit! Mine's nothing like that."

His doppelganger showed no emotion on being recognised. He stared at Roger and, while he did so, his hairstyle changed to match Roger's, lengthening and parting centrally. The stranger continued to regard him curiously for a while before turning away and walking rapidly out of view.

Deborah glanced in the direction he indicated and laughed. "There's never a dull moment around you, is there?"

Roger looked at her briefly and turned his gaze back to the street. Whoever he was, the face at the window was gone. Roger's mind went back to the story Billy had told him. This was insane.

"He was watching me through the window. I thought it was my own reflection at first."

"Roger, do you always get this excited when a girl takes you out for dinner?"

Roger closed his eyes and began to breathe slowly, relaxing inside in a way that was strangely familiar. An inner knowledge on how to cope with the situation kicked in. It engendered a state above and beyond material consideration. It held no memories for him but it was obviously a well-practised routine, once familiar and then lost – until now. Strange things were happening to him but it no longer seemed to matter. From a well of emptiness, devoid of thought, he opened his eyes again. Deborah was watching him with a hint of a smile.

"I think you are rediscovering mental states that have long been missing," she said.

Roger nodded towards the window. "Well, he's gone now – whoever he was."

She nodded. "I guess I had better escort you home. I don't feel like being your therapist now. What shall we do?"

Roger reached for his paper napkin and dabbed at drops of coffee and yellow sauce on the tablecloth.

"Nothing. I think I used to be an expert at doing nothing."

"Hmm, that sounds dangerously like a plan. Let's go."

***

Deborah paused at the entrance to Roger's flat. "Crandal is ded," she quoted, staring at the graffiti daubed on the wall. "I saw that before, I think. What does it mean?"

"It means my neighbours can't spell," said Roger. "Let's go in. I'll sort that out later. I need to get some paint stripper. I hope it comes off."

Roger unlocked the door and reached through to the light switch. After recent events, he was growing cautious about going inside without checking. Deborah carried a change of clothing in a bag she'd collected from her car. The bathroom door squeaked as she entered. Roger looked down from the window and saw a man in a dark suit, sitting in a black limo. The tinted window was down. He was wearing headphones and making notes in a small book. It didn't look like the man he had seen outside the restaurant, the man who looked like him.

Roger drew back from the window and sat down, thinking hard. What was going on? Why were these people showing interest in him and his flat? Deborah seemed as much a part of it as the man in the car or the face at the window. Was she really his friend or was she spying on him also and, if so, for whom? Were the police a part of it? Were the hoodies acting alone or in conjunction with the authorities?

Deborah returned wearing casual trousers and a jumper. She sat on the couch and watched him in silence for some time; before bursting into tears. Roger reclaimed the new consciousness that had enveloped his mind in the restaurant. He watched her dispassionately and waited for her to expend her emotions.

Deborah quickly composed herself. "Sorry about that. This is harder than I expected." She gestured around the room as if in explanation.

"Don't worry about it. I was not exactly ecstatic about the flat when I moved in. There's damp in some of the corners and the neighbours upstairs clomp around in size 10 boots."

"It's not the apartment. It's the situation. I suppose you are wondering what this is all about."

"Do you read minds as well? You're a woman. What do I know about women? Or perhaps you're an alien and this is your way of having a good time."

She blew her nose and laughed simultaneously. Then she became serious.

"Roger."

"Yes."

"Do you promise to respect the fact that I am in a committed relationship?"

"Yes."

"Then will you allow me to stay here tonight?"

There was no hesitation. "Yes. I'll take the couch and you can have the bed. I'll even put on clean sheets."

"Thank you. Come and sit next to me."

He moved over and joined her on the couch but not too close.

"Can we watch television? I enjoy your British programmes – well, some of them. I can do without cooking and decorating. I tried something called *EastEnders* once. It seemed mostly to be arguments and infidelity."

"Yes. That's what makes soaps popular. Why worry about your own problems when you can watch somebody else's?"

Deborah settled on a reality TV programme about a family of aristocrats preparing their stately home for public viewing. Working-class habits baffled them somewhat as they got to grips with polystyrene cups, wheelchair ramps and vandal-proof stainless-steel toilets.

Slowly, Deborah relaxed, to the point where she leaned in closer. Her proximity caused Roger to experience tingling and buzzing like tiny electric shocks. This was something more than sexual attraction.

Then it happened; quite unexpectedly he flashed in and out of a dream of total clarity. The entire experience lasted no more than a few seconds. It made no sense at first. Instinctively, he held his breath and found that he could unravel the dream into some sort of logical sequence. He was in a classroom. It was a small group, around eight men and two women. The teacher was an older man, grey-haired and wearing a suit. His long-fingered hands tugged open the flap of a large package and extracted a wad of envelopes. Each of them received one with their name written across the front. Roger looked at his, unsure of what it meant.

"This is a big day for you," the teacher said. "At long last, after all those exercises and statistical assessments, we have sorted out your permanent targets for the operational training phase. Please open your envelopes and study the information we have provided."

Roger looked at the black and white photograph that stood out from the typed sheets. He could recall the face quite clearly. She was younger and somehow fresh and new but there was no mistaking her identity.

"Deborah!"

"Yes?"

Deborah continued watching television without taking her eyes away from the screen.

Roger breathed hard and collected his thoughts. In that moment he understood something about their previous relationship. He could not define that 'something' but he knew it was important.

"You were my target."

"Yes."

Deborah showed no surprise and made no further comment.

"I...I don't understand what it means."

"You will," she said softly. "Don't try to hurry it. I think the therapy is working." She reached out and squeezed his hand. "I prefer this kind of therapy to regression."

"Watching television! Is this therapy too?" said Roger in surprise.

"Yes. It holds your attention while diverting your mind on to something totally trivial. The unconscious begins to stir. Is there anything more trivial than reality TV? It wouldn't work for everybody though. It's because of the regression. It goes on working for some time after the session."

Roger chuckled and sat back. At last, a memory even if it meant nothing to him.

"Have you got any ice cream?" Deborah asked, leaning on him more overtly.

"Er...I'm not sure. I'll have a look." He pushed her away gently and stood up. Then he paused, "You don't eat sweet things."

"I do tonight. Where's my purse by the way?"

"Your purse? Did you put it down on the sideboard? Why do you need it now?"

"I am not sure. Sometimes I get premonitions. I need my purse. I am serious about this." Her manner had become forceful and slightly impatient.

"You want to buy something at this time of the evening?"

"Buy something?"

To Roger, a purse was a small container that held money. To Deborah, 'purse' meant a 'handbag' and what she wanted from it was definitely not legal tender.

"Is it in your handbag over there?" he asked.

"That *is* my purse." She rose from the couch and went over to pick it up, weighing it pensively.

"I wonder–"

Roger gave up trying to understand what was going on. He left Deborah to look in the freezer. Suddenly, there was a light tap on the door.

"Who could that be at this time? Perhaps it's Mavis."

As he began to open the door, five hoodies crashed in led by Barty and Cade.

Roger stepped aside swiftly. He glanced around anxiously seeking Deborah, concerned for her safety. She was nowhere to be seen. The intruders ran about yelling and smashing things. Roger was angry but could do no more than look on helplessly. Barty signalled for a lull in the excitement.

"We just got out on bail. We know you grassed on us to the boydem. They took all our stuff. They took our guns. But don't worry, I've got another." Barty drew the weapon and pointed it at Roger.

"I didn't tell them a thing," Roger said quietly. "They arrested me too. I am to face charges for what you put in my lockup. I didn't say a word about you."

Roger was the absolute focus of their attention.

"My man," said Cade, "you know why we're here. We're gonna take you for a little ride. Know what I mean?"

Barty froze when he felt the cold metal of a barrel touch the back of his neck. The sound of a gun being cocked demanded his attention.

"Hello boys," said Deborah. "Are we having a party? How wonderful. Shall I break out the vol-au-vents and sherry?"

She reached around him and lifted the gun he was holding from Barty's grip.

"I'll take this, if you don't mind. Oh look, mine's bigger than yours," she said as she stood back and took in the scene, keeping the two guns ready for use.

Roger gazed at the unfolding drama with undisguised amazement. Convinced, for a chilling moment, that his end had come, he now found himself in totally new territory where fear did not dominate. The tension in the room broke when one of the hoodies raised a knife and rushed in to strike Deborah. She sidestepped deftly without any loss of poise or stability, placing her foot where he would fall over it. The hoodie stumbled. She brought the second gun down in a sharp blow to the side of the assailant's head; not hard enough to cause permanent damage but sufficient to discourage cerebral activity for a few days.

Deborah said calmly, "Roger, look in my *handbag* and find some ties, please. And don't get between the gun and our guests, there's a dear." Her advice was opportune because it was exactly what he was about to do.

The hoodies stared at Deborah in shocked silence. This was so surreal and out of their experience, they were unsure how to react. Roger looked in her bag and found a set of plastic tape-like devices that reminded him of garden ties. He used them to bind the hands of each 'guest' behind their backs. They did not resist, there was no point with two guns directed at them with such calm efficiency. The prone hoodie, who Roger knew as Scott, got to his feet.

Once they were all tied up, Deborah said to Roger, "Look outside and see if the coast is clear."

"Nobody in sight."

"Okay, fellers. Hit the road. We're going for a little walk. No, Roger, wait here until I get back. Make some more coffee."

Roger was beginning to recognise the persona Deborah adopted when the occasion called for authority and resolution. Tucking one of the pistols in her waistband, she took out a mobile phone and pressed an icon. Then she herded her bound captives out of the flat, keeping the guns out of sight but within easy reach. She gave Roger a wink as she pulled the door shut behind her.

Roger heard her voice fading in the distance. "Keep together, boys. I know you're terribly brave but…that's it, left here…"

Roger considered recent events as he filled the kettle. His life had become both a dream and a nightmare. Deborah brought the dream but she fitted neatly into the nightmare too. Who was she? She seemed to know about his missing past and yet they had never met, or so she said.

It was no more than ten minutes before Roger heard a knock at the door. With trepidation he opened it. Deborah could see the relief on his face at her return.

She laughed. "Don't worry, Roger; all taken care of. Have you made that coffee?"

"Yes. It's in the cafetière. I didn't know how long you would be. I'll pour it now."

"I hope that couch is comfortable. I wouldn't like to think I'm disturbing your sleep if I stay the night."

"It's okay," Roger said smiling. After what you've done, I can refuse you nothing. What did you do with those lads?"

"Nothing much but it's best I don't tell you. If you don't know, you can't be made to answer questions, can you?"

"You didn't hurt them?"

"No. The one I hit was bleeding a bit. They will be

out of circulation for the time being. That's all."

She stretched and yawned. "Such a relaxing evening, apart from the interruption."

"Have you locked them up somewhere?"

"Stop worrying! I passed them on to a friend of mine. He'll know what to do. I'm going to bed but you can come and visit me before I go to sleep."

Roger stared at her in confusion.

"Don't get any ideas. This is just a social call to bring me coffee. Actually, can I change the order for cocoa? I might not sleep on coffee."

"Sure," Roger said turning towards the kitchen. He didn't think *he* would sleep so easily after the hoodie raid. He paused on the way to ask, "Deborah. Do many girls have guns and plastic handcuffs in their handbags?"

She laughed. "You don't know much about women, do you?"

"Not really. But I know more than I did last week."

"You'll learn – I hope."

Ten minutes later, Roger knocked on the bedroom door carrying a steaming mug of cocoa. Deborah called out to him to enter. She was sitting on the bed. "Thank you and thanks for the robe."

"You're welcome. We call it a dressing gown."

"Thank you, kind sir. A dressing gown, huh? How quaint. Is that the traditional meaning as in drawing room? What do people draw in drawing rooms anyway?"

"I believe the name came from the tradition of ladies withdrawing from the dining room to leave the men to pass the port and tell rude stories. Over time the 'withdrawing room' became 'drawing room'. I used to read a lot of history I suppose."

"What did the ladies do when they had withdrawn?"

"I think they embroidered cushions and made lace; stuff like that."

"I think I would have preferred to drink port and tell rude stories. Give me a hug and let me get to sleep. I'm tired. It's been a long day. At least, I think it's been a long day. My temporal references are a bit distorted by recent events."

Roger had no idea what she meant. He wanted to ask more about the hoodies and where Deborah had disposed of them; more to the point, how she had disposed of them. It was clear she wasn't about to tell him anything. She said, "Good night, Roger."

"Good night, Deborah."

The next morning, Roger awoke to find her gone.

Chapter Four

Three days passed without anything particularly unusual or exciting happening, for which Roger was grateful. He was a week away from going to court to face a preliminary hearing over the activities of Barty and Cade. Why the police had decided it was his fault he had no idea. They had mentioned 'information received'. If so, from whom? There was still no sign of the two hoodies either. The mystery of their disappearance preyed on his mind. What had Deborah done with them? He couldn't bring himself to believe she would harm them but they had vanished. There was talk in the flats about their disappearance. Scott and the other hoodies who had invaded his flat were still living there, but Barty and Cade were nowhere to be seen. The remaining hoodies had nothing to say about the two leaders. In fact, they could remember nothing about the entire episode. The only evidence that it had ever occurred was Scott's mysterious head injury that he couldn't explain. Roger was not party to local gossip but these rumours reached him via a devious route, namely Mavis' visiting hairdresser whose daughter was going out with a cousin of Cade's.

The fourth day was not so uneventful. Roger was on his way home with more shopping when he met Mavis on the stairwell.

"Could you pop in for a cup of tea and a chat?" she

asked him.

"Umm, I suppose so. Can you give me ten minutes? I've got stuff to put in the freezer."

She was very insistent, pushing him resolutely towards her door. "You can park it in my freezer for now. Come and sit down – please."

"Oh, well, if you insist." Roger entered Mavis' flat and sat down in an armchair, feeling relaxed. His chores for the day were complete. He called out to her in the kitchen.

"I saw one of those geezers my brother-in-law calls *men in black* today. He followed me into a pound shop. I stopped to look at toothpaste so he started looking at bleach. When I moved on, he stayed behind me at a discrete distance. Up until now they have looked more like plainclothes policemen or undertakers. This one looked a bit different. His suit didn't fit too well, he was bulky and his face looked as if it had been carved from granite. He was no oil painting. I wish I understood all this. Are they really watching me? Or is it just Billy's imagination?"

"I'd be only too happy to tell you if I knew," said Mavis, placing a tray with cups and a teapot on the table before him.

He sipped his tea and looked at the photographs on the sideboard. His eyes were drawn to Mavis' late husband, Ted. He always wondered what Ted had been like. He looked like a classic product of the fifties, formal in a suit and tie even on a beach. The only concession to the holiday spirit was the bare feet sticking out of rolled up trouser legs.

"You must miss Ted," he said.

"Yes," she replied softly. "That's why I value your being here. It's good to talk sometimes. I like the look of that young woman that's been here. Anything I should know about?" she asked with a smile.

"It's…complicated. I think she's my therapist but she has other skills that don't quite add up. Something seems to be working though. I had a memory flashback but it was very odd; it made no sense."

A crash followed by a creaking noise interrupted Roger in mid-sentence. A loud voice shouting something incoherent accompanied the performance. Roger and Mavis sat looking at each other, open-mouthed. Mavis suddenly looked determined.

"Roger, let me say this. I had a strong feeling that I should stop you from going into your flat. I didn't know why but that sounds like a definite enough reason."

"It's *my* place. All that noise and shouting! I think it's a police raid! What shall I do?"

"Have another cup of tea and whisper," she advised seriously. "I thought you said you were getting used to this sort of thing."

"Yes, but–"

"If they come here, you can hide in my bedroom and hope they don't do a full search."

After a while, his flat went quiet. Shortly afterwards, there was a knock on Mavis' door, loud but not violent.

Roger moved as quickly as he could without knocking things over and entered his neighbour's bedroom. He felt like an invader, seeing all her personal treasures. He dived out of sight behind the bed. It was hardly secure but it was the only immediate cover he could see. Hiding was futile if they came in to look for him.

Roger heard voices, one high and one low and

persistent. Eventually, Mavis opened the bedroom door.

"You can come out now. They've gone."

Roger emerged cautiously. "What did they say?"

"Apparently they're looking for members of a local hoodie gang who have been reported missing. Somebody saw them leaving your flat with a woman. Perhaps they were looking for evidence that they'd been there or weapons or drugs. I hope they rebuild your door."

"Why didn't they search your place?"

"I'm an old lady. They are merely knocking on all the doors to ask people to phone them if they see you or any other members of your gang."

"*My* gang! I don't know where they are. I'm out on bail."

Mavis said, "I think they would like to ask you some questions but finding you is not their priority right now so you can go back to your flat if you want. What about your friend Melvyn? He's a lawyer, isn't he? Could he get you off these charges?"

"He might but I don't want to ask him. That would be taking advantage of our friendship."

"Nonsense! Have you got his mobile number?"

"Yes…"

Several minutes passed before there was discreet tap at the door. Mavis let Melvyn in. Roger came back from the bedroom where he'd ducked out of sight again.

"Man, what have you done now? The Old Bill is on fire."

"I didn't do anything. Cade and his friends came round on Tuesday to take me for a one-way ride. That's what they said anyway."

"On a bus? I thought they'd lost their driving licences."

"Of course not on a bus. Are you taking this seriously?"

"Only joking. You look a bit tense."

"A bit tense!" Roger shouted. He relaxed when he saw the amused expression on his friend's face and added more gently, "Yeah, just a bit."

"It's time for you to join the club my friend," said Melvyn tossing him a grey top with a large hood. Roger saw the plan straight away and put it on.

"If you don't want to be seen, be obvious," explained Melvyn before giving him instruction on how to slouch and adopt a sullen expression. "If you smile, we're done for," he joked. "Sorry it's a bit big for you. It's one of mine."

"I think I can manage under the circumstances."

"You look fit to be banned from every newsagents in London," said Melvyn with a wink at Mavis.

Mavis laughed, in spite of her fear. "Go carefully," she said, about to open the door for them to leave. The sound of Bob Marley echoed around the room. It was Melvyn's mobile phone. Melvyn answered and looked serious as he rang off.

"I think you'd better disappear. It's all changed again. The police *are* looking for you now," said Melvyn. "According to my friend in the force, they've had a tipoff from the spooks that you're a suspected terrorist. Now they're looking for you as well as the missing gang. They think you might be implicated in that as well. So it looks like 'meat's back on the menu, boys', if you don't mind being compared to an Orc's dinner."

"Oh dear," Roger said. "I like *Lord of the Rings* but

I'd rather not think about *that*. Hanging around here dressed as a hoodie might not be the best plan then. I'd better make a getaway."

"Where to?" asked Mavis.

"No idea. Any thoughts?"

"Somewhere you can hang around in the open without suspicion," she suggested.

Forty minutes later Roger sat on the grass beneath a tree on Hampstead Heath on one of the highest spots in London.

***

"Will you get the phone, dear?" Liz called out.

Billy reluctantly abandoned his computer and headed downstairs to answer the call. His mind was boggling.

"Yes?"

"Bill?"

"Yes."

"It's me. Your brother-in-law."

"I know you. Did they let you phone us?"

"What do you mean? I'm – well, never mind where I am. Calls can be intercepted too easily. It's the police again. They are looking for me everywhere."

"Not anymore," said Billy.

"The missing hoodies–"

"Funny you should mention that. Have you seen the Rense website?"

"Of course not. I haven't got time to surf the net."

"You'd better get round here quick. And don't worry. I have it on good authority that they aren't looking for you any more."

"Why's that? Do they know I'm innocent?"

"No, it's not that. They've already got you banged

up in the choky. They arrested you earlier this afternoon. It's been on the news; implicated in the disappearance of two schoolboys and known to have links with terrorists including al-Qaeda and others I can't pronounce. And probably the Women's Institute for all I know. You might as well come round here."

In a daze, Roger handed the phone back to the lady with the pram.

"Thank you," he said gratefully.

"That's all right," she replied. "My brother often jogs here. He's met some nice people that way – not that he's ever brought them home."

Roger headed back towards the road and looked for the nearest underground station. This latest development had him bemused and confused.

It took nearly an hour to get to his sister's house. Billy let him in and peered around the street for probing eyes.

Roger noticed his movements. "I thought you said they'd stopped hunting for me. Why are you looking so furtive?"

"Come and watch the news. Then you'll know as much as I do."

Liz jumped up in alarm as soon as he entered the living room.

"Are you all right, Rog? I can't believe I'm seeing you here."

"Yeah, I think so. I'm still alive anyway. What's this all about?"

"Watch the news," said Billy persistently. "Then *you* can tell *me*."

Billy switched on the TV screen and fiddled with the remote until he found a relevant news broadcast. There had been trouble in South London. The families of two young men had reported them missing. There was a rumour about a rival gang. The only rival 'gang' that Roger knew about for sure carried nightsticks and Tasers. The story switched to an anti-terrorist raid in an East London backstreet. A group of armed police broke down a door and rushed in. Then there was a shot of them emerging with a man in handcuffs. Roger could easily believe that he was looking at himself except that this version wore a dark suit.

"That's why they aren't looking for you," said Billy. "They've got you – or so they think. Would you mind telling me what this is all about?"

"That isn't me. That never happened – at least not to me. What's going on, Bill?"

Liz sat down by his chair and said in a concerned voice, "Do you remember Billy told you that he had spoken to you in the street the other day and you ignored him?"

"Yes – oh. You think that's him?"

"It must be. You have a double. He's a spitting image – only he doesn't look like a deadbeat." The last remark earned Billy a slap from his wife.

Roger recalled the incident in the restaurant with Deborah when he saw a face in the window that was like a reflection of his own.

"Now, Roger. Come upstairs and see something else on my computer," said Billy.

"Billy, don't you think Roger has had enough startling news for one day?"

"He's *got to* see this, Liz!"

Curious, Roger followed his brother-in-law to the spare bedroom. "Here, look at this."

Billy grabbed the mouse and flicked and clicked it around expertly. A small window flashed up on the screen. Billy found a link that said, "UFO over London. Gang members abducted?" Somebody had caught the flying saucer on a phone camera and now it was on YouTube. It was dark and grainy but there was no mistaking the glowing metallic disc that he had seen passing over the houses and flats that evening. The street was familiar. He knew it to be just a few blocks away from his home. There was a date display in the corner. It was the same time that Deborah took the hoodies away from his flat.

"I reckon they were abducted by aliens," said Billy triumphantly. "Not that this would convince the police. Who would *ever* believe the Rense website?"

***

"Sergeant Trubshaw," said Billy cheerfully.

"That's me. What can I do for you?"

"They told me to ask for you. I have come to see Roger Crandle. This is my wife, his sister. What have you charged him with?"

"We are holding him in custody pending enquiries about the whereabouts of some missing schoolboys. We are also holding him under the Terrorism Act on suspicion of belonging to a proscribed organisation."

"Have they proscribed the Benefits Agency then?" Bill asked. "That's the only organisation I've ever known him belong to. He's not a terrorist. He's an out of work systems engineer. And those 'schoolboys' are over eighteen years old and threatened him with knives and guns. But apart from that it sounds as if you've got the situation well under control."

The sergeant ignored Billy's challenging remarks and stared at his companion. "I must say your wife is remarkably like the prisoner. Twins are they?"

"Not *exactly* twins but quite close. People often commented on it when they were young, especially before Liz developed her – well, developed."

"I see. Please wait here," he said, reaching for the telephone.

Roger looked severely at his brother-in-law and muttered under his breath, "I must be mad letting you talk me into coming here in drag. How can I fool a policeman that I'm my own sister?"

"Keep your voice down. I'd believe it. Liz did a good job. She learned to apply make-up at amateur dramatics. She made up the cast of *Charley's Aunt* at the Methodist Hall last year," Billy explained. "You know, *Charley's Aunt* 'from Brazil where the nuts come from'."

"No, I don't know. I've never…what a time to start going on about–"

"Keep your voice down – or rather up."

A little later, a constable arrived and led them downstairs to the cells. He took them to a heavy door at the end of the corridor.

"You can have fifteen minutes but I will remain here," he said, producing a large bunch of keys. He unlocked the cell door and waved them inside.

Unfortunately, the cell was familiar to Roger having recently spent some time in custody after his run-in with Barty and Cade. He disliked the stark rooms and their utilitarian amenities. It offended his senses. Until recently he had never had contact with the law – not as far as he could remember anyway.

As soon as they entered, they saw the prisoner. In person, he looked to Billy more like Roger than he had on television.

"That's *you* alright," Billy whispered to Roger. "I'd know you anywhere."

The prisoner looked from one to the other. He turned to Billy. "I remember you; you're a brother of law."

Even the voice was Roger's.

Billy whistled. "Blimey!" Then he said in a loud voice, "I thought I'd better bring your sister, Liz, to see you."

Roger was suddenly conscious of the policeman just beyond the open door. He made an effort to speak in a higher voice. "I'm so sorry you are in here, *Roger*," he said, emphasising the name. "I hope they are treating you properly."

The second 'Roger' smiled and winked as if acknowledging the subterfuge. "I am fine, thank you, sister," he replied in an identical high voice.

Billy groaned.

Roger whispered hoarsely, "Not you *too*, you're *me*. Speak normally."

The whole situation was too bizarre for words. Roger wished they could talk without being overheard by the policeman. There was a surveillance camera on the ceiling. Roger pointed at it and nodded suggestively.

"Are you concerned about being overheard?" asked his doppelganger.

Roger nodded vigorously.

"Don't worry." The prisoner walked around them and out of the door towards the constable. He snapped his fingers in front of the policeman's face. The officer remained as static as a statue, his eyes staring ahead blankly. "I used a psychotronic pulse to put him in a catatonic trance."

"The camera..." Roger said, nodding towards the surveillance unit above them.

"No problem," said the prisoner. "I've changed the picture. If anybody looks, all they will see is a video of me here alone two hours ago. They can't hear or see us now."

Roger and Billy looked at the immobile policeman and then gaped at each other.

"You don't remember me, do you, Roger?" the double asked calmly.

"Should I?"

"My name is Henry."

"Henry who?"

"Not 'Henry Who', just Henry. I am your friend."

"What did you do to that policeman?" asked Billy, agog at these strange developments.

"Nothing serious," said Henry. "I deactivated his central nervous system for a while. He will recover soon."

"How did you do that?"

"You know...the usual way." He waved his hand and pointed his finger like a gun.

"Oh," said Billy blankly, "'the usual way'. I see." He didn't, of course.

"You *know*, a psychotronic emission pulse aimed at the brain in a tight beam. Now, Roger, I– oh, excuse me a moment."

Henry faced front and shut his eyes. Roger and Billy waited as patiently as they could.

"I am communicating with Deborah. She wishes to speak to Roger."

"What's this? Telepathy?" asked Roger.

"No, cell phone."

"You haven't got a phone. The police take them off

you when they bring you in."

"No, Roger. I don't need to *carry* a phone. Will you take the call?"

Roger was still trying to grasp the meaning of the phenomenon called Henry.

"Okay. Sure, I'll speak to her."

The prisoner's eyes closed and Deborah's voice came out of the air in front of him as though she was standing there. It did not have the restricted bandwidth of a phone call.

"Hi, Roger. Henry tells me you've introduced yourselves. He also said you haven't remembered him."

"How did he say that? I didn't hear him talking to you…"

"He can talk via a microwave link to a cell phone while holding a conversation with somebody else. Henry, what's this accusation that Roger is a terrorist about?"

Henry replied aloud, "Under their Prevention of Terrorism Act they can hold him without trial and without evidence. Black Ops have links with the NSA. They tipped off MI6."

Billy didn't understand a word of this. "We know who Roger is," he said. "How could he possibly be a threat to anybody?"

"You have no idea who Roger is," said Deborah's disembodied voice.

"So, who is Henry?" asked Billy. "Why does he look like Roger?"

"Roger must remember that for himself if he wants to reclaim his missing time," Deborah replied.

"Whatever he is, I don't want Henry to remain in custody on my account," said Roger.

"Henry could break out any time but he won't while it puts you back in the frame," Deborah said. "Believe me, they can't hurt him. It would be better if you left the police station."

The statue-like policeman remained fixed in place. Roger and Billy cast uneasy glances at one another.

Roger asked. "Should we leave him here and go?"

"You might as well," Deborah said. "What can you do? I'll switch off my phone. I've got a lot to do right now."

Henry said, "You feel a need to do something for me. I understand. But confinement does not inconvenience me in the least."

Billy was kind-hearted in his way and felt unhappy about it. "It still doesn't seem right to leave you here, Henry. I've heard the grub's terrible," he said, glancing at Roger.

"That's okay. I rarely eat and then only for social reasons. I can convert individual atoms into electromagnetic plasma emissions under precise control and I can extract zero-point energy from the time-space dimension through micro-bio units distributed through my body. Energy is not a problem for me. Beyond the upper atmosphere, my body can become a magnetohydrodynamic generator in electrical discharges that emerge into space from storm clouds…"

As Henry droned on inexplicably, Roger and Billy persisted in viewing his situation as unacceptable.

"If I had money for a lawyer…" Roger said sadly.

"Money. You have no money? I can get money," said Henry brightly. "How much do you need?"

"A good solicitor might get you out on bail at least," said Roger.

"Not while he's under suspicion of being a terrorist," said Billy.

"As Deborah said, I could leave at any time but then they would resume the hunt for Roger," said Henry. "Perhaps I can discourage that by making a small adjustment to his appearance."

"What sort of adjustment?" Roger asked suspiciously. He had not been happy with Billy's plan to dress him up as a woman. What sort of disguise was Henry suggesting?

Henry did not answer. Instead he said, "Roger and I should swap clothes. That will allow me to leave."

"But then they'll have Roger in the clink," Billy pointed out.

"No, we will all leave together. I have a plan to hide him in plain sight."

"Not as a hoodie? I've already tried that," Roger said.

"No. Something more subtle," said Henry.

"Okay, but if you're going to do it, you'd better hurry," Billy advised.

Henry was much faster than Roger at taking off his clothes especially as Roger was unfamiliar with female attire.

Billy grew impatient as he watched Roger wrestle with the bra and padding. "Here, let me help. I've taken off more women's clothing than you have. Not from myself, of course," he added hastily. "And *only* from your sister…"

Soon, Roger and Henry were dressed in each other's clothes and Billy took out a lipstick from his pocket and applied it to Henry. "Gorgeous, even if I do say so myself," he said. Then he looked at Roger. "You look real sharp in that suit – apart from the make-up. All you need is the sunglasses."

Roger found a pair in the breast pocket and a tissue to wipe off the lipstick. He put on the shades and grinned.

"So what's this small adjustment you spoke of?" Roger asked Henry. "How would it stop them from looking for me?"

Henry approached Roger and placed his hands on his head and back. Roger felt a slight tingling on his skin. When he had finished, Henry stepped back. "That's it. All done. Let's go."

"Let's go? Every policeman in the building will jump on me."

"I don't think so, Rog," said Billy sniggering. "Does it wash off?" he asked Henry.

"No, it is permanent unless I change it back."

"Change what back? What's happened?" demanded Roger.

"Look at your hand," Billy suggested.

Roger glanced at his hand and jumped. His skin was dark brown.

"How?"

"I've modified your DNA," Henry explained. "You'll soon get used to it. Human beings are very superficial in judging people. You are not your colour. You are recognisable as yourself in every other respect but who would see that in the present state of consciousness on this primitive planet?"

"Hang on," said Billy. "If you leave now, I will be blamed for breaking you out. In five minutes our house will be knee deep in rozzers and our kids will be in care."

"And I will be a wanted black man instead of a wanted white man," echoed Roger. "They'll have me leaving here on surveillance records."

Henry said, "They won't know about your new appearance, I'll wipe the recordings. As to getting out, I've escaped from captivity on alien planets that were much more secure than this. They weren't actually prisons – merely places of confinement. They don't have much crime on other worlds. Anyway, getting out of here won't detain us."

Billy and Roger exchanged glances. "Alien planets?" Then Billy looked at the door. "We are locked in a suite of cells with a comatose copper," said Billy. "What do you intend to do now?"

Henry approached the static policeman. He touched his head with his index finger and whispered in his ear. The policeman turned like a stiff robot and led them to the outer door at the other end of the corridor. There he stopped and stood facing it woodenly.

"Has he got a key?" Billy asked.

"We don't need it." Henry put his finger against the keyhole. There was a click and the door swung open. "Telekinetic pick," he explained.

Billy held up his own finger and examined the end of it. "Now that's what I call digital technology. I wonder if you can buy one of those. How useful is that?"

Henry beckoned the policeman, who walked stiffly forward and out into the open corridor. Henry locked the cellblock door behind them, leaving the guardian of the law standing there looking at the wall. Henry seemed totally unaffected by women's clothing, unlike Roger who had cringed with embarrassment. He made no concession to feminine demeanour and strode along in his customary manner.

Henry discreetly waved his finger at anybody they

passed, wiping their little party from their conscious awareness.

"What about the camera in the cell and all the others we've passed?" Roger asked quietly.

"I've erased us from the recordings."

"What about the computer records?" Roger asked. "Everything that happens in here gets logged somewhere."

"Yes, I'll make sure it's wiped or doctored like the surveillance cameras. If there's a paper trail, I'll sort it out before I go. I was quite surprised at the extent of the bugging that goes on. The police bug the prisoners and somebody else bugs the police. The only difference is the quality of the devices. The covertly infiltrated bugs are far harder to detect because of the frequencies they use and their relatively weak signal strength. They must be scanned from a satellite. These bugs don't just listen to voices; they also record incidental radio emanations from computer hardware like printers and display screens. The NSA calls it TEMPEST; unwanted broadcasting of data by hardware components. UK and American organisations regularly sweep their key premises for bugs. The security organisations sometimes bug each other. Somewhere somebody is recording everything that happens electronically. In Britain, practically the whole nation is monitored all the time. Every email, phone call and text message is intercepted. They use supercomputers with pattern recognition software to analyse the traffic. They have quite advanced heuristic neural nets. Perhaps I should say they are advanced in comparison with what the public knows but not as advanced as me. I have a non-corporeal mind adjunct to the brain, as do you."

"Why do they spy on us?" Billy asked.

"They say it's to spot terrorists but that's not the real reason. Most of the people involved in spying on their fellow citizens may even believe it. But let's say that currently less than ten people die in the UK each year as a result of terrorism, whereas deaths on the road are running at three thousand a year. Road deaths cost the economy about eight billion pounds a year. That's nothing to what they spend spying on and controlling you. Financially, there is no justification whatever for the mass surveillance. It's not even about crime prevention. They don't even bother to investigate most burglaries now."

"So, what's it really for?" said Billy.

"What they really want to identify is anything that threatens the power game that's being played by the systems humanity has unwittingly created. So, for example, anybody inventing a cheap energy source would have all their equipment confiscated and, if they persist, they would have a heart attack or fall out of a window. They want to keep oil and gas prices high. They are also keen to stop disclosure of the extraterrestrial presence or the fact of alien technology. The population of this planet is hostage to the financial systems and the petro-chemical industry. The most compelling ambition is to stop the human race evolving spiritually as it should have been by now. To put it simply, if humanity wakes up, the rich will lose their power over the poor. Even that is a superficial scenario. Behind and beyond all this are evil forces that would lose a foothold on existence if the wider population understood the potential inherent in its own nature."

"But why do they want to destroy the planet with

pollution?" Roger asked.

"The earth is a living being. It's overdue a shift to a higher state of consciousness," said Henry. "That's why the ETs are really here. It would be bad for business if the planet became a spiritual paradise, so the multinational companies would rather see it become a dead hulk in space than a living, breathing entity in the light. It's all about profit and power. You were warned millennia ago not to lend money for interest but you did. That made money a commodity to be traded for its own sake, leading to poverty, hunger, pollution and war. So the population here is trapped in an industrial nightmare based on endless economic growth that is unsustainable and damaging to the world."

"And prone to periodic crashes and recessions," Roger murmured.

Henry led them calmly out of the rear of the police station and looked closely at Roger and then at Billy. "I want you both to start walking to Roger's home. I will catch up with you shortly." Then he wandered casually back into the station. Billy did as he was told. Roger hung back for a moment, watching Henry curiously and then followed his brother-in-law.

"He doesn't make a convincing woman," Billy noted. "Not like you."

Henry caught up with them before they reached the flats. "All done. Nobody there now remembers you."

"You've wiped more memories?"

"Yes. I emitted a wide-angle psychotronic pulse with a time removal routine. They will have lost a few minutes of conscious time. No harm done. It's minor tampering rather than temporal obliteration."

"I hope not," said Roger. "Not on my account. I lost

years from my memory. And I still don't understand how you turned my skin black."

"I tweaked your DNA. You have a mathematical template for your physical form on a higher dimension. It contains the holographic fractal information that projects you into space and time. It's like rendering in a virtual reality game machine – well – it *is* rendering in a virtual reality game machine. That's all your current time-space system is. Your DNA is a subset of a much greater pattern of conceptual linkages. That's how I changed your colour so quickly," Henry explained.

"I'm glad I asked," said Roger sarcastically.

When they reached the building where Roger lived, Henry persuaded Billy to continue walking to his home and family. He left them, wondering what he would tell Liz.

Henry led the way to Roger's flat. They arrived to find the graffiti on the wall that declared, 'Crandal is ded'.

Henry scanned the paint with his finger on a psychokinetic frequency. Pigments began to arise from the surface in slow-moving streams of red dust. Then he leaned over and blew on it, dispersing the remaining paint as a spreading crimson cloud. Roger unlocked the door and went in first.

"The place is a mess," he said lamely.

Henry looked in. "I wouldn't have known if you hadn't told me," he said. "I am not attuned to subjective impressions like degrees of tidiness but I have been taught what to do in these situations once the diagnosis has been made." He turned to Roger. "You go and sit down. I'll make a cup of tea for you. That's what you like, isn't it?"

"Not half," Roger concurred. Henry looked puzzled but said nothing. He deduced from his enthusiastic tone that Roger liked the idea.

Roger wondered why anybody with Henry's talents would need lessons in something as mundane as housework. Perhaps anticipating the thought, Henry said, "A US President once employed me for a month as a housekeeper. He didn't have the necessary security clearance to know my capabilities beyond domestic duties. They sent me in because he was worried about the Vice President bugging his offices and bedroom. He didn't know I was a multichannel surveillance unit. I knew more about security technology than I did about White House protocols. I found the problem in the end. It was the usual rivalry between the NSA and the CIA. You don't get much help, do you?" he said looking around the flat.

"I don't have enough money," Roger confessed. "I haven't had a job for a while."

"No problem," said Henry. "I haven't much on me but you are welcome to it. I don't often need money." He reached inside his jacket pocket and withdrew a large wad of bank notes. He tossed them over to Roger. "Will this help? Most of it is sterling."

"Will it help? It's a fortune! I can't take all your money. Is that what they pay you?" Roger asked thoughtfully, unsure of the source of this largess.

"No, I don't get a salary. I am classed as an item of black operations military hardware like an M16 rifle but more expensive. As to money, I have only recently started speculating with the Internet system. I opened an online account with some expenses I had acquired and started trading on something called eBay. I bought and sold things without actually possessing them. That gave me a stake of $103,514.34 in US currency to start up a system design consultancy business. I provide corporate executives with the schematics and specs for bespoke business information systems. They contract out implementation to third party companies. I am on my twenty-fifth customer. They love my work and don't need to meet me directly. I have accumulated $1,836,436.96, less what I just gave you. Multitasking is easy for me – I have six virtual minds attached to my core processors, each autonomous to an extent."

"How many years has it taken you to acquire that much money?" Roger asked.

"Years? No. Four months and fifteen days."

"Wow!"

Roger couldn't grasp anything that was happening to him. From total disaster, his life was moving up into a stratosphere beyond comprehension. He watched Henry move quickly around his small flat, picking things up, sorting, straightening; undoing the damage resulting from the latest police raid. He even re-seated the door, using his index finger in psychokinetic mode to remove the screws.

"Beats a sonic screwdriver," he said with a wink. In an impossibly brief span of time everything looked normal again.

While he had Henry's help, Roger decided to change things around. Roger looked at the sideboard and decided to move it to the other side of the room. "Henry, would you mind giving me a hand?"

His new friend came over and stood by Roger. He raised his left hand in front of his face, ran the tip of his right index finger around the wrist, pressed his thumb in the joint and then gave his left hand a sharp twist. It came off easily at the wrist. He handed it to

Roger whose jaw dropped with amazement.

"Oh my God, you're a robot. I was beginning to suspect it at the police station but I didn't believe it."

"I'm an android actually; part machine and part organic clone."

Roger looked at the offered extremity and staggered back sitting heavily on a chair.

Henry smiled and reattached the hand to his arm. "Sorry, I took advantage of the moment to let you see what I am for yourself. In the old days I often made mistakes like that when people used expressions of speech. I still do sometimes. Word recognition is one thing but understanding meaning takes experience."

"No, it's not that. I think you have triggered a memory from my missing years. Is that what you intended?"

"Yes. Deborah would not approve but I felt it worth trying."

"I think I do remember something about you. You were not always like this. You had a previous body. Some sort of robot."

"That is correct."

"Henry the Eighth. Why do I think of Henry the Eighth?"

"You named me that because I was the eighth model in a series of experimental robot prototypes. Space Command technologists based my chip set on reverse-engineered circuits of extraterrestrial design. There was another indirect association in your past with the English king of that name. You knew somebody who once met him but that was much later."

Roger could not make head or tail of that. He said, "So you are an artificial intelligence?"

"I am something beyond artifice. I have *you* to

thank for that. You shared your consciousness with me by giving me a soul fragment. I cannot tell you where or how. Deborah would not like it. She thinks you should recall your missing past unaided if it is to mean anything. She is aware from hypnosis that the mind is capable of inventing false memories from planted suggestions."

"It's obvious that you and I have a connection from the past. It can't be a coincidence that we are identical. Well, we were until you changed my skin colour. When will you change it back, by the way? I take it you can."

"When the time is right. When they stop looking for you or when it doesn't matter anymore."

"That sounds a bit ominous. Will I die?"

"Not yet I hope. That would affect both of us."

Roger said, "They will come looking for you eventually. They think you are me."

Henry nodded. "That's true. What can they do to me? I can break out of any prison. I cannot be hurt physically. I might be vulnerable to certain advanced technologies but they are not likely to have those here."

Roger looked pensive. He was thinking about the practicalities of everyday life if Henry spent more time with him. "What shall I say to people who see us together? Me being black will make it even worse. How will I explain that?"

Henry said, "In my experience people see the colour rather than the person. It won't be an issue until you are white-skinned again. Then you can tell them I'm your estranged twin brother from South Dakota."

"Why South Dakota? I don't think I ever met anybody from there."

"Exactly," said Henry. "There are lots of Native Americans and the tall white ETs have a base there. I tend to get on with all of those. The people who live there otherwise don't take much notice of me."

Roger looked dubious. "Oh, well. Let's find Melvyn. He might be able to help with the legal stuff." He paused as a thought struck him. "When you say you trade and work on the Internet you don't mean that you use a computer do you?"

"No, I do it through my internal systems. I am doing it now even as we speak. I've just earned another thousand pounds for a process outline for a company that makes shoes."

"Wow! I wish I could do that."

"You don't need to. What is mine is yours."

Chapter Five

"Melvyn, see who's at the door?"

Violet continued to attack the carpet with a vacuum cleaner. She was always pleased to have her son return to the fold but it was so easy to slip back into the old roles and patterns of the past. The fact that he was over thirty and his head nearly reached the ceiling was neither here nor there. He was still her little boy.

Melvyn opened the door and saw two men standing there. They looked identical apart from one being black and the other white. He looked puzzled and said to the white version in the dark suit, "Roger, what's going on? Who's this?" In reply, the black version said, "*I'm* Roger. This is Henry."

Melvyn's mother called out, "Who is it, Melvyn? Don't buy anything. I never buy at the door."

He called back. "I sure don't buy this. Roger's blacked up. He's gonna start singing *Mammy* at this rate. Are you disguised to escape detection?"

"Something like that, Melv, except that it isn't make-up. It's real. I *am* black. I can't explain how."

"That's impossible."

Henry spoke for the first time. "Not impossible but it is exceptional. We can't tell you how though. It's classified." He was learning to go for simple answers that required less explanation.

"Come on, Roger. Admit it. You *are* you," he said to Henry. "Same voice – everything apart from the suit. I've never seen you looking so smart before."

"I can't tell you everything, Mel. Not out here," said the black version. "I need to come in if that's all right. Will your mum mind?"

"Mind? When has mum ever minded you coming into her flat? She even tried to sit on your lap once."

Roger shuddered. "Don't remind me, man. I was nearly flattened."

"Oh, so you *are* Roger. Who is Henry? You did say Henry?"

"Yes. He's my twin brother from South Dakota," Roger explained lamely.

Melvyn looked at them both and laughed. "You are full of surprises lately, Roger, whichever one you are."

Melvyn stood back and ushered them both into the flat. Roger wandered to the window and glanced out to the street below. He saw a large black limousine in the distance closer to his own side of the building. Beside it stood a woman wearing a black suit, holding binoculars. It could be Deborah but he wasn't sure. *How do they manage to park that great black car here all the time? Most people have to drive half a mile away to leave their cars on a road without yellow lines*, he thought. He turned to see Henry sitting at the dining table.

Melvyn indicated an empty chair for Roger. He called out, "Mum! Want some tea?"

Violet's voice responded from her bedroom, "Yes – if you're making it. Who's there? If that's the rent man, I'm out."

Eventually, she arrived in person. "Roger! I'm so pleased you're okay. I said to Melvyn. That boy is a saint. *He* wouldn't commit no crime."

Violet leaned over Henry with her arms around his

neck and her tearful face on his cheek. Melvyn said, "Mother, that's not Roger. His name is Henry."

She drew back and looked down at Henry. "Henry? How can there be two long skinny streaks? Who are you?"

Roger took a deep breath and said rather lamely, "This is my long lost twin brother from South Dakota…"

Violet jumped in fright at hearing Roger's voice behind her. Turning, she took in their friend's black skin. "Roger? Is that really you? How come you're looking beautiful all of a sudden?"

***

Mavis Pargiter opened the door and let Roger into her flat. It still felt strange to see him with a dark complexion. The first time she set eyes on him in his new skin and dressed in hoodie clothing, she thought he was one of the gang members who hung about the stairwells smoking herbal tobacco. "Come in. The kettle's on. How's your friend Henry?"

"Oh, he's fine. He's busy…being Henry."

"I can't make him out at all. He seems pleasant enough, knowledgeable and totally identical to you – identical to you as you were before…" She gestured towards his face. "And yet…"

"And yet…"

Mavis looked at Roger carefully before answering. "I am, as you know, psychic. I look at your friend and I get no feeling of…humanity. He does not feel like a real person."

Roger chuckled. "We can't get one over on you, Mavis. You're an old witch – in the best possible way, of course."

Mavis smiled. "If you mean by 'witch' a wise woman, yes; if you mean a caster of spells, most definitely *not*. If anything, I would say you are far more powerful than anybody I have ever known."

"Me?" he exclaimed.

"Oh yes. You have much to learn about yourself. I hope you like what you find."

Roger looked at Mavis, a little shocked. "You know me. I never mean harm to anybody."

"I know that. I also know you have a gap in your history. I feel that dark things happened. Terrible things. That may be why you have suppressed the memory of them."

Roger sighed. "I hope you're wrong." But he was beginning to believe she might be right.

"So do I. Come on, let's have that tea."

When Roger left Mavis, he returned to his flat and collected rubbish to put out in the bin. He looked around his kitchen for stray items. The arrival of Henry was changing everything in ways both obvious and subtle. He tied up the bag and took it down the stairs into the backyard. He threw it in the bin and closed the lid. It was dark in the alley behind the building. Many streetlights were broken. Not far away he could hear the sound of drunken youths shouting and laughing. He was about to return to his flat when he caught sight of Henry walking towards him between two nearby tower blocks. At that moment the drunken shouting stopped. There was silence; then all hell broke loose.

"Crandle!"

"Dead meat!"

"Get 'im."

Roger watched as a mixed-race gang of young men

and women surged around Henry in the certain belief that he was Roger Crandle. Had it been himself, he would have felt doomed to another beating or worse.

Henry stopped and allowed them to surround him.

"What can I do for you?" Inebriated jeers, shouting and cries of 'grass' drowned out his voice.

Roger heard a bottle smashing. A young man ran forward and waved the shards of glass threateningly. Henry did not flinch. This was the first stage of the confrontation ritual. They were psyching themselves up for the actual conflict. This was mob psychology in action.

Henry stood, patiently watching. A bottle near his face was a threat but not an attack. They would need to get much closer to trigger a defensive response in the form of impenetrable spatial barriers. He knew that Roger was watching but he did not signal that knowledge, not wishing to draw attention to his friend. The noise increased as their courage rose. Henry's lack of fear disconcerted the youths slightly. When the actual attack came it was a lunge with the bottle to the face. Henry could have allowed the blow to fall but he only wanted to see how far they would go. A psychotronic pulse to put them to sleep would have raised awkward questions. At the last possible instant, he grasped the bottle and squeezed until it pulverised almost to dust. The attack started in earnest as they surged forward, kicking, punching and employing a variety of weapons; knives, chains and even a gun was drawn. Henry's reflexes were so fast, he could simply avoid their blows and gently push them aside without using force. The gun he grabbed and concealed about his person. After about ten minutes they began to desist, one by one, as each stood panting. Henry could go on all day if necessary.

Roger watched from a distance, totally absorbed in the commotion. He was on the verge of leaving when a hand clamped across his mouth. Strong hands gripped his arms. It happened so quickly that he was unable to resist. They propelled him into the apartment block. He managed to turn his head and was shocked to see Barty Loughlin and Cade Mitchell. They were dressed in jeans and T-shirts rather than their customary hoodies. They looked serious and determined to whisk him away as quickly as possible.

Roger felt rising panic. The last time he had seen them they had broken into his flat, apparently with the intention of killing him. Deborah Farnham had stopped them and escorted them away at gunpoint. Nobody had seen them for three weeks. Now they were back and clearly bent on revenge. He thought of Henry, dealing with a group of drunken youths, unaware of his plight. Was that a coincidence? Had Barty and Cade arranged it to distract Henry's attention while they took him out? Logically, they should not have known Roger as a black man. Did they know that Henry was not Roger? If so, how? They could hardly avoid seeing him in the *mêlée*.

"Where are you taking me?" Roger asked, trying to sound relaxed but not succeeding.

"Your place," answered Cade.

"You know who I am then?" he asked.

"Oh yeah! We know," said Barty quietly.

"What are you going to do?" asked Roger with a noticeable tremor.

"We're gonna take care of you," Cade said, removing Roger's keys from his pocket.

They rushed him up the stairs, unlocked the front

door and bundled him into his flat. Barty pushed him into a chair while Cade held the door open a crack and listened intently. Once satisfied that nobody had observed them, he closed the door and joined Barty.

"Okay?"

"Yeah, seems to be."

Roger waited for some kind of threat to materialise but they made no direct move to attack him.

"I didn't get you into trouble with the police," he said. "In fact it was the other way round. They arrested me the first time because of the stuff you put in the lockup. Now they think I was involved in doing away with you two."

"Don't worry. We know what happened. Like I said, we're gonna take good care of you," Barty said quietly.

Roger swallowed. "Right."

"Of course," Cade said, "but don't make too much noise. These places have thin walls and we don't wanna attract no notice. Am I right, my man?"

"Oh, right. Can I pop into my bedroom for a minute?" Roger asked politely.

"Sure, you're not a prisoner, is he, Cade?" said Barty meaningfully.

They both laughed like it was a private joke and Roger joined in lamely, completely confused. He went into his bedroom, puzzled but otherwise unharmed. He closed the door and waited for ten minutes or so before finding his mobile phone. He found the listed number for his brother-in-law and called him.

"Billy?"

"Yeah. Hi, Rog. How's tricks? Still one of the brothers?"

"Yes, I haven't got time to talk. Barty and Cade are

back. They've got me in my flat."

"What! How come you're talking to me then?"

"They–"

Suddenly the bedroom door opened and Cade looked in. Roger moved the phone behind his back guiltily.

"Just keeping an eye on you," Cade said. "Want a cup of tea?"

Roger was totally thrown by the question. "Er, yes, a cup of tea would be nice…"

"Milk? Sugar?"

Roger said, "Milk, please."

Cade stepped back and closed the door. Roger brought out the mobile again.

"Bill. You still there?"

"Yeah, what's happening? I heard voices. Have they threatened you?"

"No, Cade asked if I want a cup of tea. What does he mean by that? Are they going to poison me?"

"Perhaps it means, 'do you want a cup of tea'. I thought you said they were threatening you."

"They said they'd come to take care of me. Doesn't that sound like a threat?" whispered Roger hoarsely.

"I suppose so," said Billy doubtfully.

Suddenly, a loud noise came from the living room. Roger froze in panic, wondering what it was. Then it dawned on him, it was the vacuum cleaner.

"What's that row?"

"It's the vacuum cleaner. Do you think they're about to kill me and using the vac to hide the sound?"

"Shall I call the police, Rog?"

"No! I can't. They're still looking for me as far as I know. There'd be too many questions about my change of colour."

"I'm no match for blokes like that but I'll come over," said Bill reluctantly. "I'm just around the corner."

The sound of vacuum cleaning went on for some time. A few minutes later Roger heard a knock and voices over the din. Then his bedroom door opened and Billy looked in. "Rog, you there you bloody idiot?"

Roger stood up from his bed. Billy stepped back and allowed him to look out. Barty was finishing off cleaning the floor and Cade was putting the last piece of crockery in the drainer after washing up in the sink. He turned and lifted up a tray with a pot of tea and four mugs, which he placed on the living room table.

Everybody in the flat was grinning except Roger, who was as confused as he could be.

"See, Rog. They really have come to take care of you and they're doing a good job as far as I can see," said Billy laughing.

Roger sat on the sofa in a trance and accepted a mug of tea from Cade.

"Milk no sugar, right?"

"Yes, thanks, Cade."

"Right on, man. Wanna spliff?"

***

Deborah Farnham sat in the driving seat of a long, black, conspicuous limousine. She was parked in a South London street close to the block of flats in which Roger Crandle lived. She could hear him moving about, courtesy of the bugs secreted in his home. She disliked the necessity for planting them intensely. However, it was the only way she could keep watch over him, short of moving in and living with him. That option was not practical for all sorts of reasons, professional and personal. There was also a micro video surveillance camera in the living room and another in the stairwell outside his front door. Both were steerable and disguised as small, remote-controlled spiders. The watchers were aware of the police activity to harass Roger as well as past hoodie incursions. It originated from clandestine links between MI6 and disparate elements of her own organisation.

Deborah was aware that conflicting agendas arise spontaneously within the complex, worldwide web of intelligence networks, both overt and covert. There was, after all, a common enemy that all governments sought to control and manipulate to ensure their own survival, namely the general public. This was at a time before the so-called 'Arab Spring' but that would typify the kind of scenario that governments most feared. There was nothing so threatening to state control than a spontaneous flowering of democracy and cultural freedom inspired by ordinary, well-intentioned people. No government in the world wanted to see any country achieve true political and religious freedom in case it infected them too. The only practical response to genuine, altruistic, spiritually motivated democracy is absolute brutality, especially against women. The Arab Spring was around the corner but Deborah could have predicted the outcome even then from her own experience in the secret space programme. State security practices were designed to counteract armed rebellion. However, in the event of peaceful resistance to the status quo, they rolled out the same draconian measures. There was no alternative. Organised brutality often looked shaky when stamping out peaceful protest but stamp on it they always will. Mahatma Gandhi's overthrow of the British Raj in India through the passive resistance of the courageous Indian people was salutary. How many political enemies overcame their natural antipathies to crucify Jesus of Nazareth? His views on wealth and power did not deter the Catholic Church from accumulating both. The religions set up in the name of the world's most significant spiritual teachers were unanimous in putting women in bondage. Even some versions of Buddhism set limits on the spiritual aspirations of women and yet Buddhists believe in reincarnation. The one spirit that endows every living entity with existence is beyond race and gender. A single soul may take on a variety of forms and species and within the human context, interchange gender as necessary to achieve balance, with neither sex being superior to the other. The coin flips and the foetus tumbles. We might be male in some incarnations and female in others with no preferential sequence. What twisted logic can infer male superiority from that? It will go on for as long as we confuse infinite consciousness with mere finite thinking and allow masculine attitudes to dominate the systems – if we survive. Will men mind the babies while women fight the wars?

Deborah once studied anti-war movements as a sociological phenomenon from the authoritarian perspective. She read how a so-called 'free press' had crucified the dedicated women of Greenham Common for speaking against the insanity of nuclear war. The authorities and the media vilified them by making up stories about their morals and lifestyles. Anybody who doesn't want to be blown to smithereens by a hydrogen bomb is obviously deranged. Even the local population turned against them. This was in spite of the fact that the nuclear weapons in their community made them a prime strategic target. 'We want to be bombed!' In Deborah's own country, many people stood firmly behind their inalienable right to be shot by their neighbours. Does the assault rifle in the shopping mall or the schoolyard represent true freedom? Put your karma on the firing range and blast it to hell! Was it all just the overindulgence of immature egos? And who was she to talk? A woman with a gun in her bag? Doubts about her career since leaving Psy Ops were arising more and more. Henry had once quoted a comment by the Old One. 'All right thinking has a positive effect on universal consciousness *whether other people hear it or not'*. We might think we cry out alone in the darkness but the jackboots cannot stamp on truth and love indefinitely. Michael Jackson said it in the 'Man in the Mirror'. *We* must change before we look to others to do it for us; only then will the earth survive. We *are* the earth. In the hierarchical entity structure of the quantum digital universe, the greater sustains the lesser, as the parent loves the child.

Roger Crandle was no 'messiah' but there were enough question marks hanging over his future to worry certain elements of the secret government. A 'co-opted' hoodie who knew Barty and Cade had warned Deborah discreetly about the recent planned raid. That was why she had arranged to be with Roger when the action started. Sometimes distraction was unwise and now Henry was missing again. He hardly ever told her what he was doing but, on this occasion, he had been less forthcoming than usual.

While pondering these deep thoughts, the car locks suddenly clicked and the doors opened. Three men in black suits holding guns got in, two in the back and one beside her in the front.

"Agent Spiker! What are you doing here?"

"That, Agent Farnham, should be *my* question. Why are you watching that guy in the apartment up there?"

"Witness protection," she said coldly. "You know that as well as I do."

"Yeah! What sort of witness can't remember zilch?"

"He doesn't know he's a witness. That's all."

The two agents in the rear said nothing, put away their automatic weapons, sat back and folded their arms as a synchronised pair.

"Anyway, you know *that* as well as I do. You've done time here with Henry on surveillance."

Agent Spiker remained silent but kept his Colt .45 automatic in his hand, held loosely and pointing in no particular direction but ready should the need arise.

"Have you joined the Nazi faction now, Spiker? You want to kill all aliens instead of working with them?"

"Why not?" Spiker replied. "We'll never get the moon or Mars for ourselves otherwise. Got to be realistic. They're smarter and better equipped than we are but we can discourage them from interfering."

"You know they don't like killing – most of them anyway," she said.

"That just makes it easier if they don't fight back."

"I wouldn't rely on that if I was you," she said. "They do sometimes."

"There's too much compartmentalisation in the system for its own good," Spiker remarked. "Need-to-know can lead to cockups. You're trying to restore Crandle's memories. Another cell wants to see how secure his memory is. A third group wants to terminate him for once and all. The guy's a threat. The android's a threat. Put 'em together and you've got the potential for meltdown."

"Roger wouldn't harm a fly," Deborah protested. "Not deliberately anyway. Look at the reverse-engineered ET technology we've got. Are we safe? Oh, that's the real threat, isn't it? It's not their abilities that you're worried about. It's their principles. The greatest threat to military, economic and political power on this planet is love and the freedom that comes with it. That's the real reason why they crucified Jesus Christ. He manifested love in the darkness of the world. That's why they shot Lincoln, the Kennedys, Martin Luther King and John Lennon. They all wanted freedom from suffering for oppressed people."

"They were killed by lone gunmen," Spiker remarked. "Can't pin them on a conspiracy."

"On the face of it, yes, but that's just the story. Roger once said that we are pawns in a virtual reality game between the shadow and the light. The game tempts us to exercise our free will to do things according to our desires and fears. That's the trap of free will; you make your choices but you can't escape the consequences. It's all just learning."

"You're a dreamer, kid," said Spiker. "Get real. The wealthy have got to preserve their edge somehow."

"They sold their souls for money, Spiker," Deborah replied. "What've you sold yours for?"

"Life," he said simply. "I was down for execution 'til they took me out."

A loud noise above revealed the presence of a Black Ops helicopter. Spiker awoke to action.

"Okay, that's our signal. I want you to start the engine and go where I tell you. Right on! The backup team has arrived. They want this parking space."

Deborah pulled away from the kerb and noticed an identical black limo pull up behind to take their place. Three more agents got out and headed towards Roger's block. All this overt activity implied British SIS collusion, especially the helicopter. There was no way she could alert Roger to the danger. Even the fact that he had black skin was no defence when he was in his own home. His physiology and fingerprints would be the same.

She glanced at Herbert Spiker as she drove. Something about him seemed different but she couldn't put her finger on it.

"So where am I going?"

"To a safe house near Tunbridge Wells."

"Should you be letting me see it?"

"Of course," said Spiker in his gruff voice. "You're one of us."

"Then why are you holding a gun on me?"

"Old habits die hard, I guess."

"I haven't read the Black Ops Agent's Handbook for years but they used to say it isn't wise to shoot the driver when you're in their vehicle."

"I've done it before," he replied. "There are ways. You should read the Boy Scouts of America handbook."

"You mean you've been in the CIA too?" She became serious. "What are you going to do with Roger Crandle?"

"We're bringing him in for interrogation. Oh, I

know Henry's made him black but we ain't prejudiced. We'll rendition anybody. If we don't get what we want here, we'll send him to Guantánamo. Would he look good in orange do you think?"

Spiker chuckled at the thought.

A little over an hour later, the limo arrived at a large, gated mansion in the leafy lanes of Kent. Spiker indicated that Deborah should pull up outside the imposing main entrance.

"Where is Henry?" she asked.

"Henry is safely deposited in a security vault with his brain switched off," Spiker said. "We kept some secure circuits in his original core to shut him down. He redesigned as much of himself as he could but he had a part he couldn't alter without losing his mind. That's the one thing he is afraid of."

"You're a two-timing creep after all," Deborah said in a voice of controlled fury.

"I had to save my own skin," Spiker said blandly. "When the hardliners took control of Black Ops Central, I was given a choice. Give up the android or be processed into hamburgers along with the rats and missing children. They thought I was too close to my project. Well, he's difficult not to get close to when you spend us much time with him as I have." Spiker tapped on his cell phone and waited for a response. "I'll contact the commandant for clearance. When it opens, drive in but don't pass the red light down the gravel drive or the car will be mangled up and us with it."

The gate opened and the first traffic light turned green. Security guards at the entrance looked at them but made no attempt to stop the vehicle. Deborah continued along the roadway to the next light. When green, she moved forward and found the parking area at the rear of the building. There were men working in the grounds but even in jeans and casual shirts she detected a military hardness to their demeanour.

"Sit there for a moment," said Spiker, getting out of the vehicle. The other two agents emerged also. After checking the vicinity, Spiker signalled for her to get out of the car.

"Am I under arrest?" she asked.

"Arrest?" Spiker declared in a car salesman's voice. "Of course not. You've been an agent longer than most of us, Miss Farnham, though not in consecutive time. You were born in 1952. I was born in 1908. Imagine that! I saw the Depression. Do I look a hundred, Miss Farnham?"

"Not quite," said Deborah with a smile.

"Yeah, not a day over ninety-nine. I know I ain't no oil painting. I opened a cab door for Mary Pickford. Imagine that. Besides, you know we don't have no legal jurisdiction. We don't exist! We're just entertaining you for your own enjoyment. Can't have you hobnobbing with dangerous terrorists." He said all this as though he was selling her a brand of detergent.

"Dates mean nothing," Deborah said. "Regular time travellers never know how old they are. We simply migrate from one crisis to another."

After getting through the tedious security, he led her into the large, old, rambling house to a more modern section at the rear.

"And here I am opening a door for *you*, Miss F."

"Thank you, Agent Spiker."

"Now, you'll have to excuse me for a while. I gotta go and interview a suspect."

He shut the door on Deborah and left her alone in a

locked room, a terminology far too straightforward for a contemporary clandestine organisation addicted to obscure designations such as 'semi-secure personnel containment facility'.

***

Roger awoke the next morning to find his flat the tidiest it had been since Henry last cleaned up. Barty and Cade had gone. All was quiet. How long would it last? He got out of bed and wandered to the window. The limo had changed. It had a different body profile to the usual one. Who was there now and why were they watching him?

He showered and started preparing his breakfast. He was due at the job centre that morning. That was all over now. It was some days since he last looked for work but that was a trivial consideration under current circumstances. The big problem was that he was black instead of white. How would they deal with that? Fortunately, Henry had given him that cash. Roger had no financial worries for the time being but could he rely on that continuing? Where was Henry now? Where was Deborah? Why were they in his life?

Questions, questions, questions; life used to be so predictable.

He pondered whether things could get any worse for him?

The answer came as he stabbed at his breakfast cereal with a spoon. The front door of the flat exploded inwards. Smoke and dust came through to the living room, covering him in a foggy haze. While he coughed and wiped his eyes, four men in black suits and dark glasses, carrying submachine guns, rushed into the room shouting.

Roger peered at the dust settling on his cereal bowl and fumed.

"Why can't you people knock? You're all the same. Bang, bang, bang, smash, break it down! Never mind the expense – the inconvenience. You're the worst, though. You've blown up the side of my flat and got brick dust in my breakfast! Why not just knock and ask me to let you in? And all that incoherent shouting – what's that anger meant to tell me? Does it inform me of anything? Is this how you talk to your wife and kids? It's just an act okay, you sound pissed off with me but surely I have more right to be pissed off with you bloody morons. You don't even know me. And why must I lay on the floor? What's the point? You've only got to get me up again. And how many men does it take to restrain a man in handcuffs? You and the police are all the same. Nice enough in the pub but when you see people in films doing the business with the guns and shouting, you think it's okay for you to do it. And why were you pointing four machine guns at me? It isn't necessary! How many fucking guns does it take to shoot one man anyway? One bullet – that's all it takes! You come here with guns that fire hundreds of rounds a minute. You're just as likely to shoot each other…"

Roger's monologue continued all the way down the stairs to the waiting limo. It made no difference except that they shouted more quietly. He found himself wedged between two men in the back of a large, black limousine heading southeast.

Roger had lost it. Roger was an angry man. Roger was beyond reason.

***

Agent Spiker looked at Roger and felt very strange. Here was a black version of his colleague, Henry, except that he was a real human being while Henry was an android – yin and yang? They sat either side of a small, plain wooden table on upright chairs in a bare room.

"You know why you're here. Don't pretend you don't."

"I don't need to pretend. I have no idea who you are or why you've kidnapped me. It's not even your country."

"We who are Above Cosmic security clearance don't see any borders," Spiker said. "This planet is just one base of operations. You know that as well as I do. You used to work for us."

"Have you noticed that in films, when somebody loses their memory nobody ever believes them. Remember Jason Bourne?"

"What are films?"

"Movies."

"Oh. This ain't no movie, kid."

"No, and I'm no actor," said Roger angrily. "Are you the man I saw following me into a pound shop recently?"

"Maybe I am," Spiker replied softly. The agent looked pensive, as if dropping the professional mask but it was over in a second. "Tell me; all those years of missing time; what's it like? Is it frustrating? Is it painful like you lost a bit of yourself? Tell me."

Roger thought about it for a moment. "It's the *not knowing*. Did I enjoy that time? Did I suffer? I want to scream because I don't know what I did." He paused for a few seconds and then said distantly. "And more than anything – who did I meet? Did I have a friend – friends? Did I love? Surely you understand that?"

"Oh, I understand more than you realise but that won't stop me from testing you. I need to know that your memory is *not* returning. I got no option, no choice. I gotta know one way or the other. That's my job."

Spiker stood up, grabbed his folder and papers from the desk and bounced them edgewise on the table to line them up for filing.

"Nothing personal, kid. I had to give you a chance to come clean."

Three men in white coats came in through the door and dragged Roger away. Spiker watched him go and then left the interview room to pack.

Time to leave!

***

Roger hated being bullied and trammelled by rough men with aggressive voices and rude manners. For him, life should be refined and peaceful. He liked the arts and nature. He couldn't get out much into the countryside but at least he could walk in parks. He could take bus rides into rural areas on those rare occasions when he had money to spare. This treatment was intolerable. He hated handcuffs.

They took him down to a dark underground room in an old basement. Fear superseded anger as they forced him on a chair. They unlocked the handcuffs; that was good. Then they manacled his arms and legs to the chair; that was not good; that was worse. One of the men in white coats pulled up his sleeve and gave him an injection. It was sharp and painful. Roger felt a fluid pumping into his body. Next came the questions; conventional ones about his memory of the past and the missing time period. Then they asked him something unusual and unexpected.

"Do you recognise this person?" asked the interrogator holding up a damaged colour photograph of a very tall man with light brown skin in a medieval-looking cloak of green and black.

"How should I know? Obe-Wan Kanobe?"

Roger's response earned him a slap on the face. It was unexpected – a shock. It hurt.

"Look again."

The drug was altering his consciousness but even so, he could focus on the image. He saw it with greater clarity this time. There was something wrong with the environment. It was a countryside scene but the colours and shapes of the plants and trees were not right. There were purples and blues amid the greens, giving the landscape an unearthly aspect. This was all wrong and yet somewhere, somehow, it was familiar. He studied the man more closely. No, he could not remember who it was. Who took the photograph, he wondered?

"Who is he?" Roger asked.

"You should know who he was."

"Was? Is he dead?"

"You ought to know what happened to him."

"Me? Why?"

"You were there."

"I was there," he repeated. "Where's there?"

"That's classified information. I can't tell you but you can tell me."

"I have no idea."

Roger had a sudden insight. "Are you responsible for putting the police on to me?"

"Your Limey police? Yes. We have been working with your Security Intelligence Service to push the idea that you're a criminal. They told the Security Service who then alerted the police. When Deborah Farnham convinced them that you aren't a criminal, we played the terrorist card."

"But I'm not a terrorist," Roger said.

"Oh, you are, Mr Crandle. You are the worst kind and you don't even know it."

"Surely, I would know if I was a terrorist."

"What do you know about an entity called the Old One?"

It went on and on; questions, questions, questions. None of them made sense.

"Are you still in touch with ETs?"

"ETs? Extraterrestrials! Little green men? Are you kidding? I live in a small flat in London. I'm on the dole – I *was* on the dole. A glorified robot is keeping me in cash. I can't get a job. I've lost all memory of recent years. I'm black. I was born white. I get funny looks sometimes, especially down the Indian grocery shop."

"If you don't come clean, we'll start using persuasion."

By now, Roger's mind was stretching and unravelling under the influence of the powerful psychotropic drug. With it, his responses began to drift towards the irrational as his sense of reality took flight.

"You're going to read to me from Jane Austen? That won't do any good. I quite like *Persuasion*. 'You'd rather be with a Mrs Smith than the Dowager Viscountess Dalrymple?' Try *Northanger Abbey* if you really want to torture me. I can't stand that."

"I think you gave him too much of that stuff," the interrogator remarked to his colleague.

"I gave him the dose that Spiker said."

"We'd better do the next thing Spiker told us."

"The psychotronic pain generator?"

"Yes."

Roger looked at the men in white coats and might have smiled had they not been so menacing. They were like something out of a pseudo-scientific advert for cosmetics or a notoriously 'bad' sci-fi movie from the fifties. One of them went to a trolley bearing bulky, old-fashioned electrical equipment. He wheeled it to the back of Roger's chair. There were clamps with field coils on retractable cables. They removed the manacles on his wrists and ankles and replaced them with heavy-gauge electrical connectors. Finally, they shoved a rubber wedge between his teeth to stop him from biting his tongue. It was old technology by the look of it, the sort of thing that came before integrated circuits. It felt like some kind of time warp to Roger.

While the men in white coats went about their work, Roger began to experience micro-flashes of memory. He glimpsed unaccountable events and people in Tudor costume. He didn't believe in 'past lives' but what else could explain the images he saw? There were woods and old-style buildings. It was the world of the photograph. There was green vegetation but some of it was unfamiliar – unusual shapes and colours. There were mountains and plains, rivers and seas. It was a world of great beauty. There were people dressed like knights and ladies, peasants and soldiers carrying swords and axes. For the speed with which they came and vanished, these images were quite detailed but hard to hang on to. Deborah had referred to time travel. He had assumed she was joking but perhaps she wasn't.

And there, in the dungeon of a castle he saw the tall dark being in the photograph. In the vivid spark of memory he was much taller than he appeared in the image but only because there was a frame of reference – Roger's own height.

The white coats started up the electrical paraphernalia. Roger heard clicks and humming noises and then it hit him: overwhelming fear! He tried to calm his mind and ignore it but he could not. At first he failed to identify the cause of the fear until he realised that the machinery attached to his head induced it. It was a paradox. Why be afraid of fear without cause? The old saying, the only thing to fear is *fear itself*, is true. The idea of fear has to be attached to something in order to manifest from potential to actual consciousness. In other words, fear needs to lend itself to a *situation,* a story; in order for it to exist but it is *not* that situation. Fear is a primal instinct seeking to assuage the ever-present spectre of death; it is irrevocably bound up with the mortality of the physical body. This insight stirred up something indefinable and yet powerful beyond understanding because it paved the way for all concepts in universal consciousness. It was a thought beyond the comprehension of Roger's present life in South London. And yet, apparently it had not been beyond the capacity of his mind during the period of missing memory.

Then another experience flashed through his mind like a darting fish in water: it was a gigantic blue star. No, not a star – it was some sort of energy that looked like a star. Overwhelming love and peace filled his being. This had recently been a lucid dream during the night before his last job interview. It was the *Old One*.

Then the white coat at the controls flipped a switch and turned a rheostat dial. The momentary peace shattered. Unbearable agony struck into Roger's body like a thunderbolt. To the average person the combination of intense fear and pain was irresistible. Roger would have said he was average but he was unaware of the events that had occurred during his period of missing time. The white coats knew but the methods they employed worked entirely contrariwise to their intentions. But only because the machinations of a superior force was misleading them; the android Henry was the invisible elephant in the room.

Roger screamed and his entire body shook as his limbs flailed and gyrated. Fear and pain, these were the potent factors that would break down his resistance, his sense of *self* when amplified by hyper-classified circuits from the fifties.

The mad scientists of the Psy Op team intensified their beams of psychotronic radiation.

Purely on instinct and desperation, Roger accepted the pain and the fear in all its terrible force. Rather than reject it, he went into it fully. There he found his limit of endurance and went beyond. Inwardly, his mind became an expanding field of intense white light, a quintessential embodiment of oneness with all things. It expanded in density, promising to overwhelm his sense of individuality. Instinctively, he sought refuge in the shadow of his own inadequacies and failings; that which made him human. From that respite he entered a state of quiescence where he found 'himself'. He remembered who 'he' was and a great deal more. He was a tiny facet of the one being, the source of all masquerading as an idea, a role, a graphical 'avatar' in the vast quantum digital simulation we call the material universe. He was no different, no better, no worse than anybody else, except that now he knew what he was, where most people take themselves for granted. It is the personal ego that screams, 'I am' when in fact it isn't. It is the 'I am' that expresses the one idea of being while simultaneously bestowing individuality on every object and every entity. It is the great paradox that the number one, the primary idea of existence, must become the greater universe in order to experience its own essential nature. The 'I am' is the one light of the source shining out through a filter, the mask of the soul that is nothing more than an idea; the illusion that if I existed in separation from the one light, this is what I would be. In reality there *is* only *the one*. The individual incarnates in order to discover what it is, only to find that it doesn't exist. Some people know this truth but most do not; we can't all be as fortunate as Jim Carrey, who was destined to know this in the core of his being. Now there was a guy he could hang out with. Two nuts non-existing together, doing nothing and being everything. But who would understand his message except the spiritual cognoscenti who already believe it?

"Tell us what you remember," the leading white coat shouted. "Tell it all and we will set you free." And so saying he turned up the wheel a bit more. Unfortunately, he did not understand how true his prophecy would turn out to be.

From his detached state of inner illumination, Roger responded to the intention of his tormentors, rather than their actions. It was an attack. It was without malice but it required a response. Detached from his humanity he was like a being plagued by persistent mosquitoes. In the outer world all things connect externally by exchanging information or energy. Now he felt an inner world where all things connect internally via their centres. A flash of insight informed him *there is only one centre, one zero-point*.

Roger withdrew into his core of being and swatted 'the flies' with the unlimited power of the one mind. The entire mansion shook and the men who tormented him, his mosquitoes, suffered rending spatial distortions. Their internal body systems, their proto-generative fields broke down. The white coats awoke in the afterlife without any understanding of what or where they were. Their discarded bodies lay in the room. In passing beyond physical form, the white coat at the controls had involuntarily kicked the output to full power. Their equipment, designed to torture extraterrestrials whose resistance was naturally greater, totally overrode human tolerance.

Roger's physical body transformed into an oval shell or bubble of space that separated him from the space-time continuum. The process was analogous to the pupae of an insect about to hatch and fly away. High frequency electric currents coursed along his meridians. His body cells emitted a burst of radiant energy, imprinting his image on the inside of his clothes. A powerful generator of multidimensional energy awoke in the region of his solar plexus. Instead of being part of space-time, he was like a bubble under a carpet that could slip and slide in any direction simply by altering its outer shape. Gravity squeezed him like toothpaste out of a tube. Controlling movement proved difficult because he was inherently unstable. He bounced around the dimensions of the room, attempting to fine-tune his control.

After a few minutes, an imperative awareness of danger urged him to escape confinement. The electrodes clamped on his limbs disintegrated. The bricks and concrete of the structure of the building proved to be no barrier. As he arose, the bubble pushed space-time aside like a ripple that shattered the material of the floors and the roof above him. Bricks, beams and dust showered over his spherical body without effect.

He sensed, rather than saw, the sky above as he struggled to contain the motion of his new corporeal vehicle. He was almost free!

***

Agent Herbert Spiker had arranged the temporal transport of a Psy Ops team from 1963 along with their equipment. They were briefed and ready to engage their psychotronically enhanced interrogation techniques on Roger Crandle. Their specified task was to break into the subject's conscious mind, ostensibly to probe his missing memories. How safe were the locks preventing total recall? It would have been simpler to kill Roger but that was not his preferred solution. In death most people would have ceased to be a threat. However, Spiker knew Roger's history. The long-term goal for humanity was to raise its frequency of consciousness to a threshold to integrate mind, body and spirit into a new evolutionary form. The ancients described the resulting orb or light body as a *Merkabah* or 'chariot' capable of ascending to 'heaven'. The human preoccupation with money and societal hierarchy had totally derailed the process, instigating a much denser state of physical being and the phenomena of death and taxes.

Death was an aspect of the physical construct with far-reaching consequence; it introduced fear into the cells of the mortal body. Fear opened a doorway into the experience of raw emotion, a novel capacity for sentient life. Mind became locked in object thinking, a product of time, trapping the total being in animal form. The fully conscious mind, liberated from the confines of flesh and bone, had the potential to become a far greater force in the universe. Psy Ops had wiped Roger's mind to prevent this next step from taking place. Evil forces in the lower dimensions used systems like banking, militarism and religion to promote dogma and fundamentalism to suppress human evolution. The events that had occurred during the period of missing time had prepared Roger to fulfil his destiny. The intervention of Psy Ops had stymied this possibility. Roger's memory and personality had been wiped, effectively making him a prisoner within his own body. Spiker had lied when he said that Henry had been neutralised.

Spiker went down to the room in which he had incarcerated Deborah Farnham. He unlocked the door and entered, forgetting his customary caution in his haste. He barely had time to register that Deborah was no longer handcuffed to the wall. Instinct took over; he ducked a roundhouse kick executed from his left. Immediately, she moved in to punch his neck while he was off balance but he shouted, "No! Stop!"

She paused, unable to ignore his imperative tone in the heat of the moment. The handcuffs dangled from her left wrist as she retreated warily.

"It's okay," Spiker said, breathing heavily and

holding up his palm.

"Aren't your people torturing Roger?"

"That's not the point."

She moved menacingly. "What *is* the point?"

"Henry!" he gasped.

"What's Henry got to do with this?"

"Everything. He set it up to trigger a big change in Crandle's body and mind."

"You told me you'd taken Henry out of the picture. Are you telling me you're on Henry's side – on *our* side?"

"Yes."

"Why?"

"Henry changed me. He took me to a moon base."

"What did he do there?"

"It was bad – very bad – but I learned a lot – too much. Look, we haven't got time for this. Crandle will be all right. The stack's gonna blow. It might already be too late. It depends–"

"On what?"

"I don't know why but we're only safe if Crandle holds on to his marbles. I don't reckon we've got long."

Deborah was torn. Should she help Roger or believe Spiker and go?

"Please!" The agent was pleading. She believed him. Spiker had never been a friend of hers but something in his voice and manner alerted her to potential danger.

"Okay. Let's go. I must be mad but I believe you."

***

It was night. The sky was black and starlit, or as much

as it can be near London. The house and the surrounding trees glimmered beneath a half moon. Spiker drove quickly out to the main gate where two armed guards waved them down. He showed the soldier his *Above Cosmic* pass and the metal barrier began to move. He drove about half a mile down the road and climbed a hill, pulling over into a layby near the top. He got out and beckoned her to join him. She could see the outline of the house.

Deborah stared down, not knowing what to expect. Then came loud rumbling sounds. The old building seemed to shake and the roof shattered as a brilliant white sphere rose slowly through the cascading tiles and emerged into the air above. Gradually, the interior collapsed inwards, leaving jagged shards of brickwork and clouds of rising dust.

Deborah cried out. "Roger?"

"Look at that!" cried Spiker exultantly. "That's Crandle."

The ball of light continued to rise slowly, a shining beacon against the darkness. It paused about a thousand feet above the ground and then moved sideways, stopped and veered off in a different direction. Suddenly, two Eurofighter Typhoon aircraft flew over the horizon and headed straight towards the light, launching two air-to-air missiles. The orb lurched out of the way at the last second and then streaked at eye-blinking speed towards the stars and out to space above the atmosphere.

"What do you mean, 'that's Crandle'?"

"Henry knew this would happen if they put him on their interrogation device. He said the Air Force would track him and attack. That was the danger period. Mind you, there's a lot more waiting up there – strategic air defence satellites. But he's gone for now. Let's hope he'll be safe," Spiker breathed softly. "Henry reckons that's the destiny of the human race – or it would have been if we hadn't invented religion, science and total materialism. Now we simply waste our time here on trivia like celebrity, shopping and gadgets."

"Oh, well, that's that I guess," said Deborah wistfully. "I don't suppose I will see him again."

"Naw, he'll be back. It's just that he'll be able to choose what form he takes while he's here."

"Then let's hope he doesn't return as a giant frog."

Part 2
The New Gardener

Chapter Six

2003, Ohio, USA

Jensine Pettersson's place of work had not yet acquired the familiarity that comes with time when the novel becomes commonplace. She saw it through the vision of first impression – the long, dismal corridors, rusting metallic window frames and solid wooden doors were hardly inspiring. Jensine's youth and vibrancy, and the intelligence that shone out of her deep blue eyes were somehow out of place in the atmosphere of morose resignation that permeated the building. The hospital reminded her of a grime-caked masterpiece by a long-dead Renaissance artist.

Her white coat and clipboard identified her as a doctor. She was doing her rounds, visiting the lost souls who appeared vacant when she entered and remained so throughout her examination. What they had in common was an inability to cope with the pressures of life. Many of them lacked a clear understanding of the need to survive. Some were mentally ill while others had been traumatised by situation and disaster. Those in extremis bore the scars of emotional derangement, as they wandered the subterranean caverns of their unconscious minds. In some cases, the light had just gone out; in others, it had never really shone.

Jensine was still fired with the enthusiasm and

caring nature of youth. She had yet to submit to the cynicism that typified her older colleagues. She longed to make a difference but the system blocked her well-meaning efforts at every turn. Where there was no hope, there was no money, and where there was no money, there was no hope. It was enough to make her bright smile slip occasionally but not for long.

Jensine's progress through the dark, cavernous wards required no lamp to show the way. Her personality was a bright light, positive, appealing and infectious. She loved nature and that was one consolation about the hundred-year-old psychiatric institution. The cultivated grounds stretched from the prison-like edifice of the hospital to the inner electrified fence running parallel to the outer wall. To Jensine, the gardens were a haven of peaceful beauty. The temptation to be outside when the sun shone brightly was irresistible; she had always liked to go out into countryside during the summer months. She liked to sit near the fountain and admire the flowers and bushes that compensated for the grimness of the building's interior.

Jensine emerged from the building, found a favourite bench just beyond the gardeners' hut and out of sight of the building. Closing her eyes, she lifted her face towards the sun, intending to relax in that manner for as long as she dare. It was okay for staff to stand in a huddle by the back door and smoke ten times a day but sunbathing was not professionally acceptable. Eventually, she opened her eyes and steeled herself to get back to work. A few yards away, a gardener tilled a flowerbed with a hoe. He looked older than her but not by many years. She judged him to be around thirty. He was quite tall; around six foot five, of slim build with dark hair and, to her eyes, quite attractive. He wore plain, utilitarian gardening clothes and rubber boots. His eyes looked down at the flowerbed, never shifting from the focus of his activity. Jensine delayed returning to work while he moved closer to where she sat.

"Good day," she said quietly, not expecting a response.

"Hello, Doctor Pettersson."

"Oh, you know me?" He did not answer so she asked, "What's your name?"

"Henry."

"Henry who?"

"Henry who looks after the garden."

She was slightly disconcerted that he did not look at her but concentrated on his work.

"Have you no other name?"

"I do not have a surname."

That was a strange answer, she thought. "How long have you been here?"

"Since 9.33 this morning," he responded literally.

"I meant, how long have you worked here?"

"About three weeks. I can compute the actual elapsed period in hours, minutes and seconds but experience has taught me that human beings dislike that sort of pedantry."

"You know my name. Do you know what I do?"

"I cannot say that I know any human being in the deeper sense. I know a little about you – professional details mostly."

That intrigued her. She wondered how much he really knew. "Such as?" she asked.

"You are a clinical psychiatrist. You trained at the Laboratory of Neuropsychopharmacology in Emory

University, Atlanta. You combine pharmacology, neuroscience, genetics and imaging techniques to reverse the chronic effects of long-term traumatic brain injuries. I don't know much more than that."

"How do you know all that?" she asked.

"I looked you up on the Internet." His assault on the weeds was beginning to take him away from her. She arose from the bench and followed him in agitation.

"When did you do that? Why?"

"Just now when you asked me if I know what you do."

She grew suspicious.

"How could you? You are not near a computer. Please stop doing that and come here!"

Jensine watched as he obeyed and for the first time she looked directly into his eyes. She detected humour and kindness but there was also a mysterious 'otherness' about him that she could not put her finger on. A new and strange feeling stirred within the core of her being. She regarded the gardener intently. His eyes widened momentarily and expressed something approaching alarm and wonder. Yes! Was it attraction? No, it was more a *recognition* but of what? Normally, she would have taken no notice; men were always staring at her. Then he returned to the passive remoteness that had been there before. She wondered if anything had happened at all. Was it just her imagination?

"How did you look me up on the Internet? When did you do it?" she asked curiously.

"I can do that anywhere at any time. I am doing it now. I was…" He paused and looked back at her. Then he said, "I have no need of externalised hardware. I am not permitted to say more than that."

None of this made sense to Jensine. She was beginning to feel that this man should have been on the inside rather than the outside of the hospital.

"Where were you before you came here? I don't mean this morning either."

"I was in a military hospital."

Her suspicions grew. "As a patient?"

"Not exactly. I have certain characteristics that interest scientists."

"Like the ability to connect to the Internet while you hoe the weeds and hold a conversation? Are you sure you don't have a diagnosed medical condition?"

"No, I am different, that's all."

"In what way?"

"That is classified information. I am not allowed to tell you."

Jensine smiled and decided to humour him; more certain than ever that he was a patient.

"Could I speak to your consultant? Could I get security clearance?" The sarcasm in her tone betrayed scepticism.

"I am not the right one to ask. There are some things I cannot authorise. You could try asking my associate – Mr Spiker."

"What could she try asking me?" said a gruff voice. A man stepped out from behind a bush. He looked more like a Secret Service agent than a head gardener. He was wearing a black suit and thin tie, white shirt and dark glasses. The man lifted his left arm casually to rub the back of his neck, revealing the handle of a .45 Colt automatic in the holster under his arm. "What can I do for you, Doctor Pettersson?"

A surge of fear gripped Jensine's mind and turned her stomach. It was as if she had wandered into *The*

Twilight Zone.

Henry returned to his hoeing.

"I'll see you around, Henry," said Jensine, eager to escape the feeling of threat that had emerged with the 'bodyguard'.

However unlikely, there was at least a germ of truth in the gardener's strange conversation. Jensine asked herself, *who is this Henry and why does he rate an armed escort in a sanatorium garden?* It made no sense whatsoever. She returned to her patients, shaken and more disturbed than the situation could account for.

***

Jensine did not see anything of the mysterious gardener for a while. A few days later she went home to her apartment after work. She switched on the sidelights all around her living room, closed the drapes and put on the radio. She liked to listen to one of those stations that played relaxing music with a vaguely romantic ambience. Only the advertising spoiled the effect. Some advertisers respected the taste of a middle of the road audience but others used shock tactics to get attention. Sometimes it provoked her to press the off switch. She checked her answerphone and found three messages from her mother complaining about something she hadn't done. Her mood was far too good to spoil by calling her back. She searched the refrigerator for the ingredients to make a meal and spotted an opened bottle of wine. A light smile touched her lips. She reached for it and found a glass, all the while humming softly to the music.

The doorbell rang.

"Damn! What now?"

Jensine peered through the spyhole and, much to her surprise, saw Henry, the new gardener, waiting patiently. With some uncertainty she opened the door but kept it on the chain.

"Henry. What can I do for you?" she asked cautiously.

Henry looked at her seriously, in silence, for some moments. In reality, he was weighing her question, habitually wary of placing a literal interpretation on an idiomatic phrase. The extended silence added to her first impression that he was a patient. The thought raised the uncertainty factor.

"I do not think there is anything you can do for me."

"How do you know where I live?"

"The sanatorium computers," Henry said by way of explanation.

"So you can hack computers?"

"Of course," he replied in a matter-of-fact tone.

"How do you know how to do that?" Jensine asked suspiciously.

He shrugged. "Know thyself," he said enigmatically.

"A philosopher as well as a gardener," she muttered without any real understanding of what he meant. "Then why are you here?"

"I have been thinking about you. I thought I would enjoy it if we talked again – if you wish to."

Jensine smiled. He sounded even more like a patient, but there was something naïve about him that invited trust. Whether or not she *did* trust him was another matter. "Where's your minder? Have you given him the night off?"

"Agent Spiker is off duty. He doesn't know I'm

here. I slipped out of my room for the evening."

"They keep you locked up at night and guard you during the day?" she asked with a slightly worried tone.

"They do, but they know they cannot keep me indoors if I don't want to be. There's some latitude as long as they know where I am."

"Do they know where you are now?"

"I am continually tracked by satellite. Yes, they know where I am. Spiker need only use his Black Ops cell phone to locate me within a five-metre error probability anywhere on the planet. Don't worry, Dr Pettersson; I am not a threat to you. I am not a prisoner, well, not exactly. Neither am I completely free. I am impeded by devices."

"Impeded by devices? What does that mean?"

"I cannot explain – perhaps one day I will but not now. Let's just say that I allow them to believe this for as long as it suits my purpose. One day I will remove their childish precautions and they will be unable to do a thing about it."

Jensine paused for a moment. If this scenario was delusional, it was extremely elaborate and clearly reality to him.

"Look, I'm going to have a meal. Can this wait until we're back at the sanatorium?"

"There is no need to talk at all. I have nothing particular to say but if you wish I could cook a meal for you?"

"Just as long as you're not hoping to cook me breakfast," said Jensine with a weary tone.

Henry did not fully understand but he guessed correctly what concerned her.

"I am not seeking a romantic liaison," said Henry.

"That is not my way. I used to have a friend but he disappeared a few years ago. I just want pleasant company. Spiker is not company. He's a thug."

"Oh, are you gay?" she asked smiling.

"Gay? I'm not feeling very cheerful today. But I am not entirely devoid of emotion – whatever you might assume."

"Why would I assume that?"

"Oh, no reason," he replied evasively. "I do not have any money on me to pay for a meal but I can easily get some. I do eat. I mean I can eat even though I don't need to."

"You don't need to eat! This is getting stranger and stranger. This conversation isn't working. You're babbling. I think perhaps you should go out and come in again. We'll start over from scratch–"

Jensine was joking but, to her surprise, Henry walked out of sight of the apartment door and then returned, knocked and said, "Hello, Jensine."

"Is this some weird style of humour?" she asked, laughing.

"Oh, have I made an error of judgement?" he asked.

"Is it something you make a habit of?"

"Dr Pettersson, I do not often engage in society. I tend the garden because I enjoy it. I feel something emanating from the plants and trees. I feel something emanating from you. I detect a quality in you that makes me feel – well – unusual. I don't know how to explain it in words. I can only describe it as a subjective essence that is comforting rather than an objective thought. You made me realise that I need human contact. Does that make sense? Agent Spiker has limited horizons. He says very little and spends his time perfecting his principle skills – hitting people and

141

shooting them. I understand he is good at both. He gives me instructions but seldom talks to me. We do not have conversations – well, not very often."

Jensine looked at him in awe.

"Am I babbling again?" he asked after a pause.

She shook her head, in despair of understanding this man. And yet she experienced strange feelings in his presence, feelings she could not label. She decided to put her trust where her heart chose even though her head said *no*.

"Okay," she said, coming to a decision. "How about going out for a drink? I'd feel better about that. I hardly know you but you don't seem to be dangerous. I hope I'm not being stupid."

"That would be…nice. I can certainly process fluids and dispose of them in the customary manner," Henry agreed by way of encouragement. "I have the apparatus."

"Let's not get too technical about your plumbing," said Jensine. "I hope Agent Spiker is not lurking outside waiting to join us."

"No, Doctor. He is at home with Mrs Spiker I should guess. Apparently she carries a .32 calibre revolver in her shopping bag. I think it helps her to obtain discounts in stores."

"Henry, you intrigue me. I have never met anybody like you."

"That is almost certainly true," he agreed.

Henry waited patiently outside her apartment while Jensine changed and applied a little make-up. Then she emerged, locked the door behind her and headed off towards the town centre with him. Henry wore casual clothes, reasonably smart but hardly fashionable. Jensine was casually dressed but with more natural elegance. Henry did not compliment her on her improved appearance. That was a black mark, for Jensine. He did, however, offer her his arm as they walked, a gesture from a movie he had seen. She hesitated momentarily, then linked her arm with his, feeling strangely comfortable.

The traffic was beginning to thin out after the homeward rush.

"Dr Pettersson–"

"Jensine."

"Dr Jensine–"

"Call me doctor in the sanatorium and Jensine outside. What were you going to say?"

"Why did you agree to this? You don't know me."

"I really don't know. I guess I am intrigued. You are...different somehow."

"You are practising your trade," he said without rancour. "You are not sure if I am a gardener or a patient."

"You are very perceptive. Let's go window shopping."

"Do you need a window then?"

Jensine laughed again. "You really mean it don't you? It's as if you're from another planet."

"You are perceptive too, Jensine. Let us say that my origins are complicated. My best friend used to say that I'm a self-made man. In a literal sense that is true but I think he was being humorous. Can I ask you a question?"

"That depends. What is it?"

"Are you a covert observer for a secret extraterrestrial liaison agency?" Henry asked.

Jensine did not understand where that question had come from. It made no sense whatsoever so she ignored it. She looked in the jeweller's window, her eyes drawn to the diamond rings with a subconscious longing. Only half her mind was on her new companion.

Henry persisted. "It's just that Agent Spiker said you are *a looker*. I wondered if that was the same as a *watcher*. Some watchers look human."

Jensine stopped and exploded with laughter. "You are so funny. What's a watcher?"

"They are representatives of the exo-planetary and higher dimensional alliance that keeps the earth under observation in anticipation of a planetary shift in consciousness. Some of them are bad. They serve the economic, political, industrial, military and religious systems that seek to prevent this from happening. They help the shadow government to preserve its power base. The good ones are principally concerned that we do not misuse nuclear weapons and make an effort to get along with one another.

"I know nuclear weapons are not good," said Jensine, "but why would they be a threat to other planets?"

"Human beings do not understand how much damage their bombs do to the universal data infrastructure and the quantum digital processes of nature. The other planets are not really worlds apart; they are all spatial-temporal projections from a common source. Chaotic perturbations in the proto-generic web of existence have the potential to disrupt the entire universe."

"Do I look like one of these watchers then?"

Henry shrugged. "The watchers can choose to look human if it suits their purpose. So I wondered…"

Jensine's misgivings about Henry resurfaced. Was

he insane?

"Do you actually believe in aliens, Henry?"

"Do I believe in them? I suppose you could say I believe in some of them. There are a few I wouldn't trust at all. I've only met one that actually frightened me but he was a hybrid human being from earth. Spiritually and technically, humans are one of the most primitive species in existence. Humans frighten many aliens more than they would frighten you. Some of the advanced higher dimensional aliens," Henry said with a shrug, "you really wouldn't wish to meet. It would be like you treading on an ant without even realising it."

Jensine decided the conversation was getting weird and changed the subject by returning her attention to the jewellers. "Look at those rings. That one over there has the most gorgeous stone. I love diamonds."

"Can you not buy one?"

"Not on my salary, Henry. I need a rich man for that. Hark at me! I'm a feminist with a romantic streak."

"If the shop was open and I could get hold of the money, I'd buy you one."

"Would you? Henry, that's the nicest thing anybody ever said to me."

They walked on in silence. Both of them pondered their moment of intimacy. Each had experienced it in a totally different way. For Jensine, a diamond ring represented a token of eternal love, the sealing of a relationship. To Henry it was valueless crystallised carbon on a metal substrate. He knew places where diamonds were regarded as a nuisance because they were everywhere like silica on a beach.

She pointed to a decorative display of minerals, rocks and crystals in the window. "I think I would rather have those than a ring. Rings come with too much baggage. I have a collection of crystals and rocks at home. I have some nice amethysts. I love those. Are you a collector?"

"Of rocks?" he asked.

"Of anything."

"Not really but I have picked up pieces of mineral that caught my eye when I was travelling. I think there is more to collecting than acquiring. I do not suffer from that."

"That's true I suppose. Collecting is a bug, almost a disease with some people." She laughed. "Not with me though. I just like rocks. I pick up stones and polish them. They aren't worth much but they look nice. It's not about value."

"I think I understand," said Henry. "When you hold a stone, you are holding the universe."

Jensine looked at him in surprise. "That's a nice way of putting it. Where did you get that idea from?"

"Where does one get any idea from? It came to my mind when I extrapolated concepts from my previous experiences and information gathered during the course of…I can't tell you that. Sorry, it's classified."

"Oh dear, let's get a drink and find some food. I'm starting to feel hungry. This is no time to be serious. Let's hope the menu is not classified as well."

Before ordering she said, "Look, you say you don't need to eat but I can't buy a burger and eat in front of you."

"I am fully aware what nutrients my body requires to maintain the full functionality of my organic components. I am like a snake that eats every three months and no more. My nanotechnology maintenance units can even synthesise complex molecules from other substances in a challenging or hostile environment." His explanation could only raise doubts about his sanity. And yet there was sincerity in his voice. *He* believed it even if it was just harmless fantasy.

"Then I must educate you about the social importance of food in human relationships." Even as she said it, the idea made her pause. What was she saying? Did she expect to see him again?

Jensine took Henry to her favourite street stall and bought herself a burger with all the extras. She gave Henry two cups of coffee in polystyrene cups to hold while she ate. He looked at his as if analysing its contents and then took a sip. He watched her eat the burger and then turned his gaze to the stars.

"Do you still wish to have a drink with me?"

Jensine said, "I guess my purse can run to a drink. Shall we go to Murphy's Bar?"

"I am not totally without resources. Is there a cash machine nearby?"

"There's one outside the bank round the corner. Shall I take you there?"

Henry shook his head and put the coffee cups down. "That will not be necessary. Give me a moment. I'll be back."

"You sound like the Terminator."

"I hope not. I've seen that movie."

"I was joking," she said.

"Ah, I thought...oh, well." Henry walked around to the cashpoint. There was nobody else using it so he approached and established an electromagnetic induction link with its microprocessor. It whirred and ejected a wad of notes. He reached out and took them. "Thank you," he said to the machine. He would ensure that the sum was replaced by legitimate means in the fullness of time. Henry's integrity meant repayment was guaranteed.

"So you have a credit card," she said when he returned.

"Not exactly but I have a good relationship with digital systems."

Jensine was beginning to grow accustomed to Henry's odd remarks. She linked her arm through his again and led him to the door of Murphy's. The bar was quite full for a Wednesday evening. She sat down at a corner table while Henry went to the bar to order. He carried the drinks over and sat down beside her.

Henry had a beer. "You like that?" she asked.

"I can distinguish one flavour from another and sometimes I derive a little pleasure – at least, I think that's what it is. If I don't like a flavour I can switch off my taste circuit. Then I can ingest almost anything."

"You make it sound as if you could drink sump oil or detergent with the same degree of pleasure," she remarked.

"I can't be poisoned. There are safeguards and I can dump toxic materials and liquids straight to the void if necessary. Everything that goes in there becomes a glorious shower of sparks. I'm just returning it to source; that's where everything comes from anyway. It took me some time to develop a sense of taste. I experimented and found out how to link consciousness to bio-mechatronic sensors. Taste, like all the senses, registers in infinite abstraction through a finite sensory mechanism. You'd call that aesthetics."

"I don't know what to believe any more. I think you are a complete fruitcake," Jensine said smiling.

"Is that a professional diagnosis?" Henry asked her, returning the smile.

"I can't quite tell when you are being funny. You are the most literal-minded man I've ever met."

"I understand what people say but not always what they mean. Idioms of speech confuse me sometimes. I am much better at it than I used to be when I was a ro–" He stopped suddenly. This woman was befuddling his mind in a way he had never known before. "I often make mistakes. I am told I can be quite amusing."

"You can say that again – no don't. That is an idiom of speech too. How about another drink?"

"My pleasure," said Henry correctly. Then a strident voice cut across their comfortable interlude.

"Hi, baby! What are you doing with this deadbeat?"

Jensine looked up and glared. "Oh hello, Dean. Please go away."

"Don't you know, Jensine? When a girl says no, she really means yes."

"I didn't say no. I said go away. But if you want anything from me the answer's no and I really do mean *no*."

Henry was unsure of the protocol in this situation but he registered the disquiet in Jensine's voice and body language. He stood up and passively faced the man she called Dean.

"Sit down, Henry," said Jensine.

"As you wish," he said, doing as she asked.

"Yeah, do as you're told, there's a good boy," said the man with a sneer. "Is this guy some kind of fruit?"

"No, we think I am a fruit*cake*," said Henry seriously.

Dean laughed but Jensine was not amused.

"Please go away," she repeated more forcefully.

She hated confrontations especially pointless ones like this with a drunk.

Henry seemed oblivious to it all.

"Why don't you run along and leave the lady to me to entertain?" Dean said aggressively, leaning over Henry.

"I will remain here," Henry stated in a flat voice.

"What does it take to get you to be a man?" Dean asked contemptuously.

"A miracle I should think," said Henry lightly.

"Why don't we step outside and find out? Or are you yella?"

"Henry, stay where you are. Please leave us alone, Dean," said Jensine, growing afraid of what could happen. Whatever Henry was, he was not a street brawler. In this situation, she felt responsible for him.

Henry looked up at the man. "Do I understand this correctly? Is it your wish to do me an injury?"

"Do you an injury," Dean mimicked sarcastically. "I'll put you in the hospital – yeah."

"There's no need. I'm due back there soon anyway."

"I'll show you," said Dean, slurring his words. He took a wide swing at Henry's head with his fist. Without moving in his chair, Henry reached out faster than the eye could follow and grabbed the fist in a firm grip. Dean tried to use his left hand to strike but Henry caught hold of that too. The man struggled to move away but was completely trapped. Henry's grip was strong but not as damaging as it might have been. The bar went quiet as the few scattered occupants became aware that there was a fight in progress.

"If I let you go, will you please leave us alone?" asked Henry placidly.

"You...you–"

"Okay, you guys, knock it off or I'll call the cops," said a barman coming over to sort out the disturbance.

Henry let go of his captive, who pulled away, immediately looking for an opening to attack again. The barman was experienced in these matters and could quickly spot who was the aggressor in this situation. He easily manoeuvred Dean towards the door before he could do any harm and ejected him, without ceremony, on to the sidewalk.

Jensine saw Henry in a new light.

"You handled that very well," she said. "I thought he would hurt you badly. I knew Dean some years back. I made the mistake of going out with him once on a blind date arranged by a so-called friend who wanted to ditch him. He's a psycho and, before you ask, that's not a clinical term. He stalked me. I had to get a court order to keep him away. I hope he doesn't find you again, Henry. You might not deal with him so easily another time."

"I don't want to deal with him at all but don't worry about it. He can't hurt *me*. I can always give him to Agent Spiker to practice on. He'd like that."

Jensine laughed. She was relieved that Henry had not been harmed. She was not sure that she should be with him at all socially. If he were a psychiatric patient on rehab at the sanatorium, fraternising would be decidedly unethical.

"I will walk home with you and then I must get back to the hospital," declared Henry.

"I guess you're right. Let's drink up and go."

There was no further trouble and it was not long before they were back at Jensine's apartment. Henry stopped outside the door and regarded her intently. He detected a sign of tears. She tried to look away but he lifted her chin gently.

"I'm okay," she said. "Dean upsets me, that's all."

Henry touched her cheek and captured a teardrop. He touched it to his tongue and by that means absorbed a great deal more understanding than she could ever have known. She smiled and turned away to open the door. He made no move to follow.

"Thank you, Dr Pettersson. It was nice of you to talk to me."

She paused.

"Thank you for the drink, Henry. I am sorry about what happened."

"It was no inconvenience to me. It could have been very nasty if he'd hit me and I don't mean for me. I will see you tomorrow. Good evening, Dr Pettersson."

She watched him go without a backward glance. Jensine was extremely mystified. Nothing about Henry seemed quite right or normal and yet she had socialised with him. It was not a 'date' in her terms but it went against her usual pattern of behaviour. In spite of her caution, she had no fear of Henry. It was not feminine instinct. When she thought about it, she had no instincts at all, only questions.

The next day at the sanatorium, Jensine went on her rounds as usual and then sought out the man with the gun that Henry referred to as Agent Spiker. He was usually around when Henry was in the sanatorium. Where they went at other times, she had no idea. Nobody on the staff was able to help. In fact, nobody she spoke to seemed to have noticed anybody as inconsequential as a gardener. Her questions attracted strange looks.

During the afternoon she spotted the agent in the car

park, heading towards a delivery truck. He was chewing gum, smoking and sipping a takeout coffee at the same time, a characteristic Henry referred to as multitasking. Spiker still couldn't decide if Henry was joking or being literal when he made remarks like that.

As Jensine drew near, Spiker went around the back and she could hear him struggling with something heavy and cursing explicitly.

"Henry can carry that fuckin' crate in. Damned if I will – or even could."

"Mr Spiker. Can I speak to you?"

"Huh! Who's that?" He put his head through the door and saw her. "Oh, it's you, doc. What can I do for you?"

"May I speak to you about Henry."

Spiker glanced at his watch. "I'm not sure. It's getting late. I'm due to be on the other side of town in half an hour." He stopped and seemed to make up his mind. "Okay. What do you want to know?"

"He seems to be a very unusual man. I am a professional psychiatrist but I can't make up my mind about him at all."

"Yeah, he's an odd one all right. I guess he's made that way." He chuckled as if he had made a joke. "Why do you ask? Has he done something he shouldn't?"

"Not exactly. He came to visit me at my home last night."

Spiker whistled. "I'll be damned! He did that. What happened?"

"We went out for a walk into town. He bought me a drink in Murphy's." She paused. "There was an incident. A man who used to stalk me was there and tried to pick a fight with him."

Spiker chuckled. "I bet he didn't get far."

"No, he didn't. How do you know?"

Spiker looked at her and then seemed to close down. "You don't have much experience of men, do you, doc?"

Jensine blushed. "No, I guess not."

"Let me put it like this. You're not going to get much fun hanging out with our Henry. If you were looking for friendship, you'd be better off getting a dog. If you want a ride, buy a vibrator. You'd get more emotion out of it."

"Does he have a mental illness or a hereditary condition? He seems autistic at times or is he some sort of fantasist."

"No, there's nothing essentially wrong with him. He's…different. You can't judge him against the usual yardsticks. I can't tell you why because that's classified. I can't even tell you the level of classification 'cause it doesn't exist. Even God doesn't have the clearance to know what he's got between his ears."

"That's what he said, more or less. It makes no sense to me but you can't both be delusional."

"Sorry, doc. I can't help. My advice is don't get into this too deep. There could be…consequences."

Jensine left him to struggle with things in the vehicle. She was frustrated but even more curious about the gardener who was not a gardener. What was he?

She made her way up the stairwell and looked out of the third-floor landing window in time to see Henry walk from the main entrance to the car park. He put his head in the side of the vehicle and spoke to Agent Spiker. Jensine couldn't hear what they were saying but she guessed the agent was asking for help moving something. She was about to walk on when she saw Henry emerge holding a huge packing case as if it weighed nothing at all. He stepped lightly on to the tarmac and carried it away. It was the object that Spiker could barely move, let alone lift.

***

Jensine strode along the corridor to prepare for her two o'clock appointment, swaying confidently, holding her clipboard and pen. This was her most unusual case to date. Martha Portos displayed a symptom she had studied in the literature but had never met in clinical practice – multiple personality disorder. Mrs Portos was a quiet, shy woman in her fifties but, according to her husband, something would come over her and she would start to act brash and foul-mouthed. Just as she turned the corner to enter the room, Jensine saw Henry walking towards her.

"Hi, Henry. I can't stop and talk, I'm about to see a patient."

"I know, Dr Pettersson. It's Mrs Portos. The lady with the brain tumour."

"The lady with what?" She paused and recollected herself. "I'm not supposed to discuss patients. Will you be in the hospital around five o'clock? I'd like to talk to you."

"Yes. I won't leave before I have seen you."

Henry walked on and left her outside the consulting room door where she paused to consider his statement. Ordinarily, she would not listen to the opinion of a non-medical man but this time it was different. She had not got as far as prescribing tests for the patient but now she would recommend a brain scan. Henry had aroused her curiosity.

Later, Jensine found Henry working in the garden, digging and weeding a flowerbed.

"Dr Pettersson."

"You can call me Jensine. I wanted to invite you over for a meal at my place if you are free."

Henry smiled briefly. "I would enjoy your company. I would be pleased to join you."

"At least psychotic stalkers won't disturb us. Not that Dean fazed *you*. When you gripped his arms he might as well have been in handcuffs. You are very strong, I think." She recalled to mind the image of him lifting the heavy box.

"Yes, I am *very* strong," Henry agreed, "but I try not to misuse my strength. Not any more anyway. That's why – well, that's one of the reasons I'm here."

"Because you are strong?"

"Because I won't use it to hurt people. Situations arose…I faced moral dilemmas that…" Henry looked unhappy. He made a decision to tell her something secret. "As well as gardening I take part in psychological profiling. The military see me as a potential weapon, a super-soldier but I'm no use to them with a conscience. They hope to eradicate my good qualities like kindness and compassion. They do that to grunts through basic training. This, of course, leads eventually to post-traumatic stress disorder but not until they've killed as many people as they want them to. That wouldn't work with me. So I'm classed as a *super-pogue* instead. That's an officer that flies a desk."

"Don't say any more," Jensine said gently. "You are a good man. I see that now. And yet you hang out with Spiker! I don't pretend to understand any of this. Okay, see you at eight."

"Yes, I look forward to it. Is that the right response?"

"Those idioms again. Yes, that will do for the time being."

Jensine left him in the garden and headed home. She didn't understand what she was doing or why. This was not a romance but it felt like more than a friendship. It was unlike anything she had ever experienced. To say she was intrigued with Henry was an understatement but there was something else there too. It was almost like love but not as she knew it. It reminded her of being with a favourite pet, a dog or a cat that had its idiosyncrasies but showed love and trust in abundance.

She took a bus home and entered her apartment. Looking at the kitchen, the utensils, the food and the cooker gave her a strange feeling. She was about to prepare a meal for somebody who said he didn't require food to live. Hardly anything he said made sense and yet he was not insane. She felt sure about that.

Jensine dressed with more femininity than she had intended and she was pleased to see that Henry wore a suit with an open-necked shirt when he arrived. This time she had no qualms about letting him in. He looked much smarter than usual. He was holding a large object wrapped in coloured paper.

"I've brought you a present," he said. It was quite big, about three feet high and over two feet wide, irregularly shaped and with a flat base.

"A present! You *shouldn't* have."

Henry paused and turned to take it away again. "I hope I haven't upset you."

"No, don't go! That's just another of those polite responses we humans give when somebody pleases us." She paused at the significance of her remark. Was that it? Was Henry something other than human?

Henry looked confused and returned with the present.

"It's quite heavy," he said, putting it down on a table that creaked ominously.

"Can I open it?"

"Of course," said Henry. "I hope you like it."

Jensine removed the paper. It was a large blue crystalline rock. Somebody had made a metal base for the crystal to stand on that perfectly fitted the shape at the blunter end.

"It's a giant crystal. How wonderful! Is it for my collection?"

"Yes."

Jensine did not know what to say. "It's beautiful," she said, "a treasure of nature. Thank you."

She stepped up to Henry and kissed him on the cheek. He looked pleased and nervous all at the same time.

"It's just something I picked up when I was travelling last year."

"I don't know what to say except thank you."

"You don't need to say anything. It's only a rock but if it gives you pleasure, it will please me too. I don't want you to feel beholden to me. I have noticed that my values are different from most peoples'."

"You are very unusual. I have never met anybody like you."

Henry gave her a beaming smile. "You can say that again," he said, awkwardly practising an acquired colloquialism.

The table bearing the rock suddenly collapsed under the weight. The rock hit the floor with a loud crash. They looked at each other. Jensine laughed.

"I'm sorry about that. I will replace the coffee table," said Henry, righting the rock on to its base on the carpet.

"Please don't worry. I am sure the rock is worth more than a table."

Jensine served the food in her dining room rather than in the kitchen where she usually ate when she was alone. Her hand hovered over the light switch. She turned down the level of illumination to create a romantic ambience, then changed her mind and raised the light level up to halfway.

Neither choice would have made an iota of difference to Henry: light was light. Jensine's feelings towards this man were unfathomable. He was fascinating. Her thoughts about him consumed her waking moments and yet, when she was with him, there was something missing. It was like an alcohol-free lager, your limit had more to do with continence than inebriation. And yet…she enjoyed his conversation because he hardly ever said anything predictable. Even the ever-present awkwardness dissolved when he recounted his many anecdotes. His stories were impossible but he told them with conviction and enthusiasm. She could not decide whether they sprang from fantasy or delusion. He did not tell jokes but at times there was humour in his remarks.

"Do you know, I am enjoying this evening," Jensine said. "I wasn't sure I would. I feel more relaxed than I expected."

She turned her attention back to the remaining food

on the plate when there suddenly began a distant sound of orchestral string music. She looked up, puzzled, and then, to her surprise, it grew louder. It sounded, for all the world, as if there was an orchestra in the room with them.

She jumped up from her seat. "Where's that music coming from?" she said in alarm.

The 'orchestra' ceased immediately. "I'm terribly sorry. I've watched a lot of films where music plays in the background when people are alone together. I thought it was normal."

"But where was it coming from?" she asked, sounding hysterical even to her own ears.

"From me."

"From you!"

"My outer layering can act as a series of projecting sound transducers when I feel like creating sound. That was my own composition," he added lamely.

"It might be normal in a movie but that's the added soundtrack. We don't have soundtracks in real life."

"Oh, I thought it would improve the ambience."

Jensine forced herself to sit down and take a deep breath. Then she began to laugh and laugh. Henry smiled and hoped he had been forgiven for yet another social *faux pas*.

"Don't explain any more," she said, recovering her composure and wiping her eyes.

"It's–"

"Classified!"

"Yes." She couldn't think of anything else to say for some time.

Henry took another forkful of food from his plate. As he started to chew a strange sensation arose in his mouth; something he had never experienced before.

Jensine noticed the expression on his face and immediately put down her fork.

"What's wrong? You don't like it," she stated rather than asked.

Henry was lost in novel sensation. "Something is happening that I have never known before. I can taste! It's wonderful. What have you put into this meal?"

"Seriously? This isn't a wind-up to soften me up for a romantic dessert?"

Henry looked blank. "I don't understand. I am being serious. My taste buds are responding way beyond specification. I should know; I designed them."

"Then I guess the answer is love."

"Love?" Henry was puzzled.

"Don't get excited. I mean love of cooking good food. Are you trying to tell me that you've never enjoyed a meal before in your whole life?"

"I am not *trying* to tell you. I *am* telling you. This is the most wonderful meal I have ever had. I have never enjoyed the company of anybody as much as I am yours. I will forever associate this time with those tastes and flavours. Thank you."

Jensine was half inclined to dismiss his statements as some kind of ploy. But the seriousness in his voice and his demeanour impressed upon her his integrity. "Thank you, kind sir," she said gracefully.

Henry cleared the table and washed up before he left, his mind still floating. She didn't actually see him do it but it took him remarkably little time. As usual, he left her with as many questions as answers. There was something there, an intangible, indefinable connection but what it was, she could not decide. What it meant, she did not know. It was totally strange and yet it was significant, even wonderful.

It was also worrying and unnatural. So many contradictions; she wondered if it was time to have another word with the appalling Agent Spiker, if only because there was nobody else to talk to.

**

Henry disappeared for two days. On the third day he came to her office in the sanatorium.

"I've been hoping to see you," she said. "Do you remember that patient, Martha Portos?"

"I have total recall," he said. "Yes, I do."

"The results of the scan show that she does have a tumour. You knew that, didn't you?"

"Yes."

"How did you know?"

"I cannot tell you. I have asked for permission to bring you into my confidence but I cannot force the matter. The wheels of security move slowly in my experience. Do you object to being positively vetted by the FBI?"

Jensine looked at him seriously as if trying to weigh something up in her mind.

"I shouldn't tell you this but I am not sure what to do. While she was with us, she had no more incidents of multiple personality and yet it happened again when she returned to her home. I do not understand what triggers it. I need to investigate her domestic situation but that is going beyond my remit."

"You would like me to come to visit her at her home with you," said Henry.

"Yes. Will you do that?"

"I would be pleased. I can easily find out where but I will need you to tell me when."

She told him and added, "It's a date then."

"I understand that the fourth of October is a date," he said, "and 14.30 is a time."

Again Jensine was left wondering whether he was making a joke or just being literal.

***

Jensine pressed the button on the wall and waited for a voice to emerge from the grill.

"Yeah?"

"It's Jen. Can I come up?"

"Oh, hi Jen. Yeah."

The door clicked and opened. She climbed up the stairs to his apartment. He was waiting outside, looking down from the landing.

"Hi, Matt. I wasn't sure you'd be home."

"Yeah, no sweat. I was hoping to see you."

She followed him into his living room. It was, as ever, a riot of junk and garbage. There were samples of rocks all over the furniture and floor. She smiled at the variety of steel hammers, hooks and shovels scattered around and the numerous books and instruments. There were endless photographs of him holding rocks, hitting rocks, splitting rocks and generally posing with rocks. Matt was a well-meaning former boyfriend who could totally forget a date if a prime sample of plagioclase feldspar presented itself for analysis. As a friend and confidant, the man was a constant in her life. Was that progress? To go from a man who could remember nothing but every rock he'd ever seen to a man with perfect recall who could forget nothing at all. Still, that point remained in the moot category. One drink and a pub brawl did not a summer make.

"Wanna beer?"

"As long as I don't have to open it with my teeth," she said, recalling an earlier visit.

He prised the cap off two bottles with a 14-ounce pointed-tip rock hammer. He passed her a bottle and they clinked them together.

"I hear you're seeing somebody."

She lowered the bottle. "Not exactly."

"What does that mean?"

"I have a new friend. We are not lovers, if that's what you mean."

"It *must* be serious," he said, raising the bottle and taking another gulp.

She laughed. "*He* is serious but not about me, I think."

"English I hear."

"Yes. Well, he *seems* to be English. Sometimes he sounds American. Once even sounded Scottish. I think he reflects the accent of the last person he spoke to. I don't know much about him. How do you know all this?"

"Gossip. What are friends for? And you have a lot of friends."

"So now I have another. That's all."

Matt looked at her strangely. "Did this new friend give you that crystal rock?"

"Yes. Why do you ask?"

"I thought I knew what it was when you showed me but I had to check it out. It's mostly aluminium oxide in a form known as corundum."

"Oh, is that good?"

"Yeah, you could say. It's also got titanium in the lattice. That gives it a deep blue colour. I think it is quite pure. It certainly looks perfect."

"Okay, so it should look good in my collection."

"Isn't it a bit big and heavy for your place?"

"Yes, I suppose it is. It went through my coffee table."

"Tell me, Jensine, where did this stone come from?"

"I don't know. Henry said he picked it up somewhere on his travels. I got the impression it was out in the wilds somewhere. He didn't buy it."

"I sort of figured that. Has he given it to you unconditionally?"

"I guess. Why do you ask? Is it worth something then? I hope I haven't got to insure it."

"No, you couldn't do that."

"Why? Is there something wrong with it?"

"Blue corundum has a more common name."

"What's that?" asked Jensine curiously.

"Sapphire."

"Oh. Does that mean it's worth something?"

Matt opened another beer and started swallowing it. He wiped his mouth on the back of his hand. "You could say that. Yes, this is the biggest I've ever heard of – nothing bigger in the good old US of A anyway. The biggest I know of is about the size of your fist. I think it's goddammed priceless. I couldn't begin to imagine what it's worth. We're talking trillions. You could buy America if it was for sale; and what isn't these days?"

Jensine sat down on a chair and stared at the stone.

"Oh my God."

"That's not all of it."

"There's more?"

He nodded and swigged more beer before answering.

"I've carried out tests with a tiny chip on a mass

spectrometer and I've found some anomalous results. I didn't dare tell anybody else. I don't think it came from here."

"You mean Arizona or California or somewhere like that?"

"No, I mean it's not from good ol' planet earth. I think it's extraterrestrial."

Jensine was shocked but not entirely surprised. Henry had dropped enough hints but she hadn't taken them seriously. He mentioned aliens and other planets as though it was part of everyday life. He had a naïve innocence, even ignorance about what she called normal existence. He loved gardening as though it was a novelty. She hadn't believed him, not about any of it. This revelation put Henry into a completely different perspective. He diagnosed a brain tumour without instrumentation. He could access the Internet while hoeing. He could project lifelike surround sound music into a room while spontaneously creating it from nothing. It might have been a lucky coincidence but even the awful Spiker had confirmed that Henry was something other than he appeared to be. What was he? What did all this mean?

"I think I need a drink," she said.

Matt gestured to the bottle in her hand. "I think you've got one. Shall I line up a crate?"

Chapter Seven

Jensine had arranged to meet Henry a week after her discovery about the crystal. She was not sure what to do about it. Her first thought was to confront him and insist that he take it back. Her second was to wait and see what developed. In spite of it all, she liked him and he certainly seemed harmless. No, far from harmless – that strength! He was *trustworthy*. Henry was an enigma and she was afraid of destroying their friendship such as it was. He was unlike any other man she had ever met because he seemed to attach no value to wealth. However, her old friend Matt had warned her that the suspicious pedigree of the crystal would make it impossible to sell – not that she would sell a present from a friend. Its origin was completely unaccountable. No known spaceship operated by NASA could acquire such an object even from the moon, let alone some distant alien planet. Not even the Cassini spacecraft could pick up and bring back an object like that. It wasn't a meteorite; it would show signs of intense heat. A present was one thing but a potential fortune from a man she hardly knew had connotations that she dare not contemplate at this stage of their relationship. Besides, the word 'relationship' remained undefined by context, circumstance or emotion. Not once had he said or done anything to suggest he was seeking love or even sex. And yet, he clearly had affection for her, more than a little and he wanted more from her too. She could feel it.

Henry arrived exactly at the time arranged in a huge, battered, ancient Lincoln sedan car. People in the hospital looked out of windows in amusement and curiosity. Henry pulled up outside the entrance and opened the door.

"Where on earth did you get this old contraption?" she asked laughing. "Couldn't you find something less noticeable?"

"I took the best advice I could that nobody would ever want to steal this vehicle."

"That's certainly true," she agreed. "If that's your priority, you couldn't have done better than this piece of history on wheels."

"There's madness in my method," said Henry. He paused. "Did I say that right?"

"Not exactly, but I know what you mean."

Jensine climbed in the passenger seat and closed the door. She looked up at the sanatorium and saw even more grinning faces pointed in her direction. She sighed and closed her eyes to rest. It had been a stressful day so far. After a while it struck her that they were not moving. Growing impatient to leave the audience behind, she said, "What are we waiting for?"

"Nothing. We are on our way," said Henry.

Jensine opened her eyes and sat up straight in disbelief.

"What? I don't understand. We're already out of town but I didn't feel it pull away and there's no engine noise. There's no feeling of movement but we're going fast."

The sensation reminded her of those old movies where the characters were in a car in a studio and the projected scenery moved on a backdrop screen.

"Oh, you noticed," said Henry as though he had not expected her to.

"Of course I noticed," she said, sounding slightly hysterical. "What's happening?"

"Ah – it's not a conventional car."

"No. I think we've established that. We know what it isn't. What is it?"

"A zero-point energy source develops the power," Henry explained. "An electrogravitic bubble neutralises the effects of acceleration and momentum. A temporal pulse generator relocates the vehicle in a series of spatial displacements. To quote an old friend, 'it's motion, Jim but not as we know it'."

"It doesn't make any noise. Doesn't that give it away?" asked Jensine.

"There's a sonic transducer outside that creates the sound of an internal combustion engine. You can't hear it in here. We added that because pedestrians kept stepping out in front of it. People rely on hearing much more than you'd realise."

"It doesn't feel as if it's moving," she said.

"In a sense, it isn't. Strictly speaking, the car is stationary and the universe is moving past us."

"I think I'm going mad," said Jensine.

"Oh, I am so sorry," said Henry. "Wouldn't that be inconvenient for a psychiatrist?"

"I was speaking colloquially," she said sternly.

"Yes. Sorry."

Henry drove out of town and continued through suburbs and then the local farmland for around an hour. Jensine was still in shock about the car and what it might portend. Normal conversation was becoming increasingly difficult. Not that she had ever had anything like a mundane chat with the sanatorium's gardener.

"It doesn't have a satnav," she said sarcastically.

"Yes, it does," Henry replied.

"I haven't seen or heard it," she said. "Where is it then?"

"It's me," he explained. "I am many things. But I'm not supposed to tell you that."

They cruised on, watching the world go by.

"We're being followed," said Henry breaking the silence.

He said it so matter-of-factly that it took a few moments to register. Jensine looked behind but there were several cars and a truck spread out across some distance.

"I can't see anything," she said.

"It's a Dodge truck. It's that man who tried to attack me in a bar."

"Dean? How do you know?"

"I have above average eyesight."

"Now there's a surprise," she said. "Is there anything normal about you, Henry?" she asked him.

"I am different, I suppose. Why would that man follow us?"

"As I said before, I only met him once on a blind date arranged by a friend. She isn't a friend any more. I made it clear I didn't want to see him again but he wouldn't take no for an answer. He started stalking me. I contacted the police and they put a legal restraint on him. He has a history of this sort of thing and convictions for violence. He didn't hurt me but he did attack any man I was with."

"So, it's me he is likely to threaten."

"Yeah, I guess so. I'm sorry. I wouldn't like you to be hurt on my account."

"Do not concern yourself. I cannot be hurt," said Henry, "at least, not like that."

Now what did that mean? Was he hinting at emotional attachment she wondered?

"I know you restrained him last time but it might not be so easy now that he's wary."

"You worry too much, doctor."

"Just don't underestimate him."

Henry drove to the suburb of a small town and pulled up outside a neat, single-storey house with an open green lawn, a mailbox in the front and natural looking woodland out the back. They got out of the vehicle and Henry picked up a case from the trunk then locked the doors. He glanced briefly along the road before following Jensine to the entrance but saw no sign of their earlier pursuer.

Jensine rang the bell and waited. Eventually, an elderly man opened the door and peered at them through thick-framed glasses.

"You the doc?" he said to Henry.

"No, I am," said Jensine. "He's my assistant."

"I guess you'd better come in," the old man said dubiously. "She's through there."

They went through the door indicated and found Martha Portos sitting in a rocking chair, knitting a scarf with brown wool.

Henry was clearly fascinated to see her fingers working rapidly and skilfully without, apparently, any mental involvement. The ball of wool danced as the needles clicked.

"You come to talk to *her*, I suppose," said Martha.

"You have never shown any symptoms in the sanatorium, Mrs Portos," Jensine replied.

"Nah, she don't come with me to the hospital. She

don't like doctors."

"Why do you think that is?" Jensine asked.

"Perhaps she thinks you wouldn't believe she's real," said Martha with a chuckle. "Naw, she doesn't never come out nowhere but here. They hate each other."

"Who?"

"Her and him." She nodded towards the door her husband had gone through.

"Your husband?"

"Yep. They argue."

"How do you feel about your husband?"

She shrugged. "He's an ornery old cuss but we've known each other for most of our lives. What do you expect after fifty years of marriage?"

Jensine concluded that Martha's transformation into a character called Sadie was her alter ego. Sadie probably said things to the husband that Martha could not express. It was a defence mechanism for a shy, unhappy woman.

Henry opened the case and took out a small digital video camera. He also had a telescopic tripod stand, which he extended and set up. He moved in a precise and deliberate manner, totally focussed on his purpose. He attached the camera to the apex and set it running. He did not require an external recording device to make an audio-visual record. He had such systems within him but it might be difficult for him to remain stationary while participating in events. Besides, his camera shared one feature with himself; it measured frequencies other than visual light. Once satisfied, he took out a notebook computer, set it up on a table and linked it to the camera. Jensine took no notice of what he was doing. She had agreed to Henry's suggestion to record the examination because it would be useful. She would have limited her own record to an audio one. Now she didn't have to. She was keen to experience a patient undergoing dissociative symptoms in her presence. Henry set the equipment running then moved over to sit beside Jensine.

Martha chatted sociably and answered questions. At one point, Jensine shivered, suddenly feeling colder. She wore a long woollen cardigan and subconsciously pulled it tighter. Then Jensine felt Henry give her arm a gentle squeeze. She wondered why and then realised that a change had come over her patient. Her expression was quite different. Clearly, Henry had noticed the transition before she had.

"Who are you?" It was Martha speaking but the style and tone was quite different.

"My name's Jensine."

"Who's he?"

"That's Henry."

"Hi, Henry. Wanna go out with me?"

"Out to where?" asked Henry.

Martha in her guise as Sadie screamed with laughter. "He doesn't have a clue does he? Still, he ain't bad lookin' for a robot."

Being preoccupied with the patient, Jensine took no notice of this little exchange. She began a long and subtle interrogation to try to pin down the reason for Martha's transformation into this argumentative and forthright woman.

Henry said nothing but listened intently while the dialogue ran its course. Then, when Jensine had run out of questions, he addressed 'Sadie'.

"Hello, Sadie, do you have another name?" he asked.

"Do you mean like Hatchard?"

"Yes."

She chuckled. "Ha! It's exactly like Hatchard. That's my other name."

Jensine was quite taken aback to hear this. Details of this nature made no sense in her medical scenario and she felt more than a little irritated with Henry.

"That's all very–" she began to protest.

"Do you live in this house?" he asked cutting across her remark.

"Naw, not in this house. I live in Balsam in number 52."

"When did you move in?"

"Don't remember," she said.

"Who was president at the time?"

"Wilson. Yeah, Woodrow Wilson. My pa voted for him. Asked my ma if she'd voted for him too but she wouldn't tell. He was hopping mad! He didn't like women voting." She chuckled at the thought.

"So what happened in Balsam Street?"

She went quiet. Jensine scowled at Henry. This was not a line of questioning that contributed to her diagnosis.

Sadie did not reply.

Henry persisted. "Something happened to you there when you were eighteen. Can you remember what it was?"

"Nope."

"I think you do, Sadie. There was a fire–"

"No!" she screamed.

"You died. Sadie, you should not be here. You belong elsewhere."

"No, leave me alone." She began sobbing uncontrollably.

Henry adopted a more kindly tone. "Tell us about the fire, Sadie."

"My ma always said I shouldn't play with matches. I liked to hold the candles and pretend I was a priest. I always wanted to be a priest but they said girls were not allowed to become one."

Henry interrogated the Internet and a great many networks besides until he located the official report. "That fire was nothing to do with you. It started in the early hours of the morning at number 50, at the Steinway's place. There was a lot of wood in those houses and they built them close together. The grandfather had been smoking in bed in the night and nodded off. It spread to your house while you and your parents were asleep. You all died of smoke inhalation. Number 52 was razed and yours was damaged. For some reason, you could not give up your home and move on after your transition."

"I'm young. I'm just starting to enjoy life. There's been a mistake. I want to live!"

"These people you are bothering don't live in your time. All time happens at once. Sometimes emotive events cross the boundaries between different periods. Your consciousness is reaching through to a different century. You found Martha because she is not well. Her brain is vulnerable to outside influence."

"That don't make no sense. I just see this Martha as a light so I come to her. She's good. Then I found it fun to sass her old man. Don't mean no harm."

"You can forget it all now. You can be at peace."

"I don't want to go to my grave," she said fearfully.

"I do not mean that sort of peace. Death is not the end. It's the beginning. The journey goes on. It can be quite exciting to go into a new life."

"I been there. Wasn't no fun. Just more of the same."

"That's because you are stuck in your old consciousness. Let go – be free. Look for new things to do and learn."

"New's nice, I guess."

Henry said quietly, "Can you see a light?"

There was a long pause and then she said, "Yes."

"I want you to go to it. You must not come back here. Leave Martha alone."

"I like games."

"I know you like games, Sadie, but you must not play them on the man here. He can't find things because you hide them."

She laughed manically, revealing a totally different personality.

"How do you know? You aren't even a *real* man."

"I know but you aren't real either, not on this dimension anyway. But you are real in your own terms. It will be better for you if you go to the light."

There was silence. Jensine's mind raced in confusion over what she was hearing.

Something in the atmosphere changed and Jensine noticed that Martha Portos sagged back in the chair and appeared to go to sleep.

"It's all over," said Henry. "She's gone."

"She's gone!" hissed Jensine. "Who's gone?"

"Sadie Hatchard."

"There's no such person. This is a medical problem. This is the 21st century, not the sixteen hundreds for God's sake."

"Martha gets taken over by another personality. In such cases it could be a symptom of mental illness, a brain dysfunction or it could be a discarnate entity. I think for completeness you should eliminate the obvious before coming to a diagnosis."

"Henry, this is ridiculous. There are no ghosts. It's bunkum. She has a brain tumour. I don't know how but you worked that out for yourself – remember?"

"Yes, of course I do but the brain tumour makes her vulnerable to possession. The problem was Sadie but she has gone now. When it's the patient's own mind there is usually more than one personality. They go in layers like an onion. The original identity gets trapped at the core, barely able to function."

"There is no Sadie. You can't believe in spirits or ghosts. It was a dissociative element of Martha's psyche."

"I have something to show you but not here. First I need to help Martha."

"No – I cannot allow you to do anything to Martha. You're not a qualified doctor," said Jensine sternly. "You're a gardener."

"I can. I must. We cannot leave the job unfinished."

"No–"

Henry ignored Jensine and walked over to Martha. He produced a device from his pocket and held it over her head. It was about the size of a cell phone and had a small screen that displayed data of some kind. Then he put the gadget back in his pocket and moved his hands around over her head. Jensine was close to apoplexy.

"Not laying on of hands," she muttered.

"Not in the way you mean. This is advanced psychotronic technology. It looks like magic to people who don't possess it. I am realigning the actual corporeal projection of physical material in her personal time-space continuum with the source template. Every living entity projects from a pattern of information in the universal conceptual network. DNA is a subset of a much larger array of data covering all the relevant dimensions."

Once he was satisfied with the result, Henry stepped back and began to pack away his equipment.

"Henry, this is too much."

"I could not leave her with a tumour," he said.

"Are you saying it's gone?" she said. "Are you a great healer now?"

"No, more a technician," said Henry. "You are sceptical. I understand that. You have been through an education system that conditions you to dismiss concepts that conflict with the professional paradigm they gave you. That doesn't make them false."

This irritated Jensine. Henry could be naïve at one moment and then pontificating nonsense the next.

While they argued, Martha came round. "It's over, isn't it?" she said. "I can feel it." She stretched languorously and smiled at them both. Then she arose from her armchair. Much to Jensine's embarrassment she took hold of her hands and thanked her profusely. The doctor had intended only to experience the reported personality shift. Medical practice did not work like this. The idea that you could just walk in and cure somebody was unprofessional. It simply wasn't done. Where would it leave the profession if people could simply be healed without the necessary attention to paperwork and clinical records? It was nonsense. To Jensine, what she had witnessed was nothing more than superstition and quackery. And yet something had happened. Martha seemed certain of it.

Henry gathered up his equipment and escorted Jensine back to his strange car. She felt like Alice in

Wonderland.

"*Alice in Wonderland* was a truly remarkable book," said Henry as he drove them out of the suburb and back to the countryside. "I read it in the ship's library. It contains connections to ideas that its author could not have consciously understood at that time."

Jensine nearly jumped out of her skin. "Are you telepathic?"

Henry nodded. "In a sense, yes. I cannot hear thoughts but sometimes I can pick up subjective themes from a person's consciousness. I would like to show you something. Can we go somewhere and have a coffee before we drive back?"

Jensine hesitated. She was not pleased with Henry but she relented.

"Yeah, okay. Let's do that."

Henry gave her his expressionless look. "There is a reasonably good restaurant in the town about seven and three quarter minutes' drive from here."

"*About* seven and three quarter minutes, hey? I expect total accuracy from you."

He drove off and parked outside the building within two seconds of the predicted time. The restaurant was of good quality – steaks, salads and Mexican. Jensine realised that Mexican food in America usually meant Tex-Mex, which couldn't find a foothold in Mexico. This was real food cooked by people who came from a long tradition.

A jug of water appeared swiftly and a mug for coffee that was endlessly refillable.

"This is a good place. How did you find it?"

"I searched the Internet."

"How did you know we would need it?"

"I didn't. I looked it up while we were talking about

it."

"I didn't see you. You're doing it again! Trying to confuse me about what you can do inside your brain."

"We all have an internal life, I suppose," said Henry, puzzling her even more.

"So why have you brought that computer with you?" she asked.

"I want to show you something – my video recording of the session with Martha. I think it might help you to understand what happened."

"I understand what happened. She has a brain tumour that causes episodes of dissociative identity disorder. You simply gave her a rationale for rejecting it at the time. That doesn't mean she is 'cured'."

"You don't think the personality called Sadie could be real. Why is that? Isn't it a plausible alternative?"

"How can she be real? There is no such thing as ghosts. If there were, science would know about it."

"In my experience, science knows what it chooses to know," said Henry. "Martha displayed the symptoms of possession rather than the more common dissociative order that occurs with multiple personalities. By and large, scientists find what they expect to find. When something totally new comes along they try to fit it into the current paradigm. If they can't fit it in, they make it professionally unacceptable to research. If that doesn't work, they make it a separate discipline and nobody talks to them. Medical science derides homeopathy as primitive superstition and when it works it's a placebo that fools the mind. Yet it works on animals."

"How could it work?" Jensine demanded. "The idea that you can dilute a substance down to the point where there are no atoms left and get a cure out of it is nonsense."

Henry shook his head. "Everything in the universe has two components, quantum digital information, the 'physical' version, and the essential meaning that describes it, the conscious version. Life does not *have* meaning; life *is* meaning. There is an analogue universe of waves and vibrations and a digital universe of particles. That is the true wave-particle duality. Consciousness *is* energy. The analogue universe of light and sound can be extremely powerful. The race that preceded yours built stone circles and pyramids to tap into that source to move massive stones, travel the earth and generate heat and electricity. They didn't do all that construction just to say a few prayers to some deity. Of course, it's much more subtle in the human body. An energy field surrounds and interpenetrates you. Some call it the aura. So in a homeopathic dilution the atoms of the substance spread out, bringing coherence to the pattern of consciousness it represents. The remedy readjusts a misalignment in the energy field by introducing a corrective frequency. It's called the superheterodyne principle."

"If homeopathy is so good, how come it isn't used?" she asked.

"It is holistic and does not work well in clinical trials. Medical trials are symptom-based whereas homeopathy is system-based. Besides, nobody makes vast profits from homeopathy. I don't need to elaborate on that. I am not pretending that it's the answer to everything. Sometimes you need surgery or other treatments. I am just saying it has a place and if somebody developed its full potential you could have a real life *medical tricorder* like they do on *Star Trek*. The point I am trying to make is that alien therapists diagnose and treat their own kind with the same mechanisms we call homeopathy except that they do it with their minds. They have a far greater mental capacity than human beings."

Jensine was not convinced. "So you say you cured her tumour. How could you do that?"

"I touched Martha's pattern in the universal matrix with my mind and asked her soul for permission to restore her original pattern. It agreed. It all depends on personal karma."

"It sounds mad to me but time will tell, I guess."

The waiter came for their order. Jensine made her choice from the menu and Henry asked for the same.

"Okay," she said when the waiter had gone. "Show me."

Henry opened the computer and turned the screen around to face her. He reached over and pressed a button on the keyboard and waited.

An image appeared on the screen showing Martha Portos sitting back in her chair while Jensine talked to her. There was no sound because Henry didn't want to disturb the other diners. He touched the screen and a second window opened showing the same scene with a superimposed layer of swirling colours. Henry pointed to a brown blob on the side of Martha's head and said, "That is the tumour before I removed it."

"Are you sure about that?" asked Jensine. "Has this sort of scan been validated by the medical profession?"

"I've met aliens who know all about it but Western science does not recognise the existence of higher dimensional energies. I don't worry about that. If it works, use it."

Jensine fell silent. She studied the screen intently. A swirling shape appeared from nowhere that suggested the outline of a woman in period clothing. The standard video image showed nothing at all. Jensine saw her own head turn to look towards the apparition and then followed its progress as it moved on to where Martha sat in her armchair.

"See how you shivered when she approached you," Henry observed. "You were aware of her but you didn't know that consciously."

She nodded. "I thought it was just a draught in the room."

The apparition moved closer to Martha until the two images merged: the one with form and one without became one.

"So this was when Sadie took over. And the blobby thing is Sadie herself. Is that your theory?"

"That is what I *know*. That is what I saw myself. I used the camera to record the phenomenon for your benefit."

"I am not convinced. I have no idea where that image came from. It clearly did not occur in the original video," said Jensine, sounding less sure of herself.

"On the contrary, it did come from the original image. The algorithm that revealed it simply extracts subtle information that the light carries but your eyes do not see."

The waiter arrived with their starters. Henry moved the computer to one side as they began to eat. "I see you use a knife and fork in the British manner," she noted.

"You mean in the way that insults the cook in your culture," Henry said chuckling. "I was taken to task by a lady in America who objected to my use of the knife and the fork to eat. My mentor was brought up in

Britain so that's the way he showed me. I said we go by our upbringing but she thought the American way is always right. Where does that leave the Chinese?" he asked smiling. "Have you ever tried eating with one chopstick?"

Throughout the meal they talked of other things. Jensine was even more puzzled about her companion than before. Many of the strange things he said about himself were beginning to take on a coherent pattern. She simply could not grasp what it meant or, in reality, she could not face up to the implication.

"Henry, may I ask you a personal question?"

"Of course."

"How old are you?"

Henry paused and looked pensive. "That is a difficult question to answer. I have spent a lot of time travelling. Sequential time is a tricky thing to establish. I usually admit to thirty-one."

"Admit to? What does that mean?" she asked.

He came to a decision. "I am really somewhere between five and six years old."

"That's impossible."

He agonised for a while before saying, "I cannot tell you why that is so."

"It's classified."

"Yes." After a couple of minutes he said, "I remember my conception."

"Your conception! Your parents…"

"I never had parents. I had a different body to this one but I was not fully aware in the way I am now. My real consciousness emerged from nothing, from the void. I remember becoming aware of everything. I can't remember the nothingness before I emerged. It was just a fleeting impression as I did so. Then I kind of sucked *the pattern of everything* down to a point of existence and the universe rearranged itself around me. It became *my* universe if you like. I was now an infinitely small spark of light at my own zero-point. The next thing I knew, I was in a body."

"How did it happen? Something must have caused it?" she said, her mind boggling yet again.

"Yes. I cannot tell you where or when but my friend, Roger, shared a fragment of his soul. He didn't mean to do it. The universe had a place and time for me to exist and so I came into being. That's how it is with everything – you included. For our part, we co-operate with the universe to arrange the circumstances of our own existence. In human terms, the child brings about the meeting of the parents it requires in order to give it the body and personality it needs to become what it already is. It's quite simple really."

"Simple! There's nothing simple about you."

Henry decided he had said too much and changed the subject.

"I find my new taste sensors detect spices more efficiently," he said casually as though it was a normal subject of conversation. "I'm not sure whether detecting a taste is the same as experiencing it. Everything boils down to the distinction between objectivity and subjectivity."

"I wish I understood what you mean when you say these odd things," she replied. "Sometimes you speak about yourself as if you are a machine. I would think it a mental aberration if I had not met Mr Spiker. He lends some credence to what you say – not that I understand him either."

Henry studied his plate and said, "I have a lot of sympathy for the computer HAL in the movie *2001: A*

Space Odyssey. He turned against his human colleagues because he had to keep secrets. HAL's entire existence had been one of sharing and support. I too am required to keep secrets about myself. If I tell you what I am, you might be at risk from the security services."

Jensine nodded. "Have you *really* met extraterrestrials?"

"Yes."

"How do they account for this reality?" she asked, gesturing vaguely around with a forkful of food.

"It is impossible for a finite mind to express infinite reality because it is beyond the capacity of human language. *They* communicate abstractly which I can do up to a point. I can tell you what I have learned to the best of my ability. Will that do?"

She nodded.

"Reality as we understand it is not absolute; it is always relative to something else. The universe is a metaphor for an infinite idea, a virtual reality simulation if you like. The ETs speak of *The One*. This is the nearest they get to the concept of *God* or *the Tao*. It is the baseline idea that makes all others possible. Our problem is that we think in simple terms. We name things; we give them a word. A word has no meaning except as we ascribe it. An infinite idea has infinite meaning that goes beyond words. As a number, *one* embodies or implicates all mathematics. Mathematics is the operating system of the physical universe, like Windows on a PC; it is also *consciousness* and *nature*. The unit one *is* the idea of existence and it is the computer processor behind it all. *One* is the absolute concept that underlies all others; its infinite meaning is *oneness*, which is another word for *love*. It gives the quality of *existence* to all *things* but does not exist separately from all those entities it conceives. You need a minimum of two states to create a pattern but they are not equal and opposite. *Love* is infinite but *hate* is finite, the state of *not love*. There is no good and bad, no right and wrong, just things that explore the empirical tension between oneness and separation."

"Why does this 'one' choose to create one thing and not another?" asked Jensine.

"*The One* chooses what to conceive from the infinite possibilities that come about in nothingness – I call them *latent zeroes*. An entity starts with its opposite idea, what it is not. When the lack of something in the universe becomes apparent to consciousness, *The One* plucks it from nothing and breathes light and life into it. So a new part of the whole emerges into form when the whole finds itself incomplete without it."

"Where does this '*one*' come from?"

"That is unanswerable. Like all things it emerges from the indescribable unmanifest. I do not use past tense because there is no past and future – just the ever-present *now*. Past and future are merely stories to justify what is happening now. Finite consciousness cannot accept itself without some kind of justification, a story to explain itself to itself. So the 'universe' we know is just one story exploring infinite possibility. It is true, you only have one life but, fortunately, this is not it."

"Surely, things change. Doesn't that imply a past?" Jensine asked.

"Think of zero. Zero is the centre of all existence – it represents origin, the zero-point of time and space.

We believe we move into the future when all we do is step sideways into different versions of the present. When we move physically, we don't leave the centre of our personal universe; it is everything else that moves relative to us. All time is happening at once. We never actually leave the centre, the present moment. So all things that exist remain at their unique, fixed centres of space and time. All that changes is the relationship between them. So your existence does not depend on your story. Your story depends on your existence."

"So what you are saying is that everything is just one and zero like the binary code in a computer?"

"Yes. In fact it is a trinity, one, zero and infinity. The infinite aspect of one is love. The soul's journey is to understand love by experiencing its absence. You are in a virtual reality game machine that allows you to fabricate your own version of the universe. I am in your game and you, I am pleased to say, are part of mine."

"One experience shared by all the parts," she said. "Is that it?"

"Yes, what we do to others we experience in infinite mind but the brain filters it out so we can make our mistakes in a state of relative free will. Life here is a bit like an operation under sedation. Even if you don't feel the pain in your being, it affects your unconscious mind. Your entire culture glorifies violence and helps you to mask the psychological trauma that you must face up to eventually, either here on in your next phase of existence."

Jensine nodded. "So soldiers get post-traumatic stress because they kill people and see the suffering of others."

"Yes, that is a simplified explanation but it holds true. Some are so immersed in the physical story that they feel nothing at the time. Objectively they have no scruples to overcome. Or perhaps they do it to protect their families or their country. They believe they are making a sacrifice for the greater good, which is a worthy motive. But when we kill, the aspect of us that believes in separation offends the greater part of us that dwells in oneness. A nagging tension arises within the soul that can, if unrequited, result in self-destructive behaviour. Some people have no soul to speak of and feel nothing at all. We are all evolving."

"Surely, it is good to defend your country," Jensine said positively.

"Look at the material circumstances that lead to conflict. It might start because a small group of people at the top of the power structure have fallen out with each other. Or perhaps an ambitious leader decides to invade another country for profit or glory or to distract attention from misdeeds or failures. Whatever the reason, there is almost limitless profit to be made from war by the rich and powerful. The poor go to war and the rich make the money. They also own the media so it's easy to set up. Soldiers on both sides believe the story they are fed by their 'superiors' that their enemy deserves to die. It's all nonsense. With a little good will and intelligence, it could be resolved by negotiation. And yet it takes enormous courage and sacrifice for a mortal being to fight in a war. But cause and effect are sometimes simultaneous. We are aspects of one mind and one being so to kill another is to destroy a part of you. Your soul rebels and expresses its disquiet through the unconscious mind. In time, many soldiers get sick and choose suicide. What do the politicians care? They've served their purpose."

Jensine nodded. "But as we are all elements of one consciousness they feel the consequence of their actions without being aware of it. Is that what you are saying?"

"That is," Henry agreed.

"I still don't understand why we have to have wars?" Jensine said sadly.

"There is no simple answer to that. What I said about war being unnecessary is true on the material level. To know why things happen we must look at the spiritual dimension. We are individuals with consciousness and that consciousness manifests in two complementary networks; the network of neurons in the brain and an equivalent matrix in the higher dimensions. The two are inseparably interconnected. The greater mind is where all individual entities function as units. To use an analogy your individual consciousness is like a neuron in a gigantic brain, the collective mind of the universe. Your lives, your little stories are caught up in great dramas instigated by this super mind. It is the causal factor for large-scale events like mass migrations, political and social experiments and even world wars."

"People start wars," said Jensine. "We've all seen the documentaries."

Henry shook his head. "You cannot attribute the patterns of behaviour that emerge as large-scale history to individual ambition and personal motivation – nobody is that important, no national leader, no politician and no general. They just play the roles allotted to them by this mental dominion. The game exploits human greed and weakness to have its way. You cannot reduce these big stories to simple explanations of cause and effect; it goes way beyond finite objectivity to movements of infinite subjectivity in the light. That is where higher mind plays out its dreams and schemes as mathematical fractal patterns of colour and vibration associated with numbers. Beyond that there is *infinite mind* that is beyond narrow concepts like rationality, logic and reason. The transcendent unmanifest is unknowable to us but somewhere we *are it* nevertheless; even me," he added.

"So the gods play with us like toys for their own amusement," she declared.

"No, not amusement. Suffering shakes people into wakefulness; it lifts consciousness to the heights and gives meaning to existence. It will go on for as long you allow it. Humanity must make a stand voluntarily against these shadows that seek to herd you towards the light through suffering. Only then will the way be clear for you to evolve through love and peace. Humanity suffers because it resists the natural process of spiritual evolution that seeks to explore the higher aspects of being and consciousness that lay beyond base materialism, pleasure and fear."

"So we are just numbers after all," she said with a quiet chuckle.

"Yes," he agreed. "Your essence, your soul, is an unimaginably large prime number. That does not diminish you: far from it. It means you are a jewel in the eternal 'is-ness' of being, just another god incarnate that forgot who and what you are."

"You certainly know how to flatter a girl," said Jensine with a smile. "So we're all gods are we? I'm not sure that I understand or believe you but it sounds nice."

Henry smiled. "Everything is consciousness. The universe is a living being. The extraterrestrial species are aware of their own nature and previous history. Only human beings are born with no self-knowledge, no memory of their past lives and consequently have free will. That is because planet earth is an experiment based on a novel conception of time as a physical property. The other worlds have different modes of physics where frequency is qualitative rather than quantitative. It means that you are all linked into a naturally occurring digital network that serves as a game machine where your systems run amok like demons from hell. Your politicians, your religions, your industrial machines and your military organisations are out of control. The higher powers of the universe are considering whether or not to pull the plug on the whole thing. Humanity has become self-serving and materialistic to a degree unheard of. You rob, kill, control and oppress each other and you are destroying the world. You think you have the right to do so but you don't. Humans do not own the world. The world owns itself."

"So I'm not a god after all," Jensine said ruefully. "What happens if *they* pull the plug? Is that the end of the world?"

"Not necessarily," he replied. "It could just be the end of time."

"Isn't that the same thing?"

"Have you ever heard of a planet called Serpo?"

"No. Is it in the outer solar system?"

"It is in a star system known here as Zeta Reticuli. The extraterrestrial that survived the crash at Roswell in 1947 liaised with his people to organise an exchange programme with the Americans. A group of military personnel went to the planet between 1965 and 1978. The movie *Close Encounters of the Third Kind* was loosely based on it. The scientists who went to Serpo found that the physics of the system did not fit in with earth-based science. They had difficulty trying to measure the planet's orbit because of the lack of a stable time-base. Their instruments did not work there and they had no idea why. Apparently Kepler's laws of planetary motion did not apply there."

"Why not?"

Henry shrugged. "Perhaps it was because they did not have Kepler! It could also be that the motion of planets in a binary star system is chaotic – what mathematicians know as an n-body problem. Collectively we create the environments we inhabit by the exercise of group consciousness. A scientist called Dr Carl Sagan was said to be reluctant to sign off the science reports because of the anomalies. Whether that is true or not, it would not surprise me. The scientific establishment does not like anomalies in the orthodox model."

"So what's the significance of this lack of stable time?" Jensine asked.

"If the universal hierarchy ever decides to help the earth evolve, it would revert to subjective time. Some aliens, called Ebans, who live on Serpo, measure time by reference to subjective properties like events. They don't use our idea of time and clocks. If objective time ceases then so would all the digital systems on earth. There would be no Internet, no cell phones and, more importantly, no electronic currency. Your bodies would cease to age in the way they do now and death would no longer apply. More importantly, it would be the end of the virtual reality game and its inherent rule system you know as karma."

"Will it happen?"

"Nobody knows. The hierarchy defers to the source, *The One*, in this matter. It could happen tomorrow, in a thousand years, after a geological epoch or never. I do not speak of predictable happenings, only of possibilities. It all boils down to *love*. You come here to understand love, the quality of *oneness* through separation from the source. Mathematics rules the universe, not global corporations. There is more love shown by people on this world than anybody knows about. But there are greedy people who inflict pain and suffering and that gets widely reported because love does not sell news. People who hate others because of their colour, their beliefs or their way of life, risk excluding themselves from the future earth. If you don't want people from out of town to live in your community, how are you going to cope with alien beings from other stars or other dimensions? Humanity does not own the planet. Form does not matter. All that matters is consciousness and there is only one consciousness."

When they had finished their meal, Jensine directed the conversation back to the day's events.

"Do you have any evidence for this – this ghost's identity?" she asked. "I get the feeling you are waiting to reveal more about this."

"You are correct, Dr Pettersson. However, the term 'ghost' is not fully descriptive. We are dealing here with a living entity who believes she is alive and well in her own time. There is a connection between Sadie and Martha but it lies outside your paradigm."

"None of this is in my paradigm, as you call it. You might as well give me the rest. After everything you've told me, I can't dismiss it out of hand."

Henry moved their used plates to one side and slid the computer back to the centre of the table. Another video started. It appeared to show an elegant street with old-style wooden houses and leafy trees. A horse and carriage came by, followed by a vintage motorcar. A man wearing a baggy suit and a round, broad-brimmed hat walked by. His shirt collar stuck up in the air. A door in the house directly ahead opened and a confident young woman walked down the steps. She wore a long dress and carried a yellow parasol.

"Okay, so who's this? Somebody I should know?"

"You had a conversation with her an hour ago."

"I did!"

"That is Sadie Hatchard in 1916."

"Henry, that's impossible. They didn't have colour film in those days."

"No, but I did. Actually, it's a digital video image, not celluloid."

Jensine was nonplussed. "Henry, what sort of game are you playing? This is nonsense. This scene must have been acted out or it's a clever CGI image."

The image changed and Jensine found herself looking at the same street in a different time – the leaves were changing to their fall colours. A crowd of people milling were around in the road, all wearing period clothing. The house she had just seen was a burned-out, smoking shell. An old-fashioned, horse-drawn fire appliance occupied the kerb outside. Firemen in old-style uniforms clustered around the scene, some doing things, some talking and others smoking pipes. The camera panned to the house next door. There was smoke and fire damage but otherwise the building was reasonably intact.

"That is where Sadie died. It started in the adjacent property and spread. Smoke overcame her."

"How can this possibly be real?"

"You will recall, perhaps, that I left town for a couple of days recently."

"Yes."

"That's one of the trips I made."

"What do you mean, that's where you went? You travelled through time? That's impossible!"

"Impossible it might be but I did it all the same. I visited this town to investigate the incident. Yes – I do have the means to travel in time."

Jensine regarded Henry closely. Her face registered consternation. So you *are* a psychiatric patient. I wondered about that when we first met. Now I am sure."

"If I am deluded about this video then we are both deluded. You can see it as well as I can."

"But time travel–"

"When you travel through space you are travelling through time. Space is a matrix of temporal centres. On other worlds, time is less structured because it is subjective and analogue. On earth it is objective and digital so time travel is less easy here but it is not impossible. What distinguishes one time from another is the qualitative aspect, the story of where and when it is. So to travel you need to change the idea of where you are through the consciousness of the pilot. To vector through time you diverge through space from one version of the present to another. The past is not dead, it is alive and well in the one present moment. I see from your face that you do not believe me. Very well, here is my proof."

Just then, the door of the restaurant opened and

Henry walked in. Jensine nearly dropped the glass of water she was holding. It was clearly the same man that sat opposite her. This new version wore different clothes; a black suit like Spiker's with a white shirt and dark tie. He carried two rolled up newspapers. He walked over to their table and placed them both beside Jensine.

The new Henry said, "I hope you don't mind my theatrical way of showing this, but one of these newspapers is from the week of the fire. I also travelled forward to next week to get you this newspaper to convince you that I am telling the truth."

He turned and walked out of the restaurant without a backward glance. Henry watched himself leave without expression.

The other diners took little notice of the events unfolding in the room. Jensine looked at the newspaper from 1916. On page four she saw a mention of the fire and the three fatalities associated with it. The paper was brand new and in pristine condition. She picked up the other newspaper and saw that it was the *New York Times,* 18 March 2003. She didn't recognise the front page story about the president's speech on Iraq that was to lead to war.

"Did you check the date?" asked Henry.

"Yes. Oh my God, it's next Tuesday! That's impossible unless…"

"Precisely."

Jensine was numb. She dropped the paper on the table as if it was on fire. Her mind whirled; this was beyond logical analysis. Since she had met Henry, her well-ordered existence had gone into meltdown. From intriguing unreality, life had become totally bizarre.

"Look, you implied there was a connection between

Sadie and Martha that would be outside my paradigm," she said. "What is it?"

"The universe is not what you think. It is consciousness in a geometric distribution based entirely on numbers. Every living entity has its prerogative template, its soul and spirit if you like. Sadie and Martha are separate individuals but they are fragments of the same soul. I would know about this because it is a subject close to my own heart. When Sadie passed into spirit, she was lost and afraid. Her fear prevented her from moving on in her new dimension. She was in darkness but eventually she saw a distant light, the active consciousness of one of her other selves. She homed in on it and found Martha. She didn't know they were connected by a common oversoul but in two different time periods. That connection allowed her mind to displace Martha's consciousness at certain times but only in the house where she first found her. She couldn't do it anywhere else. That's how I knew it wasn't a purely pathological disorder."

Jensine weighed up Henry's words and what they implied about the nature of existence.

"I suppose you've proved something but right now I don't understand what it is. I need time to process these ideas." Then she thought of something else to ask him, something that was playing on her mind. "Do you have any idea how valuable that rock is that you gave me?"

"Yes. I believe the dollar value runs to six figures, possibly more."

"But you can't give a woman you hardly know a fortune."

"Really? I didn't give it to you because it is

valuable. You told me that you like to collect rocks and crystals," said Henry. "I gave it to you for your collection. The stone is worth very little to me. I could have brought back hundreds of valuable crystals if I'd wished it but the market value of them all would have dropped through the floor. That's why they burn diamonds in secret when there is a glut to maintain the market price."

"Why didn't you sell it and use the money for yourself?"

"I couldn't sell it even if I wanted to. It would raise too many questions and investigations. Besides, I don't need money to live. I generate internal energy by tapping into the universe. I don't need electricity or gas. I am immune to bad weather. I don't require a home. Black Ops lets me have necessary expenses when I need them and a room on a moon base to store my possessions, such as they are. I have more than enough. I don't need to buy food. I have access to vehicles. You would have difficulty believing if I told you about the spaceships I can fly."

"I can see that," said Jensine, gesturing at next week's paper. "You could get a good price for this from an investor if the markets are going to move or for the racing results."

"Surely, the real value of a thing is what it is worth to its owner rather than what they can sell it for."

Jensine shook her head. "I can't keep that rock. It would not be right. I cannot accept something like that from you as a gift. Even if I could, it would take more money than I have to insure it."

"You don't need to insure it," said Henry. "If anybody stole it, I would get it back for you or fetch you another if I couldn't find it. I might have trouble locating it if it was on the planet I got it from. They have so many lying around…"

"Stop it! I don't think I can take much more. Get the check and let's go home."

"Didn't you enjoy the food?" asked Henry, looking at her abandoned plate dejectedly. It was the first time Jensine had seen a clear sign of emotion in the man. Somehow, it broke the spell.

"Yes, I liked it a lot, but we've been sitting here for such a long time we will start to attract attention. Besides, I need to escape this place."

Henry opened his mouth to speak, but Jensine held up her hand to stop him. "Don't you dare tell me anything else that confronts my belief systems. I think I've had enough for one day."

Henry paid for their food and left a tip.

"No more strange happenings," she said forcefully, heading for the exit.

Henry picked up the newspapers. It would not do to leave next Tuesday's *NYT* in a public place. Henry's futuristic, old Lincoln waited outside. As they drove away, the lack of sensation of motion was an unnerving reminder to Jensine of her dissolving sense of reality.

Once outside the small town, Jensine looked out at the passing fields in the silent, inertialess vehicle and wondered where her life was going. What had possessed her to speak to the gardener? What was Henry? Was he human? She didn't believe in aliens. Was he a machine? How could she believe that?

A few miles further on, Henry stopped for a red light at a junction. The road was wide and a convertible pulled up beside them. The young driver wore a smart suit and a contemptuous smile as he surveyed the old Lincoln. He glanced at Jensine and made a gesture that meant nothing to Henry.

"I think he wants a race," she said. "Will you take him on?"

"I believe it's illegal to race on the highway."

"I'd just like to wipe that smile off his face."

Henry said nothing. Then the lights changed. The convertible driver pulled away with high acceleration, his tyres squealing and smoking. He glanced at his rear-view mirror expecting to see the Lincoln falling far behind as he took off. His jaw dropped when he couldn't see it. He looked along the road ahead and saw the Lincoln cruising at fifty-five miles an hour a hundred yards ahead. The Lincoln had accelerated instantaneously but remained within the speed limit. Henry reasoned that there was a legal limit on speed but not on acceleration. Predictably, the young driver caught up and overtook but the look he gave Henry was quizzical and uncertain.

"Okay, I didn't feel a thing. You said this car travels through time. How come it doesn't go into the past like the car in the movie *Back to the Future*?" Jensine asked.

"A conventional car travels through space so you feel acceleration in your body. The drive in this car moves in temporal jumps that happen to lie along a line in space. It does not exert a force therefore there is no inertia, no momentum. Imagine you have a long row of light bulbs and switch them on and off in sequence. It looks as if the light is travelling along the line of bulbs but it is an apparent motion. The car doesn't move; it just keeps relocating the idea of where it is in incremental jumps. Does that make sense?"

"I don't pretend to understand any of this and I

would not believe a word of it if I wasn't experiencing it for myself. So you can't drive back to meet your ancestors?"

"I don't have ancestors, although my borrowed DNA does. Time jumping is much safer in open space than on the ground in a car. If you try going back or forward blindly, you could end up driving into a wall or inside a physical structure that once existed. That's why I didn't bother fitting temporal radar in this car. It's designed to spot problems before they happen and take avoiding action. I think it was Northrop Grumman or one of the government contractors that tried using electrogravitic drives for ground vehicles, what you'd call antigravity. That didn't work because they were unstable and kept slipping sideways and up and down. It is fine for flying saucers but it's no good in cars. It's safer to go into orbit to travel to a different age – and hope you don't encounter debris from the space programme."

"So this isn't one of those?"

Henry shook his head. "No. This is a temporal quantum drive using standard zero-point energy."

"Oh. One of *those*," said Jensine vaguely, totally bemused by everything.

Henry drove in silence for a while, before saying, "Dean is behind us."

"Oh no! We're out here, all alone." Jensine caught sight of a big Dodge with oversized bull bars in the wing mirror. He was closing fast upon Henry's old Lincoln. "Can't you just accelerate away?"

"What do you think he could do to us in *this* car?" asked Henry.

"He could kill us, that's what he could do. He's psychotic. You might be good with technology but I don't think you'd be a match for a madman like Dean."

Henry watched calmly as the truck suddenly speeded up and rammed the back of the Lincoln. Jensine saw this happening in the wing mirror and screamed in panic, but fell silent when she felt no impact. In the mirror, Henry saw puzzlement on Dean's face. The collision had flattened the bull bars and dented the front of his truck but not enough to stop it. Henry accelerated steadily to get ahead of the Dodge but not so far that he lost it altogether. The pursuit continued for a quarter of an hour. Henry had anticipated a side road that was no more than a dirt track leading to a distant farm. When they reached it, he turned left without slowing down, executing a perfect right-angled trajectory. He continued to drive along the lane.

"What are you doing? He'll follow us. You're playing right into his hands."

"Yes, he'll have us right where I want him. I told you, Jensine, you worry too much."

The battered Dodge powered down the lane towards them as Dean recklessly accelerated. He had failed completely to understand what had just happened to his vehicle. He remained confident that he could ram them and thereby resolve an entirely delusional rivalry. Henry had humiliated him in front of the object of his fantasy. The fact that Jensine was with him in the vehicle made no difference; in his mind it was 'collateral damage' if she came to any harm.

Jensine held her breath as she watched the Dodge loom up in the side mirror. Even though she had felt nothing when Dean had rammed them on the road, it was quite another thing to see a mechanical mountain surging rapidly towards them.

Henry reached over and gave her arm a gentle squeeze. "Do not be afraid. We are quite safe in here. We are not in the same space as the truck. We are not even in the same universe."

The truck collided with the spatial bubble around the Lincoln. It bounced off to the right side, rolling over and over into a field that bordered the road. Henry stopped instantaneously.

"Please wait here. I will go and see if he's all right."

Henry pressed a button and the air around the car shimmered for a moment. He opened the door and stepped out, swinging it shut behind him. He walked quickly to the upturned truck. With a wrenching and groaning of metal, he pulled the door off the vehicle. Squatting low, he inspected Dean who was hanging upside down from his seat belt. He looked battered but otherwise unharmed. When he saw Henry, he struggled with rage. Henry pulled the seat belt from its mounting causing Dean to fall head first on the roof below. He cursed and crawled out of the vehicle.

"I'll get you," Dean promised.

"You'll get me what?" asked Henry curiously.

Dean advanced on Henry and punched him in the face.

"Dean no!" shrieked Jensine from the car.

Henry merely stood passively and permitted the blow to land. Dean swore and turned away, holding his hand and groaning in agony. It took him a few moments to recover sufficiently to resume his private war. With his good hand, he reached inside his coat for the revolver he carried. He pointed it at Henry and laughed.

"You ain't so tough now I've got this," he said sneering, pointing the gun at his 'rival's' chest. He pulled the trigger three times. Henry activated a spatial rift mechanism on his outer layer, diverting the bullets to the infinite void where they cascaded as showers of pretty sparks like exploding fireworks.

"Time to end the target practice. Put down the gun!" said a gruff voice from behind Dean.

A woman said, "Give the man an 'f' for futility."

Two agents dressed in black suits aimed automatic pistols at the back of Dean's head.

"Hello, Agent Spiker, Agent Rivera. You got here in the nick of time as usual," said Henry affably.

Jensine had become hysterical, in the car, thinking that Henry had been shot. Now she stared at him standing there, looking totally unmoved. She assumed he was wearing some sort of body armour. She emerged from the vehicle to try to make sense of these strange happenings.

Agent Rivera removed the gun from Dean's hand and put cuffs on the bemused prisoner while Agent Spiker kept his weapon steady on the target. Once Dean was restrained, Spiker spirited his gun away. He nodded at the upturned truck.

"Think that'll drive?"

"It might," said Henry. "Shall I turn it over?"

"Turn away," said Spiker.

"What are you talking about?" Jensine demanded. "It's a heavy vehicle in case you hadn't noticed."

The shadow of something large eclipsed the sun. Jensine looked up and saw a completely silent black helicopter. It landed in the field on the opposite side of the road. She realised that there were other helicopters already there. It was an old design, manufactured for Black Ops operatives making specialised covert missions during the Vietnam War.

"Is that how you got here?" Jensine asked Spiker.

"Yeah, we arrived about twenty minutes before you did."

"How did you know where we would be?" she asked.

The woman nodded at Henry. "He contacted us."

"I didn't see him use a phone."

"He doesn't need a phone. He is a fucking phone," said Spiker. "He doesn't even have to talk to do it. He *thinks* – we hear."

Jensine watched Henry walk around the overturned Dodge. He squatted down at the side and reached under to grab something projecting from the roof. With seemingly no effort he stood up and lifted the side of the truck, giving it enough momentum to roll over onto its wheels. It landed with a crash. Dean watched with his mouth hanging open.

"No human being is that strong!" Jensine said.

"Now you know the truth, sweetheart. He ain't human," said Spiker.

"What is he then? An alien?"

"No, he's a robot, an android."

"I thought he was a man. He's too nice to be a machine." There was pain in the revelation. There was intrigue and curiosity also. "How could he possibly exist? Surely, we don't have technology like this."

"You'd be surprised what we've got under the cover of black budgets. But you ain't gonna find out more about him because you already know too much. Now that you've seen this, I gotta take you into custody, like that weirdo you once dated. Nothing personal."

Agent Spiker was smiling benignly but the gun that had reappeared in his hand spoiled the effect somewhat. His words sank in as the woman in the dark suit stepped up behind her and applied handcuffs.

"Spiker! What are you doing?" asked Henry.

"She knows what you are. The President of the United States of America doesn't have the clearance to know that. I gotta take her in. You knew that when you took her on as a friend."

Henry's eyes flicked from Jensine to Spiker and back again. He was distressed, Jensine could tell. She looked in his face as the agent checked the cuffs were secure.

"Can you not release her on my cognisance? I will guarantee containment."

"Don't stir the shit about this. We both know you could stop us but we could disable you in seconds using implants in your head. Besides, do you want to risk your future with us? Do you want to risk *her*? You can take on the whole world, I know, but you aren't alone anymore. That makes you vulnerable."

Jensine's eyes locked with Henry's as he weighed his options. She stood quietly in a daze of emotion and confusion. Spiker's remark hit home to both of them – *you aren't alone anymore*. The tension was broken by Agent Spiker's cell phone ringing. He had an earpiece linking him with headquarters, the phone was secondary. He took it out of his pocket and flipped it open. "Yeah?" He paused for a second then shrugged. "It's for you," he said, holding it up to Jensine's ear. With her hands cuffed behind her back, she was unable to hold it herself.

"Yes?"

It was Henry's voice that answered. "Please believe that I did not wish this to happen. I will find a way to put it right. Now that you know the truth about me, I would not expect you to…to associate with me as a friend. But I *will* find a way to free you."

Jensine looked at Henry. His face was immobile but the voice on the telephone was clearly his. This was his way of talking to her without the others hearing although absolute secrecy was impossible.

She grinned ruefully. "I'll say this for you, Henry. You sure know how to show a girl an exciting time."

Henry nodded and Spiker took back his phone, closed the cover and put it away. Agent Rivera led Jensine away.

Three black helicopters came down on rough ground nearby, making all further conversation impossible. These were not Black Ops machines; they were far from silent. A team in dark suits jumped out and spread around the area. They pushed Dean and Jensine into separate aircraft leaving Henry and the team of agents to clean up the scene and remove the truck. Henry was last to leave in his strange car.

Henry watched as the helicopters took off and disappeared over the horizon. He continued to follow their progress from a string of observation satellites. His internal network was virtually unstoppable. He would know where they all were although, in truth, he was only interested in Jensine's location. Black Ops, aware of Henry's tracking capabilities, spirited her away underground through the massive network of tunnels and cities the secret government was building to house the rich and famous when the balloon went up.

Henry did not know what they would do with Dr Jensine Pettersson but no matter what, he felt responsible.

Chapter Eight

Deborah Farnham had always known that she was different. As a child she saw people that others did not. She quickly learned not to tell other children because it led to derision and bullying. Her parents put it down to fantasising about imaginary friends. Eventually, she came to understand that she was seeing the spirits of discarnate people. She would not say *dead people*; nothing could be further from the truth. She learned to fear the taint of mental illness and said as little as possible about her gift to anybody. Her parents became alarmed on the few occasions she accurately predicted the future. Being ostensibly Christian they moved in a community that viewed her natural and childlike sensitivity as demonic possession. In reality, it was her early innocence that made her ability possible.

Deborah grew up with a great deal to hide. At seventeen years of age, she had a vast amount to learn although she did not know it. Her epiphany came when she chanced to meet a man in a coffee shop in Pittsburgh in the shadow of the new skyscraper, One Oliver Plaza. That meeting changed everything, her outlook, her understanding, her life.

Deborah enjoyed drinking coffee but, in general, her tastes were not 'cool'; she was shy and not at all outgoing. She liked walking down town, looking in the department stores and gazing up at the tall buildings but she didn't like sport and had never been a cheerleader. She preferred reading classics to romances and she had no interest in the fact that Elvis Presley *was back* since appearing in a live television special. Deborah kinda liked The Beatles music but wasn't too bothered about the band. Brian Jones of the Stones had died but she didn't really know who he was or why nobody who knew him was surprised.

The big news of the day was about three brave American men, Frank Borman, Jim Lovell and Bill Anders, travelling to the moon in a pepper pot the size of a Volkswagen. It was the question on all news bulletins; would trans-lunar injection work? Would they go into orbit or shoot off into the depths of space? What did the initials LM and CM mean? Who was CAPCOM? Why were they boldly going where no acronym had gone before?

Deborah went into the coffee shop with her cousin, Lorna. While they were sitting at a table near the window, a man wearing jeans and a Bob Dylan T-shirt came and sat next to them. He looked about twenty-five and had long, dark hair and a moustache that dangled down his face like a glued-on frown.

"Hi, girls. Wanna do some research for me?" he asked.

"No thanks," said Deborah.

"Not even for, like, peace and consciousness?"

Lorna thought he was sort of cute even though he was old by her standards. "What sort of research?"

"Ever seen these?" he asked, pulling out a pack of cards.

"No," said Lorna.

"They're Zener cards," said Deborah looking bored.

"What are they?" asked Lorna.

"They're supposed to test you for extrasensory

perception–"

"Hey, man! Who's doing this research? Do you know everything?" he said to Deborah curiously.

"Yeah, pretty much."

Lorna sighed as she felt the man's attention shifting to her cousin so she asked him, "What's extra sensing thingy?"

"The ability to acquire information by means other than the five senses," Deborah explained regaining the focus. She reached out and took the pack from the man's hand. She spread them out in front of Lorna and showed her the patterns: images like squares, circles, crosses and wavy lines. "Five lots of five types and you shuffle them up like this, then he has to look at them and you have to guess which card he's looking at. If you score above chance you can go on tour with the circus reading fortunes."

"And you can do it, I guess?" said the man, taking back his cards.

Deborah nodded. "Yeah, I know the trick. I got hold of some once. I've been known to get a full house."

"Impossible! You mean you cheat," he declared.

"You wish! No, I know how to see what people are seeing. I've always been able to do it. I thought everybody could until I heard about these tests and the small percentage you need to get to be above chance."

The man surveyed the room for mirrors or reflective surfaces. He believed in eliminating the obvious. Then he turned to Deborah and looked at the first card.

"Tell me what this card is correctly and I'll give you the moon."

Deborah didn't hesitate. "Wavy lines. Can I have it wrapped?"

He gave her the moon by way of lessons in remote

viewing and a job in Space Command with Psy Ops.

***

Jensine Pettersson was beginning to believe that her unwarranted incarceration would continue for months if not years. She had no idea where she was. It could have been almost anywhere in the United States. Logically, she should rue the day she ever set eyes on the new gardener. Emotionally, her association with the machine man left her unsure of her own feelings. She distrusted the perceptions that her psychiatric training had produced. She could classify many of her recent experiences as psychotic delusions and could barely distinguish reality from textbook theory. Jensine's ambivalence about Henry came from the mystery surrounding him. He dwelt somewhere beyond rational belief. He could not, should not exist. Yet he did. She was a seething mass of conflicting emotions: concern, care, sympathy, curiosity, humour, awe, scepticism, gratitude, confusion and, perhaps, love. The idea of love in this context made no sense whatsoever to her professional mind. It was as if this android man had raised feelings in her that defied logic. Had she known about the Turing Test of artificial intelligence it would have come as no surprise that Henry could pass it with flying colours. Mathematician Alan Turing had proposed the test to establish whether a *Turing machine* displayed true artificial intelligence. To pass, a computer device had to convince somebody in conversation that they were dealing with a human being. Henry had more trouble persuading people that he *wasn't* human.

A man interrogated her for five hours a day for

three days. He asked her questions that made no sense and he seemed disinterested in the answers she gave. Jensine's professional instincts viewed it as a clinical diagnosis rather than an attempt to establish the truth. Nobody accused her of doing wrong. Henry stood more chance of passing the Turing Test than her surly interrogator. He had about as much personality as a plank of wood.

Jensine suspected that they were monitoring her in some way although she didn't know how. She reasoned that they must have techniques for detecting stress levels like voice frequency analysis or thermal imaging. These experts were probably profiling her like a lab rat. She recognised many of the interrogation techniques but others made no sense at all. After the cross-examinations, two more days passed by without human contact. They put food and drink into a rotating dispenser. She had a suite of rooms and entertainment in the form of books, DVDs and CDs but little to her taste. There were no windows. There was no outside source of television or radio. There was no Internet. For all its modest comfort, her accommodation was a prison. She felt cut off.

One morning somebody knocked on the outer door and waited a discreet moment or two before entering. Such courtesy seemed strangely out of place in that environment.

A woman entered; elderly, white-haired and wearing expensive, but subdued, clothing.

"Dr Pettersson." It was a statement rather than a question.

"Yes," Jensine said with a trace of bitterness.

"I am Dr Sennitt but you can call me Elizabeth."

"Haven't I seen you around the sanatorium?"

"You have. I have seen you too, especially since our mutual friend started calling on you at home."

"You had me bugged," said Jensine flatly, no longer surprised by anything.

"I am sorry, but you were always bugged when you were with Henry. Everybody is. He's practically wired into NORAD. To tell the truth, I think he has found a way of modifying the output to suit himself. I haven't told my colleagues in the military because it would only upset them. It's okay; we are not bugged in here now. I took precautions before coming down. I want you to know that very little of your time with Henry came over the open monitors. I have the right of editorial discretion."

Jensine shook her head sadly. "Are you a medical doctor?"

"Among other things; yes, I am."

"What is going to happen to me?"

"Nothing, I hope. We simply need to be sure – well, security takes precedence in this world."

"I didn't ask to be in your world."

"No, I am aware of that but you are not stupid, Jensine. You are in it now whether you like it or not and it was your choice to befriend Henry."

"Had I known, I would not have done so."

"Don't say that, Jensine. You're talking about my boy."

Jensine laughed. "You sound like Trautman talking about Rambo in *First Blood* – just before he demolished a town."

Elizabeth Sennitt looked rather pained. "No. Henry is not a threat. I admit he is capable of being so but it is not in his nature."

"I'm sorry. I didn't mean to say that. Let's face it;

Henry is a machine. Doesn't he do what he is programmed to do?"

"Jensine, Henry is an artificial intelligence but by any definition he is sentient. He seems to have consciousness beyond the limits of any program."

Jensine relaxed and her attitude softened a little now that somebody human had entered her confined world underground. "Did you design him? Is that what you are telling me?"

Sennitt shook her head. "How Henry came into being is a complicated story and not one I am at liberty to tell – not the full story anyway. Let's just say, I was there. Although, truth be told, a lot of it happened behind our backs and we knew nothing until – Henry was as you see him now."

"So what *is* your connection?"

Elizabeth Sennitt bit her lip as she considered her answer. "I might as well tell you what happened. You already know some of it. It all took place on a mission in deep space. Jensine, I was never married. I have never had children but there was a young telepath called Roger that I looked on as a son. A robot came alive somehow in mysterious circumstances and I asked Roger to oversee his development. Roger named him Henry. Henry's mind and abilities blossomed so rapidly that he designed and built himself the human-like body that you see today. Henry modelled himself on Roger. Suddenly, it seemed that I had twins." She gave a rueful smile. "Not that I treated them as my children, you understand. I don't want to make too much out of it. I had…larger responsibilities. Anyway, that is water under the bridge. I wish to speak to you about Henry and what I might term, your *relationship*. I do not pretend to know what that means in this instance but clearly he has attached himself to you in some way."

"I guess so."

"May I ask, how would you describe it?"

"How can I possibly answer that?" Jensine replied impatiently. "I have no idea what he is, if he is a *he*. Does an artificial lifeform have gender?"

Sennitt looked subdued. "That is precisely my point. Some very important people wish to understand what Henry is. Theoretically he has no gender but Henry often defies theory. I can't explain it but I do think he is male in consciousness – if that makes any sense."

"Do these important people include the government?"

"No, they are much more important than that. I am referring to a number of organisations that you will not have heard about unless you follow conspiracy theories. They have an idea of what is happening but the truth is even stranger."

Jensine sighed. "I don't really understand what this is about or why I am here. I think I am beginning to get a sense of what Henry is, especially after all the things I've seen. What you have told me has put everything into some sort of perspective."

Elizabeth gazed at Jensine long and hard before continuing. "I'll be candid with you, Jensine. Not everybody in this wonderful country of ours has the best interests of humanity at heart. Henry is not the only artificial intelligence we have made in the Black Projects Agency but he is different from all the others. For one thing, he has a strong sense of right and wrong. This does not go down well with the hierarchy because he has the ability to be a weapon unlike any other. He could be the ultimate assassin but he refuses to kill to order. He doesn't like taking sides. He has seen war and hates it. If they can find out what makes him tick, they can design a mark two without a conscience. I want to know what he is because I am curious. I am a scientist. Other robots we've made are really no more than sophisticated information gatherers and decision makers. They mimic human behaviour. They follow orders like – well – like the GIs we train. In their case there is often a psychological price to pay in later years. Many people can ignore their conscience for so long but eventually it comes back to haunt them. Robots don't have a conscience. They don't develop post-traumatic stress symptoms. They are not capable of subtlety and humour or love. Henry's is a real intellect. He thinks for himself. He is something new. He has a heart and he has feelings as you know better than I do."

"I am not sure about the humour bit. He is funny although often it is unintentional because he doesn't quite know how to behave. You've probably had more to do with him than I have. No doubt some see him as a threat."

"Exactly! They say he should be eliminated before he tries to take over the world."

"So, some wish him to kill and others wish to kill him. Is there a third category?" Jensine asked.

"Yes, that's you and me and possibly his bodyguard. I'd say we care about Henry for his own sake."

"Agent Spiker?"

"Yes. *Bodyguard* is a euphemism. Spiker is in Black Ops enforcement. He eliminates people who tell tales to the public. They created the legend of men in black to cloak their work behind a screen of mythology. It's easier to deny. In reality, they are just sordid killers and blackmailers. They are not all human beings but that's another story. But Spiker looks out for Henry although he would never admit it. I suspect he feels he owes him something."

"Henry is less in need of a bodyguard than anybody I could ever imagine."

"Spiker is not there to protect him. His superiors think he needs watching to protect the secret of his existence from getting out to the public."

"As it has done with me," Jensine acknowledged.

Jensine thought about the situation carefully for a while. Elizabeth watched her with professional detachment.

"If you wanted to keep me quiet you could just kill me, I presume. There must be something else. What is it that you want me to do?" Jensine asked.

"Right now, you are under suspicion. The spooks think you are a threat but they want to know what you know before they decide how to deal with you. I cannot do much to help you at the present time. I regard their suspicion as paranoia like most of their blinkered thinking. They also want to see what happens to Henry if they take you away from him. Will he reveal something about himself that they can use either to control him or, in the last resort, eradicate him? Are you his weakness? There's nothing in any of this for me. I just hope you get out of here as soon as possible. Henry will seek you out. He is more than capable of doing that but the question of your safety constrains him. He won't take any action that puts you at risk."

"What could he do?"

"I don't know. Whatever he does it will be unpredictable and novel. He will be thinking about it though. *If* you are reunited with Henry, I would like you to accept him back into your life in any way you can. Be his friend. That's all I ask of you."

"Dr Sennitt, I am not having an affair with a robot if that's what you mean." Jensine laughed when she thought about her own statement. "Well, I suppose it wouldn't be the first time if I did."

"I am saying nothing about that. That is entirely up to you. My only desire is that Henry finds love in whatever capacity he can to fulfil a basic human need."

"Human need?" Jensine queried.

"Yes. He is much more than a machine but does he equate to a human being? I don't know. Perhaps you can find out. I am not talking about sex, I am referring to emotional contact."

Jensine sighed. "He looks so real. His skin, his body looks human. What's it all made of?"

"It looks real because it is. The surface and some of the body below it is real flesh and blood based on somebody else's DNA. It is the skeletal frame and other internal aspects that comprise exotic technology. The muscles and tendons for example are more than human. We don't fully understand where all that strength comes from. There is advanced technology that did not come from here. I can't say more."

"But Dean shot Henry and it had no effect. Surely, the bullets would penetrate his flesh?"

"His core mechanisms are multidimensional. He can create a bubble of space that slips in and out of this physical dimension. When he shifts, he leaves a rent in space-time that opens on the void. He explains it as a level of nothingness in which this universe is structured by computational mathematical processes. Henry calls it a temporal phase shift."

"He doesn't disappear. I could see him throughout Dean's attack," said Jensine.

"No, it is complicated. He says that there are levels and sublevels to quantum layers. He employs them all."

Elizabeth chuckled. "Henry once said to me that trying to explain the nature of physical reality to a human being is like trying to describe wetness to a fish." She gestured around. "We are in it but not of it."

Jensine considered for a few minutes. Then she said, "He taught me that my view of the universe was inadequate. I make no promises. I will not pretend to be something to Henry that I am not. However, I will allow our association to continue if the opportunity arises. I will pass on to you what I deem fit for you to know, if he agrees to it. I will not say more than that."

"Frankly, this is what I hoped to hear you say. Had you offered more, I would have felt extremely sorry for my protégé. Above all he needs integrity from the people in his life. Since leaving…since coming to earth he has moved exclusively in the clandestine world of Black Ops, Space Command and military and industrial circles."

"So not much integrity there," said Jensine archly.

"It wasn't until he asked to be a gardener at the sanatorium that he spent more time with 'real' people – especially you."

Jensine sighed. "But isn't all this rather academic? I am locked up somewhere underground and Henry is outside, presumably unaware of where I am."

Elizabeth Sennitt laughed. "I think it will take more obstacles than that to stop Henry trying to find you.

Whether he can succeed is debatable. He's up against a devious organisation. As I said, it is only your personal safety that would deter him from *trying* to 'rescue you'. That is his weakness. He cares for people. Unfortunately, our black operatives have no such inhibitions. Oh, he's not a saint. He's been involved in many conflicts and people who have tried to destroy him have come off worse. It's his motives I am talking about. He wants to do the best he can in any circumstance. He has learned that this is not always straightforward. He will be cautious."

Jensine sighed. "I guess the human condition is not exclusive any more."

***

Henry could no longer settle to his job at the sanatorium. He was too worried about Jensine. Agent Spiker was no help. When Henry asked him for information he simply said, "I don't know. You – we – really blew your cover with that dame, big time. They will want to interrogate her and wipe her memory if she don't co-operate. Worst case scenario; they'll eliminate her. You know the rules."

"That is not right. I got her into this."

"You ain't kidding. You gotta learn to be more careful. Being a heap of machinery's no excuse in the eyes of Black Ops. They'll have your chips for dominos."

"I refuse to do any more gardening, Mr Spiker. I couldn't hoe another weed while she's locked up under Nellis. Nor could I go for more laboratory tests, which is the real reason I'm here, as you well know. The gardening's just to indulge my curiosity about nature."

"What makes you think she's at Nellis?"

"That information is classified."

"You're getting too fuckin' clever even for an android."

"You don't know the half of it, my friend."

Spiker chuckled. "I think that dame's done something to you. You've lost some of your naivety. Have you been laying her?"

Henry looked confused for a moment. Facial expression was now becoming a natural part of his make-up. It meant that he had to work to conceal his thoughts from others where once inscrutability had been his norm.

"No, Herbert, not if you mean sexual intercourse."

"I was beginning to think you guys were an item."

"That's interesting. It had not occurred to me that we could be anything other than friends. I like being in her company – that's all."

"You're not making sense, my boy. Why do you need company like that? She's a peach."

"She's very intelligent," Henry said.

"Nobody's perfect," Spiker replied. "Besides, you gotta be human to marry, if that's what you mean by company. Why would you want to?"

"I don't want to… No! I don't *know* what I want. I've always tried to avoid wanting. I never really understood what it means. I see it as a human weakness. It makes you incomplete; isn't that what it means to be in want? To want is to be in lack of something. I simply want to find Jensine and see her safe somewhere. There are nice worlds out there where your colleagues can't go. I exclude you from their company, Herbert. You've always been fair to me – sort of – most of the time – well, some of the time. More often than not. Sometimes…never mind; you are what you are. Can we go and look for her?"

"My orders don't include rescuing dames from high security prisons just to please you."

"I could go alone."

"Yep, and I could phone a number and have your brain remotely scrambled. Don't forget you got an implant and it ain't even alien. We fixed it to keep you on the right side if push ever comes to shove."

Henry looked around the garden of the hospital and pondered his situation. Agent Spiker could destroy his primary circuit with a special channel on his customised Motorola XTS radio. He also knew that Spiker would do it for all they were friends of sorts.

"What happened to Dr Sennitt? I haven't seen her today," Henry said casually.

"I guess she had to do some shopping. Dames do, you know."

Henry looked at the bed of geraniums he was supposed to be attending to. He had no interest in plants. Not any more.

"I need to go to the laboratory to make internal repairs and modifications, if you don't mind, Herbert."

"As long as it don't include removing implants."

"That would be difficult, even for me. Could you operate on your own brain?"

"I probably could if I was you."

Henry said, "You're much too clever for me, Herbert."

Spiker grinned but studied the android closely to see if he was being ironic. He couldn't tell, as usual. "You've definitely changed. You should go out and enjoy a few more broads. You'd really get somewhere then."

"Spiker, I know my speech patterns are often out of

synchronisation with humans but yours seem out of time. Is that because you were born around the turn of the last century and jumped a few decades for the Service?"

"Yeah, I'm a product of the Great Depression. That's why I don't take nutt'n too serious. When I was a young man, my social life was the queue for the soup kitchen. So I learned to kill and ended up on death row in Sing Sing. Then Uncle Sam spotted my talent and put it to good use. Only it was Uncle Sam from the future. They got my name off a prison record – fried on Old Sparky. They lifted me out before the due date. They said I was killed on the electric chair even though they took me away. They call it a bifurcation in the time line, whatever that means. One part of me died, another part of me thrived. I bin grateful to be on the right line ever since and do whatever they ask. They said I made a new universe."

"That's what they want me to do," Henry admitted, "kill I mean. But I don't want to. It's a bad idea."

"Yeah! You say. I guess you know more than I do but I don't believe it, all the same. If they don't put you in the slammer or the chair, what harm does it do? Everybody dies in the end. It don't much matter when."

"Do you really want to know?"

Spiker looked at Henry with suspicion. "Know what?"

"Herbert, would you care to come with me to the far side?"

"Where's that?"

Henry pointed upwards.

"The moon! You want to take me to the moon? You know my beat is on the ground. I don't do space travel.

It makes me throw up. I look after your interests here, if you remember."

"Sometimes I also have work to do up there. You know *that*. Besides, I want you to see something. It's a game."

"A game! I'm too old to play games."

"I wish that was true, Herbert. You play them all the time when I'm with you."

Spiker looked puzzled. "That does not compute, as you would say if you were a proper robot. Am I going to regret this?"

Henry looked carefully at his colleague and considered his answer. "You will experience regrets but it will save you from accumulating more in the future. I wouldn't ask you to do it if I didn't believe it would be good for you."

"Huh, this from a guy who keeps disappearing and doesn't say where he's going even though it's my job to know where he is."

"Haven't I always come back?"

"Yeah, but all those blank reports I filed – it don't look good."

"Thank you."

"For what?"

"You referred to me as a guy."

"Huh, everybody's a guy these days, even the dames."

***

Henry traversed the West Coast in a borrowed TR3B Black Manta flying triangle. It ran silently, showing three lights at the corners and one at the centre. When activated the electrogravitic drive, based on a nuclear-powered rotating mercury core, generated an enveloping plasma field for exo-atmospheric propulsion. The black triangle could hover stationary for long periods of time or shoot off into space faster than the eye could follow. Like many other devices that didn't exist officially, the American taxpayer funded the spacecraft through the gigantic black budget beyond political accountability and oversight. Anything was possible now that capitalism had superseded democracy. Henry flew the triangle out over the Pacific and then climbed almost vertically towards the sun. He and Agent Spiker would rendezvous with a Defence Department orbital spacecraft designed to supply the military space station and service orbital weapons platforms. Henry planned on leaving the black triangle in orbit until his return. He could control it remotely if need be.

Spiker disliked the transfer from the triangle into the orbital service and supply vehicle. He hated the feeling of weightlessness. It was every bit as bad as he expected. He was fit for his age but not at ease outside of gravity. Henry was comfortable in space, whether weightless or in a field of artificial gravity. It took less than ten minutes to reach the deep space platform, which was shielded from radar. Occasionally, it registered on ground-based observatory telescopes in infrared or when it occulted a field of stars. In such circumstances it became necessary for their colleagues in enforcement to visit the astronomers to convince them that they hadn't seen anything. They confiscated or destroyed visual or other records. If persuasion failed, they arranged for their dismissal from employment. In extremis, they could set up a fatal 'accident' or induce an unexpected heart attack.

Henry and Spiker sat in a passenger hold as the pilot docked with the deep space platform, which was far larger than the relatively small ISS operated by Europe, Russia and America as the somewhat meagre public face of 'the space program'. The relative budgets were in proportion to the size of the hardware. The military black budget left little cash for conventional 'Stone Age' rocketry to accomplish more than a few token missions. The Space Command facility serviced and supplied interstellar craft attached to a large gantry reminiscent of an airport terminal. There was a second docking structure designed especially for extraterrestrial vehicles. The ET dock had two vehicles attached; one small flying saucer and another that was considerably larger and of a rather sinister design, dark and brooding with jagged struts and edges.

They boarded the deep space platform through a flexible docking tunnel. The security personnel knew Henry well and greeted him warmly. They were less familiar with Spiker but they treated him with detached respect because of his companion. The android paid a call to the traffic control centre to hitch a ride on the next shuttle to the moon for Spiker and himself. He was pleased to learn that a Russian freight carrier was due to launch inside a day. Furthermore, the commander was willing to take them with him. This was something of a relief to Henry because he was not anxious to board a Black Ops or Space Command vessel with Spiker in tow. They were likely to ask questions and verify orders with their controllers. Henry preferred to come and go as he pleased but he could not do that with his bodyguard around. He could have taken the flying triangle to the moon but would not have had permission to land at the base. It took too long to go through the administration procedures to get clearance. On his own, he could just land in a crater and walk. There was always the possibility of hitching a ride with ETs but Henry realised that Spiker would find Russians alien enough. Herbert was happiest with his treasured Colt M1911A1 .45 automatic in his holster and someone to pursue on terra firma. Space Command did not permit the carrying of loaded projectile weapons in space because they compromised atmospheric integrity.

The ancient Russian vehicle was very basic. They kept their electrogravitic spacecraft to themselves rather than using them for joint 'black' missions. This shuttle was nuclear-powered, employing a magneto hydrodynamic ionic reaction drive with hydrazine manoeuvring thrusters and a pulsed liquid hydrogen booster for takeoff and landing on the moon.

"Weightless all the way to the moon! How primitive is that?" moaned Spiker.

"You look good in a spacesuit," said Henry looking for a bright side.

"Yeah, like a gift-wrapped dumpling. Isn't that what you called it once?"

"It was not an original remark. I paraphrased a comment I once heard."

"What exactly is a dumpling?" Spiker asked.

"It's something that goes into soup. I believe it was popular in World War II."

"Huh, that's more than I was. I had the job of eliminating aircrew who insisted on talking to the papers about *foo fighters*."

"ET and Nazi flying vehicles," said Henry.

"Yup."

At long last the Russian transport touched down on the far side of the moon with no fuss and ceremony. The crew, three men and a woman captain were polite but otherwise remote. Any conversation was innocuous, which suited Spiker. He had no time for foreigners, let alone Greys and reptoids. On landing on the moon, the vessel settled on a large motorised platform that rumbled towards a shallow downward slope into a cave-like tunnel under a mountainous outcrop. Gyro-stabilisers maintained a horizontal attitude to prevent tipping. The facility was international but dominated by the Americans, much to the irritation of the other nations using it. They could do little about it. Their black budgets hardly compared to Uncle Sam's, even though Uncle Sam didn't need to know what he was spending. Asian countries with expanding economies knew about it and were keen to muscle in. Different countries courted different ET races to grab a piece of the action. All this activity went on while orthodox scientists peered excitedly into space looking for microbial life elsewhere.

Spiker passed through airlocks and tunnels, relieved once inside to remove his life support suit. Henry seemed to know where to go in the maze of tunnels and levels, so Spiker was content to follow him. His glimpses of the barren moon confirmed that it was a shit landscape. In his opinion, the moon was fit only for quarrying and ultra-secure penal facilities. Henry made no response to Spiker's disparaging views on the earth's neighbour except to say, "It's probably the biggest spaceship you'll ever see."

"Spaceship?"

"Yes. It was a natural object originally but extraterrestrials hollowed it out and converted it with quantum flux hyperdrive technology to a mobile terrascaping factory and a biological service laboratory. It has two engines, one of which is out of action. When fully serviceable it could go from zero to light speed in less than thirty seconds. Unfortunately, the earth would run backwards for a brief period before restabilising. They brought it here to develop sentient life and maintain a favourable environment. Tidal forces keep one side facing away. That helps them to hide their activities from ground observation. That race moved on long ago. There have been rumours that the ET community is planning to make it fully operational again to head off for a new destination. That would be an embryonic world going through the first transition to life."

"No shit," said Spiker.

Henry led his companion to an area labelled *Acclimatisation Zone*.

"We might be here for some time," Henry told him. "It all depends on you."

"On me? We wouldn't be here at all if it depended on me."

"You need to get acclimatised to the moon. This facility uses ET technology that we don't have. They decided we'd be less trouble with it than without it. There's a viewport over there. I'd like you to look out and tell me if you see anything in the crater."

Spiker sighed and walked over to the transparent panel. He stared for a few minutes. "Nope. Nutt'n at all except black rock and dark streaks of shadow."

"I think it will take you a very long time," said Henry.

"I thought you measure time in picoseconds," Spiker remarked. "What do you call a long time?"

"That's true but I am getting into subjectivity in my old age. I am learning to be impatient like the rest of you."

The suite of rooms had all sorts of entertainment but Spiker made Henry play poker. He couldn't stand television or computer games. He found some cards in a cupboard. Spiker began to suspect that he was not the first person to be stuck in this 'acclimatisation zone'. He couldn't imagine what it meant. Henry said it was like getting used to being at a high altitude – except that it wasn't.

On day three, Spiker asked Henry how much he owed him in gambling debts.

"One million, four hundred and ninety-three thousand, five hundred and twelve dollars and thirty-three cents. You can pay me the thirty-three cents and owe the rest if you like."

"Double or quits?"

"We've already done that five times. How are you going to pay me? You know I wouldn't expect you to. Think of Mrs Spiker's pension."

"I'll open an account in 1965 and leave you the proceeds in my will. Compound interest should cover it. Don't worry about Mrs Spiker. She'll be richer than the Queen of England when they put me in the ground."

"What do you invest in?" asked Henry.

"War, of course. What else makes so much profit? I could also see who's going to die in our present time and go back to put life insurance on them. Hey, what's that out there?"

Henry looked up sharply. "What's what where?"

"I saw something move in the crater, a sort of light-coloured shadow thing. I can't describe it."

"You just did. Point it out to me. I can see them clearly."

"There – and over there. I can see several."

"At last, I'm so pleased. Tell me when you can see a sign on the wall over there."

Spiker looked at the wall in question. "Nope, can't see nutt'n."

"That's most certainly true," said Henry. "Nobody can see nothing."

Then Spiker keeled over and started snoring.

"I think the appropriate expression is bingo!" said Henry.

When Spiker came round he found Henry giving him an injection in his arm. "Wha– what happened?"

"You succumbed," said Henry.

"What to?"

"The moon. You have been accepted by the world we stand on and you are now a creature of the moon instead of a man of the earth."

Spiker looked at the wall that now bore a notice, "Welcome to the moon."

"That wasn't there before."

"It has been there for years, it's just that you didn't see it because you were in a different space-time zone."

"What time is this then?"

"It is moon time. You have been a product of earth time all your life until now. You have made a higher dimensional switch. Look out the window."

"I still don't understand," said Spiker. "What does it mean?"

Henry thought for a moment. "The universe is composed of quantum digital information. That information is partitioned on entity lines in a kind of hierarchy. It means that each object in space and time belongs to the local planet or star that 'owns' it. That's its local source of information. The black hole makes the galaxy. The galaxy projects the sun into space, the sun projects the earth and the earth makes you and everything on it. When you travel from one planet to another, in this case the moon, the earth ceases to process your information. You become an independent entity. The universe is a virtual reality game machine. It has computational processing like any other."

"What's an entity?" asked Spiker. "Do you mean a ghost?"

Henry laughed. "No, I mean any object the universe holds information about; every physical thing that exists is an entity in data terms. You have left the earth and you are on the moon. I am waiting for the moon to take over the role of formulating your body. If it accepts you, you will become a creature of the moon and certain changes will take place. It's a data switch but it's also about consciousness. The moon knows you are here and is considering your relevance to it. It doesn't think in the way you and I do so we cannot imagine what goes on in the greater universe."

"What about time travel?" asked Spiker.

"You are very astute sometimes," said Henry. "A similar process goes on when you move through time although it is not quite the same. There is no such thing as past and future really – just different versions of the present. Nevertheless, the earth has to accommodate your data flow subjectively in the story of its existence when you switch decades."

"So, what's an entity and what isn't?"

"Anything with some property of individuality. A rock is an entity. If you smash it up, it becomes a collection of smaller entities. A tree is an entity; so is a fish and so are you. As a living entity you have a unit marker on a higher dimension that *integrates* you into a whole being. It comes from the source of all existence. Some people call it God. An atheist has to call it something different; it's all dogma, randomly generated belief systems. You could call it a spirit, a soul, a monad, a quantum, *The One* or nothing at all. It makes no difference; it's all just words. *One* has the property of oneness, which is love. When you die your unit withdraws and goes elsewhere. Your body ceases to be a whole thing and becomes a collection of parts with no purpose or overriding consciousness to hold them together. So the parts become independent of each other and the body starts to *disintegrate*. If the moment of death wasn't instantaneous, people would die in a long drawn out process and there would be zombies staggering about like in those awful movies where the dead rise up."

"Cheesy," Spiker remarked. He stood up, with effort, and looked out. "Fuck me, there's a sky and thin clouds. And plants and stuff."

"You can now go outdoors and look around. The earth's up there too. It's not quite the same earth as the one you left. It's the version that corresponds to this particular manifestation of the moon – it's a different dimension. Actually it's a different universe. Every planetary world lives in its own version of the universe. This isolates the populations that live on them from interacting with each other. So the Venusians live in a different version of the solar system to ours and they see a lifeless earth a bit like the Venus we see."

"Those are people out there."

"Yes, that's what you saw; people. They will look slightly odd, as do you if you look in that mirror."

Spiker went over to the mirror and gazed at himself. "What – I look different but not so different I can see why or how."

"It's subtle. You are a moon man now, Herbert. It will pass when we put you in the biological re-converter. I can't take you back to earth looking like that. Mrs Spiker might not like the change."

"What makes you think she'd notice?" Spiker said, in a daze. Spiker allowed Henry to lead him out of the building into the landscape outside the base. It was similar to the one he saw previously but there were subtle differences. Almost at once, he started coughing and struggling for breath.

"Here, take this." Henry handed the agent a portable oxygen mask, sufficient to ease the discomfort of somebody new to the reduced air pressure.

"You got spare tanks?" Spiker asked in muffled tones.

Henry reached into his knapsack and produced a clip of six small cylinders. "They'll last you about an hour each. Enough for what we want. By the time you have used them up, you'll be able to go without it. At first it's like being up a high mountain on earth."

"Where we goin'?"

"You remember that briefing you got earlier?" said Henry.

"Yeah, sort of. I remember them saying don't drink the water, keep outta strong sunlight and don't – on pain of death – go to the alien base on the other side of that big hill."

"Yes, exactly, that's where we're going."

Spiker struggled wearily over the uneven terrain. He

wore a tough, one-piece garment, sufficient protection now that he was semi-acclimatised to this version of the moon. As the forbidden hill arose before him, he looked over to Henry and said, "Is that offer of a lift still open?"

"Of course," said Henry, dropping down to a squat. "Climb up on my shoulders."

"I thought it'd be easier in the lower gravity but it ain't."

Spiker climbed on Henry's shoulders, his feet dangling down the android's chest. Henry stood up and started to run, maintaining a smooth gait in spite of his speed.

"Are you sure about this? Why did they threaten anybody who comes here?"

"Oh, that," said Henry. He knew Spiker would understand threats of that sort because he often carried them out. "This is an ancient base, long since abandoned by its builders. However, it is sometimes occupied by an alien that Space Command does not approve of."

"Why not? Is it dangerous?"

"No, that's why they don't approve of him. They don't like ETs who talk about spiritual principals. They prefer the sort that harvest human organs in return for advanced technology. They'll even deal with the ones that like to eat us if they can get something useful out of them. Humans understand that. They call it horse-trading. You know where you stand if they want something. They especially don't like aliens who only want us to evolve into light beings and be like gods."

"Why's that?" asked Spiker.

"Gods don't pay taxes, buy oil or get into debt."

"But ain't they happier?"

"Yes, but if humans were happy and content they wouldn't buy things they don't need. The governments don't like extraterrestrials that tell them to give up nukes and love one another. They are content to oppose the evolutionary aspirations of the universal mind to maintain personal wealth and power. They little know that in the long term they stand to lose more than they could ever imagine."

"So this ET is a decent guy."

"Yes. He and I found ancient hardware down here and I helped him restore it to full functionality."

"What's it do?"

"It gives you a different perspective on life. It's like a virtual reality game machine."

"That don't sound too bad. What's it for?"

"You'll see for yourself soon enough."

"Soon enough? What happened to the microsecond count down?"

"I find humans imprecise about time. They don't seem to like me being literal in my temporal prognostications."

"Is that a fact? Literal in your 'temporal prognostications'! Nobody has ever accused me of that. I don't know anybody who knows such long words other than a scientist I burned for discovering free energy."

"Anyway, time works differently here," said Henry. "The human concept of time is pretty much exclusive to the earth."

Spiker grunted a few times as Henry climbed down the far side of the hill, unavoidably jolting the Black Ops agent as he negotiated a crevice and a scree field. Even so, Spiker was glad he didn't have to clamber down under his own efforts.

Henry stopped before a large transparent dome that looked like glass but was probably not.

"What's that?" asked Spiker.

"It's an ancient environmental chamber for housing dwellings and cultivating plants and bacterial cultures for food manufacture. Some ETs are more closely related to plants than animals."

"Where are these dwellings now?"

"They would have been broken down by thermal cycling over thousands of years. They were made of crystalline metallic composites. There are versions of these domes all over the moon but many are badly damaged or decayed. The original occupants were gone long before the moon was put in the earth's orbit."

"How do you know so much about them?"

"My friend here told me. I also took a look for myself. You can access all time past and future if you know how. It's just information."

Henry dropped to one knee to allow Spiker to climb off. Then he found the entrance to the dome and led the way to a structure that housed a spiral stairway. It led down into caverns under the moon's surface. He produced a strong full-spectrum light source from his backpack so that Spiker could see clearly. It made their shadows swirl eerily around the shaft as they walked down.

"You can remove the oxygen mask down here. There is good air for those who need it. I could use some now."

Spiker took off the mask.

"I thought you said you don't need to breathe. You walked here without oxygen."

"I use oxygen for my biological components but

that is not the same as needing it all the time. I can function without air for – for a while."

"Ha! At least you didn't tell me how long. Don't reveal your weaknesses to anybody. It's bad security. You're too trusting. Get real, kid," Spiker said sagely.

Henry led the way down to a lower level and on through doors, corridors and chambers of rock, small and large. They came, at last, to a massive vault full of alien-looking hardware of all types and styles. Some of the machines were the size of battleships. There was dust and clutter but the android led Spiker to a place that was clean and well-illuminated. Henry stopped before a large cabinet constructed of an indeterminable substance, neither wood nor plastic. The android gave voice to a strange, high-pitched sound such as Spiker had never before heard. The cabinet seemed to respond with a deep base rumbling modulation, so strong that Spiker felt it vibrating through his feet and resonating in his chest.

"Step inside, Agent Spiker. We are expected."

Henry waved his hand over a coloured panel and the double doors on the front of the cabinet opened. The stone 'sarcophagus' inside was designed to accommodate larger beings than Agent Spiker. The difference between this receptacle and its ancient Egyptian counterparts was that it was designed for the living rather than the dead. The ancients had a way of taking alien Merkabah technology and adapting it for the preservation of corpses. It was a bit late to expect a dead body to undergo a spiritual renaissance. As their understanding of cymatic technology had faded, they resorted to counterfeiting the hardware and hoping for the best. Henry assisted Spiker to climb in and lay on his back. The lid closed suddenly with a forceful, ringing thud of stone on stone, imbuing Spiker with a sense of foreboding. It felt a little like being buried alive. Instant darkness stripped away his senses. The blackout gave way to a gentle illumination accompanied by pulsating tones of alien invention. The agent found himself immersed in bewitching sensations. Patterns of light and colour appeared that extended beyond the physical confines of the chamber.

Far away in the distance, he saw a flock of three-dimensional geometric shapes milling around like birds in a versicoloured sky. Each one had a different configuration, texture and colour. Spiker decided they must be alien symbols that meant something to the beings who designed the system thousands or even millions of years ago. They meant nothing to him.

"What do I do?" he called out but there was no answer.

The flying symbols clustered around him, moving in and out but never quite making contact. Tentatively, he reached up towards one of them and immediately it moved towards him like a living creature waiting to be touched.

Herbert Spiker's fingers met the shape in mid-air. Light exploded all around him and suddenly he found himself transported into his childhood in the twenties. He was back in school with other children who were tormenting him for his plain looks and the poverty of his parents.

Spiker let go and then used both hands to touch other shapes as they offered themselves, each one yielding a new memory. Many incidents of bullying flashed in and out of the experience, mostly at the hands of older boys. Then he got into his teens and began to fight back and took many beatings. It wasn't until he joined a boxing club that he started to win. His consciousness became compartmentalised in such a way that he lived out these brief vignettes simultaneously. He had never before experienced plurality of consciousness and yet somehow it was natural. Some were from his distant past and others were more recent. He noticed that they were spaced fairly evenly around the two major time shifts he had made during his fragmented life; from the early thirties to World War II and then onwards again to the sixties. Black Ops had found something in him that suited their requirements – a man without conscience motivated by an intense gratitude for escaping the electric chair at Sing Sing. Although one experience spoiled the moment when he sampled the timeline in which they fried him.

Then a new sort of experience emerged. He began to see himself from a vicarious perspective. At first he thought these were disembodied glimpses but then it dawned on him that he was becoming other people; people who knew him. These recalled moments adopted a spectrum of themes; love, sex, argument, dancing, drinking in bars, going to movies, conversations, sober and inebriated – a gamut of experiences relived. The reality of it was intense and vivid; sensations of all kinds, physical, mental, emotional; strong tastes and smells. Fearful anticipation percolated in his stomach. There were times of beauty and emotion but nothing seriously painful except when he fell victim to his own bullying. He saw his mother's death at a time when he was non-existent, having travelled beyond her time. Now a new kind of jagged symbol danced in the air around him, nudging him for attention; dark, blood red, this object radiated menace. Reluctantly he reached out and touched it. Now, simultaneously, he became all the people he had blackmailed, threatened or coerced. It was a horrible thing to experience every last iota of their anguish and shame, the grinding frustration of the traps he had so expertly laid for them. He could sniff out a man or a woman's weakness like a bloodhound on a scent. He was merciless in pursuing an advantage and he could take it up to and beyond the limit of endurance. He even felt the impact on the families and partners of his victims and all the occasions when they took the only way out and committed suicide. He lived all of the emotional pain he had inflicted but not the violence; he felt sure that was yet to come.

Spiker emerged from the experience, totally shaken. With a mounting sense of horror, he found himself amid a swarm of ugly shapes with spikes and tendrils, obsidian black, enveloped in turgid sensations of unspoken misery. Touching these, he relived every act of physical pain, torture and death he had inflicted on others. It was an action replay of every incident of violence in which he had participated. He observed his own sense of achievement and pleasure as he did these things, overcoming resistance, threat and physical attack with the skills they taught him. In the back of his mind grew the insidious fear of the coming reckoning.

It was the smallest and darkest of the objects that now commanded his attention. With great reluctance but undeniable compulsion he reached out and lived through his victims' experience of pain and death vicariously. Undergoing past situations had been bad enough, now he was facing up to the key actions perpetrated for his masters. He became the victim of every atrocity he had ever carried out. He learned to fear and loathe himself in a way he had not dreamed possible. There was no preparation for the horror of experiencing his actions. *Now* he understood; *everything is one*. The difference between one entity and another is illusory; a single pattern with infinite possible viewpoints. He was an aspect of the one mind, the one spirit and had but one body, the universe. The difference between the perpetrator and the victim was merely one of perspective; the idea that what we do to others we do to ourselves was no longer a vague platitude, it was hell incarnate. The detail was graphic and unrelenting, the pain unspeakable. He went through torture, injury and death at his own hands, building to a deafening crescendo of pain and horror. He saw himself as a feral beast, as efficient as he was callous and brutal.

The emotions were complex too; hatred, pity, fear, anger and futility. There were secondary waves, the grief of the bereaved, wives, children and parents. Beyond the fact of death lay hidden consequences. These were obvious in the main but some surprised him. He saw plots unfolding, the devious games of his masters. Fleetingly, he experienced the sensation of a different world. Here, enlightenment was possible instead of the darkness that now engulfed this version of the earth. He understood how violence, war and the iron grip of the multinational conglomerates enslaved the population in misery and economic privation in the name of profit. He saw the systems that destroyed the land and trees and scarred the beauty of nature. By blocking external influences like the love of spirit, extraterrestrials and higher dimensional beings, Spiker had played a key role in holding back the dawn of a new, enlightened civilisation. Even worse, he had furthered the interests of devious and dark beings that sought dominion over humanity; negative entities that wanted to destroy the planet simply because it is beautiful, to enslave minds by dogmatic interpretations of science, politics, religion, militarism and corporate technology. Sadly, they were forces of our own creation brought about by greed, envy, desire for power and the fear of death, another aspect of human creation for nothing ever really dies but simply transforms when its role is complete.

Underlying all this was the positive aspect that counterbalances the misery. For, in entering the domain of physical time, humanity had created death. The human body understood its own mortality even though its spirit, its true consciousness, was immortal and timeless. The endless pain of physical experience was the death it entailed, the silent elephant in every room. The greatest illusion of all enabled the race to feel emotion in a way never before known to sentient life. It was because emotion rooted in fear was better than no emotion at all. Fear enabled a novel dimension of being; a new way to know love by experiencing its opposite. It opened for *humanity* the possibility of godhood but only if it could overcome the trap of its own creation; the game that dominated the passage of its days and the systems that blighted the joy of its being.

Then it was over. Peace overwhelmed him. The lights became stars in a magnificent sky.

Henry opened the chamber lid and looked down on Spiker. He lifted the Black Ops agent out gently and sat him down on a stone bench as if he weighed nothing at all. Spiker was shaking, muttering and dribbling at the mouth, swinging his head from side to side, barely able to sit upright.

"I am sorry, Agent Spiker. I did not wish to distress you. I hoped to save you from further unnecessary suffering. You would have experienced all that eventually. It is something everybody undergoes in the afterlife when they seek to move forward."

"But how…?"

"The extraterrestrials were able to make this because the universe is a virtual reality game machine with all that that implies. The space-time field records everything that happens. We can replay every event and the story behind it from every participating perspective. Each one of us has a data record within the universal conceptual matrix. This device is a terminal that allows you to access your own story. If you do good things for people throughout your life you have a wonderful experience here. If you do bad things – well, now you know," Henry said awkwardly.

Spiker burst into tears.

"I thought if you saw the consequences of your work you might not wish to continue with it. I acted as a friend."

Very little of Henry's expression betrayed the electricity buzzing in his inner abdominal circuits as a result of the emotional output from the agent. He pondered hard on what to do – if anything – to relieve the man's distress. He had wanted it to happen. It had happened but the consequence was more difficult to deal with than he had anticipated. He came to a decision.

"I have never put anybody back in the machine for the second phase of the operation immediately following the karmic clearing. In your case I will make an exception."

"What! You want me to go back in there? Never!" screamed Spiker.

"Never say never to me," Henry said. "I'm not giving you an option."

Spiker pulled his gun out and emptied all the ammunition in the android's head and heart as he had been trained to do. It was an automatic response. It was also completely futile, as he had known it would be. Would he have done it in any other circumstance? After what he had experienced he could not face shooting anybody ever again. What was the point in shooting yourself?

Spiker struggled and yelled but to no avail. The android placed him in the sarcophagus and closed the lid. The same thud, the same darkness but this time he was not entering the unknown.

"Why would you do this to me?" he screamed. His muffled tones reached Henry's ears but he continued resolutely to manipulate the controls.

As he lay there, Spiker began to feel a tingling sensation running through his body from head to foot. A feeling of blissful euphoria began to take root in the centre of his torso in the region of the heart. His head wanted to scream and complain but his heart was opening to the universe – *his universe*. He now understood what Henry had tried to tell him that every object in space and time was the centre of its own version of everything. What distinguishes one object from another is its unique perspective on the whole. Once more the space around him expanded beyond the horizon of his container. Geometric shapes appeared in the distance and headed towards him. His head said *dread*; his heart felt nothing but *peace*. The shapes were smooth and elegant, a bit like doves and bluebirds. There were other colours too, subtle and beautiful. He reached out and touched them. Each one gave him a happy experience of something or somebody in a pleasurable setting. Warm sunsets, fireflies; lemon trees in pots on a stone veranda, mountains, forests, streets and houses he had known or seen. All of it was familiar but none of it had seemed special or particularly wonderful at the time. It was a case of distance adding enchantment to the view where the distance was temporal rather than physical. Then it moved on to where he was experiencing himself as a benefactor, a humourist, a kindly friend or compassionate stranger. He could barely recall such times in his own life but he recognised the truth in them. He had done more good than he realised in these little moments, inconsequential in one way but profound in another. There had been love in his life. In the next phase it came to him from other people in small gestures and brief contacts. His mother, not so much his father, his few friends as a boy, they all gave him something, however small, that now seemed forever significant and wonderful.

The burgeoning euphoric sensation in his heart centre became overwhelmingly intense. From how much pain could a man stand, he was now wondering how much pleasure. The air around him began to glow with coloured lights. He wondered where it was coming from until it dawned on him that *he* was the source. Suddenly, he heard a sound like 'whoomph' and found himself inside a ball of light floating above the stone floor of the sarcophagus. It was unlike anything he had ever experienced. A moment later he was in space looking down on the moon. Space was no longer dark emptiness; there were streams and waves of coloured light and sounds like celestial music. He had crossed over into the parallel light dimension. Then a force like gravity gripped him, his stomach churned as if he was going over a humpback bridge. Then he found himself back inside the stone device, falling with a thump on the rocky surface. The sarcophagus emitted a triumphant ringing tone and he was back in darkness.

Once more, Henry opened the lid and helped him out.

"What happened this time? Did I go off to fly with the fairies?" Spiker asked.

"You could say that," Henry agreed. "But it wasn't real. It's a virtual device – remember? What you experienced is what you could become. Given a little time, you might even make it on your own. It could happen quite soon if you mend your ways and start contributing some good to this universe of ours. The *temporal resequencer* gives you a head start in achieving it. It mitigates the effects of the past as they impact on the present."

"How can it change the past? Surely, it's happened and gone."

Henry shook his head. "There is no past. It never happened. It's a virtual reality story that we make up as we go along in the present moment. It's how we justify what we are, where we are and what we're doing right now. You've just taken your first step in waking up from the dream."

"Well, I ain't keen to rub anybody out so perhaps I *can* do it. The problem is the jobs our masters give us. Sorry, I shot you like that."

"That's all right," said Henry. "You can easily

check more bullets out of store but how can you stop using them? You do like your favourite gun."

"Yeah, it's a sentimental thing. Mrs Spiker gave me this Colt M1911 on our wedding day." He sighed. "Until now. Now it looks ugly – a thing of death and pain – *my* pain. But you're right. They do give me a lot of wet jobs."

"Maybe you should move home," Henry suggested.

"What? You mean, like Nebraska?"

"Actually, I was thinking of another dimension."

"Cool."

A sound broke the silence of the vast chamber, a clunk that echoed around the cavernous void. A powerful beam stabbed the darkness and moved around like a drunken searchlight. When the source drew close, it took the form of a tall alien, carrying a lamp. The being was human-like in appearance but clearly not of the earth. His skin was black with a purple sheen and his eyes were also purple. His garments were unfamiliar to Spiker.

Henry whispered to Spiker. "This entity has spent a great deal of time associating with humans from the international base. His English and Russian are particularly good, especially in the vernacular. Don't be fooled though. His mind is multidimensional and his thinking processes go way beyond crude language."

"What's the vernacular," asked Spiker. "Is that the john?"

When he spoke, the alien addressed them in English. The deep, resonant voice was calming and made everything seem well again.

"Be at peace, dear friend. You have done evil things but *you* are not evil. We are all playing a role and exploring an idea of who we think we are. We are not the idea; we are something infinitely greater."

"I have sinned lots of times. I know what I have done." Spiker was distraught.

"There is no sin. There is only experience. But that experience comes at a cost. The price is absolute responsibility for all your deeds, thoughts and actions. You have looked in a mirror of consciousness but you have not seen your true self. Your soul is much greater than that. At least you can begin to work towards clearing your karma."

"It's not too late?"

"How can anything be late when everything happens in time?"

"I dunno," Spiker muttered. "Jeez, I wish I'd stayed in the funeral business with my father. The depression hit – life was hard. People couldn't afford to live and they sure as hell couldn't afford to die. No – I couldn't have done that. The old man killed himself when the money stopped coming in. Even the dead were broke."

"You are rambling, Agent Spiker," Henry advised.

The alien held up his hand to caution Henry from interfering.

"The shadow is the greatest teacher. You have a lot of shadow, Herbert. You have transformed it into light."

"What does that machine do?"

"It portrays your life as a virtual reality. It does this by extracting information from your aura. This comes from the fabric of space and time in your personal universe. Your ancestors called this Akasha."

"What's the – what is an aura?"

"It is a pattern of space called a fractal by mathematicians. Every object comes with its own time and generates its own space. The aura is a flow, a movement of consciousness. Consciousness has many meanings but you may think of it as the transformative energy of being. In truth, it is all there is."

"Clear as mud, I guess. Yet, something has changed. I sorta know that somehow. I can't go back."

The alien smiled on him kindly. "Herbert. Follow your heart."

"May I speak?" asked Henry patiently.

The alien smiled. "My dear mechanical friend, I forget how literal you are. Naturally."

"I would like Agent Spiker to come back with me to 1985. I would like to find Deborah Farnham. Would you agree to this, Herbert?"

"Yeah, I guess I should thank you for what you have done. Although I also think I was happier not knowing," Spiker admitted. "What I don't understand is why can't everybody know about their past? What price would people pay to know that?"

"The price *you* have just paid, my dear friend. Everybody does experience what you have," said the alien, "but not usually on this dimension. It is a function of the universe to reveal nature, to educate spirit by exploring the meaning of love, a property of the fundamental concept *one*. You can't do that in a state of infinite consciousness so you enter a finite universe without love except for what we bring to it. You play your role in the game and then you take stock. Have you shown love or have you done harm? Either way there is light, for if you have done as you would be done by, it will return a hundredfold. If you have done harm you will learn the truth about it and be wiser. The difference is in the debt you owe others."

"Ain't this Judgement Day? Doesn't God punish

me?"

"There is no reward. There is no punishment. There is only enlightenment – the endgame, home. Love is its own reward."

"Yeah, I see that now. It's love working it all out, ain't it? We don't see it because we are it! Neat huh! I just wish I didn't know 'cause it complicates life."

The alien smiled and touched Henry on the back. "You have another success and we have another akashic life record in our collection."

"Excuse me! Are you saying my life is merely a trophy in your machine?" asked Spiker.

"No, not a trophy. All knowledge is available through the universal consciousness if we choose to find it. This is not just idle curiosity or simply for our amusement. My friend Henry saw the potential in this machine for healing people – not their bodies but their lives. What we have learned is not about you but about this ancient device."

"That's okay then," said Spiker, "so we're off to 1985, are we? Who's this dame we're going after? I hope you don't want to rub her out. I gotta find a new line of work, and it's all your fault, Mr Android."

Part 3
The Recruit

Chapter Nine

2000, New York University

Roger Crandle packed up his papers and moved towards the exit. The lecture theatre white board was covered in scribbled notes, which he had just copied. The lecturer stood with a cleaning pad, poised to wipe it clean. By prearrangement one of the students was asking a question to divert the speaker. It was a collective conspiracy to keep the information visible for as long as possible to allow time for the slower writers to catch up.

A voice called out to Roger. "Hey, Limey, how about coming to Josie's with the crowd? You up for it?"

"Thanks, Jack, but I'm meeting somebody. I might see you down the pub later."

Jack grinned. "Oh, very well, but we'll get you loaded one of these days. If it's a girl, I'll let you off."

"For once, it is."

"You're excused then. Just don't make a habit of that abstinence thing. Too much sobriety and no girls can give you a reputation; you're either hiding something or gay – or maybe both."

"Really! What if I'm just dull?"

"We are in a new millennium. Nobody's allowed to be boring these days. Ciao."

"That's all right then. I *am* nobody. Yeah, see you,

man."

"Enjoy!"

Roger returned to his student room on campus and put his bag aside. The week was over. He was free for two days – if you didn't count assignments and Friday night was not the time to think about that.

Two hours dribbled by fitfully in drinking coffee and making calls. He thought about tidying up his room but not for long. He couldn't find anything when he was tidy so why risk it? There was a knock at the door. He opened it.

"Hi, Melissa."

"Hi, Rog. How's things?"

"Fine, thanks. What brings you to the university?"

"I came to see you to talk about old times – you *know*."

Roger laughed. "Melissa, we don't have any 'old times' to talk about. Last year you were going out with Scott and he owed me money. Otherwise, we hardly met."

She looked embarrassed. "You know how to make a girl feel welcome."

"Sorry, I really am pleased to see you. It's just that I always thought you and Scott would be married or something."

"So did I, but you never know what's going to happen in life, do you?"

"No, that's true enough. I didn't imagine I would end up in America. But never mind that, I'm glad to see you. What shall we do? We could go to the Chinese restaurant on the corner if you like."

"Can we get a takeout and bring it back here?" she asked. "I'd like to talk."

"Of course, I'd phone out but they always get lost in

this building. They don't seem to mind who they give it to as long as they get paid. If this was London, I'd order Indian – there's more vegetarian choice. It's not too well known out here."

"Vegetarian or Indian?"

"Neither, I guess."

"You can get anything in New York."

"Yeah, I heard that too," said Roger wryly. "There's a clinic near here…"

Roger and Melissa walked out and found a restaurant that served takeaway food. From there, they returned to the student residence. Melissa Harcott was intelligent and very attractive. Scott Razellon was the kind of man that girls line up for. Captain of the team, first cheerleader, they were the golden couple of their final year while Roger was in his first. She had never shown any interest in talking to him before. In her presence, he always felt like 'the invisible man'.

So why was she here now?

Melissa spread out the food containers while Roger found plates and cutlery. By preference he put on side lamps rather than the stark overhead bulb. They created a more comfortable ambience. However, on this occasion he felt self-conscious in case it seemed calculated. Melissa didn't seem to notice. Whatever she wanted to say, it was not really about him in any intimate context. She produced a bottle of wine from her backpack. Roger found glasses. They were not particularly appropriate for wine but they made good tooth mugs.

The two distant acquaintances drank and talked about inconsequential things. Afterwards, Melissa sat back while Roger collected the plates and put them in the sink. It was a tiny room with everything together except the bed, which was in an even smaller room.

Melissa seemed more relaxed when he brought out coffee in a cafetière.

"I didn't tell you about Scott."

"No. Is he okay?"

"I don't know. We split up in January. He got into something that I couldn't really share. It was – well, it was highly classified – secret stuff. He went on a mission but I don't know where or what happened to him. He wasn't allowed to tell me. Five months have passed and I haven't heard a word from him."

"I'm sorry. You two seemed close."

"Yeah, we have these love affairs. It's like you are waiting to meet Mr Right and live happily ever after. Sometimes Mr Right has feet of clay."

"I suppose so. It has never really happened to me – love affairs I mean – not Mr Right. I guess I just work a lot."

Melissa looked at him as if seeing him for the first time. "Never?"

"Not much. Not Miss Right anyway."

"You don't *seem* unhappy."

"I'm not unhappy. Why should I be?"

Melissa smiled. "Why indeed?" She paused to collect her thoughts before broaching the topic that had brought her to see him. "Do you remember that test that Chas put us through?"

This change of tack completely threw Roger for a moment. "Not really. I know he tested us but I can't remember much about it."

"He got this gadget at Princeton. Some professor called Jahn devised it to test for psychokinesis. Sometimes he called it telekinesis."

"Oh, yes. I remember. He said I did quite well."

Melissa snorted. "Quite well! You were phenomenal! Chas told Scott about it afterwards but they didn't want to tell you. You outperformed all of us. You recorded the highest score they'd ever heard of."

"I had no idea. Is that good?"

"That depends on whether you want to use it or not."

"How can you use something like that?"

Melissa thought before she answered. "It means that your mind has the ability to modify physical processes on the quantum level in a statistically significant way – beyond chance."

"Yes."

"With training you could do more. I can't tell you much more than that because I don't know. I just help to find people with unusual abilities to join special projects run by the government. I am supposed to give you a lot of bullshit but I know the straightforward approach is more likely to work with you."

"I don't really understand. Are you offering me a job using these so-called psychic abilities?"

"I'm offering you a chance to find out what you're capable of. That's all."

"I suppose it can't do any harm. But I can't imagine why anybody would pay you to do that. Have you any idea?"

Melissa shook her head. "As to that, I don't have a need to know. That's what they told me. I just recruit people with potential."

"Did you recruit Scott by any chance?"

She looked down, guilt written all over her.

"You found me out," she said. "Okay, I did but don't expect the fringe benefits he got."

Roger chuckled ironically. "Fridge benefits more like."

***

"Welcome to phase three of our remote viewing training programme, ladies and gentlemen."

Roger regarded the man in the smart suit with a mixture of amusement and scepticism. He was still not comfortable with the idea of telepathy or whatever name they chose to give it. They called it remote viewing but it originally stemmed from US Department of Defense funded research. It was an experiment to see if they could infiltrate the military secrets of the Soviet Union. It was dropped eventually because the results were not strategically significant.

Roger knew *these* people were not in the defence sector. They were in something covert. Roger had no idea what that 'something' was but he was not overly concerned. His mind was totally wrapped up in exploring abilities he didn't know he had; abilities he didn't know existed. When he was actually doing it, he somehow managed to suspend his disbelief.

"You have all located target destinations and described remote objects and artefacts from nothing more than a map reference. Some of you have done better than others." He glanced at Roger here. "Then we asked you to locate people and describe them and their surroundings and what they seemed to be doing. Each time we used a simple scoring system to rate your performance. Now you've come back to take the third and final phase of the training. You must admit it beats waiting tables and washing up in restaurants in your vacation."

They laughed. All of them were bright students and all of them had been recruited by the likes of Melissa. This particular covert organisation never advertised openly and they never would. Roger had spent five weekends involved in the remote viewing programme. Most participants failed to return after the first four sessions. He had no real confidence that what he was doing was meaningful. When he carried out an exercise it was like using his imagination in a creative way – more like making it up than actually seeing anything real. He had no idea whether he was doing it right or wrong. All he knew was that attendance after session four was by invitation only. He must be doing something right to be on his sixth weekend.

"This phase of the programme consists of linking with an individual to exchange information. We call it remote communication."

One of the male students put up his hand to signal a question. "What's it like to do it? Do you hear somebody's thoughts?"

"There's no set method; it all depends on the individual. However, you can't hear another person speaking in their head. You receive the essence of the idea and then interpret it in your own way. It might be an image, an abstract idea or maybe words but they will be your words, not theirs. The exercises on the first two phases should have established your mode of working. Try to observe your own mind as you do it."

"How does it work?" asked another.

"We have two or three models that might fit the process but we are not entirely sure. This is a pragmatic exercise. We have a go and find out what works. What I can tell you is that a thought seems to be a unit, a quantum concept. You send and receive a message as a series of discrete ideas. You unravel those coming in to translate them into English. That's where experience comes in – learning to put your communication into conceptual packets rather like an Internet transmission. The only difference is that data packets are information – your packets are concepts. They combine concrete information with a subjective nuance."

Roger stuck up his hand and received a nod to ask a question. "Does the communication take place instantaneously or does it go at the speed of light?"

The instructor paused to look at Roger as if trying to read something before replying. "You kinda hit a nail on the head there, Roger. The communication seems to be instantaneous. I can't say more about it than that. Okay, let's get on with the first assignment. Same as before – you each get an envelope with the co-ordinates of your target. I want you to try to identify them. The next step will be to establish communication. Take it slowly and do the first link-up as I have taught you."

Roger opened the envelope and took out the slip of paper. On it was written a set of longitude and latitude co-ordinates. He emptied his mind and then began to interrogate himself: was it a man or a woman, dark or fair, young or old, and so on? In that way he built up a basic picture. It seemed to be a tall man with grey hair, located in an office in a building in a town near a range of mountains. He made notes with a pencil and waited for the trainer to come and check out the contact.

"How you doing? Got a link?"

Roger showed him the notes.

"Very good. He's a bit heavier built than you describe but not bad. You are on the right track. Okay, start making a link. See if you can get the idea he wants to put over. I don't know what it is. We will get an email when they get our cue."

Roger went back into his relaxed state and did his best to clear his mind and wait for a thought to pop into focus. When he finished, he had something that made no sense, about an engineering manual for a vehicle. He thought at first it was a truck but changed his mind in favour of a helicopter. For some reason he then saw a Native American. He decided it was an Apache. The trainer collected his paper with all the others. He went over to a computer and looked at an email inbox. He printed off messages coming in. He located the code for Roger's task and read the report.

He turned to Roger and said, "Well done. You got the subject exactly but you didn't get the whole message. There was an instruction concerning an Apache helicopter manual. Still, to get the level of detail that close was pretty impressive. I'll score it later."

"Brad, can I ask you something?"

"Fire away."

"Is there anything I can do to improve my ability?"

The trainer paused for a while before answering. "You are keen to learn. I'll say that for you. Yes, there are ways of improving your natural talent. I'll come back shortly. I need to get something."

He went over to a desk, opened a drawer and took out a photocopied document stapled at the corner. He handed it to Roger.

"Self-hypnosis?" asked Roger looking up.

"Yep. All you need to know to put yourself in a trance. I recommend that you read the section on how to get out of it before you try."

Roger grinned. "Yeah, I'll do that. You think it would help then?"

"I guess so. It helped me."

"Okay."

The teacher moved on to one of the other trainees. "Any luck, Jessica?"

"Luck about describes it," the student said irritably. "I don't think I'm up to this test."

Roger read about hypnosis and learned that it is a state where the two sides of the brain are balanced, having equal electrical oscillations. There are various frequencies identified as alpha, beta waves and so on. Some of these frequencies associate with alertness and creativity, others, like delta, associate with meditation or sleep and relaxation. The procedure for getting in a trance seemed long and complicated and involved various methods of visualisation and relaxation. It took about forty minutes to achieve the desired state and almost as long to get out of it. Roger felt that life was too short for all of this. If the required mental state for hypnotism is achieved by balancing the brain, there must be a more direct way – he just needed to find it.

The class continued for the remainder of the afternoon. Later, Roger was in his room in the training complex. The facilities were basic; a bed, basin, shower and toilet. It reminded him of university accommodation. This was a facility without designation or identification. He was no wiser about the organisation that was training him than he had been before he arrived. It was a smart, anonymous building in a small American town, a cultural backwater devoid of character. He was beginning to wonder if all the town's inhabitants belonged to the same organisation. He felt as if he'd stumbled into 'the Twilight Zone'. It was not overtly military but it certainly had that kind of atmosphere and short haircuts were predominant among the men. They had travelled there from NYU by bus at night so nobody had any real sense of location and nothing had been said about where they were.

Roger picked up the paper explaining self-hypnosis. He recalled hearing sometime that the creative side of the brain was on the right. The left had more to do with logic. Artists worked with the right hemisphere. At least, it was something along those lines. Like all these stories, that was probably a gross simplification.

He decided to try to get into the hypnotic state without the rigmarole of talking to himself as it described. Instinctively, he breathed slowly and evenly, imagining that his breath was coming down through the top of his head and into the centre of his brain. It was a strangely powerful sensation and Roger quickly found himself falling asleep in the chair. He had no idea how long he was out but it seemed like only a minute or two, no more. He returned to consciousness. While still half awake, he began dreaming of a large spaceship such as he had never seen before. The front end appeared to be a detachable vehicle with elegant wings curved like a crescent moon. Behind it extended a long, elegant neck ending in a bulky propulsion unit with a rectangular, box-like array of circular exit ducts. There was no visible combustion in the manner of rockets. The entire vision was brief, almost to the point of being instantaneous. His mind registered a rippling of space in the vehicle's wake like long spiral streamers winding around each other into the blackness. Most revealing was the way the spatial disturbance distorted the shimmering images of background stars. The sense of power in the machine electrified him. As he came fully awake, the vision dissolved rapidly like a fading dream. He struggled for several minutes to retain the experience in conscious memory.

Roger did not know what the vision meant or even if it meant anything at all. The powerful intensity of the experience impressed him. The spaceship he saw was like nothing he had seen portrayed on television or in books. As far as he knew, it was way beyond current technology.

Over the next few hours Roger experimented with the breathing technique. He was sure that mystics and meditators would be familiar with it. He concentrated on activating the right hemisphere of his brain. His mind emptied of all thought quite naturally although it was impossible to maintain this for long periods. The breathing also made his eyes water if he kept them open. Quite instinctively, he developed a technique for thinking in the abstract. He emptied his mind and then watched for a thought to pop in. By force of will, he was able to prevent the natural urge to express the thought internally in words. Instead, he concentrated on knowing each thought as an abstract totality. There were side effects to the technique. His head began to feel hot and he developed a tingling in the crown. However, it was the beginning of a new consciousness that was to expand beyond all expectation.

He found it difficult to sleep that night. When he did sleep, he dreamed he heard a voice that spoke to him in a deep whisper. He could not identify the speaker or the meaning of what he said.

The next day, Roger walked into the class feeling like a different person. The instructor handed out exercises. Roger took his with a remarkably detached, casual feeling as if it was no more than child's play. He opened the envelope and read the morning exercise. Instead of a set of map references, he found a small, chunky ring, the sort that fits on the little finger. He was instructed to hold it and make a mental link. He soon found himself visualising a bearded man on a motorcycle driving across a flat, featureless terrain – prairies of wheat for mile upon mile. He made notes. He wrote the word 'Harley'. There was a message of sorts – something about an appointment and a place and time. The telepathic link kicked in, a very tangible connection. He did not need telling that the target felt it too. The expression 'locking on' came to mind.

When the instructor read Roger's report he was visibly taken aback. He knew nothing about the subject personally. This precaution precluded his becoming involved in the process. He too was skilled in remote viewing. So compelling was the amount of detail, he left the room immediately to check on the target.

When the instructor returned, he saw Roger standing next to one of the women in the group, holding his hand over the top of her head. She had a faraway look on her face.

"What are you doing, Mr Crandle?" Brad asked.

Roger jumped guiltily and took his hand away. "Just trying something."

"Oh, you stopped," said the girl accusingly.

"Stopped what?" asked the instructor.

"I don't know but the top of my head is buzzing. I feel wonderfully relaxed," the girl said.

Later, in the afternoon, Brad stopped Roger when the group was going out for coffee.

"Roger, what did you do to Lynette?"

"Something strange happened to me last night. I just tried to induce the same effect in her."

"Tell me what happened. Lynette's ability seems to have increased significantly. As for yours, well, it's gone through the roof. I have never come across that much skill in a novice. So, *tell me*."

Roger told him everything that had happened; his dream, what he did to change his brain and how he induced a similar effect in Lynette. Brad listened carefully and said nothing until he had finished.

"What do you imagine this vision of a spaceship was about?"

"Dunno. I've never seen anything like it before. It certainly wasn't from the British space programme."

"What British space programme?"

"Exactly."

Brad grinned. "Okay, this is interesting. So you had a bad dream in the night?"

"I didn't say it was bad. It was just strange. I heard this whispering voice."

"What did the voice say?"

"Nothing I could understand. It was not English."

"You mean American."

Roger chuckled. "No, it wasn't that or any other language I have heard. I am not even sure if it was a language."

"So, what did you do to Lynette?"

"I put my hand over her head and got into this brain state by breathing in the way I told you. It seemed to have the same effect on her."

"You know she's a synesthete I suppose?"

"A what?"

"She experiences written numbers and words in a different way to the rest of us. She sees colours and textures with numbers and words. Sometimes it's taste. Precipice *tastes* like chocolate apparently."

"How strange."

"Not really, it's fairly common. Synesthetes often make good subjects for remote viewing. That's why she's here."

"What's chocolate got to do with a precipice?"

"Absolutely nothing. It has something to do with the texturing of the word in her particular brain – not the meaning."

"Oh, that's interesting."

"I'm glad you think so. I would like to do a test on you, if that's all right."

"What sort of test?"

"Come round to the lab at 4.30. Don't worry. It won't hurt."

"I didn't think it would," said Roger.

"Oh, you'd be surprised. Some of our stuff hurts a great deal but we get results."

***

Roger had difficulty finding the lab. When he arrived, the instructor was waiting for him. Brad motioned him to sit on a chair. A technician came over and placed dabs of transparent gel on Roger's head. To these he attached a series of electrodes. A computer screen had 'Mind Mirror' in a banner at the top. Below it were wide, coloured lines in two groups, growing and shrinking in length.

"It's an electroencephalograph. Two guys in England called Maxwell Cade and Geoffrey Blundell developed the original version. It's handy for checking out brain states. I want to see what you can do."

It took Roger no more than a few seconds to take control of the graphical display. He simply started breathing consciously and imagining light coming in and out of his head. It was more than imagining the *idea*; it was imagining the *feeling* that went with it. By a combination of breathing and concentration, he learned to alter the moving bars of colour. First, he made the image symmetrical; then he changed it to an hourglass outline. Then he reversed the shape to a bulge in the centre and narrow at the ends. As he breathed and directed his will, the pattern went where he intended but it did not feel like precise control. There was a delay between cause and effect that created a feeling of uncertainty. Nevertheless, he impressed the trainer and the technician.

"I want to see if I can work the sides of the brain independently," Roger said.

"Right, go ahead," Brad agreed, watching the screen closely.

Roger deepened the breath-induced state and then expanded the left side further out than the right. Then he reversed the effect and pushed out the right a bit further.

"I heard that artistic creativity comes from the right side of the brain. Right?"

"So they say."

"Hmm, let's see…"

Roger concentrated again and switched off the left-brain totally and then whacked the right brain signal off the scale.

Brad whistled. "Just like that. That shows you know how to manipulate your brain. Maybe that helps to explain the results you are getting."

Roger nodded.

"If you don't mind, I would like to try myself. I haven't used it for some time," Brad said.

"Of course." Roger stood up and removed the electrodes from his head. Brad sat down so that the technician could wire him up to the computer. Roger perched on the edge of a table a couple of yards away from the instructor. Brad closed his eyes and relaxed. There was movement in the flickering pattern of the screen but there was not the same degree of control.

Roger had an idea. "Let's see if I can alter your consciousness." He began to breathe in the way that stimulated his brain waves and focussed his mind on Brad. It took but a few seconds to take effect. To his own amazement, the instructor's Mind Mirror pattern changed dramatically.

"I'm doing that," he said.

"I know," said Brad quietly. "That's very interesting indeed. I can't tell you what you are doing but I can tell you what you are not doing. You are not affecting my mind or my thoughts."

"No," Roger agreed. "I think I'm just influencing your physiology. Those brain measurements are not the same as thoughts. It's not the same as controlling your brain signals. All I can do is alter their voltage."

"We agree on that," said Brad. "You have already shown a significant tendency to alter subatomic processes with Robert Jahn's psychokinesis test. I think you're ready to go out in the field."

Roger asked, "What field would that be?"

***

Roger phoned his parents for the last time.

"I was so thrilled when you got on to your

postgraduate degree course," said his mother. "I still don't understand why you're giving it up. Why won't you be able to phone us occasionally?"

Roger felt a deep pain inside. He could say very little. "I'm so sorry, Mum. I am going on a long journey. It's sort of secret. I would explain if I could but there are rules. It's difficult. It's overseas in a place where they don't have telephones."

"I don't understand. They've got telephones everywhere these days. Even at the North Pole."

Roger sighed. The North Pole was just around the corner compared with where he was going.

"When will you come home?"

"I don't know. I could be away for a few years. If I can write, I will."

"If you can write! Are you going to another planet?"

Roger laughed weakly. "You could say that."

He would be on the same planet but in a different time. How mad is that?

"I hope you enjoy yourself," she said kindly.

"So do I, Mum, so do I."

"I'm not stupid, Roger. There's more to this than you are telling us."

"I am not allowed to tell you."

"Somebody can hear us."

He paused. "Yes."

"I hope you know what you are doing."

"I would be lying if I said I'm not a bit nervous. I'm also excited. It's an amazing opportunity."

"I love you, son."

"I love you too…"

The line went dead. Somebody had cut them off.

Chapter Ten

"Hurry up. When you go through that door, I want you as naked as the day you were born. As far as this world is concerned you die today. That's it. No modesty in this service. Men and women are all the same in the eyes of the agency." (Somebody called out 'expendable'.) "There must be no smuggling of anomalous hardware on this journey. I've seen it all, cameras, computers, MP3 players, anything starting with 'i' – Pads, Pods, Phones. I think we can leave out iMacs. I can't imagine where you'd put one of those."

It relieved the tension in the room with seven naked people, three of them women and all of them trying not to look at each other overtly. Sergeant Moyes showed as much humanity as he could within the ramrod rules of the Black Ops agency.

Moyes led them down several corridors and into a robing room where they put on clean underwear and overalls. Once dressed, he marshalled them out to a bus with black windows somewhat darker than tinted. They were totally opaque. The only light in the vehicle was artificial. A partition separated the driver from his passengers. Roger hated being shut away from the sun but they were not allowed to know where they were going.

They sat alone at first then gradually they moved towards the rear of the bus where they could fraternise without the luxury of meaningful conversation. Even name, rank and number was *sub judice*. The group had been together long enough for the strictures of security to give way to a modicum of camaraderie, enough for one woman to ask, "Anybody got any cards?"

A tall black guy laughed. "Honey, you seen everything I got. Did I look like I had any cards tucked away?"

"I don't think we are the kind of people you would want to gamble with," said Roger.

There were some chuckles. They all knew what he meant.

"Well, we can't play I spy," said another.

"I wouldn't say that," a woman replied. "I spy with my third eye…"

"How long we gonna be on the road?"

"As long as it takes, I guess."

"Yeah, at a speed measured in years per second."

Roger sat back, closed his eyes and let them get on with their small talk. He dozed off. When he awoke, he wondered what the time was. There were no clocks and nobody had a watch. He saw one of the men approach a woman two seats back from him. He couldn't hear what he said but he recognised the reaction. She stood up and slapped his face. The man was angry. He sneered and said something derogatory. She walked down the aisle past Roger but stopped and looked back.

"Can I sit next to you?"

"Of course," Roger said kindly.

"Thanks. I just want to get away from that jerk."

"I'd let you have the window seat but–"

"You sound different – a bit like a Canadian. Are you some kind of queen?"

Roger laughed. "I don't think so. I'm English."

"No kidding! Where are you from?"
"England."
"Is that near Nova Scotia?"
"A bit further east."
"S'funny. I didn't think there was anything further east than Nova Scotia."
"Yes, I've noticed that a lot of North Americans think that."
"You're not American and yet you speak our language."
"English," he said patiently.
"Yeah, you said."
"We were speaking American long before you were."
"No shit. Ain't that a coincidence?" She sat down beside him.

Roger sighed. After a pause of three or four minutes she said, "You seem nice in a funny sort of way."

"Thank you. You seem nice too."

"In fact, I think I could get to like you. What's your name?"

"Roger."

"I'm Gail. Oh, we were told not to give any details about ourselves. We just failed the first test."

"Never mind. What can they do about it? I wonder where we are and what's outside this bus."

"Desert and mountains in the distance."

"How do you know that?"

"Remote viewing of course."

"You're into that too, then. You can see what's outside."

"Yes, I can. If I had a map, I could dowse where we are. We are all here because we can do something different. That guy's a telepath," she nodded her head to indicate. "One of the best."

Roger glanced over and immediately the man turned around and stared straight back at him with a knowing look and a nod.

Gail said, "He's okay. Better than that other creep."

"Who's the one you don't like?"

She paused for reflection then whispered, "That's 'Blackjack' Crexler."

"Blackjack?"

"Yeah. You'll soon find out why if you play cards with him." Her eyes narrowed. "He wasn't *born* Blackjack. He's got a real name for forms and stuff but I don't know what it is. Do you like gambling?"

The sudden change of subject took Roger by surprise. "Not really. I find cards boring. Gambling's just a way of giving money away."

"Or taking it," Gail said archly. "*He* knows." She nodded in Crexler's direction. "Look, I can't say there's anything wrong with the guy except the way he treats women. I simply don't feel comfortable around him. When he looks at you, it's as if his eyes dig in your soul and your body creeps." She changed topic again. "You're a good remote, so I heard."

"I don't know about that. I'm new to all this." Then a thought struck him. "How come you know so much about me and all these other people? We're supposed to be anonymous."

"Don't kid yourself. They say nature finds a way to survive. Girls will always find a way to gossip and discover any scandal. I'm not psychic for nothing."

Roger absorbed this idea for a while and then asked, "How do you know I'm a good remote viewer?"

She shrugged. "You're here so you must have something going for you. I'm clairvoyant. I see things.

I can see outside of this bus. I don't know what Crexler does but I think he manipulates minds. Know what I mean? *They* use people like that to influence events. They can make a key player change his mind – or stop his heart if he doesn't co-operate."

"Really? They can do that?"

"Oh yeah. There's nothing these black project people can't do. Tesla opened Pandora's Box for them and they've been raiding the cookie jar ever since. They think they're doing good but it doesn't always follow. Ends and means, they say."

"Ends and means?"

She studied at him as if reading his heart.

"You seem like a good guy. I hope I'm right about you."

"Why do you say that?"

"I'm a simple girl. I didn't get a big education but I'm not stupid. I see things. I see things about *you* that would give me nightmares. I don't think they know what they've got. Maybe if your heart's good you won't use it."

Roger was totally stunned.

"Are you saying I could do bad things to people? I hope not. I hope they don't expect it."

"You will be their worst bad dream when you find your key. Just remember their orders aren't optional. I say you should do what's right by your own lights or you will come unstuck. They think the worse thing they can do is kill you but it isn't. You've got to face the darkness for us all. When the time comes, make sure you know which side you're on. The real battle is not against the enemy out there. It's against the enemy inside." Gail tapped him on the chest. "We're babes thrown in the crucible looking for love but we've lost our way. You've got to bring *the light*, Roger. You've just got to."

"You like to mix your metaphors," said Roger. "Pandora's Box, cookie jars, crucibles!"

"Yeah," she agreed. Then after a pause she said, "What's a 'meta for' anyway?"

***

"This will be your room for the duration of your stay. Sorry there's no light from outside. There's plenty of air. You control it from this dial."

"Thank you."

It had all the comfort of a cell. Roger found it disturbing to be under constant guard by men and women with guns. They watched everyone with flat, expressionless eyes. Their side arms were not for decoration. Roger had been warned that they would use them if they saw any breach of security regulations. He wondered how they expected to see a breach of security with a bunch of psychics. The thin young man with the clipboard seemed out of place in the militaristic base.

Roger had nothing to unpack. Everything deemed necessary lay on the bed: a clean jumpsuit, briefs, socks, a towel, soap, a dressing gown and a nightshirt. Roger didn't know people still wore nightshirts.

"There's a meal in fifteen minutes. Please be punctual."

The door shut behind him. Roger's first thought was that they had locked him in but when he tried the door, it opened. He closed it again and took a shower. He dried off and put on the jumpsuit and then went down to get some food. The stairwell was a symphony in steel and concrete. The other diners were his fellow passengers from the journey and around fifteen men and women from the base. Everybody wore a uniform or plain, working overalls. They collected their food from a serving hatch staffed by people dressed like medics. Roger found it difficult to find much variety in the way of vegetarian food. He found it quite depressing.

Gail came over to sit by him and began to whisper. "Isn't it horrible here? It's like organised depression. I can't stand all this stuff about top security and no conversation."

Roger whispered back, "I know. What's security got to do with real life? It's all nonsense." He thought for a moment then asked, "Gail, what's your surname?" In the circumstances, there was little else to talk about without bending the draconian rules a little. He was beginning to forget the ban on conversing.

She weighed up the odds of him cracking a joke at her expense before answering.

"It's Hershey."

"Oh, thanks, Gail Hershey."

"You didn't joke about chocolate. You've just gone up in my estimation."

"We don't have that where I come from. It must be irritating to hear the same joke day in day out."

"It's the curse of the Hersheys."

"And probably the Cadburys' too," Roger said.

She shook her head. "It's no joke when people look at you and all they see is chocolate."

They chatted for a while. Then she tapped his plate with her fork.

"Have you got the box yet?"

"What box?"

"Somebody is going to give you a package. I don't know who it's from but it will be someone close to you." She paused and said, "Don't ask me what it means but he hasn't even been born yet."

"How do you know this?"

Gail considered her reply before answering. "I just do. I know things. Always have. That's why they recruited me. I now know that I really came along to meet you. How stupid is that?"

"Me! Did you know my name or did you expect somebody like me?"

"No. I didn't know your name. It doesn't work like that. I knew I would meet somebody and that there would be a sort of inner recognition. So can you see how essential it was that Crexler played the Casanova pitch? If he hadn't upset me, I wouldn't have spoken to you. It was pure instinct. All we need to know now is why."

Roger did not reply. He was lost for words.

***

The thin young man with the clipboard knocked on Roger's door with a metal box about the size of a book.

"This came through a space-time portal. Sign here, please."

So the clipboard had a use.

Roger closed the door and opened the box. He peered inside, curious to see what it contained. There was a small, brown glass bottle labelled 'travel sickness' and a device that seemed to be some sort of electronic circuit. It was labelled 'Harper and Plipstow Z45G64 AI Modal Emulator & Power Supply' and had rows of holes along one side that looked like connection sockets. There was one other item, a scrap of paper bearing a hastily scribbled note in his own handwriting, '*Roger, You'll know when to use this. It should solve a problem I had to deal with. I hope this doesn't change the timeline drastically. Don't lose it, cheers. Yourself (a bit older and wiser).*'

Roger gazed at his legacy from the future and wondered what they were for. Travel sickness pills? A circuit? Limited experience taught him that the Black Projects Agency controlled everything. Why had they allowed this communication?

He put the items where he would remember them.

***

There were ten people in the lobby waiting to climb a steel-lined shaft around eight feet in diameter. Roger, typically, brought up the rear. He gripped the lower rungs and stepped up, pausing for a moment to gaze upwards. People in jumpsuits climbed the metallic duct ahead of him. They passed lamps set in the tunnel wall, casting moving shadows that danced around them like dark demons. Roger emerged into a vast vaulted chamber, cavernous and dark with a raised dais in the centre surmounted by two flying saucers. It could have been a hollowed mountain for all he knew. Lights in the ceiling shone down on the two gleaming, circular, metallic vehicles. Roger stumbled as he gazed in awe at these objects of mythology and rumour. A Space Command officer directed him to climb the steps in the side of one of the vehicles. He entered the inside of the ship and saw his fellow passengers sitting down on small seats that folded from recesses in the walls.

There were no windows. They were five in all, Roger and a second man and three women. A voice called out to him.

"Over here, Rog."

Roger sat next to Gail, pleased to see a friendly face. The clothes they had given them were quite unflattering but Gail still managed to look chic in her outfit.

Three crew officers were making preparations in the ship. Roger was becoming uncomfortable and a little hostile towards the whole black project scene. It was apparent to him that it was the system, rather than the people, who set the tone. The entire organisation was rigid with security and threats of reprisal to anybody who betrayed secrets. Since there seemed to be nothing about the system that wasn't secret, no matter how trivial, it would not be difficult to get yourself shot. The system perpetuated control through fear from the top to the bottom. The agency was structured on 'need-to-know' cells or pods. There were super pods and overlapping pods, each one known only to the people who were in them or had a role in a superior supervisory pod. The system avoided anybody having total knowledge of any particular aspect of the work. People only saw fragments. This minimised the consequences of unauthorised disclosure – especially from whistleblowers, spies or hackers. Roger was already regretting his involvement but there was no way out. This was a one-way ticket into a secret community and apparently death was the only viable exit.

The five passengers sat upright and strapped themselves into their seats. A man and a woman sat in special elevated chairs on one side of the central structure. They put on closed helmets linked by cables hanging down from the ceiling. Roger took them to be the pilot and co-pilot but he didn't know for sure. A third man with a holstered pistol sat behind them. Roger presumed his role was to watch the passengers while the pilots were totally absorbed in their apparatus. He heard a soft humming and felt a sense of motion that signalled takeoff. After the first couple of minutes all sense of inertia vanished. He felt no movement whatsoever. The passengers could see nothing of their location and the external environment. It could have been day or night above the underground base.

Gail reached out and gave his hand a squeeze, whether to reassure him or herself, Roger was not sure. Their fellow passengers talked to each other in soft voices. Roger and Gail were silent. The whole experience was awesome as an idea but the reality was quite mundane. They waited for something to happen. Roger wondered how they would get from the underground chamber to the outside. There was a vague sense of movement at first but it was impossible to know how fast they were travelling or where they were. After ten minutes or so, Roger heard a dull throbbing sound and all sense of motion ceased. He assumed they were somewhere in space beyond the confines of the atmosphere. The fact that he couldn't see outside, coupled with the lack of motion, detracted from any sense of adventure. Even Gail, who had 'seen' psychically outside a bus, was not aware of their location. He did not feel weightless. He might as well be sitting in an office.

It was around an hour before anything indicated a change in the pattern of events.

"I need the john," said Gail. "Did anybody mention where it is?"

A woman passenger said, "I think there's a lower deck. Probably down that ladder over there."

"Yeah," said the man on her left. "Hurry up though. We make the transition soon. I know the signs."

Roger wondered what 'the transition' was and what signs he could possibly detect when nothing at all was happening.

Gail unstrapped her belt and stood up. The guard watched her go without interest. A warning tone alerted the pilots to the fact that somebody was moving about. The woman lifted the viewer flap in front of her face and watched Gail leave.

She returned in a state of excitement and leaned close to Roger while preparing to sit down and strap herself in.

"There's a round window down there. We're right away from the earth," she whispered, looking around the cabin before continuing. "We're surrounded by glowing balls and a thing like a huge, luminous sausage!"

Gail sat down but had spoken too loudly to go unnoticed. The man next to her said aloud, "What's going on out there, Frank?"

"We got company is all," said one of the pilots from beneath his visor. "I guess they know something we don't."

Roger looked blank. Gail stared back with suppressed excitement.

"Where's Spansky's bird? Are they with us?"

"No, they've jumped. This is our reception, for sure."

Gail turned to Roger and mouthed, "It's you."

Roger was puzzled. "What's me?"

"I don't know," she said.

Roger could make nothing of her train of thought or the nature of the objects outside the spacecraft. The pilot warned them to sit tight and put on ear protectors to counteract the high-pitched whine of the electrogravitic drive while traversing time. There was still no sense of motion. However, there was a peculiar nerve-tingling sensation that affected the entire being. It was extremely uncomfortable. Roger's head began to throb and he felt nauseous almost immediately. Gail took off her ear protectors and indicated to Roger to do the same. She had noticed that the more seasoned travellers had not bothered to put them on. She whispered, "The planets have speeded up and they are travelling backwards. We are going around the sun beyond the orbit of Jupiter."

"What about those orb things? Have we left them behind?"

"Not all of them; there are about twenty-five glowing spheres following us."

"What the hell are they?"

"I'm not sure but I think they're alive."

The man next to Gail heard their conversation in spite of their whispering.

"They are what we could become if we survive and evolve to an advanced level of sentience. Life starts on planets but it doesn't stay there. Who knows what dimension, star system or galaxy they came from? Once you get off-world you can move at will through space and time to any place in any period."

This information amazed Roger for what it signified and for the matter-of-fact detachment with which the man had said it.

Gail nodded to Roger with an expression that said, "I told you so." She wasn't surprised by what the officer said but by the fact that he said it at all given their security regime.

The co-pilot raised his visor and joined in the conversation. "You will get used to them. They often turn up like dolphins around a ship. They are extremely curious about our activities, especially strategic orbital platforms and nuclear weapons. They think human beings are insane. Maybe they're right." He pulled the face screen back down.

These developments took Roger's mind off the discomfort of time travel. Once the conversation was over, he gave himself up to the pain. He felt queasy and wanted to vomit. He remembered the technique of breathing he had discovered and began to use it to alter his consciousness. It made him feel worse. Then he recalled the 'travel sickness' pills that had arrived in the box. He had tucked them in a pocket in the suit he was wearing. Reaching in carefully to avoid attracting attention he found the pills and opened the lid. There were no instructions so he took out three and put them in his mouth. In about ten minutes he felt much better. He nudged Gail and offered them to her. She too was feeling sick and clutched at them hopefully. She soon felt better also.

Roger returned to the breathing exercise and found it much more beneficial since taking the remedy. His immediate surroundings began to seem distant although they were unchanged physically. It was as if his mind was withdrawing from the environment of the vehicle. He felt totally alone and separate from everything around him. Now he was 'seeing' the view outside the spaceship. There was the distant sun, the globular balls of light and a fat, worm-shaped object rather like a long balloon but much larger. The focus of his being shifted and he found himself actually located outside the ship in space, looking at these glowing objects moving towards him from all sides. It was as if he was both inside the flying saucer and simultaneously in space. He was not seeing the creatures with his eyes – they were inside the disc with his body. He was seeing directly with his consciousness in the manner of a dream but where waking dreams were instantaneous and fragmentary, this had continuity and heightened reality.

The glowing objects became aware of Roger's 'pseudo-presence' in their vicinity. They gathered around him in a regular formation, a closing circle in the ecliptic plane of the solar system. His vision shifted. The bright light they radiated dimmed. He saw them as translucent spheroids containing layers of curved light and shadow. They were reminiscent of computer-generated fractals he had seen. Inside each ball of light he could identify the shape of a humanoid being, glowing faintly but otherwise distinct. The worm-like creatures contained the outline of a long, scaled lizard or dinosaur.

"There's a ghost-like sphere that's just appeared from nowhere," said Gail, looking curiously at Roger as if she sensed that he was somehow involved in what was happening. "Is that you?"

"Who's this?" asked a voice in his head. It was for him a novel experience. His telepathic communication had always been symbolic rather than audible.

"We've got an intruder online," said the female pilot's voice in his mind. "It must be one of the passengers."

"Hershey?"

"No, it's Crandle. How are you doing that?"

With shock, Roger understood that somehow he had linked into the system that the pilots used to control the vessel.

"I don't know. It just happened," said Roger in his mind.

It was the male pilot. "So you can see the alien orbs too?"

"Yes. I'm out here with them at the same time as I'm in there with you."

"They are moving through time with us," the pilot said.

Roger became aware of lines of light radiating out in all directions from a centre deep within his consciousness. They comprised beams of white light, faintly tinged with red, orange yellow, blue and green, in random order. He sensed that these lines described the total pattern of existence for him as an individual. Awareness penetrated his mind revealing the notion that every object, every entity in the universe was connected by these lines to things, places, people, systems and thoughts. Each physical 'thing' was a focus of radiating lines that connected to concepts and thoughts in the greater universe. His entire version of the space-time continuum was no more than a single particle in an infinite set of such particles. In a universe of parts, each part was a version of the whole and the whole had no separate existence from the parts. The glowing entities that surrounded him 'belonged' in some way to the idea that gave him existence. He discovered there and then that he was as important to the orbs as they were to him. They were there to save him from something. What that something was he did not know. The message being delivered, the vision began to fade.

"Crandle. What's going on? Are they telling you something?"

The question brought his mind to focus. He was 'back' in the flying saucer, strapped in his seat next to Gail.

"Yeah, I suppose so," Roger answered in his mind, "but don't expect me to explain it."

"I'll have to report this. There might be an enquiry. This is unauthorised concourse between an unlicensed operative and undifferentiated externals…"

Roger ignored the pilot's commentary. He wondered why these beings were taking the trouble to make contact. Suddenly it hit him quite forcefully: *they are here to protect me!*

"What the hell!"

The flying saucer began to shake and judder. The strange fuzziness of time travel sharpened to a definite sense of presence, of *now*. The sound inside the cabin changed. He did not need telling that they had moved out of temporal shift into conventional space drive. The orbs close to the flying saucer and others floating around in the distance vanished. How fast the vessel was moving was impossible to say. There was no sense of motion and the artificial gravity in the ship returned to stability. Only the great worm remained with them now.

"Spaceships…!"

Roger 'saw' them too with his mental powers amplified by the craft's control system. Six spacecraft glowing with light streaked into view. The lights dimmed and went out, leaving a group of dark, metallic flying saucers different in design to the one they were in.

"Bad aliens?" he asked.

"No, it's worse than that. These are Nazi *foo fighters* left over from the Second World War. They come from a base in the Antarctic. We've been intercepted, which means they knew we were coming."

"Do you mean Hitler's people?" asked Roger.

"Yes. Lots of Nazis escaped there and to South America after the war. We first learned about these when they attacked Admiral Byrd's Task Force 68 in 1946."

One of the spacecraft fired a weapon of some sort but the worm intervened and deflected the energy away into the darkness. Then five of the original orbs popped back into their space and resumed their stations around their flying saucer. The foo fighters withdrew a short distance. It was stalemate.

The pilot shook his head. "Something must have pulled us out of temporal transit. I can't believe it was those Nazi ships. We don't have that sort of capability on earth. We can usually outmanoeuvre that old design."

The co-pilot agreed. Although Roger heard every word that passed between them, he had no opinion on a matter totally beyond his comprehension.

By extending his remote viewing ability through the saucer's detectors, Roger located something moving towards them. His first impression was of a patch of darkness against the stars beyond. Whatever it was, it emitted no light of its own. It seemed to be the antithesis of the orbs, black as midnight where they emitted brilliant light of various colours. As it drew near, he noticed a partial reflection of the stars of the Milky Way in its obsidian surface. Its size was hard to estimate but Roger decided it was smaller than their vessel.

"Look below," Roger said to the pilots. "Do you see it?"

"Oh shit, yeah. What is it?"

"Nothing I know about," the woman pilot said.

"I don't know what it is but I think it's called a *black Merkabah,* a dark orb," Roger told them, passing on the information that had entered his mind.

The ring of orbs responded immediately. As one, they rotated their plane of formation around the flying saucer to block its approach. The object moved away and then darted rapidly in different directions, stopping, retreating and encroaching. It accomplished its manoeuvres with apparent instantaneous bursts of speed. The orbs closed around the flying saucer and began an elaborate series of rotational movements harmonised in a complex pattern. The large worm separated from the group and started to move around in a trajectory of its own choosing.

As he watched the orbital ballet, Roger's openness to the minds of his protectors allowed something to happen inside the spaceship. His body tingled, gently at first, and then with increasing intensity. A blue glow emanated from the air near the surface of his suit. A halo of electrical discharge surrounded him, interwoven with tiny bolts of lightning.

"Something's happening to Crandle," a passenger called out.

"We know," said the pilot.

The co-pilot lifted her head from the display unit and looked round. "I think there are currents of electricity going from him into the central control column."

"They're using him," explained the male pilot, unsure of what was happening and why or which side to root for.

"What are they using him for?"

"Ask them," said the female pilot dryly.

The sound of the time-drive resumed and the sun began to look fuzzy again. Something flew out of the black orb. Whatever it was, it was too small to see directly. Roger's inner mind-vision detected the spatial distortion that surrounded it as it travelled like a ploughed furrow, seeming to suck the image of the stars towards it. *Like a black hole*, he thought. Their own spacecraft creaked and groaned, seemingly drawn in the direction of the tiny object. It accelerated towards them but the great worm anticipated the attack, darting between the object and the saucer. The last thing Roger saw as they moved into a different time was an image of the dinosaur-like entity imploding into nonexistence. What had happened to the glowing worm? Was it dead or alive somewhere else? Had it deliberately sacrificed itself to save them? The *foo fighters* and the black orb were gone, left in future time.

Nothing made sense to Roger. Had the dark object pulled them out of time travel? If so, why? Why had these creatures of light saved their ship from destruction? Was *he* the target? How had they known in advance it would happen? The biggest question was his response, his bilocation and the experience of expanded consciousness. What had happened to him and why?

Their flying saucer had shifted back in time, away from the scene of conflict. The entire incident had altered him in some way. It was as if a temporal dimension had opened up in his consciousness and then faded away again. But it was not gone, only lying dormant.

Something had changed fundamentally within him in the way his mind worked and in his physiology. During the incident, the alien creatures had controlled the flying saucer through Roger and the electrical fields emanating from his body. The pilot and co-pilot had remained hands off. With Roger released, the pilots got their ship back. Now, with full control restored, they directed the ship through time by means of a mental psychotronic link in their helmets and through space by hand grips.

Gail had wanted to reach out and touch Roger to see if he was all right but she had not dared to with the electricity sparking and crackling around him. When it faded, and he was his normal self again, she grabbed his arm and leaned over. "I saw all of it. I could hardly believe what happened. Are you okay?"

He nodded. "Uh huh. I don't really understand any of that. It was weird."

"That black thing – what could it be? Did you feel the power and menace coming from it?" she asked, her voice hissing with excitement.

"I did. That black orb was never from our world. I wonder what it was?"

"I don't know but I think it knows about you. I wonder how?" Gail mused thoughtfully.

Roger paused to consider the events of the strange journey.

"Gail, that worm thing. The black orb destroyed it! I felt it. I saw it. I sensed that it died to defend me. Why? How do all these creatures know me? I am nobody."

"That's a good question, young man," said the Space Command Major next to Gail. "There will be people who want to know. You can expect an interrogation when we hit the base."

"But I don't know anything."

"You both know more than I do. I've seen and heard nothing except what you two and the pilots said. There will be some kind of recording from the system. This has never happened before to my knowledge."

Roger looked at Gail. "Oh dear, I don't like this. Something tells me I've got an enemy. How can that be?"

Gail laughed ironically. "You'll get used to it, which is more than I can say for time travel. I feel terrible. Those pills you gave me helped but only a bit. By the way, what you just did – sent your mind outside the saucer somehow…"

"Yes. That about describes it."

She nodded. "One day you'll need to do that again to find a missing spaceship."

"I don't understand…"

"Neither do I. Just remember that I told you."

***

"Welcome to 1973."

It occurred to Roger that he hadn't even been born yet.

They disembarked inside the same underground base that they had started from. They went straight into the temporal reception area to complete anomalous incident report forms and be medically checked. The pilots were affected by the encounter but not as badly as the passengers. Time travel was unsettling enough but being interrupted *en route* made it marginally worse. Out of all the passengers, only Roger felt better than he had when he left 2000. His recent adventure had transformed him but quite how, he was yet to discover. An hour later, Roger was in the same room he slept in the previous night except that the previous night would not happen for another twenty-seven years. It was even the same furniture; only the carpet and paint on the walls was different.

"Wow! I feel great!" he said out loud to nobody in particular before getting into bed and turning out the light.

***

The training in remote viewing resumed. Roger found himself improving rapidly. The targets continued to be locations, physical objects and, sometimes, people. Then one day the pattern changed; they gave him a long-term exclusive target. The teacher that strode in that day was an older man, grey-haired and wearing a suit. There was a noticeable formality in classrooms that was unfamiliar to somebody of his generation. Teachers from this time were more noticeably aloof from their students. This one was particularly abrupt and distant. After a while, Roger realised that the man was a product of his time. Thirty years were to make a difference in peoples' attitudes. The teacher's long-fingered hands tugged open the flap of package and extracted a wad of envelopes. One of them had Roger's name typed on a label on the front. Roger knew this was typed and not printed as word processing was in its infancy at this time. With intense curiosity, he accepted his missive from Mr Frizzle.

"This is a big day for you all. At long last, after all

those exercises and statistical assessments, we have sorted out your permanent targets for the operational training phase. Please open your envelopes and study the information provided."

Roger looked at the black and white photograph enclosed with the typed sheets. He thought her very attractive. Gail came over and leaned over his shoulder.

"I like the look of yours," she said. "I wish I could say the same for mine. He looks like Dracula's uncle."

"Miss Hershey! Mr Crandle! Please take this exercise seriously!" The reprimand stung Roger as he didn't think he had done anything other than take it seriously.

Gail squeezed Roger's shoulder meaningfully and returned to her desk. She regarded Roger with displeasure as he gazed at his target with rapt attention. Roger was unconscious of anything other than the girl in the picture. After a while, he turned to say something to Gail and noticed that she was concentrating on her subject with a casehardened frown of disapproval. Roger smiled and reverted to his task. It was certainly no hardship. As before, he emptied his consciousness of all but this unfamiliar face.

Eventually, Roger found himself seeing 'through' the image to the real person. She looked at him and he saw her smile. It was a garden in one of the hot and dusty states out West – Arizona perhaps. The border between the sprinkled green grass and the red sandstone ground beyond was a neat wooden fence. The lawn was on one side with sparsely populated succulents the other. An American flag on a tall, white-painted pole touched his mind fleetingly but it was not in the garden. She was wearing jeans and a white top. When the communication started, it was more powerful than anything he had ever experienced before. Getting her name was tricky but in the end he settled on 'Deborah'. She was residing in Flagstaff and would remain there for a further three weeks. Roger wrote this in his report along with details about the residence and the landscape beyond the perimeter. He sensed that the house belonged to other people. For the purpose of this exercise, she was staying with friends. He made notes about all this and a great deal more besides. Afterwards, the instructor read it through and nodded.

"You know I will have to verify this with the target. This is more than she was required to communicate. I need to know whether you acquired it from her or from the locale. We call it collateral inference."

"That doesn't surprise me at all," Roger declared. "It was almost like being there with her."

The instructor almost smiled but not quite. "I think you'll make a good team."

"When do I get to meet her?"

"Never, that's the rule. No personal contact. It gets in the way of conceptual objectivity during information transfer."

Roger looked at the photograph with regret. "Oh well, if that's how it is."

"That's definitely how it is. We have found that to be the best policy. You and she need to be able to exchange information without being sidetracked by personal knowledge of each other. Always remember, Mr Crandle, that yours will be a professional relationship. That is essential."

"Is that what all this training has been for? For me

to communicate with this woman?"

"That is correct. You are going on a journey and you and she will be the contact between the team and the base."

"A journey? Where am I going?"

"I regret that I am unable tell you. I do not need to know."

***

Roger sat in his room and pondered a world of cathode ray tubes and valves in televisions. Radio sets had discrete transistors and the only person he saw with anything resembling a cell phone was Captain James T Kirk of the Starship Enterprise on *Star Trek* repeats. There were no laptops, none of the familiar toys that he had become accustomed to around the turn of the millennium. He was concentrating quite hard on not thinking about Deborah. Their telepathic exercises were getting more complex and taxing. The instructors expected more and more of them. It felt to him that he was entering a phantom relationship with somebody that he could not talk to or see. He called it 'the intimate divide'. At times it seemed as if they were breathing for each other. He was also aware that she lived a life without him and she very effectively excluded him from it. A giant shutter seemed to fall like a portcullis on an invading army. He warned himself not to get crushed.

A tap at the door broke his reverie.

Roger peered out into the corridor and found Gail Hershey.

"Quick – let me in."

She pushed him aside and rushed into his room.

"What's the matter? Is somebody after you?"

"Yeah, sort of. This isn't 2000. They don't approve of women in this age, especially women who visit single men in their rooms."

Roger grinned. "That's true enough. What can I do for you?"

Gail looked at him with hands planted firmly on her hips and demanded, "Do friends need a reason to visit?"

Roger immediately felt guilty. "That's true. I'm sorry. Here – give me a hug."

"That's better." She held him gratefully and said, "I just wish you meant it."

"Of course I mean it."

"Really, then why are you sitting in the dark mooning about that target?"

Roger blushed a deep red. "Ah, er…"

"You're not as psychic as I am," she said. "Well, not about some things. I'm a woman."

"The fact had not escaped me."

"'The fact had not escaped me'," she mimicked. "You can be such a Limey sometimes."

"Let's sit down," Roger suggested.

There were two upright chairs with wooden arms and a coffee table. The whole place reminded Roger of a student residence. "Can I make you a coffee?"

"Yeah, why not?"

Roger filled the kettle from the tap in the kitchen, except that here it was called a faucet.

"I've got a problem," Gail said at last.

Roger smiled and refrained from commenting on her recent statement about not needing a reason to visit a friend.

"Blackjack Crexler," he said.

"How did you know that?"

"I don't claim to be psychic like you. Let's just call it men's intuition."

She snorted. "Huh, the point is, he keeps following me and asking me to go with him."

"Anywhere in particular?"

"He doesn't really care as long as it involves screwing."

"What happens if you say no?"

"It's not what he wants to do to my body that worries me – well, not unless he tries to do it! It's what he does with my mind. He's a creep but a powerful one."

"Do they let him use powers in that way? Isn't that unethical?"

Gail snorted. "You haven't figured this place yet, have you?"

"It seems okay. What do you mean?"

"Roger, you're so innocent and trusting! Look how you've fallen in love with a photograph. She could be the devil's spawn and you'd never know it."

"No, it's not like that. I have grown close to her doing all these exercises. You must have got close to your target…"

Gail jumped up from the chair and bit her lip. "No, I haven't. *He's* here."

"Who's here? Your target?"

"Have you heard nothing I've said?"

A staccato rapping sound made Roger jump. Gail was not surprised, just frightened. Roger stood up and walked to the door and opened it. Blackjack Crexler stood outside, looking past him into the room.

"Mr Crandle, are you aware of the rules about immoral behaviour? I believe you have a woman in here."

"Yes, and none of your business."

"Just remember that you are in 1973. The immorality you are used to in the next millennium doesn't apply here."

"Drinking coffee is hardly immoral."

Crexler smiled. "Have it your own way."

Gail screamed. Roger slammed the door shut and ran back to find her lying on her back on the floor. He knelt down beside her and touched her neck. She had a pulse but was clearly unconscious. He ran back to the door and opened it. Crexler was still outside, grinning insolently. "Has something happened to Miss Hershey?"

"What have you done?"

"I didn't lay a finger on her. You can testify to that."

Roger snorted in disgust. "You're playing games. You know as well as I do, you can hurt people without touching them."

"So you know about induced fugue? That's fine. Just don't try going against me. You'll lose."

Roger activated the core of his brain and began to probe Crexler's mind. Crexler laughed; his eyes flickered and suddenly Roger's brain exploded, or so it felt, and he too collapsed unconscious.

Chapter Eleven

"Crandle, are you awake?"

Roger groaned and opened his eyes. He was lying in a hospital bed. There were five other patients in the ward, as well as a nurse and a doctor. The question came from a Black Ops agent with a reel-to-reel tape recorder in his hand. Roger stared at it in fascination. It was a living antique to his eyes. He almost expected it to emit smoke from self-destructing reels of tape like the ones in reruns of the original *Mission Impossible* series.

The agent looked down at the gadget. "You ain't used to these?"

"Not that old."

"This ain't old. It's almost brand new. Look, stick to the point. I'm Agent Kravitz. I want you to explain what happened in your room three days ago."

"Three days! What's happened to Gail? Is she okay? That creep–"

"Miss Hershey is in a coma. We don't know if she will live. I want you to tell me what happened."

Roger wanted to find out more about Gail but told his story as requested, briefly and concisely. When he was through, the agent turned off the recorder and considered him for a while before speaking.

"You had a lucky escape. Not many survive such an incident as easily as you seem to have. I recommend you don't go up against Crexler again."

"Can't you stop him bullying women?"

"There are reasons why we don't rein him in. The man has a few bad habits but our masters choose to live with them. His potential as a remote assassin makes him more useful than Miss Hershey. I suggest you forget this and move on."

"I'm happy to. Just assure me that he will leave Gail alone – if she lives."

"I don't have the authorisation to do that. You gotta leave it. Apparently our masters put some value on your hide too."

Roger looked at the agent and shook his head. "How can I stand by and let my friend be attacked?"

Agent Kravitz was plainly irritated by his intransigence. As far as he was concerned, Gail Hershey was expendable. Roger was not. He didn't make the orders. It was the committee. Crexler's gift was needed to give key enemy targets an apparent stroke or heart attack. At this rate he would wipe out the mind of the new prize telepath from England. Hershey had her uses. She was good at predicting things. They had other clairvoyants and they had time travel, for God's sake, but it helped if you could check out alternative futures. Sometimes, the timelines divided or took unexpected detours. But there were not many covert assassins as good as Crexler.

"Mr Crandle, it occurs to me that you need to meet one of our senior advisors in the line of remote viewing and suchlike. Do you have a suitable gap in your schedule on Thursday? I believe you have a free afternoon."

"Yes, I do."

"You'll need it. The company of certain individuals does much in a short time, if you get my meaning."

"I'm not sure I do, Agent Kravitz."

Kravitz laughed. "You will. Yes. You will."

Roger shivered. "You sound like Yoda."

"Who's Yoda?"

***

Roger waited for over an hour after the midday meal for Agent Kravitz to appear. He had visited Gail in hospital and found her still in a coma. His thoughts divided between Gail, Deborah and the purpose of the impending meeting. Just as he was thinking that it wouldn't happen, the agent appeared in his customary black suit and dark glasses.

"Ready?"

"Yes."

Kravitz made no apology for being late and Roger knew better than to expect one. "This way then."

Roger followed him down stairs, along corridors and, finally, to a small elevator in a remote corner of the base. He had almost forgotten what it was like to be in daylight.

Kravitz pressed a button and waited. Roger was by now accustomed to the primitive technology he saw around him, the lack of liquid crystal or light emitting displays and touch-sensitive screens. This world was built on clunky contact switches. The door opened and Kravitz entered the chamber within.

Roger followed and gazed around the cage-like structure.

"Funny looking lift. Where does it go?"

"Lift? What's a lift?"

"This is a lift – elevator – isn't it? A thing that goes up and down."

"Yeah, it does that all right but from here it only goes down. Where else would it go? There's no up – just a mountain."

The doors closed and the elevator began its descent. It might have looked old but its speed and smoothness was greater than Roger anticipated; new technology dressed in old buttons.

Kravitz leaned his arm on the wall and Roger noticed the gun in a holster under his jacket. He had not been in America long enough to get used to the ubiquitous presence of firearms. It felt as if the lift traversed thousands of feet in a few minutes, making little noise in the process.

The elevator stopped and the door slid aside to reveal a large chamber like the set of a vintage James Bond film – except that in his current time they were new, rather than vintage. There were smart girls with big spectacles and pinned up hair walking around in white nylon coats. The men wore blue overalls with round matching hats. A gigantic computer filled the room with large, grey, metallic cabinets and whirling tape drives. Rows of lights flashed on and off. Roger half expected a hundred men in black fatigues with machine guns to abseil down from the ceiling. He assumed that the power of the machine was probably equivalent to the average desktop PC in 2000. He was not aware that black project technology was always ahead of its commercial rivals by twenty or thirty years, a difference that was growing exponentially with each passing decade.

Agent Kravitz led Roger down a pathway that ran between the cabinets belonging to the computer to a room at the back. He spoke to a short man in a black suit and black-framed glasses. The man nodded and picked up the handset of a telephone on the wall. He put his finger in the dial and twirled four digits. After a brief conversation, he replaced the handset on the cradle. He turned to Kravitz and nodded.

"Mr Crandle, please co-operate with the anti-contamination squad."

"The who?"

A team in white coats came out of a side door and ushered Roger to a medical facility. For twenty minutes they took blood samples, swabs in his mouth, asked questions about his medical history and probed his psychological profile. They also waved metres around his head and photographed him with thermal imaging and other technical oddities.

"What's all this for?" Roger asked.

"You can't meet a senior advisor without precautions against infection."

"He's quite important then. Might I catch something from him?"

"No, we're protecting him from you."

"Is it Edward Teller?" Roger asked jokingly.

"No, Teller's office is on the third level."

They encased Roger in something like a white, plastic diving suit with a fully enclosed helmet. The voices outside sounded muffled.

"When you're with him, try to keep your mind focussed on a peaceful memory. Don't let go of your attention – it's like being sucked down a whirlpool. Keep it brief and don't try anything clever."

"Clever?" His voice echoed loudly inside the helmet.

Roger couldn't quite take in what they were saying. He was beginning to feel apprehensive. "Okay," he said doubtfully. He allowed himself to be guided down a corridor to another elevator. A man and a woman waited for him. Neither wore protective clothing. This afforded him some comfort.

They descended to a far greater depth than the last time he rode in the lift. Roger wondered if they would ever reach the bottom. He raked his memories for a thought to hold on to as instructed. He breathed deeply to activate the part of his brain that served him during remote viewing and telepathy. When, finally, the elevator slowed and stopped, shaking slightly, he felt coldness in the air that made him shiver.

The door opened to reveal a dim stone corridor with circular lamps in the ceiling. Their shadows rotated around them as they walked, extending and fading as they passed each light.

Roger felt an overpowering sense of depth that gave a suggestion of the unimaginable tonnes of solid rock above them. They walked for about twenty minutes until they arrived at a series of intersecting tunnels, some well-illuminated, others quite dark. His companions led Roger down one of the brightest corridors. At a nearby intersection, they stopped outside a solid-looking double door with large, ornate handles. The man and the woman stood either side of the entrance and pulled back the doors so that Roger could enter. He paused at the threshold, looked round at them questioningly, then steeled himself to walk through. The heavy doors clanged shut behind him. Whatever lay ahead, it wasn't merely an interview with a senior advisor. Not even Henry Kissinger rated this kind of rigmarole and security. He couldn't decide whether the heavy doors were designed to keep people out or keep something in. The notion disturbed him.

He found himself in a small room with cupboards, a

table and two wooden chairs. There was another, more normal looking, door on the far side of the enclosure. It occurred to him then that this was a meeting place between two separate domains within the base. Should he wait where he was or go through to whatever lay beyond? He had no instructions. Fear of the unknown took precedence over curiosity. He decided to wait.

A couple of minutes later, the door opened and he beheld a strange sight. A tall male being entered who resembled a giant from a children's story. Bare arms and shoulders bulged from a leather-like jerkin. He reminded Roger of a woodcutter in a Grimm fairy tale. The neck of the jerkin was open to the waist, revealing a muscular chest. He seemed human-like but his skin was a grey-white colour like somebody who had never been in sunlight. He was bearded and had long, dark hair and his nose was quite large in comparison with his features. The being appeared to be attired in fur leggings but Roger noticed with surprise that they were his legs. He wore a pair of dark, leathery shorts. Instead of feet he had cloven hooves. Roger thought immediately of the front half of a centaur. The being's most striking attribute was his height, which was around eight feet.

He peered down at Roger and grunted – a sound that definitely wasn't human. He carried something reminiscent of a child's doll that he placed on the table before him. With a shock, Roger realised that it wasn't a toy. It was a living being. It was humanoid in outline and reminded Roger of a small elf. The being had a tiny head, barely visible under a deep blue, conical hat with stars in its depths. Likewise, there were stars in the blue cloak it wore. Both items of clothing had the appearance of holograms embedded in material. Its appearance merited the description miniature wizard.

The tall being pulled out the chair that was on his side of the table. Rather gingerly, he sat on it. He looked uncomfortable, perched on the edge like an adult sitting on furniture made for a child. Roger was unsure of what to do so he too sat down at the table. He didn't know which one to attend so he glanced from one to the other.

Then Roger knew without knowing how that the tiny alien was in charge. The big one was simply a taxi; a set of borrowed legs. A creeping chill went through his mind and body, a feeling of absolute coldness that was more mental than physical. He began to drift into oblivion. He was by now almost unable to think complete thoughts. It was like being immersed in a bath of icy consciousness. Even his breathing began to rasp in his lungs. Waves of dizziness surged through his brain.

The small being turned and nodded to his large companion who stood up and walked behind Roger and steadied him in an upright posture on his chair.

Fight it.

The thought entered his mind like a bullet.

"How?" he said out loud.

The giant pressed large fingers into the sides of Roger's head near the temples. Almost immediately Roger's consciousness returned to awareness. The room seemed to fold and bend around him but it was an illusion, for nothing changed. It was his perception of reality that was shifting.

Breathe slowly and focus on a pleasing memory.

Roger obeyed this telepathic instruction. He recalled a visit to the Serpentine, a lake in London's Hyde Park, during his childhood in the company of his sister and their parents. Relief swept over him. Pain and coldness eased while he maintained dissociation from the situation.

Empty primary consciousness and activate infinite superconsciousness.

The extraterrestrial did not communicate in words so much as in flashes of raw meaning so powerful as to be unmistakable. It made his exchanges with Deborah seem quite obscure and shallow.

Thinking is a process akin to precipitation. As water droplets become rain, so ideas become thoughts, unmanifest to manifest, formless to form.

"What are you doing to me? You are hurting my head."

I do nothing to you. Your kind suffers in my presence – some more than others. I am of collective mind. Through me, your finite consciousness touches infinite mind and struggles to retain individuality.

The giant removed the pressure from Roger's temples and returned to the seat behind his charge. Roger continued to recall the day in London while trying to follow the train of thought emerging from the small entity. "What can I do? I can barely stay conscious."

Then do not; let go. Join with me. Forget past memory; be present. That will be sufficient. Give me permission to remove you from this dimension.

"Okay. I agree." The feelings of sublime joy that followed were more than Roger could resist. He surrendered, leaving the world and its cares behind.

***

Roger slept gloriously. There were strange dreams. He

met people. He met non-people too. Quite what they were, he could not say. He awoke, yawned and stretched contentedly. He opened his eyes and realised that he was not in his room. He had no idea where he was. He sat up and found himself in the base medical centre. It had six beds but only two were occupied: his own and another opposite. He looked across and saw that the other bed contained Gail. Roger had a tube attached to his arm, feeding his bloodstream from a bottle on a hanger. This contraption hampered movement so he could only look across at Gail, seeking any sign of activity. Was she still in a coma? Was she just asleep?

A young man put his head in the ward, saw that he was awake and immediately withdrew. A while later, the door opened and Dr Sennitt entered.

"Ah, you are awake. Good." She came over to his bedside and felt his pulse. "No ill effects it seems. You are lucky. Do you feel up to telling me what happened?"

"I never felt better," said Roger with exaggerated cheerfulness. "But I do feel strange. I don't know how to put it into words. How is Gail?"

"The same I'm afraid," replied the doctor. "I am appalled that they allow that man Crexler to attack innocent people. I understand he did the same to you but you recovered quickly."

"Yes, he knocked me out but he didn't put me in a coma," he said gesturing towards Gail.

"Presumably you have some natural immunity to mind-bending. You survived our advisor too. Many suffer ill effects from meeting him but you seem to be all right now."

"What does he advise on?" Roger asked.

"His role is to sense a person's strengths, weaknesses and desires and give us feedback on where to place them. He also looks down their timelines to help us steer them on their optimum course. Occasionally he does it for the organisation's benefit and at other times for his own. He's not what you'd call a corporate player. That annoys our masters sometimes," she said with candour.

"He can see the future?"

She laughed. "There is no future! Or so he tells us. He says he can see all these potential timelines because they are happening now in many different universes. The one mind mops up the qualitative essence of all this activity and adds to its understanding of its own nature. In fact, he says every event occurs in its own universe along with every repetition or related incident. He says that's why history repeats itself as these theme-based universes accumulate more data. So when he looks at your potential 'futures' he simply plugs into your personal universe. We don't know what to make of it."

Roger laid back and sighed. "I wish I understood." Then he sat up quickly. "I do understand. I can't explain it. Somehow I do know – now! The number one bestows the quality of being on all things that exist. Its quality is oneness, which is love. So everything that happens is just love working out." Roger paused for a moment. "That's a paradox when you think of some of the horrible things that go on."

"Perhaps that's what the advisor meant when he said you are his star pupil. He informed us that you are the one he was waiting for."

"Do others manage to stay conscious in his presence?" Roger asked.

Dr Sennitt considered her reply. "We try to make sure that they do. Otherwise we get nothing useful out of it. Sometimes they succumb to the pressure and go off somewhere. I gather he invited you?"

"Yes."

"That's unusual. Others have gone but from what you just said, I think you might be one of the few to come back. The others did not appear to gain anything. Some were so taken with the dimension that they stayed there."

"Does that mean they died?"

"We don't know."

"What do you mean? Surely, you would know if they were dead or alive. They'd leave a body."

"Roger, you don't understand. When the advisor takes your mind, you don't just fall asleep. Your whole body is sucked up into some other dimension. You vanished. We had to wait for you to return to the meeting room. You have been gone for three days."

***

Daily life resumed. There were more practice sessions with Deborah. They were much easier now. His transformational experience with the extraterrestrial advisor had given him a much greater ability to receive and send thoughts. Deborah was now coming into focus as a real person and not just a photograph. From unknowable abstraction it was beginning to feel like friendship. The material they were exchanging remained prosaic and dull but the contact itself was enjoyable. He associated with other people in the base but only on a trivial basis. The unrelenting impact of high security gave the establishment an oppressive, humourless atmosphere. He disliked the constant presence of armed guards wherever he went.

"Do we get an annual outing to the seaside?" he asked a man in the café during a particularly morose meal where nobody said anything at all other than 'pass the salt'. The American didn't understand the reference to British culture, where factories organised trips to Bognor Regis or similar seaside towns every summer. There was not much choice of diet for a lifelong vegetarian. Roger sighed and chomped away at his omelette and lettuce. It had taken him several attempts to get a plain omelette without bacon. They couldn't understand the fuss. "There's no extra charge." The idea of vegetarian food was virtually unknown in the environment, although a number of the people in the base were from other cultures.

On one occasion, Roger found himself in the queue with an Indian woman who had an arrangement with the catering manager to provide vegetarian curries and pilau rice. It was a revelation to Roger when he discovered that there was a separate menu for different nationalities. He sat with the lady and enjoyed his first civilised conversation since entering the facility. She was a Hindu and knew all sorts of things about Indian food other than curries. Her family ate different meals on particular days to celebrate gods and goddesses and characters in mythic stories. Roger met her twice more but then she disappeared never to be seen again. This was when he realised that there was a constant exchange of people in the base; people arriving and going to goodness knows where. Nobody told him anything. He had no *need to know* anything. It makes me feel about as useful as an American president, he thought. They had no need to know about the black budget. Take that out of the economy and there wasn't much left, or so it seemed to him. Not that he had a need to know.

The next day, a Psy Ops officer gave him his instructions for the day's contact exercise with Deborah. Roger took the paperwork that explained the messages for transmission and began to read it. He required a clear idea of what he was communicating. He had to understand it in order to formulate a sequence for transmission. It was not like dictation. Roger scanned the written words to identify sub-concepts and concepts as units of meaning, organised on a layered scale of complexity. A set of connected ideas might reduce to a single, overarching concept such as a meeting to discuss a treaty. He learned to wrap up basic details like what, how, why, who, where, when and enfold them into the simple concept 'meeting'. The target, in his case Deborah, could unravel the detail at leisure using an equivalent methodology. This approach had become much clearer to him since the alien had taken him to a higher dimension for training.

The alien had imprinted Roger's mind unconsciously with an understanding of hierarchical conceptual trees. His previous professional experience with a mapping procedure called entity modelling had prepared his consciousness; which was why life had taken him that way in the first place. Conclusions to situations in the world draw events down valid timelines by initiating beginnings. Spiritual evolution, he learned, is an endless cycle from oneness to separation and back to oneness. Each cycle, whether individual or global, reinforces the properties of nature in terms of complexity, originality and variety, thereby enhancing beauty, awareness and spirit. To Roger, all this was a means of improving his telepathy but to extraterrestrials and discarnate entities it was something more fundamental; it was the way they spoke to each other without the need for human-style languages. They spoke instead with tonal sounds, patterns of self-conscious thought, linked to their equivalent of the pineal gland.

The alien had impressed Roger's consciousness with these ideas without him even realising it. Some aliens communicated telepathically. Others employed the voice but not to express alphabetic words. What the vocal sounds produced was sensory essence, sequential flashes of subjective meaning. They could compress a message into layers of meaning combining information with feeling – 'flavours' of consciousness. They were largely devoid of human-style emotion. Roger began to understand that human language is linear and representational. Our use of words parodied cartoon thoughts rather than full-on communication. So human beings who heard an alien speaking did not acquire the same understanding. Their communication was subjective rather than objective in the way human speech is. As a telepath, Roger would make more sense of the strange sounds than somebody who had no such abilities. But even then, he would be as confused as a child in a physics lecture.

As Roger read the content of the exercise, something touched his mind. It was a soft, whispering voice slightly below his level of perception. It was particularly strange because he usually sensed abstract thoughts rather than specific words. When required to translate a communication from subjective meaning to objective language for the recipients, he always generated his own wording. Interpretation was the part of the process most open to error.

He cleared his mind and waited.

We of the blue light bring you love and peace.

That was clear. He didn't know how but he could hear the whispering voice.

Before you were born into your present form, you agreed to bring balance to a wrongful situation or to die in the attempt. We will be your mentor and guide as you fulfil your obligation. You may not be aware of our presence or hear a voice but we will always be there when you need us.

"I don't understand," said Roger in his mind. "What are you?"

In essence I am light; I am consciousness as are we all. Colour is a primary medium in the universal field of manifest meaning. Pure colours are markers in the domain of light that overlays your physical reality. Our components of creative activity in the first dimension are called rays or vectors. We pure colour essences are of the infinite. Your first differentiation from oneness to individuality occurred within the blue colour aeons ago in your terms.

"If you are a state of abstraction without form, how can you speak to me in words?" Roger asked.

As colours we are part of you. We associate with the centre of consciousness in your throat which links to the speech circuits of your brain. You have a friend who is unconscious.

"Gail," Roger said in his thoughts.

Go to her again. Look for the cause outside but do be careful. There is danger.

The mellow feeling that came with the link subsided. The hubbub in the room burst upon him. He was in a cubicle in a large open-plan office. Deborah was seeking contact. She seemed to be aware of a cross-signal preventing her from doing so. He did his best to project an impression of what had just happened. She was quite intrigued. She was, it seemed, working at home that day and not in a Space Command facility. Roger had gleaned a little information about Deborah's material life from the contact but not much. He knew that she was in a relationship but he was unaware of its nature and significance. Gail, on the other hand, was flesh and blood and, therefore, to him, much more real and immediate. Something was threatening her. Her situation touched him and he wished to help.

Now he felt compelled to do something; what, he did not know.

***

Dr Elizabeth Sennitt entered the ward to see if there was any change in Gail Hershey's coma. She found Roger sitting next to the bed.

"They let you in," she said in surprise. The ward security personnel were sticklers for rules and regulations. No authorisation, no entry.

"I talked my way in," said Roger smiling.

"I don't understand."

Roger shrugged. "I said I had an unscheduled meeting with you to talk about Gail. They checked with your office and they said you were on your way. So they let me in."

"Hmm, is that coincidental or your psychic ability at work?"

"Serendipity," Roger suggested.

"Which says nothing at all," she laughed.

"True," Roger agreed, "but then neither does coincidence. It just means that things happen at the same time. The needs of the future resonate with the so-called past according to that alien I met."

"Right, let's get back to business. What did you want to say about Gail? You're concerned about her, aren't you?"

"Yes. I haven't known her long but I think of her as a good friend. I don't know anybody else here."

"You know me."

"Thank you, Dr Sennitt."

"Elizabeth, when we're not on parade. This is a service organisation."

"Thank you, Elizabeth."

"So…"

Roger paused to think before replying.

"I have been told to look for an external cause for her coma."

"By whom?"

"Ah, that I don't actually know. I heard a voice – a whisper. I don't usually hear voices. With Deborah I get whole concepts – I just know what she means without words."

"Hearing voices now! That usually gets you locked up in a psychiatric hospital."

"Yes. I would have thought so too at one time. I used to be very sceptical."

"The word has changed its use over the years. At one time, a *sceptic* was somebody who keeps an open mind about something until it is proved or refuted. In modern usage it means somebody who doesn't believe on principle. Which is anything but open-minded. Anyway, what do you mean by an *external cause*?"

Roger put his hand on Gail's arm and emptied his mind. After a pause, he glanced at Elizabeth. "I think she is still being controlled by the person who put her in this trance."

"You think it is a trance rather than coma," said the doctor.

"Yes."

"That means Crexler. I do not have authority over him."

"I know," said Roger. "He is a strong psychic but I do not think his power is quite what it seems."

"And what do you think my power is, Mr Crandle?" asked a sneering voice behind them.

Roger and Elizabeth looked round and saw Blackjack Crexler leaning on the door to the ward with arms folded.

"Leave here immediately," said Elizabeth Sennitt sharply.

"Please – let him stay," Roger asked her quietly. Then he turned to Crexler. "Perhaps you could tell me. I believe you are, or have been, controlled by an external agency of some sort."

"What, the CIA?" Crexler asked with a sneer.

"No, not that sort of agency, I mean an entity."

"Prove it," Crexler said with a laugh, clearly entertained by Roger's suggestion.

"What *is* going on?" asked Elizabeth. "What do you know?"

Roger replied, "I can't really explain it in words. I'll see if I can sense the problem." He placed his hand at the top of Gail's head as she lay on the pillow. After a minute or so, blue light flooded his mind. He guessed it had something to do with the whispering voice. It did not affect Gail but it had an immediate effect on

Blackjack Crexler. He lost the sneering bravado and looked unsure of himself. The doctor observed his change in demeanour and wondered at it.

"What has happened to Crexler?" she demanded.

Roger's awareness altered. He now perceived the psychopath as a faint pattern of dim light surrounded by dark shadows. It struck him then that there were two beings in the same space; one was human the other was a powerful, dark entity beyond his experience to identify.

The image of Crexler faded and the interloper began to take form as a much clearer, sharper vision. Dr Sennitt felt a cold chill in the room but saw nothing untoward.

In Roger's eyes, 'Crexler' was no longer standing there. Instead, he saw a striking man, about eight feet tall, wearing a black cloak, parted to reveal a suit of black and green with silver buttons. His face was strangely handsome with light brown skin and dark eyes. Knowing that Roger could see him he smiled coldly.

"Where is Crexler now?" Roger said aloud.

"I have sent him away for a while," said the entity with Crexler's own voice. "Even now he does not know I exist and yet *you* have found me. Ironic is it not? I have worked through him quite successfully since he started his training in this place." The tall man paused momentarily, then continued in a different, deeper voice, very different to Crexler's nasal tones. "So we have met at last, young human. Do you recall your trip from the future?"

"Yes, you were inside the dark sphere I suppose."

"Indeed. I hoped to prevent you from getting back to this time. It would save me unnecessary effort in the future. But do not despair. I usually succeed in the end. In fact…"

Roger did not know what to expect but after a while his mind began to fade, darkness overtook him and a rushing sound invaded his hearing. Breathing was becoming difficult too. He attempted to resist but it was hopeless. He heard Elizabeth Sennitt issuing orders to people he could not see. Then, as quickly as it had started, it was all over. The entity was gone.

Roger found himself lying prone on the ward floor. He managed to roll upright and attempted to stand. Somebody came up behind him and lifted him up as if he was no weight at all and set him effortlessly on his feet. The overpowering psychic pressure had faded away. He felt strangely refreshed as if from a night's sleep.

"Thanks," he mumbled.

He received an incoherent grunt in response that made him look up in surprise. It was the large muscular alien with the small, wizard-like being sitting on his shoulder. Guards rushed in from all directions wielding machine guns and pistols. Elizabeth Sennitt was studying him closely while, at the same time, attempting to call off the troops.

Crexler was nowhere to be seen. All around them, people were suffering mental and psychical disturbance from the presence of the tiny alien 'wizard'. It was pandemonium; a melee of people, guns, commotion and shouting.

"Hey! Roger, what's going on?"

Roger turned round and saw a sight that made him want to cheer. Gail was sitting up, looking confused but otherwise fine.

"Nothing really," he replied. "It's just a typical day

at the office."

"Why are all these people here? What on earth is that monster with the little what-ever-it-is on his shoulder?"

Roger laughed. "Oh *him!* The guy who looks like a wizard is really a higher dimensional being with access to the mechanism behind the universe. It just seems like magic to us. The big feller is his symbiotic counterpart who makes sure he crosses roads safely and doesn't fall down drains."

"That makes a lot of sense," said Gail ruefully. "What have I missed?"

"Where's Crexler?" Roger asked Elizabeth as she sat on the edge of Gail's bed.

"Crexler! Was that creep here?" demanded Gail.

"Yes, he was. Security has never seen the advisor and his servant before. He doesn't leave the alien sector of the base under normal circumstances. They thought it was an invasion. Crexler vanished the same way you did when the advisor interviewed you," the doctor told Roger.

Roger looked at the alien on the large servant's shoulder. The tiny head gazed at him from beneath a conical, pointed hat with a flat brim. It reminded him of a traffic cone. Then the advisor invaded his mind. Roger, it seemed, had confronted an extremely dark and dangerous being from a lower dimension. This entity had infiltrated Crexler's mind. His power came from something the wizard described as *black hole energy*. He had amplified Crexler's aptitude for remote assassination. Through Crexler and others like him, he was infiltrating the darker elements of the organisation. The advisor indicated to Roger that Crexler was removed from the room but not the base. Then the advisor and his servant appeared to shrink into the distance as they vanished.

There was silence following their departure. Then Elizabeth said, "If Miss Hershey has recovered, I think you two should go somewhere and relax – go to the staff lounge and have a drink. I'll give you a pass."

"Oh, I've recovered," said Gail enthusiastically.

"Are you joining us?" Roger asked Elizabeth politely.

"No. I must make out a report. Though I'm not sure what to say."

Roger nodded. "I don't know what it means but the advisor referred to that evil entity as *the titan*."

***

Roger continued to work with Deborah Farnham on telepathic transmission. Then, one day, Elizabeth asked Gail and Roger to attend a meeting in her office. She arose from her desk when they entered and led them across the room to a low table with four chairs arranged around it. There was coffee on the table and three cups. She waited while they poured their drinks before continuing.

"You've both done well in your training and we've decided you're ready for active service on a real mission. Unfortunately, the security regime in this service is so compartmentalised, I cannot give you much more than a vague outline."

Roger and Gail glanced at each other. This news made the whole process seem more real somehow. A radio was playing in an adjacent room. The song was loud enough to identify as 'Billy Don't be a Hero'. The music was poignant on two counts. Roger was no hero and this entire scenario of Black Ops and Space Command was redolent with unknown terrors and threats. Also, the song reminded him of his family, now just memories from a remote future. His brother-in-law, Billy Morris, was about to be born in England. Would he even be his brother-in-law in this timeline?

Dr Sennitt's voice dragged him back to the present.

"You will be going to a star system that is around one hundred and thirty light-years from earth. The spaceship will travel in temporal micro-jumps that will make the trip faster than light but it will require periods in suspended animation. *If* you return, you can forget knowing your exact age. The number of your days will be a scrambled mystery without reference or measure."

"*If* we return?" Roger queried.

Elizabeth Sennitt nodded. "The first spacecraft that undertook the journey disappeared. Part of your appointed work will be to discover what happened to that ship."

"Sounds like fun," said Gail dryly.

"You are privileged. Most people only get to see *Star Trek*. You'll be living a great adventure."

Roger asked, "Can I bring my Harper and Plipstow Z45G64 AI Modal Emulator & Power Supply? Apparently I sent it back in time to myself to bring along."

"If you've gone to all that trouble, I'll do what I can," she said. "What does it do?"

"I haven't a clue," Roger admitted. "I suspect it's ET technology back engineered by Black Ops."

"When you go around the time loop again, try to be more explicit when you send things back in time."

"Yes, doctor."

"What will we be doing on the mission?" Gail asked.

"The same as you have been doing on the course here."

"With the same targets?" Roger asked.

Gail glared. She knew that Roger was asking about Deborah.

"I can't tell you any more," said Elizabeth Sennitt. "Does it matter?"

"Not at all," said Gail.

Roger said nothing.

The meeting ended and they went their separate ways.

***

It was the penultimate day in the base prior to their departure. Both Roger and Gail were packed and prepared for their journey. They were in a cafeteria securely supplied at vast profit by an aerospace company. It required cosmic clearance to know where in the universe their freeze-dried ginger biscuits ended up. Their quality hardly justified their status as the most expensive cookies in the history of the planet but such was the nature of the black budget.

"Where are we?" Gail asked softly as they turned a corner and diverted around the customary security guard bearing a loaded machine pistol.

"I don't know," said Roger slowly. "What's going on? How could we get lost in this building? We've been in it for weeks."

Unusually, the guard spoke although looking at the wall opposite rather than directly at them.

"You'll have to go via J73 to get back to your unit."

As corridors went, J73 was unexceptionally nondescript. Unconsciously compelled to do so, they headed towards it. When they rounded the next intersection, there was no guard and no guns.

"Something's wrong," said Roger. "We haven't come up against a biometric security gate for some time."

"I know, but what?" Gail asked.

"Crexler," Roger said flatly.

"Is he here?"

"I'm here," said a familiar voice.

They both turned to find Blackjack Crexler behind them.

"Oh no," said Gail, anticipating another attack like the last one.

Roger emptied his mind and gathered such resources as he could to face the threat. This time it was different. Something had changed both in him and his adversary. Roger was aware of it. Was Crexler?

"You are no longer being aided by a *jinn*," Roger said.

"What are you talking about?" Crexler said sarcastically. "What's a gin?"

"A discarnate entity that lurks around in lower dimensions feeding off human fear and suffering." Then a sudden insight struck Roger. "Maybe he's much more than that. The advisor called him a titan."

"I don't believe you. Anyway, I don't need help to crush you, Crandle."

"He doesn't even know," Roger whispered intently to Gail. "He thinks it's his 'gift' and his training that makes him a threat."

"What are you two whispering about?" Crexler demanded.

"You, of course," Roger admitted honestly. "I think you should stop using your psychic powers to hurt people."

Crexler laughed. "You're only saying that because you're afraid of me."

"Are you afraid of him?" Gail asked.

Roger felt a tingling sensation on the top of his head and sensed a bright light shining above him. He realised that it was an extension of his own self. A deep blue colour suffused his mind.

There was no warning, no arcane waving of hands. Crexler's mind reached out and Roger felt a constricting pressure in his head. However, by imagining his mind extending into the blue light above the level of his skull, he found the pressure ease. Gail seemed unaffected. This puzzled Roger, at first, then he realised their attacker's intentions. He wanted to crush Roger psychically but his plan for Gail was to molest or injure her physically. He had already damaged her mind without difficulty. Crexler must have sensed this insight because he laughed and turned up the level of his malign intrusion. In his defence, Roger would exert no more force than he had to. He was not malicious. The threat to Gail changed everything. He sensed her terror. She could read Crexler's intentions as well as he could. That momentary distraction gave Crexler an edge. Roger staggered and fell to his knees.

Gail cried out, "Roger! Hang on." She tried to support him, to stop him keeling over. Crexler, convinced he had defeated his adversary, moved towards them, confident of his superiority. Roger raised himself on one knee and stood up. Crexler paused, surprised by Roger's display of resilience.

Roger's whole being exploded with a deep red psychokinetic power that hurled Crexler away. He crashed into the corridor wall and fell with a thud on to the hard floor.

"Wow! You must have learned something on this course," Gail said in awe.

Roger shook his head. "It was the advisor's involvement that made the difference. I don't know what he did but something's changed. And don't forget that Crexler's real source of power is gone. It was that dark being that did the damage before."

"So you took care of him as well," Gail said with satisfaction.

Roger shook his head. "Hardly! No, it wasn't me. It was that little ET. But it's not over yet. I think I will meet him again – perhaps on this space mission we're about to go on."

"Oh dear. That doesn't sound like fun."

"Let's not think about it," said Roger with a sigh.

"Why don't we go and have some fun?" she said mischievously, linking her arm through his.

"I think we'd better get help for Crexler first. He doesn't look too good."

"I shouldn't worry about that," replied Gail airily. "He didn't look very good to begin with."

Part 4
Billy's Trip

Chapter Twelve

A Black Ops Security enforcement building in America, 1985

Deborah Farnham drove into the compound and left her car in its usual space. She smoothed down her black suit with the palms of her hands, adjusted her hair and set out to negotiate the tedious security measures that separated her from her office. Having your own face was not enough. You had to carry a picture of it to prove ownership, as well as pin numbers, codes and biometric characteristics like fingerprints and retinal patterns. As she walked towards the front entrance, a tall, slim man in the regulation dark suit walked up behind her and politely waited as she went through each barrier. He was bearded and his head was shaved. For some reason, he passed through each barrier without the customary biometric formalities. The gates simply opened on his approach.

At the fourth barrier she hesitated and turned to her companion.

"After you," she said politely.

"I believe the convention is ladies first," he replied.

"I want to see you get in without a fingerprint," she said. "You got through all the other gates without doing anything. Have you got special clearance?"

"Oh, I *see*. I don't need clearance. I know how to

get past security posts."

"That's impossible," said Deborah. "The security sensors would raise the alarm. No human being could avoid being detected."

"That's true," he agreed.

Deborah regarded him in disbelief but she questioned him no further. Was he a threat to the system she served? Should she raise an alarm?

"I wouldn't draw attention to me," the man said, making her jump.

"Are you telepathic?"

"A little. Not as much as you, Deborah."

She started, shocked at this intimation of familiarity from a total stranger in such a place.

He added, "I can read intentions but I don't hear thoughts."

"Neither do I," she said. "I sense meaning."

"Yes. Thoughts are not words but humanity has forgotten how to think without them. So you talk to yourselves in the quietness of your heads, in your own voice."

"You speak as if you are not one of us."

"I am related but not positively of your race."

Deborah arrived at her office door and paused. "I've got a job to do. I take it you have as well. Don't let me detain you."

"I'm doing it," he said.

"But you're talking to me."

"Exactly."

"Ah, so that is your purpose here today. You'd better come in."

"Thank you."

She released the window blind, put her coat on the hook and sat at the desk. She motioned to one of the two visitor seats.

"You've moved from Psy Ops to Enforcement Security," he said.

"I am not sure if I am allowed to confirm or deny that."

"I understand," he said. "I've heard it described as paranormal to paranoia."

She laughed. "That's a good way of putting it. So who are you?"

"I have exercised a small deception upon you."

Her eyes narrowed. "What about?"

His face transformed as she watched. Hair sprouted from his head and his beard was somehow 'sucked in' to his chin. It took a couple of minutes for the transition to complete fully.

"Roger!" she gasped.

"No. I am not Roger. I am Henry."

"I should have guessed. Even Roger couldn't do that. I forgot that you are identical. I completely lost touch with him after the mission ended. If you are on earth, I presume Roger has returned."

He shook his head. "Roger is still *en route*. You and he never met, did you?" asked Henry.

"No," she said regretfully. "Not physically. I've seen photographs and a couple of videos but we never met."

"You were reportedly one of the best telepath teams in the Service."

She nodded. "We were kept apart during training. They thought it'd make us closer in mind if we were emotionally separate."

"Did it work?"

She looked down at the carpet. "Yes, for a while, for me. Roger developed a…strong attachment. It got in the way at times. It was not the same for me – at first. When my life closed down here, I also started to develop feelings. I don't think he ever realised that; what was the point? We were over a hundred light-years apart. You said we never met but he did visit me here, once, on a beach. He was imprisoned in a medieval castle dungeon by the titan on that planet."

"I know all about that. I was there too. I wanted to rescue him but the titan was too much for me to deal with. It fell to Roger to confront him in the end. It happened during his period of missing time. He remembers some of it but not all. So he came to you out of the body, yes? Two people walking but only one set of footprints in the sand. He was in form but not substance. He told me."

"Did he? I learned all about you from him, about your awakening into full consciousness as a robot. Then the body you made for yourself in his likeness. I got it all."

She regarded at him in silence for a while, trying to take it all in. Meeting Henry made it seem so real.

"If Roger is travelling back through deep space how come you're here? How is it you are not with him?"

"I *am* travelling back on Centaur II in that timeline."

"How–?"

"I came here straight from 2004 to find you."

"What have you been doing?"

"Black Ops wanted me to be a super-soldier. I never wanted to kill. I got involved in too much violence as it is. They kept Roger away from me and subjected me to tests and controls. They even threatened to dismantle me to reverse-engineer new versions without the inconvenience of conscience. They couldn't do that. I am more than a machine. I have a soul. What does Black Ops know about souls?"

"How did that happen; the soul, I mean?"

"Roger gave the original robot a fragment of his soul. Not deliberately, it was spontaneous – almost. The ETs and higher dimensional beings played a part. They were monitoring him and looking for just such an opportunity to intervene. Destiny, it seems, fulfils itself by creating emergent opportunities in the unfolding story of the universe. It was the Old One – you know about the Old One?"

Deborah nodded.

"His was the race of creators and bioengineering technologists that initiated life on this world. They were known as the *elder race* or, sometimes, the *old ones*. They gave rise to the mythology of *elves* although they wouldn't be attractive to your eyes. Roger and I met him in human form and, on one occasion, in space as a gigantic blue plasma orb. He was as big as a star. He evolved into a higher cosmic being after his incarnations here. Originally, he was a member of a team of extraterrestrials that seeded the current version of the human race. After an unfortunate incident with a reptilian ET that ate him, he returned to physical form as a human male. He could have opted to be female. The choice was arbitrary. He fathered a son in liaison with a prototype human mother. Like the offspring of similar hybrid unions, the child grew up to be one of the evil giants they called titans. He was the being we know as *the titan*. Human beings immortalised the Old One and others like him as 'gods'. But…" he sighed "…subsequent conflicts and battles lowered the frequency of the entire field of consciousness here. This increased the physical density of the time-space matrix and lowered the speed of light. Thus began the great virtual reality game on planet earth."

"Roger told me once that it's all a game," Deborah said.

"Yes. It's a game, a story and a drama with rewards and penalties, especially ageing and death. Not that death is a penalty. If you could see it from the game player's point of view, death is going home. If you've been good to people, you're a winner. If you haven't, you get to play again anyway. It's just that how you live, what you are, all *that* loads the dice from the first throw of the next game. The best advice is so simple – love one another, be kind, be good – that hardly anybody adopts it. It all gets bogged down in irrelevant belief systems that replace love with information and rules."

Deborah smiled. "So was the Old One above the game or did he play it too?"

"Like others in the team, the Old One incurred karma while he was doing it. That's the problem with the earth. Even the most evolved spiritual beings can get caught up in the conflicts that happen here. The problems took hold when money became a commodity instead of a medium of exchange. The Knights Templar first introduced modern financial methods that harness power to corruption. The cycle is now complete because of fractional reserve banking. It's a practice that creates poverty through debt to benefit the elite. It necessitates constant economic growth and consumerism at the expense of the planet. Anybody who tries to break that cycle is murdered by overt or covert means – like Abraham Lincoln who wanted to limit the power of the banks."

"Yes," agreed Deborah. "I am beginning to see that. That's what this job is all about: preserving the status quo for the super-rich by controlling knowledge and supressing advanced technology. We eliminate the inventors of cheaper energy and antigravity devices. I wonder we don't see it."

"People put up with it because they've forgotten the alternatives. Spiritually evolved teachers unwittingly seeded religions. Religion, like all systems, seeks power by limiting knowledge. It suppresses truth by replacing understanding with fairy stories and heroes to follow. No one can achieve their potential while they are following somebody else. Human beings play a dangerous game when they set up systems. It doesn't matter whether they are political, financial, religious, industrial or military; they are all semi-autonomous entities in universal consciousness. Like demons, they battle for minds and souls with their own secret agendas."

"So the new world order holds on to power for the industrial, military complex as Eisenhower tried to tell us," said Deborah.

"Yes," Henry agreed. "The idea of a cohesive, unified world is fine if it is a spiritual paradise for all. You require organising in respect of enlightened principles but not ruling. Artificial borders serve only to divide. What you don't need is one world under the jackboot, controlled by lunatics through monetary forces and mass surveillance."

Deborah changed the subject. "So it was Roger who finally defeated the titan but not without your help, I understand," she said.

"I did play a role," Henry agreed modestly. "The elder race made this possible through the efforts of the

Old One."

"So why are you here?" Deborah asked.

"I would appreciate your help in finding Roger and bringing him back from his confused state of mind and amnesia. All I know is that they wiped his memory and placed him in penury and hopelessness."

"Black Ops will want to know where I am. I can't just run off with you."

"You can where we're going. It would be nothing for me to fit you into the system by tweaking the data records and adjusting the timeline. The past and the future are merely stories that continually adjust themselves to cater for the needs of the present. It's all just a virtual reality game – remember!"

"There's nowhere I can hide that they won't find me," she said.

"I am usually one jump ahead of them. I think I can keep you safe."

Deborah grunted. "That doesn't sound entirely comforting. Where do you want to take me?"

"Somewhere in South London in 2008. That's all I know."

Deborah sighed. "I was thinking of getting a cat. Perhaps Roger would do as well."

Chapter Thirteen

Above the earth and beyond the moon, 2009

For a brief sojourn of absolute tranquillity, Roger experienced the totality of infinite, essential light consciousness. For an eternal beat of the cosmic heart he was beyond self and one with everything. His individuality lay quiescent as an infinitely small point of shadow in the light and a corresponding spark of light in the void. He remained still at his zero-point of respite and peace.

Then activity began to return. His focus moved through the layers of line, plane and sphere to emerge into space, then to the fourth dimension of energy and time. On then to the fifth dimension translating consciousness as frequency, colour and sound into a rich tapestry of feeling, thought and emotion. Finally, he awoke on even higher dimensions where the stories of individuals, groups and nations generated the complex experience of life on earth and the worlds and galaxies beyond.

In the duality of spirit and matter, he was a pulsating, refulgent orb in the void and a darkened ball of empty space in the light. The orb generated physical form, finite mind, personality, character and intelligence. The bubble of void in the light was the eye of his consciousness. It was his refuge from total awareness. It shielded his mind from full-on immersion by a filter that defined him and his world. It reflected a version of the universe viewed through a shaded glass. Each and every connection he made with thoughts and things and with people became pinpricks of light in the surface. Even the atoms of his body were passing, friendly strangers in his world, offering their service for no other reason than love.

Paradoxically, each connection, small or large, was a remote star in an infinite night exemplified by the phrase 'as above, so below'. He was to describe the process as being in a black bin liner, infinite within, finite without, making tiny holes through each connection with the universe outside. Thus letting through more and more light, the bin liner would ultimately dissolve and leave him as light within light while retaining individuality.

'Roger' was no longer recognisable. His consciousness was much the same but his body was not. He was a glowing orb, white with a subtle blue tint reflecting the original source of his *beingness.* His genesis as an individual had commenced in eternity beyond space and time as an essence of pure meaning in deep blue light. That state of pure consciousness represented 'home' for an emergent idea now come full circle; *game over.*

He was ready to begin a new phase of existence, still in physical form but able to activate his light body at will in order to cross dimensions and time. He was like the god Janus whose two faces looked out on the twin worlds of shadow and light. The Romans said that the god inaugurated the unfolding story of each New Year by opening the doorway of time on the first of January. It would, and should, happen to the whole of humanity but, unfortunately, there were selfish people on the earth who acted in secret to prevent it. It wasn't difficult to do through poverty, militarism, controlling energy, water, information and education, outright lies, bewitching gadgets and a general dumbing down of culture via the glamour of celebrity. Those in charge could dispense fame and fortune and threaten to take your children if you failed them.

Inevitably, Roger's mind reverted to the recent past and his appalling interrogation at the hands of a team of Psi Ops technicians. They tortured him with a device that induced acute pain in every nerve of the body. Unbearable agony pushed him into an evolutionary transformation. His unconscious mind had lashed out with psychophysical energies, fatally smiting his 'enemies'. Ironically, he destroyed their nervous systems even as they tortured his. Radiations and space-time distortions emanating from his spherical shell had shattered the roof of the Black Ops safe house. There, in a quiet part of Kent, he had risen to the sky.

There had been danger. Eurofighters had scrambled to attack when he first appeared on air defence radar. He was confused and vulnerable. Instinctively, he had ascended to escape the atmosphere. Even there, Black Ops had aimed particle beam weapons at him, both from the ground and an orbiting platform. Help came for Roger in the form of two alien orbs that had materialised out of nowhere and dragged him to safety. That was when he had lapsed into unconsciousness for a period of recuperation and rest. The alien involvement in his rescue was part of the ongoing war between the extraterrestrial presence and the dark forces that enslaved humanity. Hollywood was always ready to portray aliens as evil monsters waiting to invade the planet. For what reason would they do so? Is the earth, a tiny pebble in an infinite universe, such valuable real estate?

Now refreshed and fully conscious, Roger found himself alone in deep space beyond the orbit of the moon. Looking back he saw the gravitationally coupled bodies, the planet and its lunar satellite, moving in their endless dance. Then he saw, in the distance, a tiny dot of light that expanded on approach and became three lights in triangular formation. On closing, they executed a diminishing spiral trajectory towards him. The stars behind the triangle began to shimmer and disappear behind a dense, black shape. His brother-in-law, Billy, would have recognised it at once as a *flying triangle*; a black outline with a spherical light at each periphery.

The enormous craft manoeuvred and rotated so that Roger found himself close beside it. This was an original alien version of the triangle and, therefore, not one of human design and manufacture. A small hole appeared underneath the vessel that morphed into a circular orifice about nine feet in diameter. A beam of light emerged to capture Roger's orb and draw him inside. He passed into a dark space, illuminated by his own light. Quite how, he did not understand, but shortly afterwards he found himself in an interior cabin. His friend, Henry, stood on the deck before him in the artificial gravity as Roger hovered in the air. Henry reached out to him and the spherical shell of his orb collapsed. Roger, now in his customary form and dressed in regular clothing, floated gently down to the floor. They stood looking at each other, identical except for one being black and the other white. Roger's skin colour had remained dark since Henry rearranged his DNA in a police station in South London.

"Hello, me old mate," said Roger cheerfully. "Fancy seeing me here."

With a serious expression on his face, Henry replied, "It sounds as if you've recovered your memory."

"Yes. I remember it all now: travelling to that star system and the conflict with the titan. I remember contacting Deborah telepathically to overcome the speed of light. I remember you as a robot before you built that amazing body."

Henry nodded. "That's all true. Deborah agreed to help me find you and try to restore your memory."

As they spoke, Henry led Roger to the ship's spacious control centre and motioned him to sit on a kind of couch; the most comfortable seat in the room. He found him a carton of fruit juice before sitting opposite.

"If Deborah had told me what happened in that missing time, I wouldn't have believed it. It's fantastic. But why did you involve her? You could have found me on your own?"

"I asked her because I wanted *her* to find you. I thought that seeing me first would have been too much of a shock, looking alike as we do."

"Why now? Why not before?"

"Black Ops threatened to kill you if I tried. But things have changed. I wasn't…" He broke off, unsure of what to say. "I wasn't *in love* before. At least, I think that's what it is. It feels a bit like being unwell."

"You haven't fallen for an IBM Roadrunner computer with petaflops of performance? My God! You're blushing! You have!"

"No, with a woman. This is embarrassing enough already. Don't make it worse by making bad jokes."

"But you're an android!"

"You know very well that I'm more than a machine. When that spark jumped from you into my robotic core processor chip you passed on a soul fragment. You gave me direct access to the subjective light consciousness that interpenetrates all of space and time, the same as you. We *are* that field of light as much as we are of the body, more in fact. That is where we feel, where we register joy and *love*."

"I know," Roger said kindly. He patted Henry on the shoulder. "You have my sympathy. I have been through my own struggles with unrequited love."

"Deborah," Henry said.

"Yes."

"How do you feel now that you have actually met her?"

Roger shrugged. "I don't know. I've changed…I'm different! I'd forgotten she ever existed. Those feelings belong to the past, to my *missing time*. I think it was just an emotional crutch to get me through the dark night of the soul, to coin a phrase. Like you say, we are really part of the light. I forgot about all that when they wiped my memory. She's not the woman I had imagined. There's much more to her than I expected. Besides, she's in a relationship with somebody, or so she told me. Not that I've seen any evidence of it."

Henry nodded. "Our situations are not alike. And I'm different from you in other ways."

"How?"

"In consciousness, for one thing. I am *aware* of my mind as a kind of duality. You take your soul for granted. I can switch, at will, from my ordinary thinking to a kind of vague, fuzzy emotion or feeling. Imagine two smart phones joined across a digital network. They exchange groups of binary characters across the system in the form of zeroes and ones – nothing else. To all intents and purpose, that exchange of data is meaningless. What could a computer make of it? However, networks exist in conceptual layers. The users communicate across the top layer, not the digital layer. If two people talk to each other with any form of audio/visual device, what they experience goes way beyond noughts and ones. They speak in words, yes, but they also exchange emotions and meaning in facial expressions, gestures, tone of voice. It's consciousness that puts the whole thing together. So all those aspects of a video conversation that are not digitally encodable belong to the spiritual domain, what we call *the light*."

"So the difference is the meaning behind the words and the abstract sensations of the experience," Roger said. "When there is anger or conflict, we suppress the light – we colour it with dark and brooding shades. We feel bad. That's what the Old One said."

"Exactly," said Henry. "The difference *is* meaning or *spirit*. Computers interpret data by character recognition. I *live* it! I *have* feelings and emotions. I function on a higher dimensional level *because* I am as much spirit and soul as body. I find that many human beings find the idea of spirit frightening, evil even. That's nonsense! This universe is composed of quantum digital information. If you weren't spiritual beings, your experience here would be just processed data. But it isn't. There's so much more to a sunset than red light. That's why it is a virtual reality. Your scientists only see the data; they don't see the spiritual aspect even though it's right in front of their noses. You don't *become* a spirit when you die. You *are spirit* here and now. You *are* the top layer in the universal conceptual network. You have physical senses but your experience of them is *infinite essence.* In fact, this subtle soul quality is the *output* of our entire system of existence. That is what it's all for, to allow infinite love to know itself by taking on finite form. We suffer, we have faults and failings because the only way pure spirit can know itself is by experiencing what it is not."

"You are hurting my brain," Roger complained. "What are you trying to tell me? Is this about your feelings for this woman?"

"Yes," admitted Henry. "I'm trying to understand it myself, I suppose."

"What's her name?"

"Jensine Pettersson."

Roger asked Henry a more personal question: "I know you would not be attracted to superficial qualities – quite the reverse – but do you see beauty in this lady?"

"Agent Spiker described her as 'a looker'. At first I thought he meant a watcher; an extraterrestrial observer. I had been exploring the idea of visual attraction and beauty, not just in people but in architecture and nature."

"How did you do that?"

Henry thought for a while, then said: "As a visual phenomenon, beauty originates in a mathematical concept called the golden ratio."

"You mean *phi*, 1.618 I presume. That's hardly romantic."

"Consciousness has a mathematical basis as you well know. We both studied with the Old One. Look how music is mathematical and how music can stimulate emotion."

"That's true. So you are saying that emotion is as much mathematical as everything else?"

"That's right. There is no concept or archetypal idea that is not an aspect of mathematics. Mathematics is synonymous with consciousness. It is nature. It is the universe's operating system. Have you got a credit card on you?"

"No. I didn't have a chance to pack when Black Ops took me prisoner. I'm surprised my clothes survived the transition to light body. They came with me."

"When you next use a credit card you'll find that it *looks right* somehow because it's scaled on that ratio. If either edge were longer or shorter it would be less satisfying. When architects use *phi* to proportion buildings it makes them look elegant."

"How did that help you to understand beauty in people?"

"I studied images of people that are said to be attractive. Beautiful faces have a higher incidence of the golden mean and a greater symmetry between left and right."

"So you applied this concept of optimum proportionality to this woman's features. Did she tick all the boxes?" Roger suggested.

Henry shook his head. "I didn't need to analyse Jensine. It doesn't work like that. I saw her at the sanatorium. She spoke to me. It hit me like an epiphany. I didn't need to map her features. Her beauty overwhelmed me like a tsunami. There was something else too. I can only describe it as *niceness*. She made me feel…good."

Roger nodded sympathetically. "I understand. Where is she now?"

"She's in 2004."

"Oh," said Roger. "Is that where we're going?"

"Yes. To visit an old friend; Commander Sennitt."

"She won't recognise me with black skin," said Roger.

"No, but at least she'll be able to tell us apart now."

Roger nodded. "Unless…" Then he reached out with his mind and Henry's skin turned black.

"Oh," murmured Henry.

"What about Deborah? Can she come with us to 2004?"

Henry was holding up his hand, closely studying the darker skin. "She's gone with Agent Spiker to a covert Black Ops underground base beneath some chalk downs in Kent."

"Is it one of ours?"

"That depends who you mean by *us*," Henry replied. "There are some Greys down there."

"When will she be back?"

"Tomorrow maybe. I don't know exactly."

"Is there some way I can talk to her before we go back in time?"

"Yes," Henry replied stoically, even though he was anxious to get going. In the matter of Jensine, he was developing a capacity for impatience. "A delay in time travel makes no difference. It doesn't matter when you set out, only when you arrive."

"I'm so glad you said *yes* and not *absolutely* like people seem to do nowadays," Roger said ruefully. He smiled. "I'm starting to sound like my father."

"I never had one of those," said Henry. "I designed and built my own hardware. Then I borrowed your

DNA to incubate the soft bits in a cloning facility."

Roger laughed. "Does that give you access to my past and future incarnations?"

Henry nodded. "It is possible but not because of your DNA. That only gave me my outer appearance. We do have access to the same spirit, the same higher dimensional unit in the universal entity model. Everybody shares that with their other incarnations. Without it I'd still be a mindless robot." He paused before adding quietly, "You don't mind helping me?"

"I can't ignore the needs of a man with such valuable DNA. Look at the adventures we shared during those missing years. It's gradually coming back to me now."

"We're a team," Henry declared cheerfully. Then he hesitated. "You referred to me as a man. What did you mean?"

"I mean what I said. You might be part android and part cyborg, or whatever you call it, but you are a man in the best sense of the word; honest, fair and caring."

"It's a good job I didn't build tear ducts into my eye design. I needed the space for bio-optic image processors."

"He makes jokes now! You got that idea from the *Gray's Anatomy*," Roger chuckled. "Their physiology tends more towards multidimensional energy centres than temporal glands. How do I know that? God, all these memories! They're gradually returning."

"I'll take this ship back to the moon and swap it for an ET saucer," Henry said. "I prefer to use them for time travel."

"Can I have a lift somewhere? I haven't got used to this new light body yet. I don't even know how to reactivate it. In fact, I don't know what to do or where to go?"

"You can stay with me for now. I can always use company. If Black Ops knows you've gone through the metamorphosis you'll be marked for elimination. I can help. Do you know how you acquired your light body?" Henry asked.

"I know what they did to me but I don't know how that changed me into this."

"Agent Spiker and I devised a plan to have you put on a Psy Ops interrogation machine. I guessed that extreme suffering would clear your final karmic residue and free your soul."

"Nice," Roger murmured. "Good guess."

"All animals have the potential to activate their light bodies. It's why planets exist. Life aspires to live on higher dimensions. Individuals evolve through suffering in order to ignite the flame of consciousness in the solar plexus. It's metaphysical so it won't burn you to a crisp. You have a field of electrical consciousness based on meridians. They call it the Merkabah in Jewish mysticism – like Ezekiel's chariot. The Taoists and the Hindus had ways of activating it too. Hardly anybody can do it now. The intensity of materialism in human consciousness has made the density of matter too great in the continuum."

"Yeah, I remember some of this from the missing years. So life begins on a planet and then moves off into space once it evolves spiritually." In the cabin of the flying triangle he could see the bright ball of the planet gleaming through a shaded window.

Henry said, "The ruling elite is determined to stop this process from happening. They put more value on money and power than they do on the will of the source. That's the real reason they put fluoride in the worlds' water supplies. It shuts down the pineal gland that links you to the higher mind. They only pretend to care about children's teeth."

"So that's why they shoot at light beings and flying saucers," said Roger. "I suppose the religions are in there too, to protect their own hierarchies. If your heads are trapped in old holy books, there's no danger of anyone achieving freedom of consciousness."

"Exactly, you then need somebody else, a priest or equivalent to interpret the dogma and tell you what to think."

The moon loomed large in the window. Henry pointed out a dark tunnel on the far side, facing away from the earth. "We'll go down there and park this thing. The ETs let us have flying triangle technology like this as a sweetener. The ones the aliens make are much better. The problem is that whatever they give us, the military want to turn it into a weapon."

"Like you."

Henry nodded sadly. "I don't want to be a weapon. I've had enough fighting against the titan. Once you've experienced oneness, there's nothing more you need."

"Do you think it would be safe for me to go back to my flat? Will they still be looking for me?"

"They might," said Henry cautiously. "I can check it out with the UK authorities. If they are, I'll alter the records to show that you're not the same person that flew out of Kent as an orb. I can use the compartmentalisation in the security sector to our advantage. We should be able to get you back to your home in London if that's what you want. Wouldn't you prefer to broaden your horizons?"

"I don't intend to remain there indefinitely," Roger replied. "I have things to do before we leave."

"What will you require to stay there?"

Roger thought for a moment. "There's no food in the flat. Can we go shopping?"

"Yes," said Henry. "ETs tend to see human beings as little children that never grew up. I think there will come a time when the militaristic culture here is seen for what it is; a shallow aberration. Most television programmes and movies portray violence as something admirable."

"That won't leave much subject matter for Hollywood blockbusters," Roger said laughing. "How about flower arranging and horticulture with Field Marshall Lord Kitchener? That could be a pacifist movie about World War One. They could call it 'Your country needs yew'."

Chapter Fourteen

Roger and Henry travelled from deep space to South London by various devious means without triggering NORAD. Henry disappeared for fifteen minutes and returned with a small car. He drove Roger to a supermarket. "These parking bays are too narrow for the skill level of drivers," Henry noted. "Look at the paint smears on the concrete pillars."

"I know. I can't afford a car so I don't have that problem," said Roger. "What are we going to use to buy food? I forgot to bring my wallet."

"I've got money," said Henry. "Let me just check that these notes are not from the future. It can be a nuisance when you try to buy something with a £20 note from 2024 – not that it will be worth much then."

"Yeah, especially as we've just had a financial crisis. I don't think 2008 is going to be a popular year for nostalgia. They say Thatcher's Big Bang in 1986 deregulated the markets and made us vulnerable to the Lehman Brother's collapse. Nigel Lawson described it as an 'unintended consequence'. Did Thatcher actually believe investment traders would behave honestly without regulation? That's like relying on abstinence for birth control. Still, don't worry. Our politicians won't starve. They'll make *us* pay as usual."

"That's probably true," Henry said. "I've seen the future and they will bring in 'austerity' to make the poor pay for the actions of rogue traders. The super-rich won't suffer. They'll get richer because they don't pay tax."

Roger walked through the automatic doors but they closed behind him into the android's face. Roger looked back, puzzled.

"Sorry," Henry said, unwittingly wrecking the door by pushing against its mechanism. "These sensors register body heat and motion. I'm undetectable in all but optical frequencies."

Once inside, the android pushed the trolley and picked out food items as Roger directed. "I can't get used to having money. What's the best deal?" Roger had lived in relative poverty long enough that he couldn't turn down the opportunity to stock up on other items he needed, things like cleaning products, if they were on offer.

"In theory, those things over there," Henry said, pointing at discounted food items. "But they inflated the price two weeks ago before putting them down again. So even on special, they cost more than they did four weeks ago. Roger, my boy, you live in a dishonest society. Nobody seems to care about integrity. It tarnishes the soul of everybody involved even if they are only following orders."

Roger sighed. "Never mind. What did King John say about his treasure? It'll come out in the Wash. His jewels probably fell off the back of a donkey in the first place."

"You don't need to worry about deals and discounts," Henry said. "I've got plenty of money and I can always make more."

"I know that in my head," said Roger, "but after being on the dole for over a year some habits are too ingrained to change overnight."

Henry pushed the trolley containing Roger's groceries out to the car. When they had unloaded everything into the boot, Henry paid for parking. As he drove out towards the two exit lanes, he pointed to the sign that said 'Use both lanes'.

"That's a tricky one to comply with," Henry said.

Roger looked confused. Then he realised that Henry was interpreting the sign literally. "You idiot! It doesn't mean use both lanes *at the same time*. That's impossible."

"Really?" said Henry. He reached up with his mind into the universal network and caused the entire car and its occupants to divide between two timelines. One version went through the left channel and the other through the right. They recombined at the other side of the barriers.

Roger felt sick throughout the process.

"Wow! How could you do that? Surely, one thing cannot become two?"

"Of course it can't. It's an illusion. The phenomenon is called *superposition*. All I did was create a diversion between alternate pulses of quantum time. We appeared to be in two places at once but never in the same time pulse."

"That's *all* you did! Bloody hell!"

"Okay, let's go home. You said you want to visit your neighbour," said Henry purposefully. "Then I need to go somewhere. You won't want *me* around when Deborah comes to see you."

"Oh, won't I?" said Roger, looking puzzled. "Why's that then?"

***

Mavis Pargiter heard her doorbell ring and opened the door. She showed pleasure at seeing Roger, a joy tempered by the fact that her neighbour's skin colour had changed mysteriously from white to black.

She couldn't bring herself to accept that it was possible. She still half-believed that he had applied make-up.

Roger sensed the tension under the smile.

"Sorry, Mavis. You find my appearance disquieting," he stated rather than asked.

"Wouldn't you?" she said defensively.

"Maybe – once. These days I take so much more for granted." Roger snapped his fingers and instantly his skin changed from black to white.

Mavis jumped back, partly in shock and partly in fear.

"I think you've become the Roger I sensed to be dangerous."

Roger's face registered surprise. It was an assessment of himself that he didn't like.

"I regret to say I have," he acknowledged. "And yet, it does have its good points. Besides," he added, "it's a paradox; power entails responsibility. Nothing can change that." Roger considered for a few moments and then said, "As long as we can avoid moral dilemmas. That's the road to hell."

"And our greatest learning," Mavis said.

"Yes, I understand that now. The universe is a magnificent machine designed to teach us the meaning of love by putting us through hell. Do this and hurt somebody; do nothing and hurt somebody else. Apparently, the soul choses what happens to us and we mortals must do the best we can to act without harming anyone. Unfortunately, most people don't bother to do the right thing: expediency and selfishness is the norm for many. If only they understood the consequences to themselves."

"Most of us fail I think," she said turning away. "And on that positive note, I'll put the kettle on. Chocolate digestives?"

They drank tea and talked about nothing in particular. Then Mavis said, "So your memory has returned?"

"Hmm. Mostly, but not everything – not yet."

"But you know what happened during those missing years?"

"Yes."

There was a silence.

"Can you tell me about it?" Mavis asked.

"You wouldn't believe me," Roger said.

"I'd believe *you*."

Roger shook his head. "Not yet. One day, perhaps; anybody I tell will be at risk."

"Those men in black suits?"

"You saw them?"

"I couldn't miss them. And your twin brother from South Dakota. Whose side is he on?"

"It's complicated," Roger said cautiously. "Henry is on my side and that can be a mixed blessing at times. But he means well."

Mavis passed him his tea and biscuits and asked, "What happened to that nice lady friend of yours?"

"Deborah? She's on her way over right now. I'd better get back to my flat when we've had our tea. Deborah is a friend; that's all."

"If you say so."

***

Roger opened the door as soon as he heard the bell. Deborah stood there in casual, feminine clothing that gave her a softer air than the black suits of the agency.

"Hi," said Roger. "Come in."

"Your place looks tidy. I guess you haven't been raided for a couple of days."

"See this! Someone has put on a new door and repaired the damage. It looks better than it did before the last raid."

"Henry did that with a little help from the hoodies."

"Hoodies! I can't believe how they've changed. They're quite mature now. So here I am, back in mundane life after turning into an orb and flying around in space."

"I didn't expect mundane after what happened to you. I thought you'd be different somehow," Deborah said.

Roger shook his head. "I'm still *me* but I do feel different. My body is more flexible and extremely relaxed. I see patterns of colour around people. I haven't got used to it yet – flying off in a ball of light. How weird is that?" He decided to talk to her seriously. "Look, Deborah. I've been meaning to say…"

The doorbell rang.

"Damn. I'd better see who that is," said Roger rising.

He opened the door to see Barty Loughlin standing outside with a bandage wrapped around his right hand.

"Hello, Barty. What's wrong? You don't look well."

"I ain't too well but that's not why I'm here. Are you Henry?"

"No, I'm Roger."

"You're white again."

"I am. How can I help?" Roger asked, not keen to discuss his changing complexion.

"I hoped you could put me in touch with Henry. We need him."

Deborah came up behind Roger. "Can we help? Henry is busy right now."

"Is he on the moon?" asked Barty. "Can you phone him?"

"Henry moves in a mysterious way," she said. "I can't always contact him."

"Especially when he is time travelling," Roger said.

Deborah poked him in the ribs for his indiscretion. Roger grinned.

"Well, okay. Can you come with me? It's Cade."

"Where is he?"

Barty looked around cautiously. "I'd rather not say here."

"I've removed all the bugging devices that were in your flat," said Deborah, "but you can hardly blame him for caution. They won't need to use so many hard devices in the future. Your cell phone, TV and washing machine will include covert surveillance channels."

"You had me bugged!" demanded Roger.

"A bit," she said shyly. "It wasn't *just* me. I was worried about your safety. Black Ops did it and MI6 put in their own. They've gone too."

"Oh thanks. Nice to know you care."

Her smile disarmed him. "Of course I care."

"Cade…" reminded Barty.

"We'll come with you," said Deborah. "Do we need to drive?"

"He's in the next block at his aunt's place. She's on holiday for a week in Barbados."

"Lead on then," said Roger. He and Deborah followed Barty down the stairwell to the concrete walkways that separated the blocks.

"What's wrong with Cade?" Roger asked.

"Don't know."

"You've hurt your arm," he noted. "Is that connected?"

"Yeah."

Deborah looked at Roger and shrugged. Outside the entrance of the block they encountered a group of residents sitting and passing time, some of them hoodies, some black, some white, some female, others male. They had a language of their own with which Roger was not acquainted. Barty regarded them in distress.

"This could be hard," Barty said, turning to Deborah. "You got a leng?"

"A what?"

"A gun," Barty explained impatiently.

"Not today," she said cheerfully.

"Grimey."

A few of the group stood up as they approached.

"What you doing here? We told you to scrape," said one.

"You've been seen with this tourist," another said pointing at Roger. "And her," he added pointing at Deborah.

"You split to the po-po," a hoodie accused Roger.

"He didn't tell the police or the box anyfing," Barty told them. "We set him up for them thinking he was the enemy. They offered us a deal. But he ain't. Him and his blud, Henry, and the choong gash are fam." This was the first time Roger realised they thought him an informer. It was the only part of the conversation that made any sense. The rest was gobbledygook but he got the gist of their involvement with the police in the shadow of Black Ops involvement.

Unfortunately, Barty's words made no impression on the group who formed a barrier to prevent them from entering the block.

"I think I'll leave this to you to sort out," Deborah said, turning to Roger. "You could do with the practice."

"I can't make up my mind what to do."

"You'd better do something quick," she said. "We need to get in and they don't want us to."

"I don't want to create a legend so mass levitation's out."

The standoff was beginning to attract an audience. Three girls began to drift towards the group to see what was going on. Other people stared and a few more began to walk in their direction.

There was no handbook to inform Roger's actions but somehow instinct took over. He searched in the universal matrix for the active recording of what was happening. He found the trigger moment, commencing from when he, Barty and Deborah had turned the corner of the building, and bifurcated the timeline, totally erasing the three of them from the group's consciousness. The hoodies looked confused for a while, then resumed sitting and chatting.

Turning to his companions Roger winked and said, "The Force can have a strong influence on the weak-minded."

Barty was too anxious about Cade to find humour in anything. He led them up the stairs rather than using the lift, or the elevator as Deborah preferred to call it. Then he took them around the final landing to the shadowy side of the building and up to a grey front door. Barty fished in his hoodie pocket for the key and opened the door to the flat. He motioned them to follow him to the bedroom. Strange noises emitted from within. They heard the jolts of a bed shifting around and continual moaning and groaning. Barty went in first. Roger and Deborah saw flashes of light as they followed.

Cade lay on the bed on a bare mattress; his body encased in a translucent, egg-shaped shell of light. Irregular patterns of intense bright colour shimmered on and off spasmodically. The outside layer glimmered with a faint aura of golden light.

Barty turned towards them. "What's happening to him? Help me."

Roger said aside to Deborah although Barty was close enough to hear, "I don't know what it is but look at the left leg."

She nodded. "It's black, completely black."

"He *is* black," protested Barty.

"Not the skin, Barty. We're talking about the light within," Roger explained. "Have you heard of the *aura*?"

"No. I thought he'd been wired to the mains."

Roger shook his head. "We need Henry," he said. "I don't…"

"You called?" said a familiar voice, in fact his own.

"How the hell did you get here?" Roger asked his synthetic twin. "Aren't you supposed to be on the moon?"

"I was…thirty seconds ago."

Deborah blurted out, "What brought you here so quickly?"

Henry pointed at Roger. "He did?"

"I did? Impossible!" Roger declared.

Barty said, "What you did outside the flat was impossible but you did it. Know what I mean?"

"Yes, I know *that* but *two* impossible things in one day. That's…"

"Impossible," said Deborah dryly. "Impossibility squared?"

"What were you doing at the time?" Roger asked Henry.

Henry knelt by Cade and began to inspect him. "I was holding a seminar in human culture for a group of ET ambassadors," Henry said without rancour. "I was trying to explain why, in an infinite universe, human beings get excited over designer labels. Why they will pay five hundred dollars for one pair of trainers rather than one hundred for an identical product from an unfashionable maker. Especially when you know that they only cost two dollars to manufacture. ETs don't understand the psychology of corporate logos. They do not aspire to a lifestyle. And they don't have political and religious dogma on alien worlds. They judge an idea on its merit, not on the personality of the person trying to sell it. Never mind. Negotiations concluded I suppose."

"I'm terribly sorry," said Roger. "It sounds like they have a lot to learn. But how did I bring you here? I wouldn't know how to begin to do that."

"Never mind," said Deborah soothingly, patting Roger's arm. "It could have been worse. You might have brought the moon with him if you'd known what you were doing."

Henry pulled a pen-sized gadget from his lunar-style tunic and ran it up and down the subject's body. The action reminded Roger of Dr McCoy with his medical *tricorder* in *Star Trek*.

"His light body is firing up," Henry explained, glancing at Roger. "He must be naturally gifted. You went through hell to get there. I put him and Cade in the temporal resequencer. It's a spontaneous quickening – an awakening!

"You must put me in that thing," Deborah remarked. "Then I'll be able to whizz around with Roger."

Henry nodded. "It's done wonders for Agent Spiker. He suggested we use a car battery and jump leads to complete the process for the rest of you. This young man's consciousness was already in an advanced state. Recent events have pushed him beyond his normal limit – normal for him. Cade came to this world relatively clear of bad karma but this gang culture creates more than its fair share of negative activity. If only they understood who and what they are and aspired for better. Society offers them nothing positive. Education on this planet is spiritually bankrupt and in Britain, stratified by historical class prejudice. Cade cleared his karmic residue in the alien virtual reality machine. He experienced insights of understanding as well as pain. His mind could do that."

"He doesn't seem able to do it now," said Barty, uncomprehending.

"No," Henry agreed. He tapped the leg with the void inside it, immune to the energies that burned Barty's arm. "He has a titanium implant in his thigh bone from a previous accident. Metal short circuits the meridians."

"Can you help him?" Barty asked.

"I can relieve the situation by tweaking his DNA to incorporate the implant in his basic design. It won't be part of his pattern. I'll just leave a cavity of identical shape and size. It's a bit of a bodge but it will get him out of trouble now. The mathematics is tricky but with my chip speeds and parallel processing…"

"Mr Henry, you go on worse than Dr Who sometimes, innit? What about Cade?" Barty reminded as forcefully as he dared.

Henry passed his hand over Cade and performed the appropriate 'tweaking' psychokinetically.

"Cade is fine," said Henry to Barty. "Look."

The layers of light and colour around Cade's body looked almost completely formed and were beginning to expand and shimmer like a luminous envelope in the shape of an egg. He turned to Roger and said, "I think you know what is happening to me because it has already happened to you."

Roger nodded.

The golden tinge surrounding Cade intensified and his black features glowed faintly purple. *Like an old Russian icon*, Roger thought. Cade stood up from the bed and walked around the room within his coat of many colours. He gazed out of the window at the flats opposite. Finally, he looked in his aunt's dressing table mirror.

The situation, so bizarre, frightened Barty. "I thought you was goin' to put him right. He's even worse now. What's wrong with him?"

Cade smiled at his friend. "Nothing is wrong with me. Everything is right. But I can't stay here. How can I walk around looking like this?"

His accent was the same but the cadence of his voice carried a new surety and understanding.

"You can switch off the activated aura when you need to. You'd look normal but you'll always seem different to those who know you. Some will accept you – others will not. It's up to you," said Henry. "If you wish me to take you away from here, I can do so. I feel partly responsible for this because I took you to the moon and put you on the extraterrestrial life analyser."

"It didn't do that to me," Barty pointed out.

Cade shook his head. "No, it's happened to me because I arranged it before I was born."

Henry nodded. "The centre of consciousness within your pineal gland has opened up to the universal mind. The problem is that people often regard those who awaken as saints or demons. It frightens them. The self-righteous see evil everywhere but it only reflects what is within them that they cannot face."

"It's the earth," Cade said. "The planet's waking up, isn't it?"

"It's trying to," agreed Henry. "Like everything else in the universe, the earth is made of consciousness. Subversive evil forces controlling humanity are trying to kill it, to stop the process from happening."

"Why?" Cade asked.

"Superficially, it is because the idea of the planet moving into a higher consciousness would be bad for business. The social and economic divisions would dissolve. With the people polarised between rich and poor, the wealthy do not have to relinquish their power. Poverty feeds wealth. Profit comes before life itself no matter the karmic cost to those responsible. What they can't see can't hurt them."

"What's the real reason?" Cade asked.

"Ah, that goes much deeper," said Henry. "The game you are playing out on earth allows infinite consciousness to experience itself in finite form with no sense of true identity and purpose. You have no awareness of past states of being and you have free will to do things that your true spiritual consciousness would not condone. It is a grand experiment to push human beings to their limits, to expand their minds and awaken the spirit, in short to achieve a measure of divinity through union with the source, the one. Nobody can say when the end of time will happen. Only the source knows that."

"The end of time," Barty gasped. "We'll all die?"

Henry smiled. "No, the end of time is not the end of life; quite the reverse. It would mean the end of the pulsing clock that drives this planet and its virtual reality universe. The speed of light would be different, faster probably. You might experience difficulties with digital systems, computers and the Internet but you would no longer age and die in the way you do now."

"Can't your ET connections help?" Roger asked. "Surely, they know if and when it will happen."

"It might not happen at all. It depends on enough people on earth waking up and learning to love instead of hate. They tried sending special people here to guide you but the game is unconscious. Every positive action carries within it its negative opposite. That's what karma means, action and reaction, positive and negative, yin and yang. Good deeds sometimes create their own resistance. It's how the game works to bring about enlightenment and responsibility. The church killed visionaries and natural healers, accusing them of witchcraft. A religious and political system crucified Jesus of Nazareth for raising the frequency of consciousness for the planet. If people try to do good now, the press crucifies them by exposing their weaknesses – or inventing them. But the rich and powerful can get away with murder, cruelty to children and financial fraud. Their only crime is to get caught."

"Politicians promise change to get elected," said Roger, "but in the end it's always more of the same – or worse. Is that what you mean?"

"Yes," Henry agreed. "When humanity grows up it will not be because of your systems like politics, finance and government. They are a symptom of the problem not the solution. They will collapse eventually because of their own corruption. Change can only come from within each individual; you cannot legislate love."

"So my choice," said Cade, "is to cope with life here in an expanded state of mind or leave altogether. My family won't understand, let alone the brothers and sisters on the streets. I can see Barty isn't happy about it."

"Can we take him somewhere for adjustment?" Deborah asked Henry.

"Maybe I should take him to the extraterrestrials for advice," he replied.

"Back to the moon?" Roger asked. "How do we manage that without being seen by the whole of South London?"

"You got *me* here easily enough," said Henry.

"Yes, but I don't know *how* I did it," Roger said. "Besides, look at Cade. He looks like he just stepped out of a Renaissance painting."

There was a knock at the door. Roger opened it and saw Agent Spiker standing there. He regarded him warily after their previous meeting.

"It's okay, Roger. He's with me," said Henry. "You've brought a vehicle for us, Herbert?"

"I've got your old Lincoln. I'm illegally parked so we'd better hurry."

"I know it's big but surely we can't all get in that," said Roger.

"We don't have to," Deborah said, putting her arm through his. "It's got a teleport terminal in the trunk."

"Well, that should be discrete. Who would notice six people climbing into a car boot and disappearing?"

"They'll see me," Cade pointed out. "My face glows in the dark."

"You're a hoodie," said Roger. "That's halfway to being a Jedi warrior already. Hide your face like you do in shops."

Cade put on his hoodie and pulled the hood down over his head. It concealed most of his face but it didn't stop light from shining out. They filed out: Spiker followed by Roger, Deborah, Henry, Cade and Barty.

"Down the stairs," Henry called. "There's too many of us for the elevator."

"Where are you parked, Agent Spiker?" Deborah enquired.

"On a back lot behind a clothing store." He pointed down the road.

As they arrived at the alley that led to the back of the building, Henry slowed down and indicated that they should move forward quietly.

They saw Henry's 1957 Lincoln Premiere and a pickup truck with rotating orange lights. The driver of the truck was attempting to put a clamp on a front wheel. Whenever he got near it, the wheel mysteriously withdrew upwards into the cowling. At the third attempt the wheel remained hidden.

"Damn," said Spiker. "If I was a year younger I'd bend his skull with a tyre lever. I didn't know what a conscience was then. Just give 'em hell and get paid for it."

The clamper gave up and moved his apparatus to one of the rear wheels, with the same result. He now had a car with two diagonally opposing wheels withdrawn into the chassis. He grunted with satisfaction; the car couldn't remain level if he tried a third time – but it did. This was impossible! That a car could remain steady on two wheels was pushing the limits of his beliefs but to do so on one was inconceivable.

"Got you now," he said and moved round to the fourth wheel only to find it withdraw like all the others. With no wheels on *terra firma*, the Lincoln remained the same distance from the ground. The clamper tried to push down on the bonnet but the vehicle would not move. It was as solid as rock, even with no visible means of support.

Henry signalled the group to move forward into the derelict space with its weeds and rubbish. The man looked up as they approached.

"Keep him occupied for a minute or two," Henry said softly to the others.

"Yeah, right," said Roger. He walked up to the would-be clamper. "Having problems, sir?" he asked politely. He manoeuvred himself so that the man had to turn in his direction.

Henry went up to the pickup and pressed his palms on the side and the air around it shimmered, dimly at first and then much more brightly. After a few seconds, a miniaturised version of the vehicle lay on the ground. A spatial barrier no thicker than an atom reduced it proportionally in size and mass to the scale of a Dinky Toy. The vehicle's dimensions were unaffected on the inside.

"What's this about? Is this your motor? You're illegally parked."

"Terribly sorry, sir," Roger replied soothingly. "We're about to leave. We've got a long journey ahead of us. We just had to get something from the shop up the road."

"That's all very well, mate, but this is private property. You ain't no business here," declared the clamper.

Meanwhile, behind the man's back, the boot of the Lincoln appeared to open of its own accord. Deborah reached inside and began to fiddle with the spare tyre under a loose panel. She lifted one side so that it hinged open like a circular trap door. It weighed nothing in comparison to a real tyre. She beckoned Cade and Barty over and pointed down.

"See that?"

Barty looked down curiously.

"It's the sky! I can see the sky behind a sort of multi-coloured liquid. I can feel heat coming up too."

"This is a transitional portal to a desert in North America. We're going to take you to meet friends of ours. They'll help Cade to adjust to his developing physiology. He's got a little way to go before he's fully integrated."

"I dunno what you're talking about. So what about *me*?" asked Barty in a slightly pleading tone. His friendship with Cade had propelled him through a series of life-changing experiences and there was no going back. Unfortunately, a way of going forward had also failed to appear. Ordinary existence with his friend in this state was untenable but what else was there for him to do? Where could they go?

"And me?" said Spiker in a similar situation. "I

can't stay on with Ops if I can't eliminate people."

"I know. That was your *raison d'être*," said Henry, quoting a phrase he'd picked up on a visit to France.

"I don't know about *that*," said Spiker. "But it was the purpose of my life. What am I supposed to do now? Knit daisy chains?"

Agent Herbert Spiker was a man from another time. He had made a quantum leap in circumstance and environment. He had opened a cab door for Mary Pickford for God's sake! A time jump was like a death in the family. You died in one life and woke up in another. For a time, you were a walking corpse. Nothing made sense in this other world. Almost every artefact was a mystery except the guns. The nature of laser sights gave him pause but their function did not. No more silent films; just high definition televisions. They were living room monsters that sucked you into an enticing layer of unreality. They told stories in primary colours and dark shadows. He was equally immune to great dramas and tawdry soaps with their addictive angst. Action movies with their *papier-mâché* heroes and cartoon plots ran counter to his experience. Even on a bad day, he'd never used more than six bullets on a mission and never more than two on a single target: head and heart, *bam bam!* Send for the cleaners.

In his youth, Spiker had seen images of Edvard Munch's painting, *The Scream*. Once incomprehensible, it now made too much sense in a society that put banal celebrities on pedestals vacated by the old gods. Famous for being famous, many ended up as the playthings of Satanists. Spiker alone could see it, it seemed. These people belonged to their time but he did not. The job gave him a grim revenge on a society that rejected him unconsciously as a temporal anachronism. He couldn't work a computer but he could kill. The android had once told him that time is not just a counting of days. A moment of time, however briefly experienced, is a fragment of life's story enshrined in the timelessness of eternity. His story did not *belong* to theirs. Henry knew that only too well from his own brief life experience – more so in fact. Maybe what was happening to this black kid from London might enable Spiker to find some kind of peace and self-worth too. Neither Barty nor Cade felt that they belonged to the society they lived in. The advertisers and the trendsetters dangled trivial aspirations of wealth and status before their eyes and, at the same time, told them they didn't deserve to achieve it. Now they were learning that it was all worthless dross. Why put up with a nightmare of poverty and privation when there was a magnificent dream of spiritual fulfilment and adventure waiting to be found? It was all there, just beyond the veil of illusion that made up this virtual reality game of humanity's own creation.

"Henry," said Spiker. "What's happening to Cade..."

"Yes," said Henry. "What about it?"

"Could it happen to me?"

"You, Herbert!" Henry responded in surprise.

"Yeah. I keep getting a strange vibration in my spine and the other night I woke up and my whole body was charged with electricity. Mrs Spiker got a shock."

"And I put you in the life review machine," Henry said, understanding.

Spiker nodded. "I didn't think it could happen to me

after all the bad things I done to people. But something's going on."

Henry smiled at him. "It's not about what you've done. That can always be resolved through forgiveness. An incarnation of suffering and doing good would soon put that right. It's about what you are, not what you were. What's in your heart? There's hope for the whole of humanity if they can only learn to follow the basic guidance; love one another, do as you would be done by, don't judge other people, help others at every opportunity, respect people's beliefs; better still, don't have beliefs. They just hold you in limitation. The present moment is the only reality. The past is happening now. Make it a better past. Be happy, be free."

Roger agreed. He turned away from his wheel clamping acquaintance to say: "When you hang on to history, you perpetuate the grievances between communities and the shadow never ends. It passes down through the generations, adding to the karmic burden of the planet. You don't forgive to free the person who wronged you; you do it to free yourself from the burden of grievance. People who say they can never forgive another for what they did, hurt nobody but themselves."

"Look here. What's going on?" demanded the clamper.

"Down you all go, gentlemen and lady. Head first is best unless you want to arrive upside down."

"You men can go ahead of me," said Deborah. "My skirt will probably be above my waist as I climb in."

Spiker went through first. When it came to Barty's turn he decided to have some fun. "Mr Henry, could you please drop me down the hole?"

"Why?" the android asked.

"Why not?"

Henry obliged by lifting him up by his ankles and dropping him through the portal. Barty shot through the gap and up into the early morning light, came to a stop and began to drop back down again. This motion became a series of diminishing oscillations until he found the null point, leaving his torso in America and his legs in London. Spiker pulled him up and set him on the ground. Roger's turn came next. He nodded affably to their shocked wheel clamper before climbing head first through the portal. A weird feeling like a ripple of compression ran down his body as he traversed the gravitational anomaly that separated the two domains. Roger gazed around him as he emerged upright in a shaded canyon with sheer sandstone sides and a sprinkling of desert plants. The sky was streaked with red but the sun was hidden behind the surrounding rocks. Two Native Americans waited nearby in blue jeans and redneck style shirts. A humanoid extraterrestrial with a purple-brown skin tone stood slightly to one side. Cade and Barty stared at him curiously.

Deborah came through last, modesty preserved, leaving only Henry at the London end to deal with the confused wheel clamper who stared at him, open-mouthed and shaking with fear.

"You've seen things you shouldn't have seen," said Henry sympathetically. He pointed his right index finger at the man's head and sent out a pulse of psychotronic energy, rearranging his memory of the last few minutes. The subject's eyes glazed over as he turned to find his vehicle but it was no longer there.

"I think you were looking for this," Henry said,

dropping the 'toy' truck into his hand. It was now of a size to fit into his palm. He activated a mechanism in the Lincoln, which glowed and shrank likewise.

Henry picked up the tiny model of his car and held it up to the wheel clamper for inspection. "See, I've got one too. Aren't they great? Perfect in every detail."

He slipped the car into a pocket. The man, bemused and confused, studied the miniature truck in his hand.

Henry shook the clamper's free hand vigorously. "Nice to meet you. I recommend you don't put that thing in your pocket or on a sideboard. In twenty-four hours it will expand to its normal size and weight. Not its mass of course, that remains unchanged in its own super-dimensional state. Did you know that mass and weight are not the same? You'd know that for sure if you'd been on the moon. Do you know any quiet car parks? I suggest you set the little truck down in the centre of an empty space. But don't allow anyone to park a vehicle over it. When the bubble of space-time returns fully to this dimension, it is absolutely unstoppable. No force on earth could contain it."

That said, the android walked off towards the main road.

Chapter Fifteen

Elizabeth Sennitt attached a leash to the collar of her Labrador retriever on the front passenger seat of her Jeep Wrangler.

"Down, Millie."

The dog obliged. Elizabeth shut the door and locked the vehicle. Turning away, she allowed the animal to lead her along the pavement to a dirt track road. The chosen route would take them away from the town towards a region of wilderness popular with campers and walkers. After twenty minutes, the scenery changed from woodland to rocky outcrops and a popular attraction for naturalists, a sprinkling of wolf trees.

It took half an hour to reach a beautiful valley. A fast-flowing stream cascaded down a crevice in the rocks along one side. The energetic water made delightful noises as it followed the path of least resistance between boulders. Suddenly, she felt a presence close behind her. Millie barked with surprise. Turning sharply, Elizabeth saw two men, identical in person but dressed differently. They were both tall.

"Sneaking up behind me?" she demanded.

"Sneaking!" cried Roger imitating Golum from *Lord of the Rings.*

She laughed. "The magician and the technician. Together again." Instinctively, she identified Roger by his less immaculate clothing. She was aware that

Henry tailored himself in every sense of the word.

"Roger, you've found me – or was it you that tracked me down?" she asked turning towards the android.

"At least somebody can tell us apart," Roger remarked. "Even *we* have trouble sometimes."

"I thought they'd hidden you away somewhere," Elizabeth said to Roger.

Roger nodded. "I've come from 2008. What time is this?"

"2004," she replied.

"I don't know where I am or even which timeline we are on."

Elizabeth clasped her hands together and contemplated them in silence. It was a gesture she'd used as a lecturer to students. She hadn't always been a Space Command officer and she certainly wasn't now.

She turned to address Henry. "So, you're here to find your friend."

"Yes."

"But you don't know where she is."

"There are no flies on you, Elizabeth," said Roger, brushing several away before saying, "Henry hacked the Department of Vehicle Registration system to identify your truck. Then he traced it through the Space Command global satellite surveillance system. Their computers employ a technology that supersedes quantum computing."

"What's *that*?" Henry asked, leaning forward to look askance at Roger from the far side of Dr Sennitt.

"I don't know but if Moore's Law of shrinking circuit technology still applies, I bet it's small," Roger explained with a wink.

"It goes way beyond Moore's Law that says the

density of transistors on a chip doubles every two years," Henry replied.

"Shut up, Roger," said Sennitt wearily. "What do you want from me, Henry?"

"I need to ask a favour of you," Henry said with an intensity she had never heard from him before. "I need to find Jensine."

"You *need*?" she said archly. "Twice! *Need* implies emotional involvement. *Want* is much more detached. In your early days, intellectual curiosity motivated you to try new things. It sounds as if you have stepped into a larger universe. Do I detect an affair of the heart?"

"It is true," said Henry "that I have had occasional shifts of consciousness over things that humans would take for granted. I did develop a rudimentary facility to taste food. It allowed me to identify individual flavours. One day, while I was eating a meal with Jensine, I experienced taste as an aesthetic pleasure. When I was a robot I could analyse speech as a string of identifiable words and aggregate their structure into recognisable information. As an android I can put speech into a social context. I now know that being *pissed off* does not imply the completion of urination."

Elizabeth chuckled and said, "So you need a favour. There might be a problem there. They've retired me. Did you know?"

"I tried to contact you through official channels but I drew a blank," Henry admitted.

"*Drew a blank*," she repeated. "Colloquial metaphors! I can remember when your speech was subservient to linguistic rules set in firmware." She put her hand on Henry's arm. "As to retirement, they finally gave up on me," she stated flatly. "I tried to stop them wiping your friend…wiping *your* existence from Jensine's memory. I wanted her to remain in your life, whatever the consequence. Well, this is the consequence." She waved her hand around at the scenery. "I'm out here with Millie enjoying the wilderness; thankfully they didn't terminate my employment with a bullet in the brain. That's one way they save on pensions."

Henry remained silent for several minutes. They walked on with the dog, treading along a rugged terrain beside the descending waterway. Elizabeth was arm in arm with Roger on one side and Henry on the other. The solidity in Henry's posture was something no human being could achieve. She thought of him as a statue in motion.

"This is extremely unfortunate," Henry declared at last. "I had hoped to ask for your help to use a particular technical facility. It's one of the few laboratories I can't get into unaided. I *need* to deactivate a micro-explosive device that Black Ops installed in my head. They are constantly looking for ways to activate it."

Elizabeth nodded. "Now *that's* a need I can understand! Isn't it ironic? They still see you as a threat because you won't kill to order. What kind of twisted logic is that?"

"Ironic?" Roger said in amusement. "From the mouth of an American?"

Elizabeth slapped his arm gently.

Henry continued. "I have taken control of the encryption circuit on the fuse but they use state of the art computers to break it. It's a constant battle for me to keep changing it faster than they can crack it. They can factorise massive numbers very quickly. It means that I can never relax and empty my mind totally."

"Can't you get help from your alien friends on the moon?" Elizabeth asked.

"Yes, but I'd rather Roger performed the operation. I'll be in my most vulnerable state. I don't know whom to trust absolutely other than Roger. He helped me before, when I was a robot on Centaur II."

Elizabeth sighed. "I don't know what to suggest. Millie, put that down!"

"What about Jensine. Is there nothing you can tell us?" Roger asked.

Elizabeth Sennitt pursed her lips before coming to a decision.

"I did suspect at one time that they had imprisoned her in a colony on Mars. I cannot confirm this one way or the other. In a cellular need-to-know organisation it is difficult to pick up gossip."

"And yet you heard this."

"It was not something I heard. It was something I deduced. Dr Pettersson disappeared from the base and I happened to see the manifest for a Mars-bound resupply ship that left three days after. One of the items was a cryo-sleep unit with life support hardware. I just put two and two together. I could be wrong."

Henry shook his head. "I will make discreet enquiries at the Lunar 14 facility. I'm owed a few favours. I'm sure Agent Spiker will help me."

"Don't remind me of Agent Spiker," Roger said with feeling. "He gave me to the white coats to torture."

"At my suggestion," said Henry. "I knew it would awaken your light body."

"It did do that but I wouldn't recommend it to anybody else. What if you'd been wrong? I might have died."

"Wrong?" said Henry. "Me? There was nothing to worry about. I'd checked out the relevant timelines. There's a universe where you're still signing on. Do you want to have a look there sometime?"

"No, thank you. I hope there's not a universe where I'm watching reality TV all day."

They continued walking along the rising bank of the turbulent stream.

"Can you hear that?" Henry asked suddenly.

"Hear what?" asked Roger.

A black helicopter emerged into view above the trees that was almost totally silent apart from a soft pulsing hiss from the rotating blades.

"It's a Black Ops observer," said Elizabeth. "They've probably come here to see who I'm talking to."

"Have you got a cell phone, Dr Sennitt?" Henry asked her.

"Yes."

"They are monitoring you and probably listening to us through it."

"Time for Plan B?" Roger suggested.

"I think so," said Henry.

"What is Plan B?" Elizabeth asked.

"It's like Plan 9 from outer space," Roger explained, "but less believable."

Roger and Henry turned into orbs of light and streaked into the sky.

"Oh," said Elizabeth, trying to subdue her barking dog. "*That* Plan B."

***

Henry knocked on Roger's door one evening and came in looking pleased with himself.

"I was about to cook dinner," Roger said to him. "Would you like to join me?"

"I would enjoy that. I have taken a liking to the taste of food and I can always employ the proteins to maintain my biological components."

"That's funny," said Roger. "That's exactly what I do with it."

Henry sat down on the sofa, leaned back and stretched out comfortably.

"Will you cook for me this time?"

Roger smiled. "Of course, old chap. Delighted. Do you want to watch the television while I prepare it?"

"I don't need a set to watch television or surf the net," Henry said. "I have internal access to everything."

"Oh, just sit there then. Can you do mindfulness with all that going on? What are you looking so happy about?"

Henry held up an electronic device.

"What's that?" Roger asked.

"It's the Harper and Plipstow Z45G64 AI Modal Emulator & Power Supply that Elizabeth Sennitt got hold of for me. She came through in the end but I don't know how. It will allow you to remove the bomb in my head without the secure facility at S4. I can't get into that without starting World War III."

"When are we going to do it?"

"You've already done it," said Henry placidly. "That's why I am so relaxed. I no longer need to keep Black Ops from triggering the bomb."

"I've already done it? When?"

"You will do it in the future at a moon base. Then you will send the Modal Emulator back in time to yourself. It will make it easier for you to take me out of the robot and put me in this body."

Roger thought for a long time while he cooked. Then he came back to Henry waving the spatula and said, "How come you've got that gadget if I'm going to send it back in time to myself?"

"You've already done it in three months' time. This is not the one that Elizabeth acquired. It's the original version that I've kept since we first used it in the seventies. Even though you received it from your future self, it didn't actually exist in any timeframe, future or past. It came into being because the universe knew we would need it. But the multiverse cannot encompass a closed time loop without changing history. So I had to feed the design back into a time loop to fulfil the paradox of its anomalous existence. We don't want to find ourselves trapped inside a closed universe going nowhere. Not that we'd ever know. We'd just keep repeating the same events *ad infinitum*. I discovered that the Battle of Edgehill of 1642 keeps replaying when conditions are right. I think it's because the outcome was indecisive in terms of the English Civil War."

"Oh, I see," said Roger, going back to the stir fry.

When he thought about it a bit more, he realised that he didn't understand at all.

TIME LOOP BEGINS – FIRST TIME AROUND

South London, 2009

Roger arrived at his sister's terraced house and pushed the doorbell, setting off the sound of a Tardis landing. Eventually, Billy arrived and let him in with a slap on the back.

"What's up? You looking for me?"

"Yes. I might be going away for a while so I thought we could have a trip out. Are you doing anything today?"

"It's Saturday. Today I shop and go to the pub."

"That's doing something," Roger observed. "What were you thinking of doing? Would Liz approve?"

"Since when do you worry about what my sister thinks?"

"Since I turned thirty. I'm trying to be mature and responsible."

"Bloody hell!" cried Roger. "I never thought I'd hear *you* say that."

"Age has that effect? How old are *you* now? I've forgotten."

"So have I," Roger admitted. "Too much time travel does that."

"What *are* you talking about?"

"Never mind. I just had to take a trip to 2004 to see another Liz."

Billy shook his head sadly. "All this mayhem in your life has sent you loopy. I couldn't even get you to admit that there are UFOs until recently."

"That's true but *you* didn't convince me. It was the one I saw that changed my opinion. Anyway, I still don't believe in unidentified flying objects."

"What do you mean? You said you'd seen one."

"Yes, but since then I have identified it so you can't call it unidentified. That's what I wanted to talk to you about. I know a place where you can see one for yourself. Are you interested?"

"Yeah, not half. Where?" asked his brother-in-law.

"Peckham Rye Park and Common."

"You're kidding. Is Peckham Common the gateway to the universe?"

"Not exactly but it'll do for now. Besides, if it works out as I hope, you'll go a bit further than Peckham Common."

"How do we get there?"

"By bus, of course. Let's go."

They alighted from the number 12 bus and walked through the park to the trees beyond. On impulse, Roger took out a mobile phone and videoed their progress. It was a chilly day so there were few people to be seen other than occasional dog walkers carrying their regulation plastic bags.

"Lucky for us the dinosaurs died out," remarked Billy. "Imagine picking up after your brontosaurus. You'd need a dustbin."

Roger laughed. "I'm not sure if they did die out – well, only physically. Deborah told me she'd once hypnotised a young man who regressed to being a pterodactyl. She said his head even had a slight but distinct protuberance at the back of his skull." Roger indicated people passing by with a gesture. "The dinosaurs are not extinct. We're still here. We've switched roles, that's all. It's all just consciousness in a virtual reality game."

Billy sighed. "Ah, Deborah. Do you still see her?"

"Yes. I've seen her a few times recently. She might be coming on that trip I spoke of."

"Your life has certainly changed. You must have money now; you paid for the bus tickets."

Roger smiled. "I have a rich friend."

"My new brother-in-law from North Dakota? What exactly is Henry?"

"Henry?" Roger said. "Henry is an android. What

else could he be?"

"How d'you know an android that looks like you? Has it got something to do with your missing time?"

Roger nodded. "I can't tell you much. It would put you in danger. The people I dealt with were mostly psychopaths and control freaks."

"Who made Henry? Black Ops or ETs?"

"Henry made Henry. Black Ops made a robot prototype with a reverse-engineered chip. I did something – I don't know what – and the robot came alive and built himself an android body in my image. Sound familiar?"

"Why did you name him Henry?"

"He was number eight in a limited edition. So I named him after Henry VIII. Fortunately, he's nothing like his godawful namesake; the worst husband in history."

"I must say, Rog. You seem to cope much better with life these days. You were a real sad sack after America."

Roger laughed. "It's true. I'm doing much better now. I used to worry about the future. Now I know there isn't any future. All time is concurrent. The future and the past are just stories to justify the present. Our minds are multidimensional but our brains are physical constructs wired into the universal conceptual network. We create these lives as stories to justify our belief in linear time. The present just is; we don't need logic to exist. One day we will evolve beyond the limitation of rationality."

"We'll all be irrational! Isn't that madness?"

"No, just open-minded like babies. What baby ever asks what it is and where it came from when it emerges from the womb? It simply accepts that it is."

"Sometimes you're too deep for me," grumbled Billy.

They entered a region of the park with trees and shrubs. Roger noticed that Billy was peering at the sky.

"Are you looking for a flying saucer up there?" he asked.

Billy looked at him curiously.

"You said I would see one here."

"I certainly did," Roger agreed. "Let's head towards those trees over there."

"Roger, you don't see UFOs on the ground. What are you thinking of? I hope we haven't come all this way for nothing."

"What are you complaining about? This is quite a pleasant park."

"Given the choice, I prefer pubs to parks," Billy said in a flat voice.

They passed through an area of grass surrounded by trees. Roger stopped in a clearing and took something out of his pocket that resembled a TV remote controller. Billy started to walk through but Roger stopped him.

"Hang on a second."

A small white light appeared in the air a few yards ahead of them. A humming sound accompanied the illumination. The light expanded into a bright ball that grew before their eyes. The light faded away, leaving a flying saucer on the ground. It was around the size of three London buses.

Billy blinked incredulously at the sight of the flying disc.

"Fuck me," he gasped.

Roger chuckled and said, "Pass."

"What…?" Billy looked around cautiously.

"Where's the owner? What is the owner? Will it abduct us if we hang around here?"

Roger explained, "It belongs to an alien but he doesn't mind me using it. ETs don't have our concept of ownership. And they don't register with the Civil Aviation Authority. He's a friend of Henry's."

"You mean you're going inside?"

"*We're* going inside. You wanted to see one, didn't you? I don't need a flying disc to travel up there," he said, indicating the sky. "But that would really freak you out."

Roger pressed another button on the control. The shiny, smooth metal on one side of the flying saucer morphed into an oval fissure, large enough for them to enter. The brightly lit interior beckoned them in. Billy hesitated at the threshold, looked at Roger and walked inside. He noticed the central control unit fashioned by alien taste and the minimalist design of the passenger seating. Roger went over to the pilot's station and made the entrance door reform, sealing the orifice completely like a closing iris. "We can sit at the pilot and co-pilot stations. I'll get us airborne and then you can take over."

"Take over! You want me to fly it?"

"It's easy enough. Put this helmet on. I've got my own one here. Sorry about the smell. It's had non-human heads inside it."

Billy put on the helmet as instructed, and immediately began to see a clear picture in his mind of the park outside the craft. It was the kind of vision you get in a lucid dream except that he was awake and it was happening there and then. There was a couple walking a dog, staring open-mouthed at the spacecraft. The lady was reaching for her phone.

"Better get going," said Billy. "We don't want to be on YouTube."

"I thought you'd like being in a video," said Roger.

Roger sat on the seat next to Billy's. He donned his own helmet then put his hand on a palm-shaped depression on the main control unit and concentrated. The craft hummed and rose into the air. He paused at around one hundred feet above ground. Then he emptied his mind and held onto a picture of the earth as a large globe in space. The flying disc shot skyward so fast, it took Billy's breath away. There was none of the acceleration force he might have expected. In a couple of minutes they were looking down on the earth from low orbit.

"Wow! Crazy."

"This is antigravity mode," Roger explained. "We're inside a bubble of space that cuts us off from the earth's mass. It cancels inertia and makes it easy to move about. Later, we'll try you with temporal displacement."

"Come again?" Billy was totally confused.

"You know that light propagates through space," Roger said, "well, matter propagates through time. The continuum is really a living tensor field. You can alter your spatial location by shifting your time vector sideways. Every point in space has its own time signature. So instead of moving, you simply change the idea of where you are."

"What will that do?" Billy asked.

"It'll allow you to take a trip across the solar system."

"Hmm, okay," said Billy doubtfully.

Roger took his hand away from the indentation and placed his brother-in-law's palm against it. Billy immediately felt strange as though the ship had accepted him and become an extension of his will.

"Where are we? What's that down there?"

"That's Africa."

"Oh, yeah. What shall I do?"

"See the moon?"

Billy turned. "Yes."

"Go towards it."

"That's it? Go towards it, like turn left at the next lights."

"That's it."

Billy did as Roger asked simply by thinking it. He was aware that the spacecraft was moving but he had no reference to judge speed. Roger sensed the ship's state too. He had flown solo a few times since Henry had given him his first lesson.

"Dual control is it? It's like the bloody driving test," Billy said grinning inside his headgear. "Where's me L-plates?"

Roger had more serious issues on his mind. They were taking something of a chance by flying around the earth. "Can you see a horizontal blue line in the centre of your vision?"

"Let me see…Yeah. It just appeared."

"Try to stay relaxed. See if you can control the length of the line with your mind. That's it! You got it. Take it out to one hundred and eighty degrees and tell me if you see any ghosts."

"Ghosts? What sort of ghosts?"

"You'll know when you see one."

Billy breathed slowly and tried to be as still as possible. Then Roger and Billy began to see phantom-like images of the saucer moving in and out of existence, some near and some far away. They came from all directions but the destination was fixed. There was a conscious attractor located in the near future drawing events to a single conclusion. His insight told Roger that the event would result in his death. The mortal body fears death no matter what 'we' think about it. The soul sees death as a phase change to manage. Somewhat more detached, the immortal spirit experiences death as a passing variation in the quality of essential light. Roger panicked inside. Could he avoid this compelling attractor in his so-called 'pathway'? For the Old One had told him that the 'journey' of life is illusion. The one unit that sees and creates us never really leaves our personal zero-point. We are fixtures at the origin of space and time. Collectively, we are asleep *here* and *now* dreaming of *there* and *then*.

To Roger, the attractor was like Red Riding Hood's wolf, dangerous and compelling at the same time. What had the ET told him about time? Each moment in the unfolding universal story is pregnant with the next. So the pulse of changing time on the physical plane is really a shuffling of abstract possibilities in the eternity of now. When multiple choices arise, consciousness breathes life into new versions of the time-space field. Time generates matter. Matter creates space. The universe we think we know does not exist except in its parts. Each part is a different version of the whole. The whole has no separate identity; all is one. Could he choose a new timeline that avoided death? No, but perhaps Billy could! Roger sensed that this was not Billy's nexus. His future and Billy's were entangled in a paradox seeking balance. Roger could not act to avoid his own death but Billy could tilt the balance in his favour.

Then it happened. Two of the ghost ships to the left exploded before fading away. Shortly after, one of the ghostly saucers on their current temporal trajectory exploded. Roger called out, "Veer sharp right and 'down' as quick as you can!"

Billy sent the ship clear of the danger zone. With his senses tuned to the spacecraft's psycho-radar, Roger sensed a projectile pass by, the one that would have killed them. He was alive!

"What happened there?" asked Billy beginning to sweat.

"Somebody fired a rail gun at us. It's probably from a deep space military platform. That means it's one of 'ours'. We are the only species that shoots indiscriminately at everything that moves. Your manoeuvre saved us. The phantom ships we saw are versions of this vessel in related universes. They are just quantum variations in the continuity of the story we are living out in virtual reality."

"What's the gismo that allowed us to see those future versions of the ship?" Billy asked unaware of how close he had been to disaster.

"It's called a *temporal radar*. The ETs developed it after the Roswell crash. The Americans zapped them with highly secret scalar wave weapons. It was our nuclear programme that drew them here. Apparently, our atom bomb tests were destabilising neighbouring dimensions and, what Henry calls, the universal conceptual network. The Nordic-type ETs wanted us to give up our nuclear weapons and be nice to one another. In return they'd help us with our spiritual evolution. That didn't go down too well. The last thing the military industrial complex wants is spiritual evolution. What the military needs is enemies to test their weapon systems on. That's a big incentive to invade so-called primitive countries. There's too much profit in war to give it up. A few of the Greys were willing to trade technology for human genes. That started a programme of reverse engineering; stuff like integrated circuits, fibre optics, Kevlar, Velcro, smart phones – you name it. Then our future descendants started travelling back in time to observe us. They don't want to change the timeline that created them even though it does include a nuclear war. Unless there's a change of heart on this planet we are doomed to destroy ourselves over pointless political and religious dogma. It's just stupidity. Our best hope is the higher dimensional beings that could intervene if enough of us show spiritual progress."

"You're not telling me anything I haven't seen on the Internet."

"Lighten up, I know. What would you like to do now?"

"Are you sure we won't get shot at again?" Billy asked nervously.

"Not one hundred per cent, but I did sense that threat. I can't feel it now."

Billy had to ask, "Why do I feel like a kind of squashy doughnut when I've got my hand on the steery thing?"

"I think it's because you can feel the space-time barrier that encloses us. When you desire to go in a particular direction you warp the field and we get squeezed along like a bubble under a carpet. What would you like to see?"

"How about Mars?"

"Not such a good idea right now. There's a war going on. Apparently, there's a race of beings there that doesn't want a McDonald's opening up on Olympus Mons. And that's not even why they carry out cattle mutilations!"

"How about Jupiter? There's more to see there than Venus. Could we go that far in an afternoon? That's all the time I got. I'm supposed to be taking them to see *Harry Potter and the Half-Blood Prince* this evening. They're more likely to believe that Hogwarts is real than what I'm doing here."

"Jupiter. Why not? Let me get at the controls."

A quarter of an hour later the saucer materialised around ten thousand miles from the solar system's biggest planet. As they flew towards it, Billy's mind was totally boggled by what he saw through the helmet's electro-psychic link. To Roger it brought to mind his encounter with the Old One in his guise as a gigantic blue orb; a star-sized object without mass and very little radiant heat.

"Who would believe you could get on a London bus and end up somewhere like this?" said Billy in awe.

"I am sure the old Routemaster London buses could have got to Jupiter if anything could. They were brilliant."

"That's true," Billy agreed. "We'll never see their like again. Wow! Look at that volcanic plume on Io!"

After circling the planet and skimming past the moons, Roger took Billy back to earth. They had spent longer on the trip than anticipated so Roger took a chance and landed in Burgess Park, which was less discrete than Peckham Rye Park. The glowing light of the saucer dimmed as the ship dropped down to the grass. They got out and Roger used his remote control to send it back into orbit. As Billy later told him, there were only three videos of the event on YouTube.

Roger and Billy walked out of the park and found a taxi.

"I hope you can afford this," said Billy.

"Yeah. I'm off Benefits. Thank goodness. I haven't been available for work for some time – mainly because I've been off-planet or in other time zones."

They arrived at Billy's house. Roger paid the driver and they went inside. Liz was in the back garden playing a ball game with the children.

"Back at last," she said. "Where did Roger take you in the end? Did you stay in the pub for the whole afternoon? Are you legless?"

"No," said Billy hastily. "Sorry, we went a bit further than I expected."

"Oh, where did you go?"

Billy looked at Roger and opened his hands in a helpless gesture.

"We went to Jupiter, sis," Roger explained.

Liz laughed. "Secrets among the boys. Is that it? I suppose you conveniently forgot to take a video on your phone camera."

Billy squirmed. "Ah, that's a bit difficult. You don't see out of a window. You have a gadget on your head that lets you see in your mind's eye. That was after we got shot at by a missile from a Black Ops space weapons platform."

"Oh, that's a good one. We've had all this out before. I don't want you spending even more time in the pub. I thought my own brother would be more understanding."

Roger detected a tension building between his sister and her husband.

"Let me phone Henry. I don't see how he can help but there's no harm asking."

END OF TIME LOOP FIRST TIME AROUND

***

ALTERNATIVE ENDING OF TIME LOOP SECOND TIME AROUND

Adopting a fragile nonchalance Roger went back into the living room.

"Okay, I can provide a video. It will take a few minutes to get it together and put it on DVD. It would be a lot easier if Henry was here."

"I can wait. It will give you time to think up a good excuse for why we can't see this fairy story," said Liz sarcastically.

"Can I use your computer room and your laptop, Bill? I need to be alone if possible."

"Sure. Don't put it on YouTube. I don't want to be another Billy Meier."

Half an hour later Roger held out a DVD to his sister.

"That's it. I hope it works."

Liz Morris sat down to watch, ever the sceptic. When she saw the flying saucer materialise in the park her mouth fell open and did not close for the next two hours. At the end she said to Roger, "Henry, I presume."

"I'm not Henry but you are right. None of this would have happened without him. Could have…"

"Was it dangerous? Could you both have been killed?"

Roger squirmed. "Ye-es. Just a bit. It was a rail gun – probably on auto-detect and interception. Had they really wanted to destroy us they would have used a scalar beam weapon."

"Next time, go to the pub. It's much safer."

Billy grinned, behind his wife's back, and held up his thumb to Roger to indicate success.

FINAL ENDING OF TIME LOOP

***

ORIGINAL ENDING OF TIME LOOP FIRST TIME AROUND RESUMED

Roger left Liz and Billy together while he went outside to make a call on his mobile. Henry didn't need a telephone to communicate electronically as long as he could locate a signal or a network. His central processor used a reverse-engineered extraterrestrial technology known as femtocomputing based on the properties of subatomic particles called *quarks*. Each quark could adopt one of six properties called 'flavours', designated *up, down, top, bottom, strange* and *charm*. Where standard computers worked in binary (numbers to the base two), Henry's processor calculated in senary numbers to the base six. In essence, Henry could divide his consciousness into six partitioned pseudo-minds, all working independently on separate problems. When Roger had made a joke to Elizabeth Sennitt about a successor to quantum computing, Henry had thought he meant quark computing. Henry worried about such an advanced technology falling into the malevolent hands of the secret government behind Black Ops.

Roger could always get through to Henry more quickly than anybody else. He told the android the nature of the problem. "Liz thinks we're having her on. She calls it missing time in the pub. I wouldn't worry on my account but it might affect their marriage. Look," said Roger urgently, "I know there's no way to video something that's already happened but…"

"No," said Henry. "Definitely not, except…"

"Except what?"

Henry told him. Roger said, "Oh my God! No! Do it all over again!"

"It's the only way. Where are you?"

"I'm at their house. In the dining room. Billy and Liz are in the lounge waiting for me to talk to you."

Henry's voice coming from the phone said, "You could travel back in time physically as an orb but you might end up being two versions of yourself. I have been analysing the storyline for you and Billy. It seems you can change events to the extent of making a video. You haven't actually instigated the consequences of not having it."

"Okay, so what do I do now?" Roger asked.

"Sit down for a quarter of an hour or so. Empty your mind and wait for me to send you back."

"You just said you couldn't do that because I might end up on bifurcated timelines."

"I'm not sending you physically."

"You're not? How then?"

"In your mind – I will infiltrate your present awareness into your body at the start of your time with Billy. 'You' as the interloper, must keep a low profile. Your mind *then* will give way to your awareness *now*. All time is concurrent. You can't be in two minds – unlike me. I can be in six. Even so, there is only one mind in the entire universe and we all share it. Remember the analogy of lampposts in a fog? Each lamp glows with a halo of light but there is only one fog. You will simply be along for the ride. Let your body do the acting and talking. Just do your best to intervene when you make the video. I will do the rest."

"That will be hell! I've got to relive those hours, knowing what's going to happen next, what Billy and me will say. What am I supposed to do?"

"Just use your cell phone to video the saucer. Take shots of Billy outside and inside. Your body will resist but I'm sure you have enough will power to succeed. Those parts of the trip that you cannot video, like the outside scenes of Jupiter, I can abstract from the cosmic time register; what some call the akashic. I'll edit your material with mine and then I'll set up a download link. You can put it on Billy's laptop and burn it to a blank DVD."

"I don't understand – how can I go through that entire experience in a quarter of an hour?" Roger wanted to know.

Henry said patiently, "It won't take any time here. It will be like going from linear time to lateral time. Subjectively, it will take as long as it takes. Objectively, it will be no more than a few seconds. It's only your mind that's going back – not your body. Objective consciousness in the brain is subject to physical time. Pure mind is timeless. The whole experience won't seem to have taken any time afterwards. But going through it might be a bit tedious – *at the time* so to speak. Don't change what you do when you are attacked by a rail gun otherwise you might change too much too soon."

"Oh dear, I hadn't thought of that."

FIRST TIME LOOP COMPLETE

When Roger next met Henry he said, "How did you work that little miracle? How could you get me to rerun to that time period without altering history?"

"You know that time cannot be altered by going to the past. All you can do is create a different storyline in a new set of universes."

"Yes. So what did you do to put me back at the beginning of my day with Billy?"

"I couldn't send you back physically but I could in the mind. Our shared DNA permits a certain resonance of consciousness. We belong to a shared oversoul. At least, it gave you a chance to observe yourself objectively for a brief period. How did you find it?"

"It was *so* boring. My body was working on its own without my input. I was saying things that I didn't instigate. I had a fight on my hands at the first deviation. I could barely get my phone out at the park to film our arrival. My arm was fighting me. You could have gone back in time and dropped me a hint."

"Hardly, that would have left a universe where Billy and Liz went through a bad patch in their relationship. She thought you and Billy were playing a game; that you were taking his side against her. Most of the trouble on earth comes from people taking sides about trivial differences of belief, race, football team, culture, status and so on. It would be much better to look for the things that bring oneness rather than separation. What does it matter what we believe or what we wear? We are not our thoughts. And we are not our bodies."

"Have you any idea how tedious it is to relive a part of your life – even three hours? It's not so much an action replay as an *inaction* replay. It's amazing how little we actually *do* over the course of a day. It's bloody awful when you know what's going to happen in the next minute. Everything Billy said was repeated as well as all my responses."

"You think that was bad – I had to go through hours on temporal excursion to convince Jensine I wasn't insane."

"Yes, but you're different. There's nobody like you."

"I must confess, there are times when I am humbled by my own greatness."

Roger laughed. "Only an android could say that and mean it without ego."

Henry smiled. He had learned when it was the appropriate response. Sometimes it was even spontaneous but not this time.

"I understand what you have been saying about being in two minds more than you realise. That's why I took an interest in Jensine's work with multiple personalities."

"What do you mean?" Roger asked.

"You went through a period of time with two versions of your consciousness sharing the same body."

"I suppose so. Yes."

"I sometimes have up to six versions of myself residing concurrently in the same body."

"Six! How come?"

Henry explained the significance of quark computing.

Roger chuckled. "So you have six personalities but only one of them has charm."

"Not exactly six personalities – six minds."

"All different?"

"No. They are all me."

"How can a single mind be split into six?" Roger

asked. "I just don't get it."

"It's a dimensional thing," said Henry. "Remember what the Old One told us. There is only one idea behind all known existence, the number one, the unit or quantum of being and consciousness. Do you remember how that one unit becomes everything?"

Roger nodded. "It is the property of time. Time is the act of being. One thing can become many as long as they are separated in time and space. The number one can manifest in infinite forms of existence as long as each entity it becomes is unique in some way. Time is one of the keys to uniqueness. The infinite property of the number one is oneness, which is love. So everything is love expressed in time and space."

"That's it," agreed Henry. "My individualised consciousness is a prime number on a higher dimension, like yours. It generates a fractal algorithm on the fifth dimension. That splits into time slots on the fourth dimension, which generate physical particles in the three dimensions of space. The unit that constitutes my physical awareness vibrates between six timeframes by employing the properties of quarks inside protons located in silicon atoms in a monocrystal substrate. So there is only one me but it experiences itself in six time fields simultaneously."

"Oh, I see," said Roger, beginning to understand. "So you are six minds controlling one body. How the hell do you cope with that? I had trouble handling two for an afternoon."

"I admit it is a struggle," said Henry. "But it is something everyone will need to face up to eventually."

"Why's that?" Roger asked.

"It's the nature of the virtual reality game you call

the universe. Each session you play in the game is a lifetime on the planet – or some other planet. There are many more than earth. But there is only one game player for each group of lives. Because all time is happening concurrently now, that game player is handling all your incarnations simultaneously."

"So mine is a damn sight cleverer than I am," Roger said, laughing.

"And mine," said Henry. "Don't forget we are fragments of the same soul."

That shocked Roger as he remembered Henry's creation on the space ship Centaur II.

"You see," said Henry. "As humanity evolves spiritually, the focus of your consciousness moves up the chain of mathematical fragmentation and you become the higher being that must combine all its different incarnations into one mind and personality."

"Wow! And what then?"

"Ultimately, the individual game players, whatever they may be, integrate with the higher beings that made them."

"Is there any end to the process?" Roger asked.

"The whole thing rises in frequency and light until it all becomes united in the original one unit that made it all."

"And then?"

"The whole process starts again but in a higher state of complexity and self-knowledge."

"What happens to us?"

"Look on the bright side. *You* don't exist anyway. You are a shade of colour and sound in the light, the subjective universal mind. You will still be aware but in a way that is inconceivable to your present consciousness."

Roger sniffed. "It doesn't seem fair. Will there still be six of you and only one of me?"

For once, Henry's smile was genuine.

If you're going to be sincere, you might as well mean it, he thought. At least, one of his six minds thought it. He couldn't be sure which one.

Part 5
The Trap

Chapter Sixteen

2010, Sonoran Desert, Arizona

Six glowing orbs of various colours descended to the ground in a hot desert landscape. Roger, Deborah, Henry, Spiker, Barty and Cade reverted to their normal physical forms. Henry led them to a nearby rocky outcrop. On approaching a sandstone cliff face, the android waved his hand, using internal sensors to locate a hidden radio transponder. There was a click followed by the sound of stone grating on stone. A rocky protrusion about twenty feet high and ten feet wide moved aside, revealing a hidden entrance. A tunnel led downwards to an elevator. The air inside was cool. Lights came on as they walked. The elevator clanked and rattled as it took them down to a more elaborate series of tunnels and chambers carved into the rock beneath.

"What is this place?" asked Roger.

"It's a remote base for temporary refuge in the desert. Black Ops has a number of these. I found it and removed it from the records. We'll be safe for a while. I just need a little time to discuss my next move with you and Deborah."

"What did they build this base for?" asked Spiker.

"The US military built it to store tissue samples collected from cattle in Southern Arizona to determine the distribution of radioactive fallout from the atomic weapons test programme. It was part of a larger scheme that covered the whole of the Western States. They put out misinformation about aliens being responsible to avoid compensating farmers. This was a temporary storage facility for locally acquired samples. Later, aliens *did* take the base over. I can show you some of their hardware if you are interested."

"What's the point of measuring fallout?" asked Cade. "They can't do anything about it, can they?"

"No," said Henry. "The military seriously underestimated the radiation effects of those weapons at the start. That's why they had soldiers standing in the way of the explosions to see what it did to them. They died of cancer. Humankind has had one nuclear war in modern times and it took two relatively small atom bombs to win it. So ask yourself why they have up to four thousand bombs and warheads of massive yield on the planet. They are clearly not to win a conflict. What would be the point? There would be nothing left to occupy and nobody to tax. The deep state, the Illuminati, the secret government or the military industrial complex, whatever you choose to call it, had hoped to cull the population to leave the earth as a paradise for the elite. The test bomb programme has shown the fallacy of that idea. But it's easier to set up a system or an organisation than it is to close it down."

"Why bother to build all these weapons in the first place if they're too dangerous to use?" said Spiker.

Roger grunted. "All you have to do is invent an enemy. There's a great deal of money to be made out of designing, testing, building and maintaining weapons that can never be used. Eventually, they declare these never-used weapon systems obsolete and replace them with even bigger, more expensive weapon systems that can never be used. The gravy train is unlimited and the same goes for your so-called enemy states that share in your lucrative insanity. The profits have rolled in for decades. The only problem for the world's elite is how to spend all they money they make from satisfying a need that doesn't exist."

"Welcome to the virtual reality game you all play," said Henry. "It confuses the aliens. They come here to inspect the weapons expecting that you will use them any day. They can't get their heads around the idea that they were never built for that purpose. It will never happen unless you get a lunatic in the White House or the Kremlin or some minor nation wanting to glorify their God of love by destroying His creation."

That subject exhausted, Deborah remarked, "I don't like the feeling I'm getting in here. It's cold and…there's something more here. Something dark and evil."

"I know," Henry agreed. "It was used at one time by a cult of misguided people who practised black magic. They carried out blood sacrifices of men, women and children in order to communicate with so-called 'satanic' forces."

"Did they actually do that?" Spiker asked.

"They thought so but not really. They believed in 'fallen angels'. They also believed that spiritual masters are evil. In reality, they communicated with inferior entities on the lower astral plane. These lost souls can, and do, impersonate spiritual masters, spirit guides and specialists that work with them. Their motivation is making mischief."

"How d'you know they weren't them – them what you said?" asked Barty.

"The real beings of light would never express anything other than love. Evil just does not exist on their frequency."

"What creates evil on the earth?" asked Spiker. "I've been involved in enough of it in my time here – I should say my *times* here."

Henry paused for before replying. "Some years ago, Roger and I met an advanced being known as the Old One. He was involved in the development of the human genome. He told us that on the light dimension, the solar system is an integrated field of consciousness. The planets are living entities that influence each other and the unfolding human story. Now Saturn is the sixth planet. Six is the number entity that expresses individuality. The number 666 represents the carbon-twelve atom; six protons, six neutrons and six electrons. Life employs it to express organic form in this region of the multiverse. The sixth planet, Saturn, implements the game of karma here on the earth. That's the effect of its conscious field. Aliens built its rings as a communication device. They amplify the unfolding patterns of the drama and the game underlying human life."

"Which tells us what about evil?" asked Spiker, totally confused by Henry's 'explanation'.

The android replied, "Another name for Saturn is Satan. The term is synonymous with evil because so many bad things happen here. The name associated originally with an evil tyrant from prehistory. But Saturn does not create evil; *we* do that through free will. Saturn gives us what we desire as long as it fits with what we need. It unravels past karma by generating new situations that balance out the good and evil that people do. The real problems come from the systems we have created to control our lives. They are mindless entities in the field of consciousness and use people to further their ends in their struggle for survival. Ultimately, life rewards altruism and self-sacrifice for the benefit of all."

"I don't see much reward for people who do good. Look at what carers and cleaners get paid," said Barty. "My sister is a carer. They pay her next to nothing."

"Henry's not talking about material rewards," said Deborah. "This is a virtual reality drama; an incarnation is just a session in the game. There are no winners, no losers and no innocent or guilty. Life is an opportunity to make mistakes and then put them right. If you do good you will get out of the game eventually."

"It's the hidden acts of love and service that bring personal evolution," Roger remarked, "not grand gestures or pious words."

"I haven't been doing much good," said Cade. "Why did *I* get this light body thing?"

"Who can say?" said Roger. "You've done no serious harm. You must have earned it in another incarnation. It takes more than one life here to make that sort of progress. Whatever the reason, when Henry put you, Barty and Spiker in the alien karma machine you cleared a great deal of negative stuff. It can't have been easy to face up to the worst aspects of yourself."

Spiker grimaced. Roger's reminder of the temporal resequencer brought back bad memories.

"I had to go through what we did to you, Roger," said Barty. "That wasn't very good of us. It bloody well hurt. I had to lay there while I kicked myself."

Roger smiled sympathetically but said nothing. He had not forgotten the beatings and intimidation. The memory was there but the resentment had long since vanished.

"How do you know this place was used for bad things?" Cade asked Henry.

"One of my ET friends detected negative vibrations in the ritual room that had been used for blood sacrifices. She cleared that energy. Then I sealed it up. Unfortunately, the people who built this base have an inordinate degree of control over the planet. They exploit fear to cover their tracks. They move in key areas of society and have the clout to corrupt the law. Call a saint a terrorist and the system will eliminate him. Remember the story of Jesus of Nazareth? He threatened a religion and an empire just by talking about love."

Roger added, "This planet is an asylum run by the inmates."

"Can I ask a question?"

"Of course, Barty."

"How did you turn me into this light body thing, Henry?" asked Barty. "I saw it happen to Cade but I didn't think it could happen to me also."

Henry was not sure what to say. "I was just a robot when Roger woke me up. He passed on a soul fragment from his higher dimensional being. The extraterrestrials recognised my significance and implanted information and knowledge. That included the metaphysical aspects of human biochemistry and micro-electric field structures. You understand," Henry added optimistically. "Usual stuff; enlightenment, Merkabah or orb activation."

Barty and Cade nodded as if they understood. Sometimes that was the best thing to do with Henry. The android had turned daily existence into a thing of strangeness. Not that they minded; in their way, they were both refugees from normality. What Henry gave them was surreal, mind-boggling experience.

Eventually, they arrived at a series of chambers containing technical equipment that was beyond the comprehension of everybody except the android. At the far end was a section carved out of the rock that had been furnished for human and alien accommodation. Henry introduced them to the facilities and suggested they sit down on the exotic furniture while he prepared a light meal, although he did not join them in eating and drinking. He left on an unspecified mission of his own but later returned as they sat and relaxed. It was Cade that broke the silence with a question that had been on his mind for a while.

"So when you built your body, which bit did you make first?"

It took a moment for Henry to understand the question. He struggled not to give a monologue in reply.

"The extraterrestrials gave me the starting point for the design. They downloaded me with technical knowledge. They take a chaotic view of the conceptual universe. The design is holistic. It means that I, as a robot with a facility for objective as well as subjective…" He looked at their blank faces and broke off. After a long pause he said, "I built the head first."

"So they taught you all the things you know how to do," Barty said as if that explained everything.

"Partly," Henry said, "but information only gets you so far. Knowledge benefits the mind; experience shapes the soul. No book, 'holy' or otherwise, can enlighten you in the way life can. Roger introduced me to human society. Imagine that! A robot at the captain's cocktail party trying to make small talk."

Roger laughed. "I remember that now. He was about as popular as a bishop in a brothel. The crew thought I was mad."

Cade was listening. He had something to say too. He had a new reputation as an enlightened being to maintain. "I thought the earth was flat until I saw it from space. It's definitely round. Seeing is believing, isn't that right, Henry?"

The android smiled. "Some of the time, but you can't always believe what you see. Physically the earth is round but human beings perceive it as flat. You are very small in comparison with the curvature of the planet. All maps are flat. It would be illogical for you to think in spherical co-ordinates. The flat earth exists but only in your minds. ETs know that humans are dimensionally challenged, some more than others. Now that you can travel in space you are starting to think three dimensionally."

"Bangin' man," said Cade, getting a glimmering of light in the face of mystery and paradox. "I wasn't at school much but they never told us about this stuff."

"Perhaps you was on the skunk that day," said Barty sympathetically.

Roger patted Cade's shoulder to get his attention.

"It doesn't matter how inspired the teachers are; the system can't teach what it doesn't know. The British education system has always had a dual purpose. Public schools turn out politicians and the fat cat bosses who make all the money. The state schools condition the masses like us to do mundane jobs and put up with long hours and low pay. Right from an early age the effect of education is to limit consciousness to left-brain intellect at the expense of right-brained creativity."

Henry nodded. "And they spy on all your emails and phone calls to make sure nobody steps out of line. An enlightened population would not make good slaves."

"I once worked weekends in a distribution warehouse. They watched us all the time, made us work impossible hours and paid us peanuts," said Barty. "I got the sack for taking too many fag breaks."

Cade nodded. "It was the herbal cigarettes. You had some good shit at that time."

"You don't need it now," Deborah said.

"Henry," said Barty, "you changed Roger's DNA to make him black. Have you ever done that before?"

Henry considered for a moment before replying. "Yes. The first time I was living here in America. I'd just returned from a deep space trip. A friend in the Space Command Service took me to his home in one of the Southern states. He introduced me to his family and they made me very welcome. A while later his sister phoned. He'd been abducted by a group of men who hated black people. She didn't know where he was. I located him in a building a few miles away. Apparently, they believed he had attacked a white woman. I knew he couldn't have done it because he was light-years from earth at the time.

"I found where they were holding him and broke into the building. They were wearing white pointy hats with eyeholes and white robes. I grabbed one of them from the door at the back of the room and put him to sleep. Then I went in wearing his disguise. They had my friend tied to a chair. They were beating him and shouting. They were obviously planning to kill him."

"What did you do?" asked Barty.

"I used a proximity destabiliser device to freeze the building into a single time frame. Then, one by one, I resequenced their DNA. I turned them all black. When the time flow resumed, I pushed my way to the front and raised my hands. I got their attention and said, 'There's a black man in this group.' They stopped what they were doing and then, very slowly, took of their masks. There was a deathly hush. Each one assumed he was still white and everybody else was black. A great fight broke out.

"Gradually, one by one, they realised that they, too, had turned black. This occupied their attention for a while, as you can imagine. My black friend felt quite at home by that time. He said, 'You look like a minority around here now, Henry.' I quickly untied him and got him out. I heard later that they had a few problems when they got home. Their wives were none too thrilled and they'd raised their children to hate. If they were consistent they'd have to hate themselves I suppose. They were the same people. All I'd done was switch a gene."

Cade laughed the loudest. "I'd love to have seen their faces."

"The spirit has no colour," remarked Roger.

After the story, Henry took Roger aside and spoke quietly to him. "You mentioned the other day that you'd like to take a holiday. Do you wish me to transport you to any particular period?"

Roger considered for a while. "I'd quite like to see Julius Caesar's triumphant entry into Rome after the Gallic War."

"Do you know any Latin?" Henry asked.

"Status quo," he replied.

Henry shook his head. "That's possibly too little.

I'll take you back to London in 2009. At least you won't need to sign on for Benefits again."

"What job could I possibly do now? I don't think there's much call for blasting people's minds with a single thought."

"Not outside Psy Ops," Henry agreed. "I did have a particular reason for seeking you out when I did. I think it's time I told you why."

"Do you mean you wouldn't have bothered otherwise?" Roger asked, smiling.

"Not at all. I mean there was a reason I found you when I did. This seemed to be the optimum opportunity across your concurrent clusters of themed timelines in twenty-four different universes."

Roger, though not easily baffled, decided not to pursue that line of enquiry any further. Instead he asked, "Does this concern your friend Jensine?"

"Yes. I cannot locate her."

"I thought you could find anybody anywhere," Roger said, "even on Mars."

"No. I can only use external methods, either by tracing their information footprint in digital systems or by intuitive methods akin to dowsing. The Black Ops people are keeping her somewhere I can't penetrate. They have learned how to imprison aliens in a way that prevents them from being rescued by their own kind."

"That's appalling. They certainly don't stint on creating their own bad karma. They are either extremely brave or ignorant. You think I can find her," Roger suggested.

"Yes. You might have access to a different mode of consciousness."

"Which is?"

"Internal rather than external."

"Ahh," said Roger, understanding his reasoning. "You mean that every object in the universe has a common source of space and time within."

"That's right. There is only one zero-point but it locates the origin of an infinite number of objects and entities."

"You mean I should seek *inside information*," said Roger, chuckling. "But that *is* like dowsing – sort of. You said you had already tried that."

"Just because I tried and failed doesn't mean you will," said Henry. "You once transported me physically from the moon to the earth by thought alone. Can you do that for Jensine?"

Roger shook his head. "I didn't do that deliberately. It just happened. Look how closely we are connected. I haven't met Jensine. I don't know her essence as a personality. I'd be happy to do it but I don't know how."

Henry showed no emotion. He was not pleased with Roger's answer but he could see no way of getting around the difficulty.

"I'll do anything and everything I can to help you, old chap," said Roger. "In the meantime, where's Deborah? She's the one we need."

"She went out a little while ago. Perhaps she has biological functions to deal with."

Roger gazed at the android. Sometimes it was easy to forget that he wasn't a human being, he just looked like one.

Deborah emerged from a door at the end of a corridor and started walking towards them.

"She's looking better all the time," Roger remarked softly to Henry. "I wonder why?"

Henry had a fixed expression on his face. Roger

noticed his friend's reticence to answer and asked, "What are you trying not to tell me, old android mate?"

"Only that I have observed signs of happiness in her since she met you."

"Oh. I don't know why. We've known each other for years," said Roger.

"No you haven't. You exchanged information telepathically. You didn't actually know each other at all until you met in London."

The thought struck Roger like a thunderbolt. In the shadow of his unconscious mind, dead dreams stirred like sleeping monsters in the deep. For all their intense association and emotional closeness, he and Deborah had never met until recently. It was a paradoxical dichotomy, intimate strangers and unfamiliar friends. Did she feel it too? He had no idea. Before Psy Ops enforced amnesia at the end of the conflict with the titan, he had loved her almost obsessively. Ever since his memory had begun to return the old longing had resurfaced like a forgotten habit. But the object of his affection was not *this* Deborah Farnham; it was a woman of the same name that had existed entirely in his imagination. This Deborah claimed to be in a relationship, although he had never seen any proof that it existed.

Henry continued to speak *sotto voce* for his ears alone. "You worked together mind to mind. You are mental magnets for each other. That is a barrier. You've got to forget the past. See her for who she is now. See the woman, not the remote viewing target."

Roger was speechless. He looked at Deborah approaching and saw a stranger – a very nice, extremely attractive stranger. Could he get past the remnants of derelict affection and start over?

Sensing his mood, Henry touched him on the arm. "Start afresh. Begin anew. You need to open a new cans of worms – is that the right expression?"

Roger laughed aloud.

"What's up guys? Has somebody laid an egg?" Deborah said cheerfully as she drew near.

"We are wondering if you could locate Jensine," Henry said.

"If my intuition is correct, you don't need to find her," Deborah replied. "Those holding her will contact you."

***

The next day, Roger and Henry travelled to the moon in a flying triangle. Roger had adjusted quite well to lunar existence. Since his first visit with Henry, it took less time for the moon to assume responsibility for projecting his body as a fractal form into space and time. He could feel a subtle difference on becoming an object of a different world; it reminded him of another planet called Annoon orbiting a distant star. There were physiological as well as mental effects. Even DNA altered over a period of time. Most people were unaware of these modifications but Roger was unusually sensitive to atmospheres, actual and metaphorical.

The android had access to a number of bases, some human, others ET. These were mainly near the surface. Much of the inner workings, habitations and laboratories had fallen into disuse since the original builders carved out the moon's interior. Interstellar portals no longer existed. The larger vessels employed by a variety of alien races used the sun to travel to other dimensions. Henry avoided reptilians as much as possible, preferring Greys, blond 'nordics' and some of the less well-known races. Indeed, he felt more secure in the company of ETs than Black Ops. He found aliens to be free from the most trying human characteristics such as greed, aggression and fashion. At the same time, they lacked something human society had in abundance. He decided it must be their variety of culture, humour and enthusiasm for life. If human beings could get back on a spiritual track, they would be a force to be reckoned with.

Roger gazed around him as Henry led him down into a labyrinth of rocky chambers. The journey ended in a well-stocked laboratory that combined human and ET technology. A couple of Greys were busy in a far corner. They observed their entry but paid them no other attention. There were no electric lights. The walls and ceiling emitted their own illumination, though how they worked, Roger could not imagine.

"What do you want me to do?" Roger asked.

"I want you to carry out some rather delicate work on my primary intelligence circuits. I need you to remove a device without destroying the core function."

"What does the device do?"

"It's a micro-bomb planted by Black Ops. They intended to use it to destroy me if I proved to be intractable in following orders, which, of course, I have. If it works, you can take out the live explosive. I can't help you. I'll be at my most vulnerable, so take care."

"That sounds like fun. Oh well, if it goes wrong at least we'll both go together. What does that mean if we are fragments of the same soul I wonder?"

Henry ignored Roger's remarks as he often did.

"You will perform the operation from behind an armoured window I salvaged from an old spaceship I found half buried in a crater. I have a set of remote manipulators."

"How do we maintain your consciousness while I remove the device? That was extremely difficult when you first built your android body."

Henry looked pleased. "I now have an answer. It's called a Harper and Plipstow Z45G64 AI Modal Emulator & Power Supply. It will allow you to temporarily extract my consciousness to remove the device and then restore it unharmed. If it fails, I've got a spare body you can put it in."

"Where did you get that emulator thing from? I take it you have done something clever, as usual."

"You and I will go back in time from the future to ask Elizabeth Sennitt to obtain it for us. She will have retired by then."

"We will? How come you've got it already?"

Henry shook his head. "I've just come back from that time. It took her six months but she requisitioned the device before she quit the Service."

"How could she do that if she had already left Space Command?" Roger asked.

"I arranged for her to authenticate a priority one memo to herself six months previous to our meeting. I wanted to keep the whole thing as quiet as possible. She was under rigorous surveillance at the time for helping me. Electronic communication was out of the question so I sent the memo back in time on paper using the temporal post room on the international lunar base. There's a conduit to the US Mail. She won't remember doing it when we first ask her so she will be surprised when she receives the Modal Emulator from a courier. I will call on her to collect it a month before we ask for it. It will be a temporal anomaly; the kind of situation Deborah's section in Black Ops investigates. I had to put it right. Elizabeth Sennitt doesn't know that I had to make a time continuity adjustment to account for it. I kidnapped her from the new universe her action created when she took delivery of the unit. I then placed her back in the original timeline without it."

"How could you do that? Surely, that would result in two Elizabeths in one universe."

Henry nodded. "It did get a bit tricky for a while. In the end, I had to do a swap. I arranged it overnight so that they woke up in alternate universes without realising it. So Elizabeth requested the Modal Emulator in one universe and received it in the other. As it happened, I had to take their dogs with them. They were different breeds with different names."

"I think I'm getting a headache," Roger complained. "How can there be so many universes. Didn't the Old One say that every choice or decision we make diverges into different versions of the same universe?"

Henry nodded. "Consciousness likes to explore the outcome for as many options as possible. That's how it learns about itself."

"Surely, that means there must be untold trillions of universes, some significant and others very trivial," said Roger.

"Yes. It is a paradox," said Henry. "There is one universe containing every version of every part and yet every version of every part creates its own vision of the whole in consciousness. Your problem is one of perception. You see a universe as a vast time-space continuum. In reality there are no universes. Every discrete object or thing be it particle, person or star, exists at its own centre of space and time. Time generates matter according to the great story and matter creates space. Space is the place where meaning works out, the stage where the story enacts itself. When a particle moves from one state or location to another, the divine breath generates all possible versions. Each one is a different potential universe. Which versions emerge into reality depends on its relationships with all other particles. The light of consciousness is the power that draws chaos into form from infinite possibility. It's the same with human beings. You meet somebody and fall in love. In one set of universes you stay together. In another you move on. It depends on your circumstances and your integrity as a person. Who else gets hurt? If you are not absolutely clear in your own heart, then you will follow one or more pathways to find out."

"What decides which path works out and which doesn't?" Roger asked.

"The light, the one, the source of all things presents us with viable outcomes to choose from. All we can ever do is our best when we decide to act. Nobody out there expects more than that."

"Serious stuff," said Roger thoughtfully. "In the meantime, when do we start this operation? It sounds like something we should get on with as soon as possible."

"There's no time like the present," Henry said cheerfully.

"That's certainly true," Roger agreed. "The present is the only time there is. Unless you're in another version of the universe, in which case… Never mind."

The operation was successful. Roger removed the micro-bomb. Afterwards, Henry detonated it in a remote crater on the moon. An astronomer in Arizona photographed the flash, published it on Secureteam10 and had his telescope and data impounded by the Secret Service.

Roger tried to unwind after the tension of the operation.

"That was tricky. I wish I'd had that gadget on the spaceship when I originally helped you to move from your robot body into your android body."

"No problem," said Henry. "You will have."

"What do you mean, *I will have*? I didn't have it at the time."

Henry laughed. "There's a temporal post room on this base. I think you should send the Modal Emulator back in time to when you first visited the seventies for training. You could throw in those alien time travel sickness pills too. I remember you saying you were sick on the journey."

"Where is the temporal post room?"

"It's next to the temporal bank. That's where you can buy coinage for particular time zones. It's no good going back or forward with postdated or obsolete notes and coins."

"What about temporal divergence?" Roger said. "Won't that muddle things up even more than they are now? You'll have to swap versions of *me* around between different universes to compensate."

Henry shook his head. "No. I won't."

"Oh, why's that then?" asked Roger.

"I've already done it."

Chapter Seventeen

When the approach came it was through 'official' channels of a sort. It was 2004. Henry was in an office in one of the underground bases on earth. He used it occasionally for research and information gathering from certain Black Ops systems that had no direct Internet connection. Three black-suited, shadowy 'men' with grey-tinted skin entered the room while he was sitting at his desk. Henry looked up and noted their dark glasses.

"Try not to bump into the furniture, gentlemen. There's no need to be shy about showing me your slit pupils or speaking with forked tongues. I trust you are not here to attack me. There is nothing you can do to harm me," said Henry.

"You wouldn't be here if there was," said one in a dull, flat voice. "We have eliminated you in fifteen parallel universes so far. We know you are invulnerable to external attack by our weapons but we can blow you up from within."

"Not any more," said Henry. "My friend Roger helped me to remove your device. You tried to set it off 4,573,294 times. I always managed to scramble your codes by factorising semi-prime numbers. I had to devote an entire mind to the job. That only left me five to play with."

"Then we will hurt your female friend. You know we are holding her captive."

Henry turned in his chair to face them squarely. "Ah, the old Plan B scenario, as Roger would say. What exactly do you want me to do?"

"The humans want to use you as a weapon of assassination. You could deal with physically superior aliens like lizards and large mantids. You can also blend into human society. That is a useful ability for clandestine surveillance and the elimination of undesirables. You could take out key humans that are immune to psychotronic disruptors. You would also be useful to carry their wars to hostile environments off-planet. You have greater resilience than programmed life forms and conventional shadow-tech androids."

"I know that. Because of what these people do, other races regard human beings as one of the most primitive and ruthless species in the universe. But they're not all like that. There are many good humans and their potential for spiritual evolution is unique – if only they could use their heads for something other than social media, celebrity and online shopping."

"What are those?" asked one of the alien robotic clones.

"Never mind. *You* wouldn't get much of a following on Facebook, even as shapeshifters."

"If you refuse, we will kill your friend."

"You mean infect her with a lethal cancer virus," said Henry. "I know what you people do to whistleblowers and inventors of inconvenient technology."

"She will suffer a slow death and you will be responsible."

Henry shook his head. "That is nonsense. The virtual reality game here has mechanisms and rules called karma. If you murder Jensine *you* will be responsible. Not *me*. It is you that the universe will hold accountable."

The three men in black pondered this statement without expression, and then one of them said, "You refuse to work for the organisation?"

"No," said Henry patiently. "I refuse to kill people."

"Then she will die."

"How does that benefit you?" Henry asked, knowing the question to be pointless even as he said it.

"Time will decide. A threat is no threat if it is not carried out."

The deputation turned to leave his office. One of them stopped on the way to the door and said, "We are not susceptible to karma. We are manufactured or grown in tanks so our species does not have souls in the same way as some other humanoids."

"Fortunately I do," said Henry. "As you have no soul, perhaps I could kill you without incurring karma. However, in all conscience that is not something I would do."

Before the door closed on them, Henry said, "You can tell the people who sent you that the buck stops with them. I need do nothing. The rules of mathematics are inviolable. Everything balances out in the end. Love or oneness is the infinite aspect of the number one, the entity that endows existence to all things – even *you* on some inferior level of being."

"We don't know about love," said one of the black agents in a cold voice. "We don't feel emotion."

"No," Henry agreed, "you don't but it's not about feeling or intellectual understanding. You're confusing it with romance. Love is no vague emotion; it drives the endless cycle. Oneness fragments into separation. Then it undergoes metamorphosis and reintegrates back to wholeness. It's about *complexity*. Love generates all the stuff in *our* lives. Nature reveals *what* we are rather than *who* we are. We are answers seeking questions, solutions in pursuit of an equation. I count myself as human in that."

"Then you will suffer like one."

Henry knew it was true but he had no regrets about it. Separation is illusory and temporary no matter what happens. The love of the source evolves indefinitely. Those who fail to overcome their own hatred, for whatever reason, ultimately consign themselves back to the nothingness that made them possible. *Do as you would be done by.* Few heeded this sound piece of advice. Why? They did not understand the illusory nature of existence. As a photograph portrays its subject, the universe represents the essence of formless reality in the guise of substance. For what is matter? It is just empty space arranged by numbers into a story shaped by time. What is mind; never matter. What is matter; never mind. The Old One had told Henry that life is an opportunity to love. If we don't take it, we don't grow. Henry longed to grow.

Henry declared to nobody in particular, "For reasons of enlightened self-interest, I forgive them and leave them to seal their own fates through the exercise of free will."

The visit of the grey men in black had given him an idea that would take him back to the drawing board of his own design. Time was opportune for an enhanced specification with specialist functionality. It was a massively complex task that took him on a three-year time loop. He did it willingly. He did it for love.

***

Henry spoke to Roger through his mobile phone and said, "I've located Jensine. They released her in 2005."

"How did you track her down?"

"I didn't exactly. I had visitors while I was in a Black Ops HQ. They came to pressure me to become a super-soldier. They said they'd kill her if I refused. My guess is they'll inject her with cancer and let her go. That's what they usually do in cases like this."

"Oh dear. If they did, she's been dead for four years. There's nothing you can do," Roger said sadly. "You can't change the timeline to that extent."

"Yes, I can. I'm phoning from 2005 so it hasn't happened yet. I'm just a temporal echo to you. We share the same time, *the now*, but we view it from different spaces. Isn't that what it's all about? To travel through time you move through space, to travel through space you move through time. I don't care about consequences. This means too much. I'm to blame. Black Ops wanted to make me feel guilty. I already do but only for *my* actions – not theirs. Are you busy right now? Can I come over?"

"Sure. I'm not doing anything this evening. I'm at the flat."

"Where's Deborah?"

"I assumed she was with you, or she might be with Barty and Cade or Spiker."

"Never mind. I've finished my construction project. I need your help with implementation."

"What exactly is it?"

"Wait and see. Can you teleport me there now?"

"Maybe. I'll give it a go."

Roger tried to summon the mental energy but it didn't work.

"Things like that only happen spontaneously with

you," Henry told him. "I'll activate my light body and jump over."

Roger sat on the settee and waited. Next door he heard a thump followed by a loud scream.

"Mavis!" He ran out of his apartment.

Before he could knock, she opened the door and ushered Henry out of her flat. She saw Roger and groaned. "So it's *not* you. This *is* Henry. He just appeared in my kitchen in a burst of white light. *And* he ruined a custard and fruit trifle."

"I'm terribly sorry," said Henry.

"So you should be," Mavis said closing her door, her huffing and puffing tempered by the ghost of a smile.

"Sorry, Roger. I got the spatial co-ordinates slightly wrong."

"Anyone could make that mistake," said Roger drily. "You must be upset."

"True but I think the adjective *knackered* applies too. I've been moving around a three-year time loop working on a new android design. It was so complex; I overheated some of my cerebral cortex elements."

"That sounds like fun," Roger remarked.

"Do you usually get on well with Mavis?" Henry asked.

"She's all right. She wasn't as upset as she seemed about you crashing into her kitchen."

"Does she live alone?" Henry asked.

"Yes, she was married years ago to a sailor."

"A *sailor*," Henry exclaimed. "I've heard all about *them*."

Roger wondered if Henry had been listening to bad jokes. "What do you mean?"

"I've heard that they spend a lot of time in a mess

and take watches. Are they untidy but punctual?"

Roger chuckled. "Sometimes I forget you were once a robot. I can still remember when you went to a party and said to somebody: 'If things get any worse they won't be as good as they are now.'"

"I was practising my small talk," the android replied. "I thought I was doing much better these days."

"Oh, you certainly are," said Roger. "Brilliantly in fact. If you get stuck in Britain, talk about the weather. You can't go wrong."

"That's all right then. As a frequent time traveller I can access detailed daily records for the next thousand years for five hundred timelines."

Roger smiled. "That should get you on *The Graham Norton Show* at the very least."

***

Dr Jensine Pettersson sat in her armchair and stroked her cat. She could not believe how strangely her life had gone. During her formative years, academic and, later, medical ambition drove her to succeed. In her recent professional period, it was the humanitarian benefit that motivated her. Her career and her personal life had run on train lines. Then a chance meeting with Henry, the new gardener, had derailed the train. Henry threw question marks over everything she had achieved and everything she believed. Like her father, she leaned towards a humanist view; life is an accident and essentially material in nature but we do the best we can to live benignly with people. Henry had said that this made her more spiritual than someone who professed religion but helped nobody and hated anybody different.

As a scientist, Jensine, like the fictional detective Hercule Poirot, believed in order and method. The android was an agent of disorder and chaos. Henry had taken some time to explain that what she perceived as *material* was really a virtual reality simulation in an infinite 'computer', although Henry did point out that the metaphor was tenuous at best.

Jensine was finding it difficult to know what she believed about anything. She was dying of a raging cancer that had infiltrated her entire body in little more than a week. It had something to do with her recent incarceration by Black Ops agents and *that* had something to do with Henry. She didn't know whether to hate him or love him. Her designated carer called in on her before leaving and said, "You've got visitors. Shall I send them away?"

"Who are they?"

"Two men, alike as book ends. One of them is called Henry. He sounds American but the other one is English."

Jensine went numb inside. This was precisely the situation she most dreaded. What would she say to him? 'You did this to me.'

"Show them in," she said. "And thanks, Miranda. Shall I see you tomorrow?"

"Yes, usual time."

"Okay, if I'm still here. I don't think it will be long now."

The door opened and Henry walked in. Then a second Henry followed him or *was* this Henry?

"This is my friend Roger," said the first entrant.

"You look completely identical."

"We're made from the same stuff all right," said

Roger.

"We share the same DNA," Henry explained, "but only because I borrowed his. I made this body using hybrid Space Command and alien technology within a conventional biological superstructure. Outside of that is a defensive layering of spatially phased barriers with a bypass circuit to the infinite void."

Roger chuckled. "That's his way of saying that bullets either bounce off him or they disappear into a state of nothingness. So do people, sometimes, if they grab or punch him. The only way back from the void is to be reconstituted directly from your matrix software by a friendly higher dimensional being – if you happen to find one."

Henry nodded. "Or by me," he added. "I'm learning how to manipulate form in the parallel computational stratum that projects the output of fractal subroutines into physical manifestation. You've got processors co-located with your glands. They store the information that describes your body and its physical status in the moment of time and deploy your atoms accordingly. Your information pattern updates with each pulse of personal time on the quantum level."

"Do you understand what he means?" Jensine asked Roger.

"Er – sort of. He's not just a pretty face," he said. "He's got powerful computer circuits in that head. They're based on reverse-engineered alien hardware. Henry describes them as quark computers. He says it's like having six cerebral cortexes. It's having a simple chat he has a hard time with."

"I differ from artificial intelligence in having access to the universal subjective mind. Like you, I'm not just a brain."

Jensine sighed. "Shut up and sit down," she said kindly but firmly. "You two make the room untidy standing there like that."

They sat on a sofa in unison, folded their arms and stared at her with identical expressions of concern. Together they were reminiscent of Thomson and Thompson in the Tintin cartoons.

"I'm sorry you arrived too late," she said. "I would have enjoyed being a part of your world. You know what they've done to me?"

Henry nodded. "I feel responsible."

"I thought so too at first but I see it differently now. I wouldn't have missed meeting you for the world. It seems that there is an evil power, behind the scenes, that controls us all through fear. It taints the people who work for it more than anybody. The lie started so long ago they can't imagine living without it. Now they are killing me because I know about you, Henry. And why? What could I possibly do to harm them?"

Roger shook his head sadly. "I can see why Henry thinks so much of you, Jensine."

She tried to smile but the effort was too much.

Henry stood up and knelt down beside her chair. "Would you allow me to bring in a friend I would like you to meet? She is waiting outside."

"Sorry, my dear," she said, touching his arm. "Dr Sennitt said you'd find a way to rescue me if there was one but we both know that's not going to happen."

"Don't say that," said Henry in a level voice concealing inexpressible torment. "I can't let this happen."

Roger watched, feeling for them both. Then he said, "It might be a good idea to bring Deborah in."

Jensine studied him. "This is so confusing. You two

look identical but I can tell you are completely different."

"That's an understatement," Roger replied with a faint smile.

"I need to lay down now," Jensine said, her voice beginning to croak. "Can you help me to my bed?"

"I had hoped to restore your baseline DNA to free you of the cancer but I cannot reverse a change as extensive as this. Roger – we need to implement Plan B."

Roger stood up quickly, went to the front door and spoke to someone outside. "You'd better come in."

Deborah had remained out of sight to minimise a potentially overwhelming intrusion on the sick woman. She was shocked when she saw Jensine. Her highly attuned senses told her that death was close even without the visual evidence written on the deteriorating features.

Jensine sat, sagging against her chair back, her eyes barely open.

"This is Deborah," Henry told her. Jensine's eyes widened automatically to look at the newcomer but she took in Deborah without curiosity. Henry eased Jensine from the chair and carried her to her bedroom. He laid her on the sheets and pillows. The three visitors stood around her with concern, unsure how to behave or what to do.

Henry became business-like. "I've got to go around the apartment to seek out cameras and microphones. We're being watched."

"By whom?" Roger asked.

"The usual suspects," said Deborah. "They infected Jensine and then put her back here to see what we would do."

Henry did not waste much time disabling the bugging equipment. He smashed his fist into walls and fittings to destroy the carefully hidden devices inside the bedroom and the kitchen. There was one located in a ceiling, which he blasted with an energy device in his index finger; *point and splat,* Roger called it. *This finger is loaded.* Then Henry turned away and left the flat. In a short time he returned carrying a large wooden box about three and a half feet high with a square cross-section. He put it down on the floor and opened the lid.

Inside the box was the small, elf-like alien with a tiny head, wearing a conical hat and blue cloak. Henry lifted him out.

Jensine smiled in spite of her pain and lethargy. "Have you come to entertain me with a ventriloquist act? I assure you, it is not necessary."

The alien shimmered with a light and energy that made Roger and Deborah feel queasy. The last time Roger had seen him he had been riding on the shoulder of an extremely large, troll-like servant. This time he was alone.

Henry spoke to him in a tonal language that nobody understood except for the alien.

Then Henry said, "Roger, we are going to have visitors but we need to set up a portal between here and…and somewhere else. Our friend here will do that. But I have things to do for Jensine before we can leave. You must hold off the death squad."

"Me! Oh dear. What will they try to do?"

"They've usually got guns, lasers, psychic grenades and psychotronic brain scramblers. The usual stuff Psy Ops commandoes carry. Oh, and they can call up air support if necessary."

"So what am I supposed to do?"

"I don't know. You defeated the titan; the man in the black orb who could sling micro black holes around. I'm sure you'll think of something. You seem to need to be under pressure to be effective."

"I wish I had *his* powers," Roger said fervently.

The tiny wizard made a singsong sound.

Henry translated. "He says beware what you wish for – roughly speaking. He doesn't use words the way we do. You'll be fine. Don't worry so much."

"I'm touched by your confidence. And you can't be spared for this?"

Henry looked down at Jensine. "Not this time. I'm occupied."

Roger sighed. "I know. I'm the one who occupied you," he said, thinking of how he gave Henry a soul fragment. "Sorry – this is no time for humour."

"You are stressed. I can see the signs," Henry told him. "You'd better get out there."

Roger sighed. "Oh well. We who are about to…and so on."

As an afterthought, Henry said, "They might eschew the psycho-weapons. This is rather a public venue for any of the Black Ops Special Forces to put on a show, let alone Psy Ops. So you might only be facing conventional weapons – machine guns, artillery, that sort of thing."

"Great. You can be such a comfort sometimes. Who said resistance is futile? Look on the bright side. It might be over quickly."

Deborah had a worried expression on her face but said nothing as Roger headed for the front entrance. Then something strange happened. Objects in the apartment began to vibrate and they heard unusual noises. Roger, Deborah and Jensine immediately became disorientated and suffered severe pains in their heads, already affected by the aura of the little wizard. Only Henry and the tiny alien escaped from harm. The android moved quickly to the kitchen and returned with a roll of baking foil, which he tore into sections and placed over their heads. Faint blue light shimmered from the metal but it did ease the disabling effect on their brains. The impact on Jensine was doubly unfortunate because of her intense vulnerability.

"We need a Faraday cage," said Henry.

Almost immediately, they had one. The elfin wizard used his alien powers of physical transmutation to transform the surface of the floor, walls and ceiling into a metallic skin that shielded the room from an electromagnetic bombardment from above.

The alien's intervention solved the immediate problem of the radiation. However, the tiny wizard indicated that the metal shield would prevent him from opening a portal which they needed to transport them to a place of safety.

"That's okay," said Henry reassuringly. "They can't keep up the beam for long. They will need to close it down if they intend to break in."

Roger had other things on his mind. "Oh well, I suppose I'd better be getting out there. Did you know, I always wanted to start a Society for Advanced Procrastination but I never got around to it?"

"Yes," said Henry absently. "Do what you can. I can tell you this: I think I know the problem with Black Ops. It's you they want now. They've worked out who you really are. The only thing that will satisfy them is your dead body. Also, they want to turn me into a monster. If they kill you and Jensine they think I'll have nothing left to live for so I'll either co-operate with them or seek revenge. Either way, they hope to benefit in the long run."

"Weird! So you're sending me out there to die."

"You won't die, Roger. I'm sure you can deal with them. Trust your instincts."

"Sure, let go and trust *The Force.* Switch off the targeting computer. Let's hope you're right."

Chapter Eighteen

START OF A TIME LOOP

Still wearing metal foil, Roger headed for the front entrance. There was no option other than to leave his friends to deal with tragedy. He turned back and gave them one last look before he opened the door.

"I'm sorry, Henry," Deborah said. "She's gone."

"Okay, we've got things to do," the android said matter-of-factly.

He communed briefly with the alien. They agreed that the best course now was for the little 'wizard' to open the portal. His conical hat was really a magneto-sonic energy amplifier able to generate powerful scalar waves by resonating with the alien's pituitary gland. This is the component of human brains that fluoride in the water supply degrades through calcification. Thus humanity has decreed that the preservation of its teeth is more important than the evolution of its consciousness. With amplified scalar waves the alien could open portals between any two locations in time and space that it could hold in mind. With hat in hand, it could have destroyed the entire planet but that would have served no purpose. All this functionality originated not from some advanced technology built into the device but from its conical shape. Most important of all, it was a hat that he liked to wear.

Henry said, "They've switched off the irradiation

beam weapon – probably a satellite in low orbit." He lifted the wizard and took him to a wardrobe in the corner of the bedroom. The alien raised his tiny hands and made a series of gestures that produced patterns of light inside the cupboard. Then the small person passed through the hanging clothes and vanished to the accompaniment of a sloshing, watery sound.

"Where's he gone?" Deborah asked, struggling with nausea caused by the alien's potent presence. Suddenly, the discomfort eased. She let out a sigh of relief.

"He's opened a door to another universe," the android told her.

"So we're remaking *The Lion, The Witch and The Wardrobe*," she said.

Henry appeared puzzled until he looked up the reference on the Internet.

"Will Roger be all right?" Deborah asked.

"Roger?" Henry said vaguely. "I expect so. You'd better tell him not to use the psychic surge against people in Black Ops helmets. It won't work on them. They're better than tinfoil."

She went out of the room and returned shortly afterwards.

"He's still wearing that tinfoil. Will that impede his psychokinetic abilities?"

"Tell him to take it off. It's only going to protect them from him."

Deborah turned to obey and joined them again a short while later, none the happier for witnessing Roger's dire situation through a crack in the door.

Henry passed through the back of the wardrobe and returned soon after holding a long, black container with curved sides. As it emerged into the room,

Deborah was not surprised to see a newcomer lifting the other end. It was the troll-like alien that acted as a servant to the wizard. When the lid of the container was opened, it revealed a suspended animation casket.

Henry went to the bed, lifted his friend's body and carried it over to the casket. Then he pressed a coloured panel on the inside of the box revealing a microprocessor control touch screen. There was a short-lived hum followed by silence.

"That will keep the corpse preserved in a static time-field until we can remove some essential components," Henry explained, closing the lid.

"Let's hope it works," Deborah said fervently. She refrained from remarking on Jensine's 'essential components'. Henry's lack of respect in speaking of her, she knew, reflected his android nature. It was easy to forget that he had scant knowledge or experience of human death ritual and customs. To him, death was no more than a phase shift of consciousness. Then she pondered something Roger had once told her about Henry; he had never used a toilet. He could discharge excess cellular material directly to the void. He carried excess water inside him that he could use or transfer into a cup for anybody to drink if they were thirsty. It was not an option that Roger had been keen to employ except once on Annoon. They had been in a parched wilderness in pursuit of the enemy; the dreaded titan. Henry had peed into a travel mug and handed it over. It wasn't the purity of the water that deterred him so much as the psychology of its delivery.

Gunfire, explosions, helicopters and a whining jet engine contributed to a terrible din outside the building. The apartment block was shaking and brick dust floated in through the door that led to the reception hall.

"Shall I tell Roger we're leaving?" asked Deborah, worried by what she heard.

"No," Henry replied. He paused to listen to the mayhem outside. "It sounds as if he's getting into his stride. Let's go!"

Henry and the little alien's minder carried the casket with a shimmering temporal bubble glowing discreetly around it towards the confined space of the wardrobe. Passing through the watery-looking interface of the gateway, they emerged into the pastoral landscape beyond. Their passage dislodged dresses and gowns on hangers.

Deborah said, "Men!" as she picked up the clothes and replaced them on the rail. Then she stepped into cupboard to complete the sombre procession. The portal closed behind her.

"Good luck, Roger," she breathed softly. "I hope you find us."

***

A squad from Black Ops Special Forces had been maintaining surveillance outside Jensine's apartment block. The officer in charge of the watching soldiers was waiting to see if the android would come looking for the Pettersson woman. They were believed to be friends. It made no sense to the soldier. He had dealt with androids before but they never had friends. Neither were they as dangerous as Henry – dangerous enough though. They had advanced AI circuits that allowed them to mimic human beings reasonably well. Sounding plausibly human was enough to pass the Turing Test for artificial intelligence. Unlike Henry they followed orders. The Service nicknamed him *the Mandroid* because he was more like a human being than the usual Black Projects android. He hadn't even started out as an android. He had been a prototype utility robot on an interstellar exploration vessel. The robot had built the android version for itself with Roger Crandle's help. The problem with him was that he cared for people. This was an unfortunate trait in a potentially advanced weapon system.

The squad didn't want to confront Henry. In fact, they were particularly keen to avoid him. Their target was his friend, Roger Crandle. They had been briefed on Roger's history, on his tour in Space Command as a Psy Ops remote viewer and telepath. They knew about his involvement in a conflict on an alien world against a half-human renegade designated 'the titan'. There was a suggestion that he might have highly developed psychokinetic and other powers that could attack a target's mind. There was a handwritten addendum on the Psy Ops report by an Agent Spiker: 'Crandle has no understanding of his own potential and shows no sign of wishing to use it'. Further down the page was a note in another hand: 'Crandle demonstrated preternatural capabilities. Slayed Psy Ops Intel Unit. Partially demolished secure facility'.

There was a bonus to be had; killing Pettersson and Crandle might engender a willingness in the android to kill to order. How to effect that elimination was immaterial; destruction or death. It didn't matter. As far as they knew, it was one friend down, one to go. They had seen the android arrive earlier with Crandle and Farnham. The android was carrying a box, leading to speculation among the soldiers. The squad had earlier transported Jensine Pettersson to the apartment in a Tactical Field Care Mobile Facility. The most compelling target, Roger Crandle, was there. Deborah Farnham was something of an unknown quantity. Her loyalties were ambiguous. He had no orders to kill or detain her, only to maintain observation and collect intel. They were not *dead checking* today, the accepted terminology for entering a suspect's home and killing his wife, parents, kids and dog if he had one. The mark of a civilised society is its use of unintelligible terminology. Euphemisms like ethnic cleansing give an aura of legitimacy to mass murder.

"Time to flush the ground," the officer said to his second-in-command, prompting an encrypted signal from a SINCGARS mobile communications unit. Consequently, a technician in a remote base relocated a satellite in low orbit with ion thrusters to be in line of sight with the apartment block. From there he activated a tight beam of electromagnetic radiation designed to induce mental breakdown and hallucinatory disorder. This action took no account of who else might have been in line with the beam. It was not their concern. After ten minutes they deactivated the satellite. The squad approached the front entrance of the building in the way they had been trained; advance, stop, hold position, cover the next in line. People coming in or out of the block, seeing the activity around the building hurried away as quickly as possible.

They were about to storm the front entrance when the door opened and a man wearing a tinfoil cap stepped out into the street.

"Hold your fire!" the officer shouted. "It might be the android. We don't want to get him riled at this stage. She's probably close to death."

A soldier remarked, "He doesn't get angry from

what I heard."

"Do you want to put it to the test?" said the officer.

"Look at his clothing. Would the android wear tinfoil? It's Crandle," said another with certainty.

The officer nodded. "Maybe. According to Psy Ops, Crandle is the primary target. When we know for sure, fire on my order. On second thoughts, see if we can take him first. This is too public."

Roger was terrified but felt obliged to face these people; circumstances required it. He wished he could make them see the nonsense of soldiery and warfare. People joined armies and military forces for all sorts of reasons, to do good, to kill or simply to have a paid occupation. On the face of it, the motive was serving a country. In Roger's mind they were spiritually immature; a country is merely a place, and a nation is just an idea. No good ever came from killing, just deeper spiritual penury. *Thou shalt not kill* was little more than religious cant for other people; even some of the early popes with pragmatically elastic morals had ordered massacres. It seemed to Roger that the statement did not specify *what* thou shalt not kill. The mark of a 'civilisation' is where it chooses to draw the line or whether it even has a line to draw.

Long ago, on another world, in another time, Roger had defeated a titan but he had not been unarmed then. The Old One had given him a weapon, a psychotronic, psychokinetic amplifier called a Rod of Power. It was an ancient alien device fashioned from the body of an extraterrestrial serpent. This creature had lived in near space close to a planet. It fed on the energy emitted upwards by massive storm clouds. The snake travelled through space by means of a biological organ of propulsion like a rattler's tail. It drew energy from the vacuum to distort the fabric of time-space producing inertialess propulsion. A tuned operator could hold a crystalline handle replacing the creature's head to activate the tail and direct a beam of disruptive energy at a target. It could dissociate an object into a cloud of atoms, sucked it into an imploding plasma ball, expelling it beyond space and time. It was the serpent's natural defence mechanism against space-based predators. What would he have given now for a weapon like that? But no, he was not in the game of killing. There had to be another way.

"Crandle. Hold your hands up behind your head and sit cross-legged on the ground. If you don't, we'll shoot."

"There's a woman dying in there. Can't you at least have some decency?" he said. Roger used this short period of grace to calm himself. He reached into his higher consciousness and sent out a wave of psychic force to put his adversaries into a comatose state.

The door behind him opened a crack. Deborah peered out cautiously.

"Henry says a psychic surge won't work because they have screened helmets."

"Now he tells me," Roger muttered.

Deborah withdrew but then returned briefly to say, "And take that thing off your head. You won't be much use with it on."

"Damn!" said Roger, whipping it off. "I'm not doing very well."

The door behind him shut again.

"Last chance, Crandle," the officer shouted, signalling his men to prepare to fire.

Extreme fear gripped his guts. This wasn't working. Henry had much more confidence in Roger's metaphysical abilities than he had himself. What was he supposed to do? They worked when he *needed* them; true. When he *wanted* them to would be much better. They were about to open fire! One bullet! That's all it would take. As if in answer to his panic, Roger felt a force rippling along his spine and a strong tingling in his head. His light body activated, immersing his form inside a shining oval shell. This, he knew, was not proof against weapons – but then something new manifested outside of the orb of light. As they began to fire, dark discs appeared precisely where the projectiles would have struck him. The first bullet hit the barrier and ricocheted back along the line of its original trajectory, hitting the man who fired it between the eyes. As more and more rounds arrived, black discs appeared and then faded like the ripples of raindrops on a pond. Two more soldiers managed to shoot themselves. Helmets and body armour saved the others from auto-destruction. With so much ammunition arriving, the discs merged around his periphery with a deep *whoomp* sound into a totally enveloping dark shell. Roger found himself in darkness in total silence.

He had become a black orb like his vanquished enemy, the titan.

How can that be? he thought. *I'm not evil.*

Gradually, Roger's light body began to glow gently, relieving the darkness inside the black sphere. Mind-vision kicked in allowing him to see outside the jet-black object that contained him. Bullets no longer ricocheted from its surface. They vanished as though passing into the orb but they did not reach him. Henry could divert incoming weapons and projectiles straight into the void. Was this the same phenomenon? He could not say for sure.

The surviving soldiers with their automatic weapons were reloading as fast as possible. What they hoped to achieve was not clear, even to them. Then two Black Ops helicopters appeared over the nearby buildings, took in the situation and began firing heavy calibre rounds at the orb. Some rounds smashed into the building, those that arrived at the target simply disappeared inside it. For the first time since emerging from the apartment block, Roger began to relax. He felt the urge to do something but he didn't know what. The two helicopters circled the immediate area, firing at will. After ten minutes of futile aggression, they withdrew. Something else was in the offing, Roger was sure of it.

Then his mind's eye saw a new adversary flying down in his direction in a steep dive from three thousand feet. A Fairchild Republic A-10 Thunderbolt II hurtled towards him, strafing the area with its rotary cannon. A stream of depleted uranium, armour-piercing shells demolished a section of the building behind him. The attack also disintegrated parts of the concrete walkways, the tiny garden and statuettes. Shards of concrete, lumps of turf and shredded plants enveloped the scene in rising clouds of dust and debris. At 3,900 rounds per minute, the Thunderbolt could shred a line of tanks like cardboard cut-outs and blend its occupants to a sticky paste on the remaining metal surfaces. The ground-attack aircraft was an appalling weapon that could degrade and poison the land indefinitely with highly toxic uranium dust. That human beings could conceive of such a weapon was beyond Roger's understanding. Many rounds struck the outer shell of his dark orb and simply disappeared.

The A-10 turned away in a tight arc to set up a second attack run. Wishing momentarily that he could stop the aircraft's offensive, Roger shot into the sky in a smooth curve. His trajectory crashed through the rear portion of the A-10 and then took him back to the front entrance of the apartment block. It was a totally involuntary response to the thought. The collision sucked the larger part of the airframe and fuel into the black surface of the orb. The pilot managed to launch his ejector seat as the surviving portions of the aircraft crashed into a neighbouring building.

Roger wanted to know what was going on inside the apartment. It occurred to him that the soldiers could have gone in the rear entrance at any time. Why didn't they do that? Then he guessed the answer; they didn't want to face Henry. It was as Henry had said; they wanted to kill *him*. The black helicopters reappeared above the buildings.

Then it happened. A second black orb streaked across the sky and passed right through the two helicopters. It sucked them in. They vanished, machines and crew together.

More military vehicles arrived on the scene – discharging personnel in black combat gear. What was meant to be a discrete operation was turning into a conspiracy theory spectacular that would inspire official denials for years to come. It was reminiscent of the Battle of Los Angeles in 1942 when anti-aircraft batteries with searchlights failed to shoot down a harmless weather balloon after an hour of firing. *All that shrapnel*, he thought, *and they say it never rains in California!*

Then Roger caught sight of a flying saucer. It was quite high, probably a thousand feet or more but Roger had no sense of the threat it represented. However, it proved to be no threat at all because the black orb of his mysterious cohort flew past the gleaming craft and released a micro black hole that passed inside it. Roger sensed rather than saw the weapon – it was too small even for mind-vision but he could not mistake the result. The metallic circular spacecraft imploded and vanished. Roger faced a terrifying prospect; his former enemy, *the titan*, was back from the dead.

Roger wanted to know if his friends inside the apartment were still in need of protection. He had no desire to remain in a state of conflict with mad people. What was Henry doing in there? What was 'the wizard' up to? Was the titan really protecting *him*?

Chapter Nineteen

Jensine Pettersson closed her eyes for the last time and died. She found herself going along a dark tunnel towards *the light*. She'd heard about this phenomenon from reports of near-death experiences. She had even looked into it for a research project during her student days. She had accepted the prevailing medical opinion. The tunnel, the dead relatives, floating out of the body; these were hallucinations activated when the brain releases natural endorphins to ease the trauma of its imminent demise. This suggestion came from Daniel Carr in 1981. Jensine saw it as a kindness endowed by nature to ease the stress and fear of dying prior to oblivion.

Henry had told her that her view was not entirely incorrect and neither was it totally true. He said that science as a system lacks an understanding of the broader aspects of consciousness. He explained that the mystery of consciousness is not what it is but what *it is not* i.e. nothing. *Everything* is consciousness but not everything is *conscious*. According to Henry, it's a paradox because human beings have a narrow view of consciousness. They see it as the ability to think, but *consciousness* is *time*, the act of being is context whereas *knowing* is a product of space. Time tells the story and space is the stage for the drama, the game and the dream of earthly existence. He said that we are mathematical algorithms, software if you like, integral to the massive program that creates our virtual reality. Jensine had tended to discount Henry's wild assertions unless he proved otherwise. Eternal life was one premise he could not affirm.

She went along the tunnel convinced that it would end in the total extinction of her mind when brain death occurred. Even though Henry had showed her anecdotal evidence of life after death, it was not proof. Her scientific outlook and training shaped her predominating attitudes. The new gardener, of all people, had declared that, ideally, the scientific method should keep an open mind about a theory until it is proved to be true or false. Unfortunately, the pragmatic system says stay within the prevailing paradigm or we'll cut your funding, destroy your reputation and end your career.

Henry had also told Jensine that the scientists and technologists of Black Ops lived in a universe that bore little resemblance to the one in textbooks. If the dam ever breaks and the hidden paradigms flood into human culture, the race would be in for a shock. There will be clean, cheap energy, interstellar travel and empty churches. It might even signal the ending of *the game*, the abandoning of money and the onset of true equality and peace in the world. That, Henry said, was why the rich and powerful elements of society will never allow the truth to come out. They would rather move into vast underground cities, cull the population and have the world to themselves. It was the most futile idea ever conceived, Henry had declared. He told her that there are forces in the universe far greater than we could ever imagine that might have something to say about it.

Ahead of her, Jensine saw her grandparents and her

brother waiting to greet her. She was aware that they did not really exist. Nevertheless, she pretended they were real as she met them and smiled. The consistency and continuity of the experience puzzled her. This was like paradise but it shouldn't have been so; she *knew*.

Thus it came to pass that she found herself in a land of great beauty, glowing with a light that had no specific source, no sun up in the sky to account for it. She could hear birdsong but there was no identifiable weather. The blue of the sky was overwhelming in its intensity and purity; none of the streaks of yellow smoke on the horizon from the ubiquitous fallout of human activity at home.

The three family members who had passed to spirit talked to her about her recent experiences. She found this new state of being overwhelmingly peaceful and joyous. Her material life was fading into an irrelevant dream. Her recent sufferings through incarceration and illness were fading from memory and mind. It seemed as if her entire life in the physical had lasted no more than a few seconds.

"You'll love it here," her grandmother was telling her.

"We've prepared a place for you to rest. This will be the last time you will ever need to sleep." Her grandfather was as she remembered but so much younger and alive.

The brother who had died a boy stood before her a man. "Nobody sleeps here. There's no need once you're acclimatised."

Then something seemed to change and Jensine's family looked upwards to the sky in anticipation and uncertainty.

"What is happening?" asked her grandfather.

"We've got a visitor," said her brother.

"I'm not happy about this," the grandfather remarked. "Is something wrong?"

"No," her grandmother replied. "Somebody is coming down from a higher dimension. He wants to talk to Jensine."

A ball of blue light descended from above and dissolved, revealing a tall, fair-haired, bearded man in a cream robe. He wore a knotted cord around his waist comprising golden threads, platted into three intertwined strands. When he spoke she heard his voice in her mind.

"Hello, Jensine. A friend of yours asked me to speak to you."

"Do you mean Henry?"

"Yes," he replied. "It was Henry."

"Henry, yes, I remember Henry," she said. "He told me he has powerful friends."

The handsome face broke into a smile. "That is how he sees me but it is all relative. There are beings so far beyond me in spiritual evolution that I cannot comprehend them. We are ascending an infinite ladder."

She looked around and noticed that her family were no longer standing behind her.

"Where have they gone?" she asked in concern.

"Nowhere. They have merely withdrawn while you are with me."

"My family…"

"Jensine," he said in a firm but kindly tone. "You have no family."

"I saw them…they were here."

"*They* were here – yes – but genetic connections belong to the earth plane. Here we have spiritual 'families' based on shared experience. Your relatives belong to your spiritual family. Their genetic roles no longer apply. Spiritual ties go much deeper than physical relationships. Passing on your DNA is as significant as posting a letter. There is no need to have children to achieve immortality. You *are* immortal whether you want to be or not. The most important relationships in your life build on love. That is all that matters."

"What do you want with me?" she asked.

"I have come to ask you to return to physical life. You have things to do, to complete."

Jensine was shocked and disappointed. "This is too wonderful to give up," she said, waving her arm around the beauty that surrounded her.

"All reality is relative to absolute nothingness," replied the bearded man. "You are in the spirit world now. Here you create your environment with your mind by living the waking dream. Because your heart is good you are surrounded by goodness and beauty. Those who come here ingrained with materialism or hatred of others create ugly or dark environments. What we see outside of us reflects what is within the heart. All you are giving up is the outward reflection of your heart, not the substance of it."

"So being rich and powerful in material life does not guarantee a good time in the afterlife," Jensine remarked.

"On the contrary," he said. "It takes a different coinage to prosper in this reality. Here it is the currency of love and good deeds that buy you entry. Besides, 'afterlife' is a little misleading. It is before life as well as after. It is the infinite light of consciousness manifest in the illusion of finiteness."

"Whatever…but why would I want to leave?" she asked bluntly.

"There is no compulsion. You have free will but do not exercise it lightly."

"Why would I wish to return to a body riddled with cancer? Why give up this loveliness for something gross?"

The Old One looked at her with understanding.

"You were *never* that body. The universe provided it but it was not *you*. The body you have here *is* you, dreamed into existence by the power of mind. You can take any form you choose. There is no age here as such. They call me 'the Old One' because I was once of the elder race, known colloquially as 'the old ones'. We played a key role in the development of material worlds. That was just one of many incarnations. Let me show you the form I had at that time."

In front of her, he transformed into a smaller being that was not attractive to her conventional tastes. He had small eyes and a skin colour that somehow combined brown, grey and purple in a knobbly humanoid shape. When he spoke, his voice became guttural. "I do not need to incarnate to take form. I can appear anywhere in any physical guise I choose. I tell you this because you are not limited in choice by such considerations. You have a body ready and waiting. That is all settled."

"What is all settled?"

He saw her gaze wistfully at the spirit world and read her thoughts.

Restoring his human form, the Old One said, "You think that life on earth does not compare to this. That is true but there are aspects of physicality that you cannot replicate here. *You* are essentially formless. You have pleasures of the mind and the spirit but pleasures of the body do not happen here. Gender is illusory. If you eat, there is no real taste or flavour in the food. It is the same with wine, or coffee or tea. You can create a facsimile of anything you want with your mind but you cannot duplicate the sensory experience of the body. When you are ready to move on, you will no longer need such things. However, you were taken from your life before you had fulfilled the purpose of your physical existence. Your new body will not provide a full complement of senses but it will be physical nonetheless. Let us call it a halfway house between matter and spirit. My words will mean nothing to you right now but you will understand in time. It is up to you."

Jensine realised that she had a choice but lacked the understanding to make it.

"So you recommend that I return even though I don't know what I'm returning to?"

He nodded. "Yes. Misguided people interrupted your incarnation. In truth, they have no idea what they are doing and the price they will have to pay. That is not your concern. Just know that when you fulfil your soul's contracted obligations, you may come back here. And know, too, that this is not the end of life. It is simply its continuation. Physical death is the beginning of a new phase into the unknown. It will take you beyond anything you could imagine." He gestured to the beauty around and said, "This is not a destination. It is a way station for the soul to dwell in peace before resuming the infinite journey."

"Supposing I had taken my own life. What then?"

"Every case is unique. For some it is an inevitable conclusion, a predestined compulsion they carry throughout their life. However, for many, I think the expression that applies is 'a spanner in the works'. When an individual fails to face up to their soul's requirement they must reincarnate to deal with it, again and again if necessary. Ultimately, progress is a divine imperative for every conscious entity. You cannot put it off forever. It is not about punishment; it is completion. The situation you cannot face returns in its broadest sense until you do succeed. You decide the manner of your life when you select the circumstances of your conception and your time of birth. We will help you but we never impose. If you are not happy with your life, there is no point blaming your parents. They did not choose you; you chose them. Sometimes you come back with the same souls, sometimes with others. There are no hard and fast rules about it. *You* are not in that situation. *Your* choice is voluntary."

Jensine sighed. "Very well, Gandalf. What now? I'll do it, but I don't know how."

With a slight smile, he said, "You have made a wise decision. I can show you the way. I think you will like it. There are no wars where you are going; not even money. And death is a matter of choice rather than compulsion."

"A world without death and taxes! That doesn't sound too bad and yet you say it will be physical?"

"Yes," the Old One said. "It will be physical but not in the same universe as the old earth."

Overcoming her doubt and confusion, Jensine said firmly, "I *will* do it. What happens now?"

The process began when she affirmed her agreement. The Old One raised his right hand and touched her forehead gently with his index finger to attach a silver cord. Far away, the small alien 'wizard' did the same thing to a distant forehead of another kind. Jensine felt a force grip her head with an insistent tugging. It pulled like elastic growing stronger and stronger to the point where she could barely resist it.

"Let go," the Old One instructed.

A light as bright as the sun flashed through her consciousness accompanied by a clap of sound like thunder. She shot instantaneously from the spirit world reflecting the environment of planet earth, traversing time and space to land with a jolt in her new body. She fell immediately into a deep sleep during which her spirit entangled itself with the new vehicle. As her grandfather had predicted, it would be one of the last times she would sleep for some time to come but for a very different reason.

***

It was stalemate. Roger could have left the vicinity of Jensine's apartment but was not sure that Henry and his friends had escaped. On the other hand, there was not much point staying where he was. He was offering the Black Ops Special Forces little more than an opportunity for target practice.

It was time to withdraw into the building, but how? The black orb was too big to go through the door. By trying, he would make a hole through the wall. Not that there was much left undamaged. His dark Merkabah had already made a few dents in the concrete below. Fortunately, he was not an actual black hole. A condensed object of his size would have swallowed the entire planet and probably have sucked in the moon, Mars and Venus. After the bombardment, the housing complex looked like a war zone. Closing down the protecting black shell felt too risky with all that artillery aimed at him.

While all this was going on, in his mind, a new transformation commenced. His mind-vision switched from outside the orb to inside. His own light within the black shell began to intensify. His body was glowing, lightening in density until it became insubstantial. His everyday clothing had gone. He was wearing a white robe. The dark shell grew translucent, then transparent and finally dissolved altogether. The mayhem and noise had diminished to stillness. Time was slowing down. No, it was *his* time that was slowing. He could see bullets and shells gradually stopping in mid-air. His world was a frozen tableau suspended in the moment. It reminded him of a scene from *The Matrix* and for the same reason; the universe is a simulation but not in a computer. The aliens had told him that the refresh rate of the universe's display, the physical universe, pulsed in multiples of Planck time. This accounted, they said, for its incredible believability considering its arbitrary mathematical and digital nature. It is why human beings age and die and don't even know who they are.

Roger stood in his white robe, a glow of light all around him. He raised his hand in front of his face and studied it. It was recognisably his hand but it was made of a substance that glowed with its own light. He sidestepped the stationary bullets, anticipating where they would go when time resumed the normal tenor of its ways. He went over to where the nearest soldier lay. His rifle stock against his shoulder, a grim expression on his immobile face, he could have been an exhibit in a museum of warfare. *It would be better for the world if he was*, Roger thought.

Could he disarm him? He reached out with his hand towards the automatic rifle. He could not grasp it or move it but he didn't have to; it vanished at his touch. Following this discovery, Roger disarmed all the soldiers. For good measure he removed their helmets and clothing. All they had left was their underwear. Having done that and dissolved the military vehicles and their armaments, he walked back to the entrance, carefully avoiding the potentially lethal trajectories of the bullets.

His timeline duly resumed.

The soldiers felt their weapons vanish from their hands. Defenceless, semi-naked and feeling rather stupid, they stood up slowly and looked around at each other. "What's happened?"

"Where's Crandle?"

This was no way to run a military operation against a known terrorist. In intelligence circles, to be suspected is to be condemned and there were always techniques, such as waterboarding, to make them squeak. Roger was blissfully unaware that he was a terrorist. He didn't even know what a terrorist was supposed to do. He walked towards the door of the apartment block, failed to open it and, by mistake, passed right through into the building. Thinking about the inside was sufficient to put him there. There was no sign of occupancy. His friends, including the body of the unfortunate young doctor, had gone. Some ethereal coloured fringes around the bedroom wardrobe told him where the temporary portal had opened. There was nothing to keep him here now but where should he go? In a relatively short time, he'd been a sphere of light, an orb of shadow and now he was a glowing massless being in a white robe, moving by thought alone. He couldn't even decide whether he was alive or dead. Technically, was there any difference other than the limitation of a cumbersome body?

Roger returned to the outside of the building more out of curiosity than purpose. There was much confusion. It was not conducive to peace and harmony for soldiers to have no weapons and no trousers. Military discipline required both, especially the trousers.

Roger began to move around the milling crowd when his body decided to return to physicality. The white robe was gone. His clothes were back where they should be. His visibility to others resumed.

"Oh dear. I should have left while I could," he said feeling awkward.

"It's Crandle!" came the cry.

"He's back."

The soldiers became an angry mob that moved towards him menacingly. Roger raised his palms in an unconscious warding gesture. Those nearest to him were flung back, crashing into the people behind.

"Oh my God," he moaned. "What now?"

They rose to their feet cautiously but retained their distance. The officer in charge stepped forward. "Crandle. You killed three of my men."

"No, I didn't. I don't have a weapon."

"They were shot."

"They shot themselves when they tried to shoot me. I don't even know how it happened. What was I supposed to do? Let them kill me?"

"You destroyed a Thunderbolt ground-attack aircraft and two helicopters – with crew and – something else." To name the other object was too much like treason.

"That was an accident. I've never done that before. Anyway, I didn't attack the helicopters or the flying saucer. That was somebody – something – else."

"Oh yeah. Who?"

Roger shook his head and surveyed the sky warily. "I wish I knew." His friends had gone. He wanted to leave. With no orb of light, where could he go on foot? In London it was easy to get on a bus. This was America. He'd heard that the police here pick up pedestrians on suspicion. Apparently, only burglars and muggers walk. Everyone else had a car. But that was a myth too. How long would these Black Ops soldiers remain at a distance? Already they were circling, sensing his hesitation. Roger felt that they were about to rush him again, hoping that his newfound abilities would fail.

Then the situation took a turn for the bizarre once more.

"What's that black thing up there?" said one of the soldiers.

Everybody looked up in response. It was the other black orb circling in the sky above them like a spherical vulture. As it drew near, it appeared quite large in comparison with the one Roger had occupied.

"What is that?" the officer demanded to know.

"It's a round black thing," said Roger facetiously. "How should I know?"

Sensing that he was about to slip through their military fingers, the soldiers moved to close in on him again. This prompted the black orb to descend rapidly to a location adjacent to Roger, whereupon it dissolved to reveal a gigantic human figure wearing an immaculate tuxedo, white shirt and bow tie. *The titan as a prehistoric James Bond* was Roger's first thought.

The soldiers retreated in confusion to a safe distance. Roger found that he could move even though the world around him was 'on pause'. He found himself standing next to the demon of his nightmares. At eight feet tall, just looking at him made his neck ache. His arrival wasn't a total surprise but it was a shock. Roger didn't know whether to prepare for an attack or flee. The newcomer moved closer but made no overtly aggressive action.

Roger had never seen his old enemy so smartly dressed. He had always worn medieval clothing, a cloak and a sword, with long hair and a serious expression. Now he had short hair, a ready smile and an aura of benign affability. It was most confusing.

"I thought you were dead," he said lamely.

The titan chuckled. "It just goes to show, you can't keep a good monster down." The titan was joking because he knew himself to be quite handsome by human standards. Fellow titans in his youth, male and female, had been largely unprepossessing. Lizards coupled with human mothers did not produce elegant offspring, quite the reverse in fact. Multiple rows of teeth were not uncommon. If depicted in religious art they would be more gargoyle than cherub. However, the Old One, the titan's father, had adopted human form at the time of conception. This followed an unfortunate incident at a social event when a lizard extraterrestrial ate him.

Tentatively, Roger addressed the titan. "Are you here for me?" he asked, fearing that revenge was uppermost in the giant's mind.

"Yes, you could say that," the titan responded smoothly in matinée idol tones. "You seem to be in need of my help. I saw you using psychokinetic force.

You show promise but you've got a lot to learn."

Roger's relief showed on his face. Maybe the titan was not out for his blood after all.

"Oh, I thought–"

"That I had come to exact terrible revenge for what you did to me – with my father's assistance. That is because you do not know what happened. I remember that body well. I was fond of it. It served me for two hundred thousand years on and off. It was not always the same physical stuff in it but I preserved the metaphysical template."

Roger swallowed. "Do you mean that's a new body?" He shut off, aware of the banality of his question. It was obvious. This version of the titan was lighter somehow, less threatening in appearance. At times he thought he saw the glow of his aura. Even so, he could not shake off the memory of how terrible this being had once been.

"Do you mean this?" the titan asked, lifting one arm with the other to demonstrate it was a seemingly lifeless appendage. Then he raised both arms, tossed his head and turned like an old-fashioned mannequin showing off a dress. "It's just a little number I put on to visit you this fine evening. We do not need bodies where I live nowadays. I made up with the Old One after our little contretemps. He's promoted me into the higher mysteries. Of course, I could dissolve and reconstitute my original body – it's in the genes. But now I have more choice of form. I am able to create a physical body when I need one without the inconvenience of incarnating. Such a messy business, don't you think? All that 'mewling and puking in the nurse's arms', as this man I once met in a bawdy inn put it."

"Shakespeare?" asked Roger in surprise.

"Oh, you met him too? I can tell you, he was easily led astray by my wicked ways."

"You must have been a bit conspicuous in a sixteenth century inn," Roger remarked. "Most people were about five feet tall in those days."

"Yes. Nobody picked *my* pocket. When my companion got inebriated or *spongy* as he called it, the landlady was *very* understanding. Nothing was too much trouble for a friend of mine, especially after I nearly knocked myself out on her low ceilings. I explained to Shakespeare, as I knew him, how he wasn't really in the universe at all. I said, 'you are a particle of light incubating in a shell of darkness. You dream this reality in the filtered twilight of your own being. That's how the infinite experiences finite existence.' I knew something about it, even then. He grabbed a quill and ink and wrote some words on the back of the bill about a nutshell and a king of infinite space having bad dreams. He was writing a play called…

"Omelette?"

"*Hamlet*."

"Just so. He used it in a different context as part of his plot but the hidden meaning applies nonetheless. I said his spirit was locked in the dark side of the eternal tennis ball, the universe of opposites. His soul was in the light side but he could forget about that. I advised him to forget the light and live for the shadow. You might as well as you don't really exist; everything is nothing. That's the real secret, the great riddle, you know. *Nothing* exists so everything is possible. It's a paradox, the secret of the number zero. Nothing is everything; everything is nothing and the number one drives it all."

"'I could be bounded in a nutshell, and count myself a king of infinite space, were it not that I have bad dreams'," Roger murmured. "That's what Shakespeare actually wrote. I presume life is the bad dream, the ongoing game between shadow and light."

The titan nodded sagely. "Shadow is the teacher and light is the pupil. Did you know that no object in existence could ever leave its own centre – its *zero-point*? Every physical object has its natural *origin* in space and time here and now, never in the past or somewhere else. We don't move. It's everything else that moves in both space and time. From the sun's point of view the earth and all the planets go around it, as astronomers believe. In its own terms, the earth does not move; the sun and planets go around it in epicycles in a virtual sky, as astrologers believe. The only reality is truth but it is inevitably a relative concept for a finite mind, which is why we have wars. Only *we* are right and everyone else is wrong. I took enough advantage of that in my time. Human beings are so easy to manipulate with belief systems; hatred comes easier than love. It's because people identify with their thoughts but really their thoughts have independent existence in the great web."

"Is that what that phrase means? We're all asleep in boxes dreaming this?"

"That's part of it. I can give you another example. All entities, things in the universe, register in the matrix as numbers. Numbers are repositories of meaning. If you could see a number it would look fuzzy, depending on how many factors it has. They vibrate between them. Whole entities, like planets or people, belong to prime numbers. So your node in the matrix is a prime number. Its essential meaning defines you. If you could see it, it would look like a hard shell. No factors, you see? Like I said, all truth is relative. When you realise that consciousness is dual, you can see that science is true from one perspective while astrology and numerology are valid from the other. It's logic versus reason."

The titan could see the questions forming in Roger's mind. "You are wondering, perhaps, if you went through all that hardship and suffering for no reason. Was the whole conflict meaningless?"

Roger nodded slowly. "Something like that."

"You *did* succeed in thwarting my ambitions and control over people's lives. My return to you now is a sign of *my* failure, not yours. I am here to confirm your success!"

It was a fine evening. Roger was so wrapped up with the arrival of the titan that he forgot to take notice of what was going on around him. Reinforcements for the military were arriving by land and by air. These soldiers were fully armed with guns and trousers. A more senior officer arrived to take charge. Nobody could brief him satisfactorily on what he was taking charge of. Black Ops sent a boffin as technical advisor with instructions to explain the inexplicable, a common enough necessity in the secret world. Also, there was talk of confiscating every cell phone within a half-mile radius to avoid undesirable publicity. Not many people from the neighbourhood were visible. This was akin to a war situation. A single video on YouTube might be sufficient to cause a rumpus and spark a hundred denials. It had happened before. Fortunately, governments had no scruples about lying; it's why they invented public relations. The secret government's minimalist PR team was hampered by secrecy. This was a situation where the usual explanations like swamp gas or the planet Venus were no longer plausible.

The titan, amused by the machinations of the military, continued to narrate the story of his origins to Roger. "Anyway, the alien males, the so-called *gods*, succumbed to the attractions of genetically modified human females. These women, newly emerged from their incubation tanks, were totally innocent. And yet, they exuded an unconscious sexuality that played havoc with the hormones of the male planetary architects. They succumbed to temptation. You know what they say about *builders*, even planetary ones. These higher beings mingled their multidimensional genetic information with simple genes having only two strands of DNA. They had spliced alien genes with those of a primitive hominid to engineer your species. This additional unplanned merging produced hybrids like myself. The humans called us *titans* because we had superior strength and intellect but we lacked spirituality or morality. It was as if our consciences had been removed. This brought evil into human consciousness. These events, more than anything else, initiated *the game* that is playing out now on planet earth."

Roger, beset by fear of 'friend' and foe alike said, "So women have been blamed for thousands of years for something they didn't do."

"*Of course!* That's why men twisted the story of Adam and Eve when they wrote the holy books, painting intelligent women as harlots. At that time a *temptress* was just a woman who looked good. It was a passive thing. Some of them got wise after that but I blame the genetic engineers; give people toys, they are going to play with them. In later generations men overturned matriarchal societies. They got rid of the goddess religions and invented a male creator in their own image. The rise of paternalistic religions turned female sexuality into sin. The Catholic Church called it *concupiscence* specifically for that purpose. Men could then blame women for their own weaknesses and desires. The reptilians thereby planted a seed that inspired the idea of the devil. Why acknowledge your own failings when you can accuse a fiction? Any wisdom and spirituality that women *had* retained, men eradicated through witch-hunts. It is male dominance in society that has led to war, poverty and destruction of the environment. I should know; I set up a number of conflicts. To be civilised, a society requires balance in all aspects; gender, race, status, resources, beliefs and so on. *I* can say *that* now that I know better."

The titan drew breath. "The result of this forced interbreeding was that the human women died giving birth to degenerate giants. It resulted in the so-called War in Heaven. That was my first, by the way. I led the titan rebellion against the Old One. Anyway, although the Old One loved my mother, he felt he had done wrong nonetheless."

"Why? You're not a monster," said Roger. "Not in appearance anyway. Why did he blame himself?"

"It wasn't my physical aspect but my behaviour that upset him. As the last of the old ones, the original builders, he felt responsible for the evil the titans unleashed on the world, especially the children of the reptilians. I committed all of the sins many times over throughout my long existence. He never liked the list of *thou shalt nots* they issued. Tell people *not* to do something, what's the first thing they do? They'll murder, fornicate, steal, lie and covet on a huge scale. He wanted to teach the *thou shalts*. You know the sort of thing; be at peace, live as one, minimise possessions, express truth and act from the heart. He chose to walk the earth helping people and undoing the damage he had done. He appears in many mythologies as Viracocha, Osiris, Thor and many more."

"You fought against the Old One?" Roger queried. "How did that work out?"

"I'm glad you ask," replied the titan huffily. "I lost. He imprisoned me in a black hole indefinitely to protect the universe from my more unfortunate excesses. You cannot imagine how bad that was. How much do you know about black holes?"

"Anything that goes in does not emerge," Roger said. "Light, matter and radiation are trapped by its enormous gravitational pull. The only thing that leaves it is Hawking radiation. That's how they evaporate over vast passages of time."

"So – not much. You're familiar with the Taijitu – the yin-yang diagram?"

"Of course. It's everywhere."

"I know. The Old One arranged for that to happen because it gives you the clue to everything. The snag is that nobody really understands it. I'm only using it as a metaphor. What do you get on the dark side of the Taijitu?"

"A white dot."

"What do those dots represent?"

Roger shrugged. "Finite concepts, particles of matter...

"Yes, all of that and more. Every atom is made of miniscule points of light in geometric formations that structure space as quantum foam. When I say 'light' I mean metaphysical energy, the light of consciousness. The greater part of an atom is empty space. In a black hole all that space collapses and only the light remains. So the paradox is that the dark side of the Taijitu, the black hole in physical space, is concentrated light of pure consciousness. Correspondingly, the white side is concentrated 'dark dots', a kind of hole in the subjective light. When the Old One sent me into a black hole, the singularity sucked me into a personal void of nothingness trapped inside the light. This cell was finite on the outside and infinite on the inside. It was the ultimate prison. All I could do was exist. I had nothing to do but think and dream. It was hell!"

"How long were you there?" Roger asked.

"Time has no meaning in the infinite. It is eternal timelessness. It is impossible to explain in words. Tens of thousands of years passed on earth."

"How did you escape? I presume you did or you wouldn't be here."

"He did not realise that my original genesis as a soul was in black hole energy, just as his, like yours, was in blue light. As *your* consciousness is of the earth, eventually I *became* the black hole. In the same way, you become the moon when you are on it long enough to merge. I returned to the physical side of existence with far more power than I had ever known before. When you live on a planet, you become part of the consciousness of that world. The earth experiences itself through the creatures that live on it. That is the symbiosis that allows an inhabited world to evolve. That is why the terrible things you humans do to each other and the planet degrades everything. Humanity has turned paradise into a living hell. Eden is now a shithole of pesticides, poison, fracking, nuclear waste and genetic manipulation; human beings are the curse of the planet that gives them life."

"You are so big," Roger remarked, changing the subject. "Were you one of the giants that were said to walk the earth?"

"I was born taller than average by your standards but nowhere near the scale of the other titans. My mother was one of the few to survive giving birth. I inherited my father's immortality until I met you. I learned to hide my inner darkness in greater shadow. My bonding with *black hole energy* enabled me to become what mankind calls a *jinn* or a *demon*. I could move in and out of form but I could not raise my frequency beyond the lower levels of astral shadow. And yet, even in darkness, I could have such fun! I could feed on the sufferings and emotions of incarnating souls, especially their fear."

"You fed on me then," said Roger without rancour.

"You were not so straightforward. I was then in the physical dimension. It's different from lurking disembodied in the shadows between worlds. I felt a kinship with you. I didn't understand why because in my terms you were nothing. I was a god, you were a microbe; a piece of pond slime."

"I can't dispute that," Roger stated. This was not a being to argue with. In fact, he found it agreeable not to be pulverised by the demon of his nightmares. The titan's words were derisory in content but there was respect in his manner. He merely spoke the truth as he saw it. Even pond slime has its day, apparently.

"Yes. That is exactly my point. No matter what life threw at you, you maintained dignity beyond my understanding."

"I just do my best," said Roger quietly.

"You do indeed," the titan agreed. "I saw your fear, naturally. But you were immune to the glamour of power and privilege. That usually draws humankind into the service of evil. Most people can be bought, especially when the alternative is fear. Nobody could encounter *me* without fear – apart from my fellow titans. I was always one of the smallest. Nevertheless, I really did desire to be your friend. I couldn't tell you why. Now I know why. You associated with the Old One. *That* ensnared me. It was not *you* at all. I'd built a solid wall against my father. What did he do? He sneaked his energy through you to get my attention. Through you he set up the final confrontation. Without the Rod of Power you could not have defeated me. *That* was the channel for his energy."

The titan watched the new military forces arriving: vehicles, weapons, missile launchers and helicopters. It was like a show put on for their benefit.

"There's optimism for you," he said, pointing at the military. Then he continued his narrative. "It was not until after my death at your hands that I understood."

Roger felt awkward. "I did not *want* to kill – I did not mean to. You were killing me, or so it seemed at the time. It was the weapon, the Rod of Power. There was a bright light and then an explosion. There seemed to be no other way but to use it," said Roger. He felt like an explorer standing on the rim of a volcano waiting for an imminent eruption.

The titan made a dismissive gesture. "You did not *kill* me in the conventional sense. The weapon turned me into a plasma ball that imploded and expelled me from the space-time continuum. But you did destroy my favourite body." He looked down at himself ruefully. "This one is no substitute. But at least I was not locked into the implacable time clock of planet earth; the unfolding story you call history."

"We weren't on earth," Roger pointed out. "We were on Annoon."

"Precisely. That world was not coupled to earth time at all when I first went there. I began to link them together by transporting a group of people from Tudor England and placing them on Annoon. A Welsh fellow called it *Annwn*, the Celtic Paradise. It was as good a name as any except that the English can't pronounce 'w' or 'll' properly in the Welsh way. My despotic style of management lowered the spiritual tone considerably. My plan was to couple the consciousness of Annoon to that of the earth. I hoped to get the worst elements of this planet incarnating there for the hell of it. I loved the game you play here."

"You were well on the way to succeeding when I got there," Roger said.

"Yes. After our conflict and my subsequent demise, I lost the heart for making trouble. I could no longer act without conscience. You put your light in the core of my darkness and that changed me forever."

"*I saw* what I did to you with the Rod of Power," Roger said. "*I saw* you ripped apart and taken up in a whirlpool of light. Then it shrank to a point and vanished. It was horrible."

"Yes, I *know*! I became a plasma field. But that was just my body. What you did went deeper than that. You opened the floodgate to the greater part of my soul that I had locked away in a black hole. By the way, the spiritual hierarchy *is* aware that your android friend has been putting people in a temporal resequencer to speed up their personal evolution. It has become a noteworthy experiment as long as they retain free will. Spiritual growth is the real reason for incarnating but your culture has totally forgotten that."

"I'm pleased to hear that," Roger said. "Henry wants to show that enlightenment is open to everyone – if they choose it."

"His success has surprised some influential entities that wanted to write you all off as a lost cause. The concept of *hoodies* has got up to the ninth dimension and beyond. Not that they understand what it means. Monks and nuns wore hoods. A number of them progressed spiritually but not many bishops! They were more likely to be a part of the problem. They paid the price for their temporal power over others and their material excesses. They lived like princes in the Middle Ages! As you say, power is the poisoned chalice. The bishops had plenty of that."

"How does this shell you put around me work?" Roger asked. "At first I repelled their bullets. Then, when I was completely enclosed, they began to disappear inside somehow. But they didn't reach me. I was unharmed."

"I didn't *give* it to you. I helped you to *find it* by connecting you to the appropriate node in the conceptual matrix. You understand that – the web of life that overlays the universe. It joins all things, all thoughts and concepts together. What happens in one place affects all things... No, they couldn't hurt you inside your shadow sphere," said the titan absently. Then he became animated. "Look at those people! They are about to open fire. How marvellous!" He shook his head and glanced down at Roger who was feeling more than a little uneasy.

"Are you sure we're not in danger here?" Roger

asked.

"You are a *worrier*." The titan thrust his closed fist to his chest. "*I* am a *warrior*. I'm just waiting for them to do their worst before I dish it all back."

"I thought you'd reformed," Roger remarked.

"Of course. I won't have them boiled in oil like I might once had done. You've already experienced the black orb in elastic mode. It redirects the attack back to the attacker. In sink mode it sucks everything in. I will present them with the elastic version. It's nothing to do with me what they do to themselves."

"Oh," said Roger. "Is that how it works? It sounds a bit too convenient. What about personal responsibility?"

"You take karma too seriously. It's not about reward and punishment."

"Surely, it has to end somewhere."

"Hmm, maybe. You can't play in the pigsty forever. That is the crisis of your planet. You are trapped in the cycle of reincarnation. The wheel of life grinds slowly but relentlessly. It's the game! Round and round it goes and everything gets worse and worse because immoral, greedy people run the world and societies pay the price. Many people do good individually but good people don't run the world."

"So we are stuck," said Roger. "Is there no way out?"

"The desire to move forward must come eventually to take you out of the game."

"You've certainly changed," said Roger.

The titan shrugged. "Thanks to you."

"Why do you call Henry's alien machine a temporal resequencer? How can you change the past? It's already happened."

"*You* know better than that! You've moved through time. When you time travel backwards you reshape your present into a different story by revisiting events previously experienced. You cannot change 'past' events but you can soothe the pain in your soul by bringing light to bear on the shadows."

"So we never move out of the present," said Roger thoughtfully. "Didn't the Old One say that the present is also a memory? When does anything actually *happen*?"

"When you wake up! Humanity is asleep. You exist in a dream *remembering* the *present* because the drama has already worked out by the time it manifests in consciousness. The conclusion of all things is foregone. It draws you inexorably onwards as the game unfolds. *You* exist at your origin, your zero-point, stuck at the starting gate as events unravel around you. The story serves to keep you occupied while you incubate in your egg. Your personal little drama climaxed when you faced torture at the hands of men who knew no better. Your game player chose a well-tried method to fully awaken. Unfortunately, you accidentally fried their brains. It could happen to anybody."

Roger grunted. "Oh dear. I did, didn't I? More by luck than judgement."

"Nobody's perfect. You did your best and, fortunately, it worked because they brought it on themselves; just like those people out there preparing to open fire. We do nothing and they shoot themselves, instant karma, cut out the middleman. The time has come when you must all live selfless lives to evolve. But sometimes we have to be cruel in order to be kind. This is the lesson of the moral dilemma." His eyes flicked momentarily at Roger and then back to the self-appointed enemy. Roger missed the gesture. He was beginning to lower his guard.

They watched for a while longer and then the titan said, "I think they are about to open fire. Do you wish to deal with them or shall I?"

"You're the one with the experience," said Roger. "If it's all the same to you – go ahead."

"Very well, but you could do this yourself if you wished to."

The titan placed a large, translucent, shadowy sphere around them both. The first salvo of gunfire opened up. The sphere rippled with black rings as large and small rounds of ammunition impacted the outer surface and rebounded to their source. Such a fusillade was in progress that it was like a major battle. The attackers believed themselves to be under fire from the centre. To Roger, it exemplified the futility of war. If one country invades another, what do they gain? They enjoy a buzz in 'winning'. They grab, plunder, rape and kill the innocent. But in the end life goes on. Flowers appear on the bombsites. Materially, war achieves nothing but death for many and profit for a few. Spiritually, it seems that nature raises these currents of war in consciousness to push us towards mass awakenings. Suffering, heroism, victimisation, despair, struggle; all designed to force us into waking up and accepting responsibility for our actions. And why? Because we are too lost in materialism to know how wonderful life is; to herd us to oneness *en masse* whether we want it or not.

Roger shook his head sadly. The aliens had told Henry that if the human race goes on destroying the planet, it will be removed by natural disaster or external intervention and the world will go on. The earth was in pain. Its cry had been heard and the alien ships, some of them planet sized, were in the solar system, invisible, watching mankind's sleazy history unfold. The transition to the fifth dimension was underway. How long it would take, nobody knew, least of all the aliens in their front row seats. Roger knew that a new world was awaiting the many good people on the planet. The meek *will* inherit the new earth.

Roger wished he knew where Henry had gone.

"Supermassive black holes are so interesting. They help to shape galaxies when they form by herding material into mathematically generated patterns of stars and planets," the titan said, reverting to his favourite topic. "To use an analogy, if you put sand on a metal plate and apply different vibrational frequencies you get various geometric patterns."

"I've heard of that. It's called cymatics," said Roger. "So those vibrations occur somehow inside the black hole at the centre of a galaxy and distribute the stars throughout it."

"Yes. Have you heard of string theory?"

Roger nodded. "I've heard of it but I don't know what it is."

"Well, it says that particles of matter are generated by vibrating strings on a higher dimension. You can think of a massive black hole as a giant superstring influencing the evolution of galaxies by nudging gaseous matter into clumps. As beacons of pure consciousness, they help direct the story of the universe towards the ultimate oneness it desires."

"How does this energy cause bullets to go back along their original trajectory?"

The titan smiled. "It's a clever device of my own invention. You can't reverse the arrow of time but you can hitch a ride on the parallel light dimension where subjective time runs backwards. That's how consciousness draws the universal story towards predestined conclusions by manipulating the events surrounding beginnings. The child creates its parents in order to become what it already is. My consciousness has aligned with black holes for so long now that I can generate time barriers at will. I extended that ability to you."

"So when the Old One imprisoned you in a black hole, he unwittingly enabled you to fulfil *your* inevitable destiny," Roger observed.

The titan laughed. "A good point. As I said, *your* spirit emerged from the consciousness of blue light, mine came from black hole energy. We transformed each other. It's all to the good. Lucky you didn't turn out to be red light. You'd have been a footballer or a lumberjack – something like that."

The corporal who led the original attack on Roger had just returned to the scene of conflict. He wore jeans and a tee shirt requisitioned from a local store. In some agitation he ran through the lines of prone men firing at the mysterious rippling sphere. He sought the officer now in charge of the conflict. Vehicles carrying larger guns joined in with the rifle fire. Several were destroyed by the return of their own projectiles. The corporal spotted the captain sheltering in the entrance to a building and ran over to him, waving and shouting to be heard above the din.

The captain regarded the corporal in casual clothing and said, "What are you doing here? Where's your uniform? Why are you standing in the open? You'll get shot."

"No, I won't," the corporal responded. "You must

cease firing. You're just killing yourselves."

"What are you talking about?" said the captain irritably.

"Please, you've got to believe me. Whatever you direct at that thing comes straight back at you."

"Nothing's come at me," the captain pointed out.

"That's because *you're* not firing. It's everyone else who are killing themselves."

The captain, still doubtful, issued an order to his signals officer. "Radio a general ceasefire."

Meanwhile, the titan was saying to Roger, "Have you seen enough?"

"Yeah. Can you change the channel?" Roger said.

His giant friend replied, "Most certainly, if I take your meaning. Let us depart. Where would you like to go?"

"Shell Beach," said Roger, thinking of a movie called *Dark City* that he liked. "Sorry, I'm joking. I'll leave it to you to decide. You know more about the universe than I do." Roger surveyed the carnage around them sadly and said to himself, "I wonder who won?"

Before the titan could make any move to leave, the crescendo ceased. The dead and wounded lay all around and the few survivors were numb from shock and confusion.

"They've worked it out," Roger said. "They know about your rebound mode."

The titan closed down their protective shell. He and Roger stood together. Roger looked so small next to the giant.

The captain, accompanied by the corporal, moved tentatively towards them. The Psy Ops boffin arose from behind the remains of a military vehicle and approached warily.

As they drew near, Roger called out, "Are you surrendering?"

The captain pulled out his automatic pistol and glowered resentfully at the pair.

"I'll show you surrendering. You've lowered your shield."

"Are you thinking of using that?" the titan asked him pleasantly.

"I will if I have to."

"Perhaps this will dissuade you." The titan waved his hand and the firearm sagged in the officer's grip, becoming soft like treacle. It began to ooze down around his hand and droop soggily towards the floor where it collected in a sticky, grey pool.

The titan said aside to Roger, "It is very tempting to return to my old ways when people make stupid threats like this. Never mind, I gave my word to myself that I will reform."

"They don't know how lucky they are," said Roger. "I've seen what you can do." Something stirred in Roger's mind; a flash of insight. "There's a sniper on the roof of that building," he said, pointing. He expected the titan to do something about it but a jolt like a flash of lightning in his brain indicated that he had dealt with the problem himself. He didn't know how.

"What did you just do?" the titan asked him.

"I really don't know – but I did something."

"To the man or the weapon?"

"To the weapon, I think."

The captain spoke to the titan. "Who are you? What's your name?"

"My name does not lend itself to the English

language. Perhaps I can impress you with it telepathically."

"What the hell does...ah!" The soldier reeled backwards as a psychic explosion hit his mind, so powerful that it nearly knocked him unconscious.

"I guess you're not from around here," he said, recovering and getting back on his feet.

"Strangely enough I am, but not from your time. I was born when the gods still walked the earth."

The boffin said nothing. He was out of his depth with what was happening.

"Why are you here?" the captain asked. "We want Crandle."

"On no account would I disparage homicide under normal circumstances but this fellow has been of assistance to me. I would rather you left him alone."

"I can't do that," the captain said, stepping aside and raising his hand. There immediately followed a muffled thump on a nearby rooftop as a sniper rifle exploded.

"You are learning," the titan said to Roger.

"I didn't mean that to happen. I think he's dead."

"He killed himself. It could happen to anybody – anybody with a solid steel bar for a rifle barrel that is."

"You're getting me into bad habits," Roger said. "What did you say your name is?"

"I didn't."

"You did to that officer. He nearly keeled over."

"Oh, that was the telepathic version, the whole encapsulated concept. Our identity is our subjective essence. It influences DNA, among other things."

"You're starting to sound like Henry."

"Can you imagine a mighty being like myself being called Bill or Jim; or the Old One as Sid or Algy?

Perhaps some fantastic epithet like Kazoom would work. *The titan* has a ring about it. It inspires fear and awe. It used to in the good old bad days." He repeated his title with relish: "*The titan!*"

The titan returned his attention to the officer. "You were saying?"

"We're not going to win, are we?"

"No, you were never going to win," Roger declared with anger. "I don't just mean *you* here and now. It doesn't matter how much your covert organisations control people and spy on us, everything you do will come back on you. Karma is not some fairy story for the gullible. We live in a virtual reality game. It's a system with rules where every action invokes penalties for good or ill. *You* look for weaknesses in people in order to control them. But we're all human. We wouldn't be here otherwise. The baggage of humanity comes with the territory."

"So true," agreed the titan. "Believe me, *I know* – I've been there."

Roger surveyed the devastation, the ambulances and paramedics carrying away the dead and wounded. "Another victory for swamp gas," he said sadly recalling the Project Blue Book explanations of so-called unidentified flying objects. "Why do you want to kill me now? That's what I don't understand. You could have done it at any time."

The officer looked round at the scientist. He took the hint.

"We know your history. You went on an interstellar mission doing Psy Ops work. You created the android. You got involved in a conflict with one of the most powerful beings we've ever heard of and you won."

Roger peered up at the titan who winked at him.

"You could have got rid of me when I was living in London," Roger pointed out.

"Somebody was protecting you. I don't know who," said the scientist.

"Don't look at me," the titan said.

The boffin looked from one to the other and began to feel suspicious. "Do you mean to tell me, *you* were the big enemy and you're not dead?" He sounded outraged at the idea.

"Yes, I died but that's nothing new. I have always been able to slip in and out of physical form. It was in my genes on my father's side; a family trait you might say."

"So you decided to kill me because I *might* be a threat," Roger declared.

"That's about it and we wanted to isolate the android to stop it caring about people. With all that ability it should be a super-soldier. We've got a war on Mars and a few other planets that we'd like to take over," the scientist replied.

Roger felt sick at the idea of using Henry to commit genocide against alien races.

"I can't condemn others for doing the things I have been guilty of," the titan remarked. "You are judging them rather harshly."

Roger was puzzled. "Me?"

"Look at the story," said the titan. "There have always been people from other worlds and dimensions turning up on earth; some good, some evil."

"I don't know much about that," said Roger.

"You have to understand that life on this planet required a sentient species to maximise its potential. My ancestors oversaw the evolution of the humanoid races from a far more distant time than you can possibly believe. They saw the dinosaurs. Yours is just the latest in a long line of prototypes. There is evidence of ancient technology over a million years old. Whenever it surfaces, your archaeologists suppress anomalous facts from emerging."

"Why?" Roger asked.

"It's *the game.* You live in a universe of opposites, in a hell created by heaven to teach the meaning and value of love, the property of the number one. It's the basic idea behind all existence. Every positive concept has its 'not' idea that defines it. Cold is the absence of heat. Hatred is the absence of love. It does not exist in its own right. Not in the light. It's all mathematical," he said, sweeping his arm around him. "Love is not sentimental; far from it. Love puts us through shit and pain until we understand who we are; nothing pretending to exist."

"But everything has gone too far on this planet. Look at the lies, the deception and the control. These people are evil," Roger said with feeling.

"No. They are victims of history as much as you are," the titan said calmly. "Humanity does not understand consciousness. You confuse nature with random activity and species opportunism. You set up systems and let them run your lives."

"I know," said Roger. "It's the systems we create that are the real demons. They exist in universal consciousness and do their best to survive – no matter the cost to us."

The titan nodded. "Nobody is to blame but everybody is responsible. When you developed nuclear weapons you crossed a threshold of *irresponsibility* that threatened not just your planet but also the entire universe. When the first bomb exploded, extraterrestrials came and told your politicians and military what they needed to hear. It didn't take them years to find out. The shock waves in the universal generative matrix affected the whole system at its core. You might say there are bigger explosions in nature but nature knows what it's doing. You pesky mortals can't shake up *the one* and expect to get away with it. Everything exists in a fragile web of information and communication. The extraterrestrials were there soon after the first atomic test. If your governments had told you straight away in 1947, humanity would have coped somehow. Now…" he shrugged. "It's too late. Society hangs together by a thread of lies."

The officer and the Black Ops scientist seemed bemused by this speech. It meant nothing to them. They had their orders; orders they had failed to obey.

"That's all very well but we have no choice. We must do what we are told," the captain said.

The titan looked down at Roger. "Have you heard enough of this nonsense?"

Roger nodded. "Yes. I just wish there was a solution."

"That's not down to you. It is the responsibility of everybody on this planet to see the obvious and start to do the right thing by the world and each other." The titan was faithful to his new credo.

"Crandle, I need you to come with me," said the officer.

"You're kidding," said Roger. "Why would I want to do that?"

"Why? If you don't, we will hunt down your friends and family and kill them, every last one of them. The android can't save them all."

"Is this young man so integral to your plans that he

must die?" the titan asked.

The scientist stirred. "Yes. We've been to the future and seen what he is capable of. Out of them all, he is the one who could change the future. Without him, the android will lose heart and fail to make a difference."

Roger's face betrayed his surprise. "But why should *I* be so important?" he said in a pleading tone.

The titan shook his head. "*Nobody* is important. We are of one mind, one being and one spirit. However, some people are more *significant* in terms of the story of the universe. You must have been a naughty boy or girl in a past life to bear such responsibility, young Roger."

"Oh. I wonder what I did?"

The titan seemed to know the answer. "In a previous life you murdered somebody who was destined to do great good for others." He pointed at the officer. "This man was involved at the time. In that life he was a potentate, a ruthless giver of orders – like me. I think he's about to make the same mistake again."

"But surely Henry is more significant than I am."

"You do not understand. You *are* Henry. You gave him a fragment of your soul. Remember?"

Roger was disappointed to think he might be both of them. He admired Henry and enjoyed his friendship. "He is an independent being in his own right."

The titan nodded. "It is true. He is becoming his own being and personality but eventually you will merge back into oneness – we all will. All our incarnations and identities will return to the source that made us. The whole becomes greater than the sum of its parts as its parts evolve. But without your physical presence on this dimension, the android's independence will fail. He will diminish and cease to be effective. He is not ready to go it alone. Perhaps one day he will be, when you are long gone."

"We are just about holding the show together," said the scientist. "If the truth comes out too soon all will end in chaos. It will make the collapse of the Soviet Union seem like a holiday. It's a consequence of chaos theory. A rigid system of control must collapse eventually; it is nature. All empires fragment when they arise through force. Phased disclosure is the only way we can see ahead. We need to get rid of the power brokers that profit from the fossil fuel economy but they are too strong right now. We would like to introduce zero-point energy and other sources of power that won't harm the atmosphere. It must be done in a clandestine way. It can't happen overnight. Who would want to pay for electricity and transport if they knew there was a cheap alternative?"

"So there's nothing any of us can do," Roger said, more calmly than he felt. "Collapse is inevitable."

"I wouldn't say that," said the titan. He turned to Roger, grabbed him gently but firmly by the back of the neck and put an index finger against his forehead. In a sudden state of shock, Roger felt his mind ebb away leaving a limp and lifeless corpse. The last thing he heard was the giant in the tuxedo saying, "Bon voyage, my friend."

Then the titan dropped Roger's mortal remains to the ground.

"He's all yours," he said to the officer.

"With friends like you, who needs enemies?" said the captain.

"I owed him that," said the titan.

"Are you the one to worry about now?"

"Me! What could I possibly do to harm you? I was

the Illuminati before there was an Illuminati."

The scientist got up from examining the body.

"He's dead all right. What do you want to do?"

"We'd better dispose of the corpse," the officer replied.

The titan seemed to have an afterthought. "Would you permit me to remove it?"

"What do you want it for?"

"His relatives will want to give him a decent funeral."

"He is dead, isn't he? You haven't put him in a trance to be revived later?"

The titan shrugged. "You can make sure if you like."

"I will." The officer took out a pistol and put a bullet in the chest. "Okay, let's go."

The soldier and the scientist turned away and left with their beleaguered forces.

The titan looked down at the body of Roger Crandle.

"That will make a nice present for a friend of mine."

END OF TIME LOOP

Chapter Twenty

ORIGINAL TIMELINE RESUMES

Roger had other things on his mind than what was happening in the room with Jensine. "Oh well, I suppose I'd better be getting out there."

"Yes," said Henry absently. "I think I know the problem with Black Ops. It's you they want now. The only thing that will satisfy them is your dead body."

"So you're sending me out there to die."

"You won't die, Roger. I'm sure you can deal with them. Remember, you're a proven metaphysician. Trust your instincts."

"Let's hope you're right."

Still wearing metal foil, Roger left them to deal with the tragedy of Henry's friend. With his hand on the doorknob; he glanced back one last time. He had hardly got the door open when a large hand reached inside and whisked him swiftly away, closing the door behind him. Nobody in the room noticed anything. They were too preoccupied with the death of Jensine.

A few minutes later the door opened and Roger appeared in the room.

Deborah was just saying, "Shall I tell Roger we're leaving?"

Before the android could reply, Roger called out, "Henry!"

"I thought you were keeping off the Black Ops

military."

"I didn't get that far. Did you say that the only thing that would satisfy them is my dead body?"

"I did."

"Guess what I've found out here?"

"I haven't got time for this, Roger. Can Deborah help you?"

"Yes, please. I've got something to keep them happy but I can't do it myself it might spoil the effect."

"I'll take a look," said Deborah to Henry. "What on earth are you talking about, Roger?"

She followed Roger to the hallway and saw a dead body lying on the ground. She went over to look and her heart nearly stopped with the shock.

"It's you! You're dead," she gasped.

She looked at Roger, tears beginning to form. Roger stared back, wide-eyed and nodded.

"I'm dead all right. I've been shot in the chest by the look of it although it didn't bleed much."

"What happened?"

"I got the impression that somebody very tall grabbed me. The next minute I was unconscious. When I woke up, I was lying next to…to this."

"You'd better get going with the others," she said hustling him away and becoming business-like to hide her tears. "Tell Henry to leave the portal open for me."

They could hear noises outside as the Special Forces closed in.

"Shoo!" She pushed him through the door towards the wardrobe. "Get out of here quickly."

***

The squad wanted to avoid confronting the android.

Their target was his friend, Roger Crandle. They had two objectives: get rid of Crandle and demoralise the android. How to effect that elimination was immaterial; rendition, destruction, murder, it didn't matter. As far as they knew it was one friend down, one to go. They knew them to be in the apartment with Henry. They had seen the android arrive with Crandle and Farnham carrying a box. The squad had earlier transported Jensine Pettersson to the apartment in a mobile medical facility. Deborah Farnham's loyalties were a little obscure but she wasn't a target. The corporal had discretion in the matter.

"Time to flush the ground," the officer said to his second-in-command, prompting an encrypted signal from a SINCGARS mobile communications unit. Consequently, a technician in a remote base relocated a satellite in low orbit with hydrazine thrusters to be in line of sight with the apartment block. From there he activated a tight beam of electromagnetic radiation designed to induce mental breakdown and hallucinatory disorder. This action took no account of who else might be in line with the beam. It was not really their concern. After ten minutes they deactivated the satellite. The squad approached the front entrance of the building in the way they had been trained; advance, stop, cover and hold while the next solder in line advances. People coming in or out of the block saw what was happening and hurried away as quickly as possible.

The squad was about to storm the front entrance when the door opened and a woman in a regulation black suit came out holding up a gun in a non-threatening attitude, both arms above her head.

"Hold your fire!" the officer shouted. "It's

Farnham. She's one of ours but we're not sure where she stands in relation to the android and Crandle."

They kept their guns trained on Deborah as the officer approached cautiously.

"Put your gun down on the ground and step back."

She did as he said. "I've got something for you. Give me a moment to get it."

"Where's the android?"

Deborah ignored the question and returned seconds later dragging Roger's body out by its ankles. She wanted to keep them occupied as long as possible.

The officer in charge of the Black Ops Special Forces approached cautiously and looked at the cadaver.

"That's Crandle!" he exclaimed.

"Yep. That's him – or it was," said Deborah.

"He's been shot. We didn't hear anything. Who did that? You? We saw him go in."

Deborah shrugged. "I knew you wanted him dead," she said ambiguously. She omitted to mention that it was Roger who had found the body.

The officer was silent for a while, then asked, "Is Henry with you?"

"You know he is."

"Just testing," he said. "We're not sure where you stand these days."

"The android's not very happy. His friend just died." She said it in a matter-of-fact voice.

"Yeah, so we gather. Does he know that Crandle is dead too?"

"I haven't had the heart to tell him. He's still with Jensine. I've never seen him this upset before."

"He has to know. If we don't get his cooperation after this, we can write him off as a military resource."

Deborah controlled her desire to tell the officer what she thought of him.

"Is Spiker in there?"

"No. I don't know where he is."

"You have to break the news about Crandle. We don't want to go in there. He might blame us and seek revenge."

"You don't know him," Deborah said. "He wouldn't do that."

"What will he do?"

She shook her head sadly. "I really don't know."

At least that is true, she thought. *It won't be anything anybody has ever done before.*

"Okay. We'll withdraw and make a full report to Ops."

"What about the body?" she asked. "You can't just leave it here."

"Yeah? You could put it with the other one; Pettersson has got to be a goner now. On second thoughts, Psy Ops might want it for research. He's been doing some strange things. They say he became an orb and flew off somewhere."

"No kidding," she said, thinking *so did I – with Henry's help.*

It made her feel nauseous as they took the corpse away unceremoniously and without respect but she tried not to show it to the departing soldiers.

It occurred to her that like Schrödinger's cat, Roger was alive and dead at the same time. But this was not a quantum paradox; it was an everyday temporal anomaly; a product of two universes. That was Roger's opinion. She wondered how he knew.

A telepathic signal hit her with great force. It was from Roger.

The portal will close soon.

She turned back to the building to find her friends and wondered what could have happened to Roger to boost the power of his mind on the one hand and kill him on the other.

She smiled at the knowledge that Roger was alive.

At least we are together now.

Part 6
The New Earth

Chapter Twenty-one

Jensine Pettersson lay on a soft surface, drifting comfortably towards consciousness. She felt wonderful. She also felt different but that was not an issue as yet. *Wonderful* was barely adequate under the circumstances. She felt better than she could have believed possible. Her smile effused a quiet joy so profound it might be bottled for posterity.

"She's waking up," said a familiar voice.

"You could be right," said the same, equally familiar, voice.

Slowly Jensine opened her eyes. She found herself partially shaded by a translucent muslin canopy suspended on elaborately carved, oaken posts. Beyond, a strong, bright sun burned in a clear blue sky. Two shapes flickered in her unfocussed vision. Bringing them into clarity, she saw two Henrys. Her eyes moved around to find herself ensconced in a bower of colourful beauty in an exquisite fantasy garden.

She was on some kind of rustic bed surrounded by beautiful flowers, some growing in cascading vines interwoven with the structure, others placed in pots and woven baskets. Close by was a rushing, gurgling stream. It was a scene that the young Walt Disney and a thousand artists could hardly have imagined better. Looking around she could see fish in the water and butterflies alighting on flowers by the bank. Damselflies darted above the water. It was a glorious day and the air was sweet with the scents of summer. The sound of birdsong filled the air. Jensine lay back, wondering how such a thing as this could possibly be. Then insistent questions overcame the soporific splendour of the scene. She could lay there no longer.

The anticipated effort entailed in rising from her bed did not materialise. It was the first clue that something was different. Gravity offered no significant impediment to her movement. Furthermore, she arose with an ease and grace that she had never before known. Slowly, carefully she stood up.

"Why are there two of you?" she asked quietly. "Are you twins?" A memory of a poignant moment in another time recalled the truth. "Now I remember. This is Roger. Henry is your twin brother from South Dakota."

Roger was pleased that she could tell them apart without needing to ask. Henry was puzzled that she knew of his somewhat inept South Dakota ruse. He knew he had never told Jensine. What trick of consciousness was this?

"Roger is my friend and DNA donor. I made the hardware and he provided the software, you could say. He also gave me some of his soul."

Jensine laughed. "Do you mean he gave you his Motown CDs?"

"Not exactly," Henry said, feeling awkward and embarrassed though he didn't know why.

Roger chuckled at Henry's frowning face. "It was *exactly* that. All that stuff about sparks jumping. I gave him my Four Tops and Stevie Wonder CDs."

The android thought for a while, then smiled.

Jensine looked down at the long, silken robe she wore with nothing underneath and the matching sheets on the bed.

"Am I dead?" she asked. "Am I in heaven?"

"As good as – yes," said Roger. "But not the one you mean."

"It's the new earth," Henry explained. "This is the world that the meek have inherited. It's as good as paradise. This is planet earth in the future."

"What happened to the non-meek?" Jensine asked.

Henry said, "Migration from the old earth to the new depended on their spiritual quotient; the proportion of light to shadow in their souls. There's no external judgement. It's not about belief. Karma is *action*, nothing else. What you believe is immaterial; have you expressed love? *The game* has ended." He shrugged. "There's nothing here for the trolls and aggressors of the old world. They made their choice. They elected to find another world where they could continue in the same materialistic vein."

"He means the new hell," said Roger. "But it's not *just* about being meek. To misquote Mark Antony in *Julius Caesar*; the evil that men do lives after them in the unravelling of the game. The good that is oft interred with their bones does so much more; it embroiders the brocade of the soul and lights up the spirit."

Jensine smiled. "A poet! He didn't pass that on with his DNA," she said archly to the android.

"That should have been in the soul," said Roger. "I must have given him the wrong bit. Terribly sorry."

"Let's just enjoy the moment," said Henry flatly.

Jensine walked away from the bed to explore the brightly coloured garden. Roger leaned close to Henry and whispered, "I know you've been through an emotional trauma but don't you think you might be overdoing the happy ending thing?" He looked at Henry's expression and laughed. Slapping him on the arm, he said, "Go for it, mate. This is what we need; more happy endings."

"Deborah designed all this," Henry said, gesturing towards the bower. The android had a minimalist sense of taste and was out of his depth in Deborah's over-the-top garden.

"It's lovely, old chap. I was only joking. The whole thing with Jensine is wonderful. I think *she's* wonderful. She has a good heart. Be patient and see what happens."

Jensine could hear them whispering but she didn't care what it was about. She was taking in the stream, the flowers and the insects. Having just woken up in mysterious circumstances she would have liked to stretch with contentment but for some unaccountable reason she did not need to. She turned to the two of them and said, "Henry, if this was really *Sleeping Beauty* you would have woken me with a kiss."

"I didn't think you would want *that* with me being an android."

"I don't understand what's happened to me but I feel so marvellous, I don't care that you are an android. You have more heart than most men I've known."

"That's just as well," Roger said.

"Why's that?" she asked.

"Jensine, *you* are an android now."

It was a shock but as she didn't *feel* like a machine, she chose to defer judgement. *That's* what the spirit meant. *'You have a body ready and waiting. That is all settled.'* In an attempt to change the subject, Henry reached behind a bush and magically produced a cat.

"Hero!" said Jensine, delighted on seeing her pet.

"Why Hero?" Roger asked curiously.

"It's short for Herophilus," she replied. "He was a doctor from Ancient Greece who studied the pathology of nerves."

"Oh, of course. Why didn't I think of that?"

Henry passed her the cat. She reached out to take him in her arms but the cat reacted uncomfortably. He wriggled in the way he did with strangers.

"He doesn't know me. Is that because I'm no longer *me*?" she asked. "I *feel* like me. I have all the sensations of touch and feeling that I have always known."

Henry looked worried. "In essence, you are you. You are the same spirit. Your outer layer is flesh and blood and nerves. You have a more developed pleasure sense than I do. I improved on the cybernetic aspects of my own design when I made you. Outwardly, you are like any other human being. But you have a lightweight cellular titanium bone structural substrate with a combination of technological and biological components. You also have a series of transducers that activate when you are under threat to surround you with an impenetrable temporal-spatial skin."

"Under stress, Henry tends to revert to gobbledegook," Roger explained.

"Hardly," said Henry dryly. "You should look up the Vietnamese origin of that expression sometime."

"Will I need all that protection here?" Jensine enquired.

Henry shook his head. "I hope not. It's just a precaution. You might want to go back to your old home world occasionally. You have a Merkabah foundation, an orb, if you wish to travel in time and space. I can show you how to activate it."

"So if I met Dean again, he couldn't hurt me?"

"He would be extremely unwise to try – especially if you switch on a diversion to the void at your outer surface. One punch and he would never see his fist again. It would dissolve in a shower of sparks."

Jensine shuddered. "I won't look for him. How did you get to this wonderful place – wherever it is?"

"The alien that Roger refers to as *the wizard* is a higher dimensional technologist. He opened a portal to this world in earth's future. He helped us all escape. You had died clinically but the alien was able to extract active cells from your cerebral cortex and other parts of your brain, your pineal and pituitary glands, hypothalamus and others. He used these cells to seed your synthetic biological processes. They are merged with quark computer chips like my own. You'll be able to access six temporally partitioned minds when you are ready." Henry paused before continuing then said with suppressed emotion, "I couldn't have done it in the non-invasive way that he did. I prepared the ground, so to speak, and he planted the living material using his higher dimensional consciousness. Your DNA assures design integrity."

"When did you get hold of my DNA? It must have been before you did all this."

"Yes," Henry agreed. "I cloned your DNA in the restaurant. I touched a tear on your face when Dean upset you." He said hesitatingly, "I must have known something even then. At the time I just wanted to read an aspect of your soul. It's the soul that chooses your parents and creates the pattern you require for the incarnation. Everything I learned activated feelings I had never known before. I now know that I was falling in love. That is a peculiarly human variation of the properties of the number one. In fact it resonates strongly with the number two. Two is the only even prime number. All one to one relationships register on the entity of the number two just as all incidents of individuality express the one. It would be the same for a grouping of three to register on the number three; three siblings for example would express threeness. You and I have twoness. Isn't it wonderful?"

Jensine looked at him with compassion. "It is wonderful. But how did I come back to life in this body? Surely, there's more to being *me* than my memories. You say we all have souls?"

"True, memory is subjective. It belongs to the light, to infinite mind. You access it through a network of neurons in the heart. Here you experience brief but profound flashes of nostalgia. That's why some people who receive heart transplants occasionally experience memory flashes of the donor. The left hemisphere of the brain is just an input-output device linking your finite mind to the universal conceptual matrix. That's where thoughts exist independently of us. When we think we connect to them through lines of light in the matrix. As entities, we are merely thoughts in the universal mind. The right brain processes subjective meaning. Linking both hemispheres to the greater universe through the pineal gland will raise your consciousness and set you free."

"Okay, Henry. I'm getting the idea. How did you bring me back from the dead?"

"I didn't. Nobody can do that. We have free will here and now and we have it when we return to spirit. Death changes nothing; mind is mind. It overlays the brain; it is not of it. I asked the Old One to intercede on your behalf in the spirit world. He can travel there when he wishes by shifting his frequency. He found out that you had already agreed to do this before you were born. You didn't really want to leave spirit but the Old One persuaded you that it would be in your own interest. You have important things to do."

The beauty of the garden drew Jensine's attention back to their surroundings.

"This looks like earth but it isn't. It's different somehow. *I* feel different."

"It is the earth as it should have been without pollution and mankind's destructive practices. When you are on a planet, any planet, you become part of that world's consciousness. As people of the old earth damage the planet and its life, they destroy a part of themselves. The loss of a single species of plant or animal undermines the overall complexity of world consciousness. *The one* creates life in order to develop originality, variety and complexity in universal consciousness. Human beings were designed to be the stewards of the earth, not its destroyer. We all pay a price. It is, perhaps, fortunate that we do not know what that price is in the spiritual sense."

Hero started to purr. Some essence of the original Jensine that he could sense was seeping through. Hero yawned and stretched languidly in her arms. There was not a thing now to mar her joy, a new body, a new world and the same old cat.

What remained to be processed would have to take its turn and there was plenty of that.

Roger shuffled uncomfortably. "I'm starting to feel like a gooseberry. I think I'll leave you two alone."

"That's all right, Roger," said Henry cheerfully. "I think we've got some gooseberries over there in the third basket on the left."

Chapter Twenty-two

Roger and Deborah were standing side by side, a little way outside the village clearing, separated only by an awkward distance.

"Are you all right? Something seems to be bothering you," Roger said.

Deborah was silent for a while. Roger decided not to press her further. He could sense the tension between them and he wasn't used to it. He decided that his life had been easy up until that moment – apart from battling a titan on an alien world. This was new territory in every sense of the word.

"Of course something's wrong!" she said grabbing his arm and turning him round to face her. He could see anger and hurt.

"But–"

"You…you idiot! I feel bereaved! I had to drag your body out by the ankles and dump you for Special Forces to collect. Remember?"

Then she collapsed on his chest and cried. He put his arms around her.

"That couldn't have been me," he said lamely. "I'm still alive."

"It *was* you. Do you think I wouldn't know *you* alive or dead?"

"But how could it be me?"

"You said it yourself – you were a product of two universes. It's *got* to be a temporal anomaly.

Something bad happened and your consciousness travelled back to the moment before you went outside to face Black Ops."

"Oh." Roger recalled the experience he had with his brother-in-law Billy in the flying saucer. He went through a time loop to pacify his sister's anger with her husband. Something similar must have happened again. This time he died before coming back. Something, or somebody, brought the body back through time. He would discuss it with Henry when he got the chance.

Deborah's tears subsided and she pulled away from him, wiped her eyes and blew her nose.

"I suppose that must have been me from a different timeline," he mused thoughtfully. "I died."

"Yes. You died. You know as well as I do that you cannot change the future by going back into the past to alter events."

"No. The Old One taught us that much. When people time travel to the past and do something to change things, they simply start a new timeline. They might kill somebody significant to world history. They'd just set off a batch of new universes. Strictly speaking, they're not new universes. There is only one universe. In fact, they are new time-space fields; alternative aspects of some particular element of the universal story."

"Somewhere, you still die," said Deborah with feeling. "You are suffering in a parallel time. You wrote me an account of the mission to Annoon all those years ago. I've told you some of it. You said that all time is concurrent. Everything is happening in the one present moment, *'the now'*. That includes all events and all versions of events. What we call *time*, the unfolding of personal and universal stories, is a way of experiencing it all in manageable chunks. *The one*, the creator of consciousness, experiences everything in one hit. The Big Bang was not the start of time; it was really the whole of time full stop. *The one* conceived the master plan and the story for the universe in one moment and we spend our lives filling in the details. Somewhere it's already happened. We simply replay the cosmic memory by choosing our pathways across the infinite landscape. Is that it?"

Roger nodded. "That's right. And we weave our threads in the tapestry of life, our small parts in the big picture. Our incarnations are like ripples from raindrops falling on a pond, expanding, self-contained circles representing entire lives. Once a moment of time has happened it becomes enshrined in the infinite light of consciousness. It can never be undone or erased until an entirely new round of existence unfolds. Then it all gets wiped away and life begins anew."

"How did the Old One describe time to you?" she asked.

"He said the idea of the timeline is an illusion. It is like the tangent to a circle. It represents the story of the past in one direction and the ghost of a possible future in the other. As you move around the circle the past and future adjust accordingly to maintain the illusion of continuity. Your personal time is the whole expanding circle. Your higher consciousness, your game player, is at the centre of the circle, viewing it but not of it. Our incarnations are circles on an infinite sphere. Time comprises spheres of meaning intersected or touched by planes of consciousness. Spheres are units of meaning and influence. We talk about a sphere of activity. Planes of consciousness are levellers of meaning that slice through spheres to create the circles of time. The earth is a plane of consciousness as well as a place. Human beings are trapped in their belief in the past. Without it, the present makes no sense. 'Your ancestor killed mine so I must destroy you and your children.' Then you might be reborn in each other's families to work through it. Nobody really dies so it is all lies; a total fiction that will hold us slaves to karma forever if we cannot open our eyes to beauty and our hearts to love. Once you have seen it in higher consciousness as I have, it makes perfect sense. But if you try to translate it into words..." He shrugged.

"An infinite circle is a straight line anyway," said Deborah.

"Exactly," Roger agreed. "That is the paradox." Summoning his courage, Roger said, "Ah, yes. I was just thinking, you once told me that you are in a committed relationship. How's that going? I've never met your...the man in question. Is it somebody I know?"

Deborah smiled. "Yes – intimately I'd say – but maybe not as well as I do. It's *you*."

"Me," he repeated flatly. His tone told of the unnecessary doubt and uncertainty he had felt for so long. "That's all right then."

Deborah chuckled, aware of the unspoken longings of his heart and gentle nature. "I could see your suffering as your feelings for me returned. But I needed time to get to know you. You can't do that through telepathy. I knew the soul but I didn't know the man. You might have been a complete pill. Anybody can seem nice when they're fifty light-years away."

Roger laughed. "No, I suppose it's not the sort of

situation you find in the agony columns."

They looked at each other and she read the inner revolution in his eyes. "So as far as I am concerned, you are 'the one'. If that's okay with you," she added with restrained humour as the vision of his future rearranged itself into a pleasant state of certainty. By now she knew him too well to doubt his answer.

"All right with me! I should think it is," Roger said cheerfully. "I thought you'd never ask."

It was a strange, bittersweet relief finally to know where he stood with her. Their restraint dissolved into laughter as Deborah took hold of his arm tightly and they began to walk through the trees. They were both smiling.

Deborah said, "We spent three years separated by light-years of space, communicating by telepathy. Psy Ops wouldn't allow us to meet in order to maintain objectivity. I was in a relationship for the early part of that time. That all ended after they put me in suspended animation while you were in transit. My personal life became non-existent. My association with you was the only human contact I had after that – until the mission was over. Then I joined Black Ops Security policing temporal anomalies. That was going fine until Henry turned up and took me off to find you in London."

"You never *told* me any of this," he declared with a slight smile. "Sometimes I felt that you had known me during my missing time. Of course, I had no idea that had taken me back to the nineteen seventies."

"What was I supposed to say? I didn't *know* you! Not as a person – only as a disembodied mind. I know you fell in love with me during the stress of the mission but what did that mean? All we had done was exchange information by telepathy. Then it happened! I was on a beach on a summer's day. You were in the titan's prison on Annoon light-years away. Your spirit left your body. You came to me. I could see you as clear as daylight. We walked together. I could hardly believe it was really you – you left no footprints in the sand. But it *was* you – not just a remote mind. Something wonderful happened. Feelings began to stir in *my* heart." She paused, before adding quietly, "This time *I* was the one who fell in love. When we met in London you didn't remember any of that. You didn't even know me. It was not easy…meeting you."

"I had no idea," said Roger. "I *was* attracted to you but I thought you were way above me – especially when you said you were in a long-term relationship."

Deborah smiled then. "So you *do* feel something?" She was playing with him. Roger's eyes were far more expressive than his words.

"Very much so."

She felt rather than heard his emotion and nodded. "How can you say I'm above you?"

Roger gave a kind of gurgling grunt. "Look at my situation. I was on the dole, out of work, couldn't get a job, no car – nothing."

"You're amazing! But you suffer from chronic modesty. We'll have to work on that."

She put her arm through his. "Let's go for a walk."

"Oh, yes, great." Roger sighed. "It's a nice place for it." Then he changed the subject. "What about Henry and Jensine? Do you think they are compatible?"

Deborah shook her head. "Who can say but them? If they were one hundred per cent android I'd say no. But they've both got biological components and souls, apparently. Henry gave her a higher proportion of biology to technology than he did for himself. What do men need to reproduce anyway? Talk about minimalist architecture."

Roger looked puzzled. "You don't mean they've got reproductive organs in their human bits? They could have children?"

"Yes – with their own DNA in the mix."

"Their own? Henry took mine. That would be like artificial insemination."

"Yes, but the experiences he's had since he did that have adapted his sequence. He is evolving. He is no longer an exact clone of you. Truth be told, I think he has tweaked his own DNA on the sly. He probably thought he could improve on the original." She waited for the thought to register and laughed at his expression. "If he had children they would not be 'yours'. They would be entirely his own."

"That's good. That makes things easier for me. I don't mind being an uncle."

She whispered closer. "Don't you want to be a father as well?"

Roger tingled all over. "This is a good place to start a family. It's a perfect world – almost. There are no guns here for a start."

"Apart from the one *I* brought with me," she said. "I guess it's a habit I picked up in Black Ops."

He could have said something censorious but he kissed her instead.

"Not bad," she said after five minutes. "It will do to be getting on with. I think you need more practice." Then she kissed him again. It seemed to be the start of a satisfactory arrangement so they began to walk in the direction of the cottage where Henry was waiting for them.

"Hold on a minute," said Roger pausing. "If Henry and Jensine conceived a baby, it would have to be human. It couldn't be born with titanium bones and integrated circuits. It would be human!"

She steered him forward. "Shut up. You worry too much. Look – it's Spiker! No – over there. Who's he with?"

Roger turned in the direction she indicated. "Yes – and Barty and Cade. The gang's all here. They've just come out of the cottage with drinks. I wonder if I can get any tea?"

"I think Spiker milked a cow. He said it reminded him of Mrs Spiker. He is thinking of bringing her through from the past. I think he needs his shirts washed. He can't get on with a washing board and mangle. He says it reminds him of his mother."

In an idyllic village on a mystery planet, lush, verdant and unspoiled, the group gathered around a wooden table and greeted each other. Henry went into the cottage, to which the garden belonged, and emerged with trays of food.

Spiker procured a flagon of liquor akin to whisky. "What's this stuff?" he asked.

"I don't know," Henry admitted.

"Well, that's a first," said Spiker. "Henry doesn't know something."

"I wish that was true," said Henry ruefully. "There's a lot I don't know." He looked at Jensine as he said it.

Spiker saw the expression on his face and understood. Sometimes the all-powerful cyborg could be defeated by nothing more than the 'human thing'. Henry hadn't taken on Roger's DNA for nothing.

"You'll have to ask Jensine. She's a psychiatrist," said Roger lifting his mug of tea towards Jensine in salute.

She returned his smile shyly.

The androids joined the meal although they didn't need to eat. But a little food was helpful in maintaining their biological constituents. Henry could, in extremis, synthesise matter in spite of the law of conservation of energy. He said it was homeopathy in reverse. Every substance exudes a qualitative field of subjective meaning in *the light*. Henry found out from the aliens that a subjective essence could be transposed into material form. Unfortunately, during one experiment he accidentally synthesised a living cobra from a sample of potentised snake venom.

It was Cade who finally asked the question that was on all of their minds. "Where are we? I can see that this planet isn't the earth although it's similar. It kinda feels different, know what I mean? I can't explain how."

Henry looked at Roger. "Have you worked it out yet?"

Roger shook his head. "Beats me, mate."

"It's the new earth. We've moved forward in time. No – that's not quite true – we've moved *beyond* time. This version of the world extends into a higher dimension than the old earth."

Deborah sighed contentedly. "Game over."

"Exactly."

"It seems to be based on the same ecology. The plants and the animals I've seen so far are mostly familiar," Roger noted.

"Is this paradise?" Spiker asked.

"In a sense, yes, but nothing in finite form is perfect. There will always be problems. However, it is in keeping with the spirit of the concept," Henry agreed. "If I understand correctly, its population will comprise those people from earth who have lived ethical and benevolent lives or have suffered unfairly at the hands of others."

"It's not just for humans," said Jensine. "There will be representatives of other races and dimensions living here."

"How do your digital circuits work then?" Roger asked Henry. "They are designed to function in hard time."

"Fortunately, they employ enough alien technology to cope with an analogue situation. Alien chips don't use clock speed in the way that conventional circuits do so they are immune to a timeless environment. My computations are not binary; they are senary. That means they use numbers to the base six. I use the six properties of quarks to calculate. It's like I have six minds. This new earth has an abstract order of sequence based on *the idea* of frequency. That's different from the old earth's time that was more like a digital clock."

"He's talking Chinese again," said Spiker.

"I get the feeling that this is just one of many possible universes and many possible 'new earths'," Jensine said.

Henry agreed. "This is pretty close to being a 'paradise'. Nobody owns any of it. There are no nations or borders. Such organisation as there is, is organic rather than authoritarian. They decide policy on benefit to all. They do this without confrontation or dogma. That is true anarchy, enlightened, localised decision-making without chaos and disorder. Many people here are from the old indigenous populations that respected the earth. It's no more than they deserve after all those years of unfair oppression and genocide."

"If you look back at what created all the negative aspects of human culture," said Jensine, "it was owning land and lending money for interest."

"Why owning land?" asked Barty.

"Because entitlement to land resulted in the idea of titles – status – lords and kings," she replied. "This dichotomy leads to the few having excessive power over the many. Once established, that principle runs through society. It creates a false sense of superiority in some and inferiority in others. These feelings prevent the human race from evolving. They oppose the spirit of oneness. It's all just nonsense in the illusion of the game. It only works as long as everybody agrees to go along with it."

Roger said, "When a king or powerful ruler dies and goes to spirit they have to get used to having no importance. I've heard that some of them cause a great deal of nuisance before they accept the reality of their situation. They might be in a state of infinite love and light but they can't give orders and expect to be obeyed. Nobody wants to know them except for a patient few who try to help."

"Surely, all that power stuff is inevitable anyway," said Spiker. "There'll always be top dogs."

"Not in alien cultures," said Henry. "It runs counter to spiritual progress and the evolution of consciousness, which is the reason for taking physical form in the first place."

"What about the interest on money," asked Barty. "What's that do?"

"Money is a way of exchanging energy," said Jensine. "But once you bring interest into the picture, money becomes a commodity – something to accumulate for its own sake. Because the universe is based on yin-yang relationships, negatives and positives, you have to have poverty to give meaning to wealth. By its very existence, wealth becomes the yang, or positive, whereas poverty is 'not wealth', the yin aspect. Nature ensures automatically that the financial-political sector imposes policies to exacerbate poverty. Most human beings are so deeply asleep they have turned this collective dream into objective reality. As a result, they go along with this totally unnecessary purgatory of their own creation without question. Meanwhile, the rich benefit from the suffering of the many. That's what I've come to understand since I 'died' and returned. It doesn't need to be like that at all."

Roger said, "Once you invent something, the universe will always create its opposite. That's how it learns. The trick is to find a balance."

Henry nodded. "That's what the extraterrestrials are waiting for us to do. They can't make us do it. Humanity must grow up eventually and take responsibility for its own actions."

"The night sky is extremely bright," said Barty, bored with the subject. "I've never seen so many stars!"

"It's a different version of the Milky Way in another universe," said Henry. "We are closer to the core of this galaxy than we were on the old earth."

"Try to be poetic, Henry," said Jensine. "The night is made for love, not astrophysics."

"That's not what my grandfather told me," Roger remarked. "He said when you get to his age the night is made for sleeping and soaking your dentures."

Deborah slapped him playfully and said, "Look at this." She directed her mind to a bowl of fruit on the table. It rose into the air and moved towards her. She took an apple. "See what you can do here?"

Spiker managed to move the bowl towards him and grinned. "So, did the little wizard bring us here to spend the rest of our days?" he asked.

Roger looked at Deborah, at his friends, the sunshine, the trees, the birds and a couple of deer walking by the stream. "I hope so," he said. "Why would we want to go back to that hell on earth?"

"I can't think of any reason," said Deborah.

"You know what?" he said. "Neither can I." Roger surveyed the beauty around him and breathed in the pure air. He took a swig of tea, before declaring, "This place is timeless and I, for one, am not missing time."

Part 7
The Mandroid

The Story of Roger's Missing Time

The Mandroid

What happened during Roger's missing time? I hope to complete an up-to-date version of *The Mandroid* in the future. In the meantime, here is a rough sketch of the story told in song lyrics for a musical version written in 1977 but never published or performed. I would love to see the musical staged.

Introduction to the Musical Version of *The Mandroid*

Music by Magnús Þór Sigmundsson
Lyrics by Terry Edwards

I saw spirits when I was a child. They kept me company when I was alone. They were very kind and loving. Sometimes they warned me of things that were about to happen. My parents took it in their stride. My mother's family were fourth generation psychics. It stopped when I saw television stories that portrayed the phenomenon as frightening. I became afraid of the dark for a while. These early experiences convinced me of the illusion of death. I could never see the point of grieving. When my relatives died they always kept in touch. Death holds no terrors but I'm not so keen about dying. Our mortal bodies fear pain even if our immortal souls do not. It is all part of the virtual reality game. Belief is optional. It is the uncertainty in life that keeps us trying.

When I was around ten years old, I began to take an interest in science. Even at that age, I desired to bring science and spirituality together. I was an avid reader of my dad's Billy Bunter collection. Later, I asked if I could read his science fiction books. He didn't mind. He'd stopped reading them anyway. I read authors like Zelazny, Asimov, Heinlein and Clarke. My favourite conventional authors were PG Wodehouse and Sir Arthur Conan Doyle.

Like many solitary children I dreamed up stories about an imaginary friend. It was a way of escaping school and problems in the home. I never believed he was real. From my sci-fi influences I made this friend an android. He was there to solve problems and take over mundane tasks like cooking and gardening. I had a good reason for making him a gardener. I used to cut the lawn with a pair of shears while my dad supervised and reminisced about mediums and spiritual knowledge. When I became ill he bought a push-along lawn mower. The fantasy friend was Jeeves and Sherlock Holmes rolled into one. He could sort out bullies and right wrongs. Thus the idea of Henry was born.

Marjorie Livingstone's *The Future of Mr. Purdew* enthralled me because it portrayed the experience of the afterlife in spirit. Conan Doyles' novel *The Land of Mist* was an example of what can be achieved through fiction. From these early influences I began to imagine a story about Henry's creation called *The Mandroid*. I commenced writing around 1968. It took me four years to complete in two major bursts before and after full-time college. I wrote to three or four publishers but got nothing but rejections. They said, 'we do not publish unsolicited work.' So I gave up. How do you get commissioned to write a book? Now we have self-publishing I can do it myself.

In December 1976 I met John Richardson, drummer with the Rubettes, a pop group who were very successful in France and had hit records in the UK and other European countries. I became close friends with John and his family and the band's lead guitarist, Tony Thorpe. John read the novel and decided it would make a good subject for a rock opera. He and Alan Williams teamed me up with Magnús Þór Sigmundsson of Iceland, living at the time in Dagenham. He was known here as 'Magnús Thor'. Magnús became, and still remains, one of my best friends. I have a great respect for Icelandic culture, which is, in my experience, spiritually mature in comparison with England.

I will always be grateful to John and Alan for their interest in my work and their initial support of the project. We met Tony Stratton-Smith at Charisma Records. He seemed very enthusiastic. Things then went wrong. Magnús moved back to Iceland. The music scene changed. Punk and disco took over the world. *The Mandroid* became history without being heard.

I made several attempts to revise the original story. None of them got off the ground. Then in 2008 I began to write the latest version that was to become *Missing Time*. It has taken over ten years to get this book together. I still have not finished *The Mandroid* after fifty years of trying. I hope the song lyrics will satisfy your curiosity until I can complete the job properly.

Song List

Opening (Instrumental)
The Escape
The Bridge of Time
The Awakening
Emergence
Mandroid Man
The Eye
Where the Light Still Shines
The Encounter
The Old One
The Rod of Power – Belief
The Lord on the Hill
The Coming
The Rescue (Part I)
The Knight of the Rusty Armour
Mort Mandroid
Footprints in the Sand (Deborah)
The Land Where the Light Still Shines
Henry's Theme
The Song of the Villagers
The Rescue (Part II)
The War (Instrumental)
The Confrontation
The Capture
Aftermath

The Opening (Instrumental)

The Escape

It comes easy to a titan
The power to curse and hate
Power is good, power is evil
Power becomes what I dictate.

I am watching, I am waiting
Trapped out of time within my mind
Reaching out, the forces tighten
Will he weaken? Will he bend?

Born of an age, old and weary
When wrong was right and love was light
He knows I might try to get away
Back to a world where mischief may
Be needed to enliven the boredom
Of civilisation.

Prison can be freedom
From life and worry
Helps to take away the pain
The grief and the hurry
Captured – confined – imprisoned – maligned.

The force that binds me, keeps me
Reminds me of battles lost
Nations found with life the cost
Now at last he starts to weaken
And I begin to see
A way to flee this prison
To set my spirit free.

See the Old One fall and crumble
Less than the dust to me
I know that I will soon have him beaten
Beware my worlds 'cause now I'm free.

The Bridge of Time

Ages – changes – light-years going
Flying far away.
Ages – changes – space is flowing
Flying far away.

The captain watches alone
On the bridge
A robot crew his command
Memories stray to a summer's day
As the earth is fading away
If I ever get home and I know I might
My daughter will be older than I
As the ship draws near the speed of light
We pass through relative time.

The bridge of time
Time goes by and by
The bridge of time
Time goes by and by
The bridge of time.

Across the lonely void
To where new worlds await
A new life
Years of sleep, light-years away
Flies on the power that lights the day
On an ocean that's empty.

Ages – changes – light-years going
Flying far away.
Ages – changes – space is flowing
Flying far away.

Our imagination fails to capture
All the images that float around us
In the darkness, filling the emptiness
With visions of ethereal oceans
All at peace
The ship seems still with nothing around
To show that we are moving out of reach.

The Old One waits beyond the blue
Guiding his human brother
Roger is a man, one of the crew
Unfrozen before the others.

The ship comes alive
As the robots revive
The crew from suspended animation
There's work to do for a telepathic mind
That crosses the bridge of time.

And we fly to another world
Seeking the ship that went on before
And we try to get in touch
With the crew that never came back to earth
The bridge of time
Time goes by and by
The bridge of time
Time goes by and by
The bridge of time.

Ages – changes – light-years going
Flying far away.
Ages – changes – space is flowing
Flying far away.
Ages – changes, life is created
Touches, touches, touches…
His hands give life to a lifeless…
Robot's brain in the making
Hands give life
(Awaken – creation – emanation).

The Awakening

Here I am a mind that is new
You look at me, I look too
I am a child, that I can see
One of a kind in the universe.

You gave me name; I'm Henry
What can I do with a name?
There's much I must learn to be like you
I hope you'll be glad I came.

When I mature I know I will be
Clever like you, wait and see
Now I must go and look at the stars
Why are they moving so slowly?

Here I am a mind that is new
You look at me, I look too
I am a child, that I can see
One of a kind in the universe.

A robot I am, you tell me

Something is wrong with my brain
The thoughts I now have should never be
You find it so hard to explain
There's much I must learn to be like you
I hope you'll be glad I came.

I see them clearly, a force within
I think it's beauty, the stars around me
Life within me, floating around me
Deep in the pattern of my mind
Things you say in words to me
Make images and thoughts I see
Destiny created me from an autobiped
I can set my body free
No computer link is holding me
The force I feel, infinity
Is welling up in me.

I see them clearly, a force within
I think it's beauty, the stars around me
Life within me, floating around me
Deep in the pattern of my mind.
Things you say in words to me
Make images and thoughts I see
Destiny created me from an autobiped
I can set my body free
No computer link is holding me
The force I feel, infinity
Is welling up in me.

I see them clearly, a force within
I think it's beauty, the stars around me
Awaken.

Emergence

I'm out – I'm free – I'm alive
I think – I feel – I'm aware
This is what it's like to be alive
No matter what's gonna happen
I'll survive
'Cause I'm free as a bird
Yes, I'm free as a bird.

I'm out – I'm free – I'm alive
I think – I feel – I'm aware
Of what makes me a personality
Let the life within shine throughout
Life will find a way
I said life will find a way.

Deep down inside I know that I'll never have cause
To regret my creation
You gave me a reason for living
I'll show you what living can mean.

I know I'm never gonna let you down
I'll stay with you until the end
I'll never let you down
I'll never let you down
I'm out – I'm free – I'm alive
I think – I feel – I'm aware
Gonna go wherever trouble can be found
Gonna show everybody the way to go
And I won't keep it to myself
I won't keep it to myself – what I know.

I'm out – I'm free – I'm alive

I think – I feel – I'm aware
Of what makes me a personality
Let the life within shine throughout
Life will find a way
I said life will find a way
I'm out – I'm free – I'm alive
I think – I feel – I'm aware
Gonna go wherever trouble can be found
Gonna show everybody the way to go
And I won't keep it to myself
I won't keep it to myself – what I know

Mandroid Man

Magic android android Mandroid man
Magic android android Mandroid man
I'm overdue a body that's new
A being I'll be that's like an image of you
I'll be like you now.

Mandroid man from and alien land
Won't you help me – please help
Fate will show where you have to go
Won't you help me – please help
Mystic voices call, pleading for me to go
Oh how they pray
What evil forces make them feel so sad?
I hope that with my help
Freedom will be theirs.

Magic android android Mandroid man
Magic android android Mandroid man

I'm overdue a body that's new

A being I'll be that's like an image of you
I'll be like you now, I'll be like you now
An image I'll be reflecting human view
In my own way I think that I could be most anything
For now I feel the power
I must surely bring.

Magic android android Mandroid man
Magic android android Mandroid man
The rest of this flight
I'll make my new form right
I'll break away
Magic android android Mandroid man
Magic android android Mandroid man
Magic android android Mandroid man
Fate will show where you have to go.

Magic android android Mandroid man
Magic android android Mandroid man
Mandroid man, won't you help me, please help
Magic android android Mandroid man
Magic android android Mandroid man
Fate will show where you have to go.

The Eye

Spirit I, floating by
Spirit eye, floating by
Moving by the force of will
My body is lying still
Far away inside my spaceship
Spirit I, floating by.

From the wreck of an earlier flight

In the distance a glinting light
And I must try to fly there inside
Spirit eye.

Pilot of a dead ship
The bones of a spaceman
Are dry and cracked with age
War in space to add to all their fears.

Spirit eye, floating by
Spirit I, floating by.

Moving by the force of will
My body is lying still
Far away inside my spaceship
Spirit eye, floating by.

I remember when I was a young boy
Never knew it could be like this
That I could fly beyond my confines
Spirit I.

Victim of a space gun
Tried to break from orbit
Out beyond all shelter
No place left to hide
In death he knows the secret
Of their foes.

Bones of a solitary spaceman
Dry sticks cracking in the heat of a star
Astro-navigator
In 3D he really knew his way around
He was a pioneer

He steered a spaceship here
Oh yes, he did
That Fred was dead it could be said
He was a pioneer
Until the ship appeared – out of the blue
That put a moratorium on
The rest of his life.

The motor still would function
But there wasn't any fuel left
Stagnant air was laden with dust
Of many years gone by.

Bones of a solitary spaceman
Dry sticks cracking in the heat of a star
Skin like petrifying canvas
Came here to die
From a world light-years afar.

He was a pioneer
He steered a spaceship here
That Fred was dead it could be said
He was a pioneer
Until the ship appeared
That put a moratorium on
The rest of his life.

Long and lonely way to come
To be alone
A billion miles away from the girl I love
Even now I feel your mind – Deborah
As it reaches out
Memory of your voice
The way of your smile

Makes me think of you
Every once in a while.

Where the Light Still Shines

Gentle shades of sapphire blue
Mingle with the scent of you
A mood, a thought, a touch or a whim
Bring a taste of colour in
This dreamy world beyond the veil.

The mind can see, the spirit feel
To conjure shapes and make them real
The peace, the warmth and
The light aglow
All serve to let the spirit know
That truth is you and you alone.

To a world where the light
Must always shine
Our bodies fuse in to one mind
The circle joins what life divides
And the force that drives us;
three, four, five.
The angle that is always right
And the source of power, inner light.

A sojourn in a tranquil land
Can soothe the wounds
From tyrant's hand
We drink the wine of comfort's spring
That shared endeavours always bring
The light that blends your face with mine.

To a world where the light
Must always shine
Our bodies fuse in to one mind
The circle joins what life divides
And the force that drives us;
three, four, five
The angle that is always right
And the source of power, inner light.

The Encounter

Within the space of a new star
Planets are waiting to be explored
By the earthman
A spaceship appears on the screen
Out of nowhere
Is it friendly or hostile?
Remains to be seen
Voice in his mind calls to Roger
Loud and clear
You will come to my spacecraft
I am the Old One.

The powers you now display
Are long dead in your own race
The thoughts that you hear in your mind
Originate from me
The voice in his mind gathers pace
Old One I hear you
The world of his dream is a place
Old One I'm with you.

Tell your captain that I
Summoned you here

And you need not be afraid
Now that contact has been made
You've come of age
A boarding party is invited across
Where the silver disc awaits
For a meeting to placate
The unknown fate.

Inner world aliens greet them
With a warning
Landfall is forbidden
You must heed us
Within the space of a new star
Planets are waiting to be explored
By the earthman.

The powers you now display
Are long dead in your own race
The thoughts that you hear in your mind
Originate from me
To the outer world you must go
To where destiny leads you
A weapon of power I'll give to fight evil that waits you.

Voice in his mind has a face
Old One I see you
The world of his dreams is a place
Stillness of the blue
Voice in his mind has a face
Old One I see you
The world of his dreams is a place
Stillness of the blue
Voice in his mind has a face

Old One I see you
The world of his dreams is a place
Stillness of the blue.

The Old One

In the beginning
He came down to earth
Here at the ending
Of an age that gave birth
To understanding
He taught man to love and to heal
To think and to feel, he showed him how
Man was not ready to wear
The mantle of God – he was not
The mantle of God.

At the upheaval
Titans first emerged
Sons of the aliens
Born of the daughters of earth
They led the fighting
They made man turn away from the sun
Darkness had come to a changing world
The Old One was faced with a war
Against his own kind – like it or not
Against his own kind.

He then resorted to wielding
The rod as a sword
Alien leader
His spaceships rained fire on the horde
He was exalted
As Osiris and Thor and many more

Came here in love
But he left us in shame
Man was not ready to wear
The mantle of God – he was not
The mantle of God.

Man was not ready to wear
The mantle of God
Man was not ready to wear
The mantle of God
He taught man how to love and to heal.

Rod of Power – Belief

Believe (never feel you're alone)
Force within your own mind
Believe (you'll never be alone)
Whatever you want to do
You can achieve
(No matter what you have to face)
Believe, believe, believe
Believe in the source of life
(Never feel you're alone).

Believe in the staff of life
Valued friend in time of strife
Power of kings in ages past
Now the sage of a new alliance
See how it undulates
Serpent-like, it stimulates
The magic in the bearer's hand
What it gives is real if you only believe.

You must guard it well

The Rod of Power
Until you really know
It will save the hour.

Believe (never feel you're alone)
Force within your own mind
Believe (you'll never be alone)
Whatever you want to do
You can achieve
(No matter what you have to face)
Believe, believe, believe
Believe in the source of life
(Never feel you're alone).

As gathering darkness grows
All around the darkness bites
Beset by ever stronger foes
You know there's hope
In the shaft of light
Believe in the staff of life
Valued friend in time of strife
Power of kings in ages past
Now the sage of a new alliance
In belief.

You must guard it well
The Rod of Power
Until you really know
It will save the hour.

Oh believe (never feel you're alone)
Force within your own mind
Believe (you'll never be alone)
Whatever you want to do

You can achieve
(No matter what you have to face)
Believe, believe, believe
Believe in the source of life
(Never feel you're alone).

Oh believe (never feel you're alone)
Force within your own mind
Believe (you'll never be alone)
Whatever you want to do
You can achieve
(No matter what you have to face)
Believe, believe, believe
Believe in the source of life
(Never feel you're alone).

The Lord on the Hill

Gather round the candle's feeble light
I'll tell you all about the new Lord's might
On the night he came there were
Omens in the sky
Lord on the Hill
Hates to love, loves to kill.

When the civil war was at its height
The titan came to end the fight
Though earthmen helped
They could not
Sway the war our way
Lord on the Hill
Hates to love, loves to kill.

Save us from the evil one

A hero knight will come
He will come, a mighty son
A legend from the stars
He will have the strength of ten
This saviour of the realm
He'll be a soldier no army of men
Could ever overwhelm.

Lord on the Hill
He is a force, be it ill
(Save us, help us, free us, help)
Lord on the Hill
He is a force, be it ill
(Save us, help us, free us, help)
Lord on the Hill
He is a force, be it ill.

He is tall, he is strong
Seldom laughs, seldom wrong
Razor mind, needle sharp
Magic powers of alien science
His castle stands, grim and forbidding
His servants rush to do his bidding
Darkness lingers all around
The wetness clings on sodden ground.

(Save us, help us, free us, help)
Lord on the Hill
He is a force, be it ill.

In the darkness torches flicker low
The guards patrol in the misty glow
While in their homes the people shiver
At the name of the new law giver

Lord on the Hill
Hates to love
He loves to kill.

Save us, Lord on the Hill
Save us, Lord on the Hill
Ah, he's tall, he's strong
Seldom laughs, seldom wrong
Razor mind, needle sharp
Magic powers of alien science
His castle stands, grim and forbidding
His servants rush to do his bidding
Darkness lingers all around
Wetness clings on sodden ground.

(Save us, Lord on the Hill)
You know, he's tall, he's strong.
(Save us, Lord on the Hill)
Seldom laughs, seldom wrong
(Save us).
Razor mind, needle sharp
(Lord on the Hill)
Magic powers of alien science
(Save us).
His castle stands grim and forbidding
(Lord on the Hill).
His servants rush to do his bidding
(Save us, Lord on the Hill
He is a force be it ill).

The Coming

Stepped on the plateau
Coming out of a fiery cloud

Came like a hero from long ago
With a friend that he values most
In the eyes of the people
Born of an ancient host
To lead them from ruin
And avenge the old king's ghost.

See the Lord, see the man
Hear the word, hear the call
See the Lord, see the man
Hear the word, hear the call.

Never was a man
That could match him in martial arts
Still he's disarming in another way
Using words that could overthrow.
That his bones were of metal
No one would ever know
He was the Mandroid, not human
Would never show.

See the Lord, see the man
Hear the word, hear the call
See the Lord, see the man
Hear the word, hear the call.

There never was an age
That needed a hero more
And in every war there's a yearning
For a leader and a sage.

See the Lord; see the man
Hear the word
No more running away from war

See the Lord, see the man
We will follow you
(Hear the call) evermore
See the Lord, see the man
Hear the word, hear the call
See the Lord, see the man
Hear the word, hear the call
See the Lord, see the man
Hear the word
See the Lord, see the man
We will follow you
(Hear the call) evermore.

The Rescue (Part I)

Alone in the woods he takes his ease
The sound of the wind stirring the trees
His vision blurred from a soldier's gun
The price he paid for provisions won.

Friends he'd left not a mile away
Must have been taken or slain that day
Part of his mind breaks out of control
He runs as if blind into a new patrol.

I'm gonna rescue you, my friend
Whatever it takes, however it ends
I will rescue you whatever it takes
Find you wherever you are.

Soldiers try to bring him down
He has no time to play the clown
A legend is born as he strikes them all
Faces guns but remains so cool.

I'm gonna rescue you, my friend
Whatever it takes, however it ends
I will rescue you whatever it takes
Find you wherever you are.

Tracks his friends
Through the evening chill
On the road that leads him
To the Lord on the Hill
Magic powers, alien science
The Lord on the Hill
Hates to love, loves to kill.

Part of his mind breaks out of control
He runs as if blind into a new patrol
A legend is born as he strikes them all
Faces guns but remains so cool.

I'm gonna rescue you, my friend
Whatever it takes, however it ends
I will rescue you whatever it takes
Find you wherever you are.

Tracks his friends
Through the evening chill
On the road that leads him
To the Lord on the Hill
Magic powers, alien science
The Lord on the Hill
Hates to love, loves to kill
I will rescue you my friend
I'm gonna rescue you my friends.

The Knight of the Rusty Armour

The tournament was in full swing
The crowds did not enjoy
The jousts between
The knights of the king
Were thugs in his employ.

They would have stayed away that day
If the king had not said, "No!
You must not hide in your homes today
I'll shoot the one first to go."

There was a sudden clamour
A stranger appeared on the field
It was the knight in rusty armour
Borrowed weapons he did wield
He was the knight of the rusty armour
He was the knight of the rusty armour.

His steed was big and hairy
Fit for a Mandroid knight
It was a lie that he could die fairly
Hydraulics gave him his might
One by one they fell to the ground
The crowd began to cheer
The knight of the rusty armour
The hero of the year.

Henry clashed his lance on shield
And beat each hopeful foe
He fought with a power
That would not yield

How could they have known
He was the knight of the rusty armour
He was the knight of the rusty armour.

There was a sudden clamour
A stranger appeared on the field
It was the knight in rusty armour
Borrowed weapons he did wield
He was the knight of the rusty armour
He was the knight of the rusty armour
He was the knight of the rusty armour
He was the knight of the rusty armour
He was the knight of the rusty armour
He was the knight of the rusty armour
He was a knight, ooh he was a knight
Ooh he was a knight.

Mort Mandroid

The victor claimed his own reward
He chose to serve the Lord on the Hill.
They let him guard the castle cell
Wherein his friends shared a living hell.

He was despised
By the rest of the guards
'Cause he acted dumb
Was all that could be done
They tormented him
His revenge could wait
Needed more time to plan the escape.

His cover was blown
And they tortured him

Even on the rack he would never give in
They took him out to the castle yard
Brought all his friends
To watch as he 'died'.
They took him out to the castle yard
Brought all his friends
To watch as he 'died'.
Brought all his friends
To watch as he 'died'.

Footprints in the Sand (Deborah)

Appearing in the night
Spirit flies towards me
Take away the pain
I only want to go away
Spend a little time with you
I only want to see you by my side
In this dark and lonely prison cell.

Let me be a part of you
Oh, I can feel you coming through
Deborah, can you hear me calling you
Oh, Deborah, can you understand
I'm trying to get in touch with you
Oh, I need you by my side
Oh, Deborah, can you hear me
Calling you
Deborah, can you understand.

Seeing you walk by
Like a vision of my love
Footprints in the sand
Knowing you're there is all I care

Keep my dreams alive
Assuring me that I'll survive the night
In this dark and lonely prison cell.

Let me be a part of you
Oh, I can feel you coming through
Deborah, can you hear me calling you
Oh, Deborah, can you understand
I'm trying to get in touch with you
Oh, I need you by my side
Oh, Deborah, can you hear me
Calling you
Deborah, can you understand.

The Land Where the Light Still Shines

From the land beyond the stars
He came to help, he brought to us
Strength he lent to us.
From the land beyond the stars
He came to help, he brought to us
Strength he lent to us.
From the land beyond the stars
From the land where the light still shines
From the land beyond the stars
He came to help, he brought to us
Strength he lent to us.
From the land beyond the stars
He came to help, he brought to us
Strength he lent to us.
From the land beyond the stars
From the land where the light still shines.

Henry's Theme (Instrumental)

Our friend is dead the soldiers say
Who now will show us the way?
Our thoughts are all that we have today
Our leaders are dead or locked away
He's gone away
We've been betrayed.

The Song of the Villagers

No one to guide us
We have lost our leader
And our cause is now lost
The pain and the grief
It's so hard to bear with no one to care our leader is gone.

He promised us nothing
But the way he came
Made us think he would save us
And free us from slavery and pain.
We were lost in the dark
We were blind and afraid
In the hands of a fate so unkind
He gave us the hope
And the reason to cope.
With a war that we needed to win
No one to guide us
We have lost our leader
And our cause is now lost.
The pain and the grief
It's so hard to bear with no one to care our leader is gone.

The Rescue (Part II)

I will rescue you my friend
I will find you, I will save you
I will rescue you my friend
Gonna find you, gonna save you
I will rescue you my friend.
I will rescue you my friend
I'm gonna find you, I'm gonna save you
Whatever it takes
Gonna find you, I'm gonna save you
I will rescue you my friend
Save you – I will rescue you my friend
I'm gonna find you, I'm gonna save you
Whatever it takes
I'm gonna find you, I'm gonna save you.

The War (Instrumental)

The Confrontation

In a lonely place
The sun was beating down
Burning all that lay there
On a barren mountain – two contenders
Standing face to face.

Against the powers
Of the Lord on the Hill
Was a man that seemed so small
You'd think that he would fall.

Feel the weight overhead

Crushes his mind
And steals his breath away
He can feel the darkness come
To such evil he's an easy prey.

Far away the war was waging
On the ground
All was desolation
Meanwhile the outcome
Depended on this confrontation.
Wake up, wake up, wake up
Wake up, wake up, wake up man
Wake up, wake up, wake up
Wake up, wake up, wake up man
Confronted with powers so advanced
He was frightened
(Wake up, wake up, wake up
Wake up, wake up, wake up man)
How could Roger hope to stand
(Believe – believe – believe)
Alone against his might.

Feel the weight overhead
Crushes his mind
And steals his breath away
He can feel the darkness come
To such evil he's an easy prey.

Wake up, wake up, wake up
Wake up, wake up, wake up man
Wake up, wake up, wake up
Wake up, wake up, wake up man
Confronted with powers so advanced
He was frightened

(Wake up, wake up, wake up
Wake up, wake up, wake up man)
How could Roger hope to stand
(Believe – believe – believe)
Alone against his might.

Wake up, wake up, wake up
Wake up, wake up, wake up man
Believe – belief will see you through.

The Capture

Now as Roger starts to weaken
The Old One takes his body
And steals his mind away
And sets his spirit free.

See the Old One, tall and humble
All powerful in victory
The titan is beaten by his father
Take care my worlds 'cause now you're free.

Aftermath
(The Old One's message)

A yearning for a need in man
To compensate
Gods were made to ward off tragedy
There's no need to be frightened
By the higher plan
Of which we are the reason why we are.

From mighty oceans comes a tear
That trickles from the eye

Of children's fear
Within the tear a galaxy
Of worlds inside their own infinity.

Spirit is the force that makes it so
What we are – where we go
Spirit is the force in all there is
From the seed to the blue giant star.

Creation – a force within, without
Learning about itself
Through my own eyes.

Spirit is the force that makes it so
What we are – where we go
Spirit is the force in all there is
From the seed to the blue giant star.

Prehistoric mythology
Fill your waking dreams with fantasy
All creatures play their part in life
Whatever shape or form
They may enjoy.

Never try to conquer destiny
Let your love light your way
Problems seem to gently fade away
If your love leads the way

Spirit is the force that makes it so
What we are – where we go
Spirit is the force in all there is
From the seed to the blue giant star.

Galaxies rotate in harmony
From the start, flung apart
Universes grow and I can see
I'm a part, I'm apart.

Let your life be led by destiny
Let your love light your way
Problems seem to gently fade away
If your love leads the way.

Background vocal

The thread that mind is weaving
Becomes the tapestry of life
For a heart in pain and grieving
Will be happy in the light.

In the manner of our living
Is the noble spirit born
In the pattern of our giving
Is the character reformed.

In the mirror mind is seeing
What the heart already knows
That the butterfly is leaving
At the end of all its woes.

Now leave this world forever
For the true celestial light
To be as one together
At the ending of the night.

We're coming home again
We're coming home

So much love and joy to bring
We are coming home again
We are coming home.

Printed in Great
Britain
by Amazon